D0094813

DISCARDED
WIDENER UNIVERSITY

Displacing Homophobia:

Gay Male Perspectives in Literature

and Culture

Displacing Homophobia:

Gay Male Perspectives in Literature

and Culture

**Edited by Ronald R. Butters, John M. Clum,
and Michael Moon**

Duke University Press   Durham and London

PS
173
.M36
D5
1989

The text of this book was originally published,
in slightly different form and without the
present index, as Volume 88, Number 1 of
the *South Atlantic Quarterly*.

Copyright © 1989 Duke University Press
All rights reserved
Printed in the United States of America
on acid-free paper ∞
Library of Congress
Cataloging-in-Publication Data
appear on the last printed page.

Contents

Ronald R. Butters

Foreword

In 1974, Louie Crew and Rictor Norton began their special gay issue of *College English* with a nineteen-page "editorial" entitled "The Homophobic Imagination."[1] One measure of the progress gay and lesbian studies have made in the past decade and a half is that such an editorial introduction seems unneeded for the current volume. The essays printed here evolve in a context in which their right to exist—indeed, the necessity of their existence—grows increasingly unquestionable. Crew and Norton wrote with no little wonderment at "the positive thrust of [their] collection of essays as a whole," despite "the lack of a traditional groove in which to work."[2] Their landmark issue was an important project in the emerging tradition which the present efforts, we hope, continue to create.

This is certainly not to say that "the excommunication of homosexual literary history" has now ended in every nook and cranny of the Modern Language Association, nor that whatever progress we have made toward "reclaim[ing] homosexual literary reality" is in any sense complete—or less subject to "deletion" by future homophobic political forces than was, say, James Halliwell's expurgation of the gay material about Sir Francis Bacon's boyfriend Godrick from the 1845 edition of Sir Simonds D'Ewes's *Autobiography*.[3]

Moreover, in many areas of the humanities outside the literary and historical disciplines represented by the essays in this volume, reclamation has scarcely begun. In my own discipline, linguistics, Stonewall and after might almost never have existed. In 1935 Allen Walker Read, a known heterosexual (now retired from the faculty of Columbia University) wrote *Classic American Graffiti: Lexical Evidence from Folk Epigraphy in Western North America*. It contained data, collected "in the field" (largely men's-room walls in the United States) such as the following:

> . . . All wishing to be sucked off get a bone on and
> wait. I will choose the best looking pricks . . .
> Yellowstone National Park, Old Faithful Camp,
> Geyser Baths Swimming Pool
> August 11, 1928.

The book was privately printed in Paris in a limited edition of seventy-five, with a second subtitle and a caveat printed on the title page: "A Glossarial Study of the Low Element in the English Vocabulary . . . Circulation restricted to students of linguistics, folk-lore, abnormal psychology, and allied branches of the social sciences." Though such "folk epigraphy" might seem inconsequential to the nonlinguist, what Read later called his "pioneering work" is virtually the only public record we have of such early twentieth-century usage compiled by a trained linguist.[4] It sheds light on a number of linguistic issues; for example: the absence of the word *gay* from any of Read's collected graffiti tends to confirm the general belief among etymologists that the term did not exist in its popular meaning of "homosexual" before the 1950s.

Read's is also one of the few works by a linguist in which gay or lesbian materials figure at all. Indeed, any notion of what might constitute gay sociolinguistics, and gay linguistics in general, is virtually nonexistent. One looks in vain for references to materials on homosexual subjects in either the standard introductory textbooks or such important recent overview works as Frederick J. Newmeyer's *The Politics of Linguistics* or Michael J. Shapiro's *Language and Political Understanding*. Dennis Baron's *Grammar and Gender* is concerned only with heterosexual issues.[5] Racial discrimination based on language has been an important subject for discussion by linguists and has been the target of numerous occasions of social activism based on linguistic research; however, collections of essays with titles such as *Discourse and Discrimination* continue to be produced with no mention whatever of gay men and women.[6] There are a few exceptions, mostly in the field of lexicography (many of which have appeared in *American Speech*, the journal of the American Dialect Society—and I have edited that journal for the past five years).[7] Richard Spears's dictionary, while not exclusively gay in subject matter, is certainly an important contribution to the field.[8] Deborah Tannen notes that two of the six subjects in her book are gay males (and lovers)—though the significance of their homosexuality is ultimately of little importance to her conclusions.[9] Except for dictionaries, homosexuals appear in linguistics only in passing—and disparagingly and secondhand, as in the occasional black English studies where informants are quoted as speaking once in a while of *punks* and *fags*.

In great part, the proper work of linguists is still being done by others (including many of the authors of the essays in this issue). For example, Jan Zita Grover, who is not a professional linguist but who "currently works as medical editor of an AIDS textbook," offers a penetrating and incisive discussion of the popular vocabulary of AIDS and how this vocabulary contributes to the social and cultural construction of AIDS as "artifact of social and sexual transgression, violated taboo, fractured identity—political and personal projections."[10] Bruce Rodgers's *The Queens' Vernacular* remains the most important work in gay lexicography (indeed, Julia Penelope Stanley's article in *The Homosexual Imagination* did little more than interpret Rodgers's data), though written by an amateur.[11] *GaySpeak* is a significant collection of essays—by scholars in the field of communications, not linguistics.[12] The author of *Homolexis* is an art historian.[13]

Much less study language in a gay context, linguists, even gay ones, have rarely informed their work with a sensitivity to gay and lesbian issues or reviewed the field from a homosexual perspective. For example, linguists—some of them, presumably, gay—*make* dictionaries, those cultural and social repositories where words and meanings are freeze-dried for later use. Gay linguists need to unfreeze and reconstruct the dictionaries. Why, for example, should *Webster's Ninth Collegiate Dictionary* (1983) have two sets of usage labels, one applied mostly to derogatory terms for homosexuals (*fruit, faggot, dyke, queen, queer*): "often used disparagingly"; another applied to most racial and ethnic slurs (*kike, Frog, nigger, coon*): "usually taken to be offensive"? It is a subtle point—one feels slightly paranoid to say it—but why is *fruit* only "often" pejorative (for that matter, when is it not?), while *kike* is "usually" so? More important, why emphasize the offended feelings of only the ethnically slurred, while taking an objective, agentive approach to the homosexual? The creature slurred by *nigger* or *coon* is presented as one of "us," the writers of dictionaries, an offendable human; the creature slurred by *fruit* or *dyke* is some "other."

It is easy to dismiss such observations as homosexual paranoia, or, worse, trivial and unimportant. But so too was it once easy to dismiss the homoerotic sentiments of *Leaves of Grass* as the homosexual reader's fantasy, or, worse, trivial and unimportant. In 1959, when I was nineteen, I read *Leaves of Grass* and listened to Clark Griffith lecture on Whitman in an American poetry course at the University of Iowa. Griffith didn't say very much about the homoerotic element (though he did say more than most people were saying in 1959), but I knew, in spite of my own homophobic wishes, that the homoeroticism that so tortured and delighted my private reading was no fantasy of my creation, and certainly not unimportant.

Is there any need for gay linguistics in general? The authors of the following essays write in a context in which such a question has likewise been asked, disparagingly and discouragingly, concerning literary criticism, history, and cultural studies. While it is true that the literary and cultural discourses discussed in this volume focus on the homosexual male, we began our project with the hope that the essays we collected would further the ongoing enterprise of both lesbian and gay studies. This particular co-editor hopes as well that the volume may prompt a beginning of gay studies in fields such as linguistics, where little work has yet been done.

Postscript

This volume is a reprinting of the essays originally published in the Winter 1989 issue of *SAQ*. The editors have added to the original title, *Displacing Homophobia*, the subtitle *Gay Male Perspectives in Literature and Culture* in order to indicate clearly that the articles herein are almost exclusively by and about men. The editors' original charge was to select writings which considered homo/heterosexuality within the framework of male experience. We do not wish to suggest in any way that a consideration of homophobia as a whole is at all possible without the inclusion of the experience of more than half of its subjects.

Notes

1 Louie Crew and Rictor Norton, "The Homophobic Imagination," *The Homosexual Imagination—in literature—in the classroom—in criticism, College English* 36 (November 1974): 272–90.

2 Ibid., 273.

3 Ibid., 277.

4 Allen Walker Read, *Classic American Graffiti: Lexical Evidence from Folk Epigraphy in Western North America* (1935; reprint, Wakesha, Wis., 1977), 48, i.

5 Shapiro is not a linguist, but a professor of political science; nonetheless, his book (New Haven, 1981), like Newmeyer's (Chicago, 1986) and Baron's (New Haven, 1986), is a pioneering work on the political aspects of the field of linguistics.

6 *Discourse and Discrimination*, ed. Geneva Smitherman-Donaldson and Teun A. Van Dijk (Detroit, 1988).

7 For example, Julia P. Stanley, "Homosexual Slang," *American Speech* 45 (1970): 45–59; Fred R. Shapiro, "Earlier Citations for Terms Characterizing Homosexuals," *American Speech* 63 (1988): 383–85. A number of pioneering articles have also appeared in the annual journal *Maledicta*.

8 Richard Spears, *Slang and Euphemism: A Dictionary of Oaths, Curses, Insults, Sexual Slang and Metaphor, Racial Slurs, Drug Talk, Homosexual Lingo, and Related Matters* (New York, 1981).

9 Deborah Tannen, *Conversational Style: Analyzing Talk among Friends* (Norwood, N.J., 1984).

10 Jan Zita Grover, "AIDS: Keywords," *October* 43 (Winter 1987): 18.

11 Bruce Rodgers, *The Queens' Vernacular: A Gay Lexicon* (San Francisco, 1972).

12 *GaySpeak: Male and Lesbian Communication*, ed. James W. Cheesboro (New York, 1981).

13 Wayne Dynes, *Homolexis: A Historical and Cultural Lexicon of Homosexuality* (New York, 1985).

Stephen Orgel

Nobody's Perfect: Or Why Did the English Stage Take Boys for Women?

My title is the last line of that most Renaissance of modern comedies, *Some Like It Hot*. Joe E. Brown reacts to Jack Lemmon's desperate revelation that he is not the woman Brown thinks he has been wooing, but a man in drag. Instead of indignantly withdrawing his proposal of marriage, however, Brown responds with cheerful complacency, "Nobody's perfect." The moment provides an appropriate setting for my own scene.

I want to rethink some basic information about the English Renaissance theater. It is a commonplace to observe that the stage in Shakespeare's time was an exclusively male preserve, but theatrical historians tend to leave the matter there, as if the fact merely constituted a practical arrangement and had no implications beyond its utility in a number of disguise plots. But it has very broad implications, which are both cultural and specifically sexual, and those are what I want to address. To begin with, the male public theater represents a uniquely English solution to the universal European disapproval of actresses. No contemporary continental public theater restricted the stage to men. Spain, in this as in so much else, offers a useful parallel: the Spanish authorities worried the question of histrionic morality with far greater zeal than the English, and in 1596 they banned women from the stage; but the spectacle of transvestite boys was found to be even more disturbing than that of theatrical women, and the edict was rescinded four years later.[1] So the first puzzle, if one is looking at English Renaissance theater in a European context, is why this seemed a satisfactory arrangement to the English and not to anyone else; or, to put it more directly, why were women more upsetting than boys to the English?

Second, the fact of a male theater in England is more problematic than it has been made to appear: the English stage was a male preserve, but the theater was not. The theater was a place of unusual freedom for women in the period; foreign visitors comment on the fact that English women go to theater unescorted and unmasked, and a large proportion of the audience consisted of women. The puzzle here would be why a culture that so severely regulated the lives of women in every other sphere suspended its restrictions in the case of theater. The fact of the large female audience must have had important consequences for the development of English popular drama. It meant that the success of any play was significantly dependent on the receptiveness of women; and this in turn meant that theatrical representations—whether of women or men or anything else— also depended for their success to a significant degree on the receptiveness of women. When we see dramatic depictions of women in Elizabethan drama that we consider degrading, it has become common to explain the fact by declaring them to be male fantasies and to point to the exclusively male stage to account for them. But this cannot be correct: theaters are viable only insofar as they satisfy their audiences. The depictions must at the very least represent *cultural* fantasies, and women are implicated in them as well as men.

Next, it is in an important respect not quite true to say that the English public stage was exclusively male. Elizabethan theatrical companies contained no women, but Italian troupes visited England on occasion, and performed not only at court but throughout the country, often in conjunction with royal progresses, and therefore under the queen's patronage—theater in this respect, as in so many others, was an extension of the court. Since Italian theater companies were family affairs, they always included women, so that the English did in fact from time to time see women on the stage. What they did not see were *English* women on the stage: the distinction they maintained was here not between men and women but between "us" and "them"—what was appropriate for foreigners was not appropriate for the English.[2] We can tell something about how the gender question was regarded by asking whether women were seen in English Renaissance plays as "them" rather than "us," as the Other. A case can certainly be made for this; there is a large component of male bonding in Shakespeare, what Eve Kosofsky Sedgwick calls the homosocial; and plays like *The Merry Wives of Windsor* and *Othello* certainly have powerful elements of the-men-against-the-women, though it is not at all clear, if we think of these plays in this way, who are "us" and who are "them." The men in *Merry Wives* lose hands down to the women, and Emilia on the relationships between the sexes—

> 'Tis not a year or two shows us a man.
> They are all but stomachs and we all but food;
> They eat us hungerly, and when they are full,
> They belch us. . . .

or,

> . . . jealous souls will not be answered so;
> They are not ever jealous for the cause,
> But jealous for they're jealous

—certainly is not speaking as an outsider. In the context of *Othello*, this is the normative view, the one we are expected to agree with. But in a larger sense, we would have to say that there are lots of *others* in this theater; in fact, Elizabethan drama is often dependent on otherness. Comedies are Italian, French, or provincial, tragedies Spanish or Scandinavian or ancient, pastorals take place somewhere else. Dekker, Jonson, and Middleton placing comedies in contemporary London are doing something new. The Other, for this theater, is as much foreign as female—Othello is the Other. And in the largest sense, the Other is theater itself, both a threat and a refuge.

Women are commodities in this culture, certainly, whose marriages are arranged for the advantage or convenience of men, either their fathers, or the male authority figures in their and their prospective husbands' families. But this too does not distinguish women from men: alliances were normally arranged for men just as for women —the distinction here is between fathers and children, not between the sexes; this is a patriarchal society. Fantasies of freedom in Shakespeare tend to take the form of escapes from the tyranny of elders to a world where the children can make their own society, which usually means where they can arrange their own marriages. Whether this is conceived as ultimately benign and restorative, as in *A Midsummer Night's Dream, As You Like It, Twelfth Night, The Winter's Tale*, or disastrous, as in *Othello* and *Romeo and Juliet*, it works for women as well as men: the crucial element is the restrictive father, not the sex of the child. Rosalind and Orlando, Lorenzo and Jessica are free to choose each other; Bertram's marriage to Helena is no less constrained than the one proposed for Juliet to the County Paris. The problem is the father or the king or the structure of authority, not one's gender. This is not to say that it isn't preferable to be male in the Renaissance world: obviously it is. It is the context of that preference that I am concerned with.

I want to begin by considering what seems to me a particularly subversive version of that fantasy of freedom, the return to childhood. In *The Winter's Tale*, Leontes, after his first flash of violent jealousy, explains his distracted manner to Hermione and Polixenes in this way:

> Looking on the lines
> Of my boy's face, methoughts I did recoil
> Twenty-three years, and saw myself unbreeched,
> In my green velvet coat, my dagger muzzled,
> Lest it should bite its master, and so prove,
> As ornaments oft do, too dangerous.

The return to childhood here is also a retreat from sexuality and the dangers of manhood exemplified in unmuzzled daggers. Leontes sees himself "unbreeched," not yet in breeches: Elizabethan children of both sexes were dressed in skirts until the age of seven or so; the "breeching" of boys was the formal move out of the common gender of childhood, which was both female in appearance and largely controlled by women, and into the world of men. This event was traditionally the occasion for a significant family ceremony.

The childhood to which Leontes imagines himself returning has been described by Polixenes as Edenic, and specifically presexual:

> We were as twinned lambs that did frisk i'th'sun,
> And bleat the one at th'other; what we changed
> Was innocence for innocence; we knew not
> The doctrine of ill-doing, nor dreamed
> That any did; had we pursued that life,
> And our weak spirits ne'er been higher reared
> With stronger blood, we should have answered heaven
> Boldly "not guilty," the imposition cleared
> Hereditary ours.

This is a world without vice and without temptation, in which even original sin appears to have been dealt with. There are no women in it, only the best friend, an emotional twin.

At this point Hermione enters the fantasy with a pertinent observation: "By this we gather / You have tripped since." Polixenes agrees; the fall from grace is a fall into sexuality:

> O my most sacred lady,
> Temptations have been born to 's, for
> In those unfledged days was my wife a girl;
> Your precious self had not yet crossed the eyes
> Of my young playfellow.

Hermione both protests and concurs:

> Of this make no conclusion, lest you say
> Your queen and I are devils. Yet go on,
> Th' offences we have made you do we'll answer,
> If you first sinned with us, and that with us
> You did continue fault, and that you slipped not
> With any but with us.

However good-natured their banter, Hermione's projected conclusion is the logical one: "your queen and I are devils." Her teasing view of marriage as a continuing state of sin with diabolical agents repeats the view of sexuality implicit in the men's fantasy.

It is impossible to say what particular word or gesture triggers Leontes' paranoid jealousy, but the translation of the inseparable friend into the dangerous rival and of the chaste wife into a whore is similarly implicit in the fantasy, its worst-case scenario, so to speak, replicating the situation Shakespeare had imagined with such detailed intensity in the dark lady sonnets. And when Leontes retreats from it he is retreating not only from women and sex: he is retreating from his place in one of the very few normative families in Shakespeare—families consisting of father, mother, and children. Most families in Shakespeare have only one parent; the very few that include both parents generally have only one child, and when that configuration appears, it tends to be presented as Leontes' marriage is presented, as exceedingly dangerous to the child: we may take as examples Juliet and her parents, Macduff and Lady Macduff, Coriolanus and Virgilia, the Duke and Duchess of York arguing about whether to denounce their son as a traitor. It is a configuration that, with the single exception of the Page family in *The Merry Wives of Windsor*, never appears in comedy.

Marriage is a dangerous condition in Shakespeare. We are always told that comedies end in marriages. A few of Shakespeare's do, but the much more characteristic Shakespearean conclusion comes just before the marriage, and sometimes, as in *Love's Labor's Lost* and *Twelfth Night*, with an entirely unexpected delay or postponement. Plays that continue beyond the point where comedy ends, with the old fogies defeated and a happy marriage successfully concluded, depict the condition as utterly disastrous: *Romeo and Juliet*, *Othello*. Most Shakespearean marriages of longer duration are equally disheartening, with shrewishness, jealousy, and manipulativeness the norm in comedy, and real destructiveness in tragedy: Oberon and Titania, the Merry Wives, Capulet and Lady Capulet, Claudius and Gertrude, Macbeth and Lady Macbeth, Cymbeline and his queen, Antigonus and Paulina.

In fact, relationships between men and women interest Shakespeare intensely, but not, on the whole, as husbands and wives. I might even go on to say not on the whole as men and women: a significant number of plays require the woman to become a man for the wooing to be effected. The dangers of women in erotic situations, whatever they may be, can be disarmed by having the women play men, just as in the theater the dangers of women on the stage (whatever *they* may be) can be disarmed by having men play the women. The interchangeability of the sexes is an essential assumption of this theater.

≡≡≡≡

It is also an assumption of the culture as a whole. For us the entire question of gender is controlled by issues of sexuality, and we are quite clear about which sex is which. But for the Renaissance the line between the sexes was blurred, often frighteningly so. Medical and anatomical treatises from the time of Galen cited homologies in the genital structure of the sexes to show that male and female were versions of the same unitary species.[3] The female genitals were simply the male genitals inverted, and carried internally rather than externally. Sexual experience was conceived to be the same in both; during coitus, both not only experience orgasm but ejaculate, and female ejaculation with its component of female seed is just as necessary for conception as male ejaculation is. Both male and female seeds are present in every foetus; a foetus becomes male rather than female if the male seed is dominant and generates enough heat to press the genital organs outward—if, that is, the foetus is stronger, with strength being conceived as heat.[4] Analogously, and logically, many cases were recorded of women becoming men through the pressure of some great excitement or activity. The crucial point is, however, that those transformations that are attested to as scientific fact work in only one direction, from female to male, which is conceived to be upward, toward completion. Indeed, the function of sexual pleasure is generally said in the medical literature to be that it enables men to overcome their natural revulsion at the imperfection of women, and enables women to overcome their natural distaste for and fear of childbearing, which would mean, in Renaissance terms, their distaste for being women.

Such claims, of course, are not merely scientific, but imply (like the scientific claims of all eras, including our own) a political agenda. The homologies they cite are only anatomical, and imply no egalitarian bias; most of the scholastic opinion codified by Ian Maclean in *The Renaissance Notion of Women* stresses the differences between men and women, not their similarities. Women are less intelligent, more passionate, less in control of their affections, and so forth. The difference in degree of perfection becomes in practical terms a powerful difference in kind, and the scientific arguments are used to justify the whole range of male domination over women. The frightening part of the teleology for the Renaissance mind, however, is precisely the fantasy of its reversal, the conviction that men can turn into— or be turned into—women; or perhaps more exactly, can be turned *back* into women, losing the strength that enabled the male potential to be realized in the first place. In the medical literature we all start as women, and the culture confirmed this by dressing all children in skirts until the age of seven or so, when the boy, as Leontes recalls, was "breeched," or put into pants, and began to be trained as a man. From this point on, for a man to associate with women was felt to be increasingly dangerous—not only for the woman, but even more for the man: lust effeminates, makes men incapable of manly pursuits; hence the pervasive antithesis of love and war. Thomas Wright, in *The Passions of the Mind in General*, warning against the dangers of love, writes that "a personable body is often linked with a pestilent soul; a valiant Captain in the field for the most part is infected with an effeminate affection at home"[5] (the effeminate affection being his passion for women), and Romeo, berating himself for his unwillingness to harm Tybalt, cries out,

> O sweet Juliet,
> Thy beauty hath made me effeminate,
> And in my temper softened valor's steel!

Such formulations are all but axiomatic in the period, and the word "effeminate," over and over, serves the basic explanatory function in them. Women are dangerous to men because sexual passion for women renders men effeminate: this is an age in which sexuality itself is misogynistic, as the love of women threatens the integrity of the perilously achieved male identity. The fear of effeminization is a central element in all discussions of what constitutes a "real man" in the period, and the fantasy of the reversal of the natural transition from woman to man underlies it. It also, in a much more clearly pathological way, underlies the standard arguments against the stage in anti-theatrical tracts from the time of the church fathers on. In this context, the very institution of theater is a threat to manhood and the stability of the social hierarchy, as unescorted women and men without their wives socialize freely, and (it follows) flirt with each other and take each other off to bed: the association of theater with sex is absolutely pervasive in these polemics.

But in England, the sexuality feared is more subversive than even this suggests, precisely because of the transvestism of the stage. It is argued first that the boys who perform the roles of women will be transformed into their roles and play the part in reality. This claim has its basis in a platonic argument, but in the puritan tracts it merges with a general fear of blurred social and sexual boundaries, of roles and costumes adulterating the essences that God has given us. Jonas Barish, in his exhaustive and indispensable study of the anti-theatrical material, relates the hostility to transvestite actors to the synchronous revival of medieval sumptuary laws, the attempt to prevent members of one social class from appearing to be members of another (thus tradesmen were enjoined from wearing silk), and he quotes William Perkins to the effect that "wanton and excessive apparel . . . maketh a confusion of such degrees and callings as God hath ordained." "Distinctions of dress," Barish comments, "however external and theatrical they may seem to us, for Perkins virtually belong to our essence, and may no more be tampered with than that essence itself."[6] This is certainly the way the polemicists view the situation; but it is precisely the essence that is the problem. What *is* our God-given essence, that it can be transformed by the clothes we wear? Philip Stubbes, in a passage that bears directly on the question of transvestite actors, deplores a current (and recurrent) fashion of masculine dress for women. "Our apparel," he says, "was given us as a sign distinctive to discern betwixt sex and sex, and therefore one to wear the apparel of another sex is to participate with the same, and to adulterate the verity of his own kind. Wherefore these women may not improperly be called *Hermaphroditi*, that is, monsters of both kinds, half women, half men."⁷ It is the fragility, the radical instability of our essence, that is assumed here, and the metamorphic quality of our sinful nature. The enormous popularity of Ovid in the age reflects both its desires and its deepest fears.

But the argument against transvestite actors warns of an even more frightening metamorphosis than the transformation of the boy into a monster of both kinds. Male spectators, it is argued, will be seduced by the impersonation, and, losing their reason, will become effeminate, which in this case means they will lust not after the woman in the drama, which would be bad enough, but after the boy beneath the woman's costume, thereby playing the woman's role themselves. This fear, which has been brilliantly anatomized by Laura Levine, is so pervasive in the tracts, and so unlike modern kinds of sexual anxiety, that it is worth pausing over.⁸

John Rainolds says the adoption by men of women's clothing kindles "great sparkles of lust," and, citing the authority of Socrates, compares the homosexual response engendered by transvestite boys to the sting of poisonous spiders: "if they do but touch men only with their mouth, they put them to wonderful pain and make them mad: so beautiful boys by kissing do sting and pour secretly in a kind of poison. . . ."⁹ Here the attraction of men to beautiful boys is treated as axiomatic; the assumption behind this hysterical (and very ambivalent) warning is that to try boys will be to prefer them to women; though the passage, as it continues, is equally vehement against heterosexuality. Similarly for William Prynne, the transvestism of the stage is especially dangerous because female dress is an important stimulant to homosexuality: the "male priests of Venus" satisfy their companions, the "passive beastly sodomites of Florida," by wearing women's clothes, the "better to elicit, countenance, act and color their unnatural execrable uncleannesses."¹⁰ The implication is that the heterosexual titillation is a cover for the homosexual response beneath. Notice also that the transvestite is not the passive one in this relationship.

Rainolds, Prynne, and any number of other anti-theatrical writers offer observations such as these as models for the theatrical experience. For such writers, the fact that women are prohibited from the stage reveals the true etiology of theater: what the spectator is "really" attracted to in plays is men—the deepest fear in anti-theatrical tracts, far deeper than the fear that women in the audience will become whores, is the fear of a universal effeminization. The growth of desire through the experience of theater is a sinister progression: the play excites the spectator and sends him home to "perform" himself; the result is sexual abandon with one's wife, or more often with any available woman (all women at the playhouse being considered available), or worst of all—and this is a claim that recurs throughout the literature—the spectator begins by lusting after a female character, but ends by having sex with the man she "really" is. Philip Stubbes gives a particularly clear statement of this anxiety: "the fruits of plays and interludes" are, he says, that after theater, "everyone brings another homeward of their way very friendly, and in their secret conclaves they play sodomite or worse."[11] What is worse is presumably the sodomized.

The assumption behind all these assertions is, first, that the basic form of response to theater is erotic; second, that erotically, theater is uncontrollably exciting; and third, that the basic, essential form of erotic excitement in men is homosexual—that, indeed, women are only a cover for men. And though the assumption in this form is clearly pathological, it is also clearly related to anatomical theories of the essential homology of male and female—to claims that male and female are versions of each other, that the female is an incomplete male, and that it is therefore possible for her even, given enough excitement, to mutate *naturally* into the male. The fears, that is, are grounded in what is recognized as fact.

═══

But why, then, if boys in women's dress are so threatening, did the English maintain a transvestite theater? It is necessary to remember that anti-theatrical tracts are pathological. They share assumptions with the culture as a whole, but their conclusions are eccentric. Stephen Greenblatt, in a brilliant essay, relates the development of the transvestite stage precisely to the cultural tropes of the body as they are anatomized in the medical and gynecological theories of the age, and he concludes that "a conception of gender that is teleologically male and insists upon a verifiable sign to confirm nature's final cause finds its supreme literary expression in a transvestite theater."[12] This is an exciting and attractive thesis, but the problem with it is that the medical theorists are for the most part French and Italian, and France and Italy did not develop transvestite theaters. Why did only the English public theater resist the introduction of women on the stage? I should say at once that I cannot answer this question, but the reasons must have to do with culture-specific attitudes toward women, and toward sexuality.

Despite the anxiety expressed in the anti-theatrical literature, English Renaissance culture, to judge from the surviving evidence, did not display a morbid fear of homosexuality. Anxiety about the fidelity of women, on the other hand, does seem to have been strikingly prevalent; this is clear from nonliterary sources. Katharine Maus cites recent studies of sixteenth-century ecclesiastical courts in Essex and York which reveal that most of the defamation suits were prompted by three insulting terms: cuckold, whore, and whoremaster.[13] The fear of losing control of women's chastity, a very valuable possession that guaranteed the legitimacy of one's heirs, and especially valuable for fathers as a piece of disposable property, is a logical consequence of a patriarchal structure—as the figure of Prospero makes clear. One would have to have parallel statistics from Spain, France, and Italy to know how much explanatory value the defamation records have; certainly cuckoldry seems to have been very much on the Italian mind in the Renaissance. But these figures help to indicate the extent to which theater served as a means of managing specifically sexual anxieties: Maus notes that the incidence of cuckoldry plots is much higher in the drama than in the other imaginative genres in the period.

As far as paternal prerogatives were concerned, there were sufficient ambiguities within the English system to justify the anxieties of a father who assumed his rights over the disposition of his child to be absolute. Fathers were legally entitled to arrange their daughters' marriages as they saw fit, and of course had control of all property that accompanied the daughter; but the legal age of consent was twelve for women (fourteen for men), which meant that daughters over the age of twelve were also legally entitled to arrange their own marriages. They might make themselves paupers by doing so, but they could not be stopped.[14] The horror stories of enforced marriages—there are many in the period—relate primarily to upper-class matches, where political alliances and large sums of money were at stake. In such cases, what the age of consent meant in practice was merely that a woman could not be forced to consent to a marriage arranged by her father before she reached the age of twelve.

Middle- and lower-class arrangements, however, would have been much less constrained. Indeed, middle-class London was a place of unusual liberty for women, and this certainly bears on both the popularity of the London theater with women and their relative freedom to enjoy it: the professional theater drew its support largely from London's properous mercantile and artisan classes. It also probably accounts for the proliferation of plays about both love matches and cuckoldry, the two sides of the notion of liberty for women. Such liberating theatrical freedom, of course, could be seen as dangerous and anarchic, and the source of the danger was generally claimed to be sexual.

Public theater is regularly associated, moreover, not only with loose women but with homosexual prostitution; the latter charge is found not only in puritan polemicists but in the playwrights themselves. Yet the attitude implied in the charge tends to be, surprisingly, liberal and permissive. In Middleton's *Father Hubburd's Tales*, a budding London rake is advised "to call in at the Blackfriars, where he should see a nest of boys able to ravish a man."[15] In Jonson's *Poetaster*, Ovid's father, learning that Ovid has become a playwright, and fearing that he will go on to be an actor, says, "What, shall I have my son a stager now, an ingle for players . . . ?" (1.2.15–16). An ingle is a catamite; Alan Bray cites this and several other examples to show that the association was a common one.[16] But the theaters were not therefore closed or avoided by decent folk. The crime of sodomy is inveighed against repeatedly and energetically in legal and theological contexts; but, as Bray demonstrates, it was scarcely ever prosecuted. When cases of homosexual behavior reach the courts, they are dealt with on the whole with surprising moderation—admonitions, exhortations to abstain. In fact, again, women are felt to pose the more serious problem: heterosexual fornication was much more energetically prosecuted. Magistrates took an interest in such cases because they resulted in illegitimate births, which increased the poor rolls, whereas, unless the activity involved coercion or malfeasance, there was rarely anything in homosexuality worth bothering about.

In one extraordinary case discussed by Bray, a laborer named Meredith Davy was brought before the magistrate on what certainly could have been a charge of sodomy. Davy slept in the same bed with a twelve-year-old apprentice, and a third man slept in the same room. On a number of occasions the third man heard activity in the other bed, and heard the boy protest and cry out in pain. It took about a month for the witness to realize what was happening, and he finally reported it to the mistress of the house, who referred the case to the magistrate. The defendant appeared baffled by the charge, and clearly had no conception that what he was doing was related to the abominable crime of sodomy. This, surprisingly, seemed sufficient mitigation to the magistrate, and to the household as a whole; Davy was sent home with an admonishment to leave the boy alone, "since which time," the court report concludes, "he hath lain quietly with him."[17] The two, that is, were allowed to continue to sleep together; and it is conceivable that things quieted down not because Davy stopped making advances but because the boy stopped objecting—it was not, after all, the boy who made the complaint.

Bray argues that such a story does not testify to any remarkable tolerance on the part of the English, but rather to a selective blindness: sodomy was something that, despite a number of explicit and well-known prosecutions—the cases of Nicholas Udall, Francis Bacon, the Castlehaven scandal—the English associate on the whole only with foreigners, not with themselves. Travelers observing it in the relatively tolerant climates of Italy, Turkey, North Africa, and Russia use it as an index to the viciousness of Catholic, Muslim, or barbaric societies.[18] And yet when, at the opening of *Epicoene* (1.1.23), Clerimont is shown with a page boy who is described as "his ingle," the fact serves as nothing more than one of a number of indices to the easy life of a London playboy. Charges of sodomy always occur in relation to other kinds of subversion; the activity has no independent existence in the Renaissance mind, just as there is no separate category of the homosexual. It becomes visible in Elizabethan society only when it intersects with some other behavior that is recognized as dangerous and antisocial; it is invariably an aspect of atheism, papistry, sedition, witchcraft. The puritan charge that theater promotes homosexuality appears because to the puritan mind theater is felt to be dangerous, not the other way around; sodomy becomes the visible sign of its subversiveness. King James's public and overtly physical displays of affection for young men are frequently remarked in the period; they are considered to be in bad taste (as are the king's manners generally), but not even the most rabid puritan connects them with the abominable crime against nature.[19]

And yet the Jacobean court, at least from the perspective of Charles I's Whitehall, was felt to be especially hospitable to homosexuality. Lucy Hutchinson, whose husband was a Roundhead colonel, saw in this a significant element in the transition from Jacobean to Caroline:

> The face of the court was much changed in the change of the king, for King Charles was temperate, chaste and serious; so that the fools and bawds, mimics and catamites of the former court grew out of fashion; and the nobility and courtiers, who did not quite abandon their debaucheries, yet so reverenced the king as to retire into corners to practise them.[20]

The disapproval of this puritan woman discussing the debaucheries of catamites is colored by neither anxiety nor outrage. Tastes, she merely observes, change. Here, for comparison, is a passage from a letter written to Buckingham by King James:

> . . . I cannot content myself without sending you this present, praying God that I may have a joyful and comfortable meeting with you and that we may make at this Christmas a new marriage ever to be kept hereafter; for, God so love me, as I desire only to live in the world for your sake, and that I had rather live banished in any part of the earth with you than live a sorrowful widow's life without you. And so God bless you, my sweet child and wife, and grant that ye may ever be a comfort to your dear dad and husband.   James R.[21]

The metamorphic quality James adopts in this rhetoric is notable; he proposes marriage to Buckingham, and then imagines himself in succession as widow, father, and husband, and Buckingham as his child and wife. The interchangeability of gender is here an essential element of the language of Eros; this is the other side of the fear that love effeminates.

≡≡≡≡

Though there are any number of passionate heterosexual relationships depicted in English Renaissance literature, it is a commonplace to find a generalized misogyny in the work of the period, even in its idealization of chaste and beautiful women who are also cold and untouchable. What is less often observed is that along with the varieties of conventional romance, romantic and even erotic homosexual relationships also figure from time to time in the literature of the period, in a context that is often—though certainly not invariably —positive, and registers again surprisingly little anxiety about the matter. I am not talking here about what in modern terms would be called male bonding, where no explicit sexual component is acknowledged; though there certainly is a good deal of that in Renaissance literature. I am talking about explicitly homosexual relationships. Consider the fact that Rosalind disguised as a boy can play a wooing scene with another man under the name Ganymede. The peculiar and pathological element in this is not that Orlando is therefore involved in playing a love scene with a man. It is that so few critics (and none cited in the Variorum) have ever remarked that the model for it must be a homosexual flirtation; the name Ganymede cannot be used in the Renaissance without this connotation. But there is no indication whatever that Shakespeare is doing something sexually daring there, skating on thin ice. Counterexamples in which homosexual behavior leads to disaster are exceedingly rare. The only clear-cut theatrical one is in Marlowe's *Edward II* (and in the career of Marlowe generally), and I shall return to this; but first I'd like to cite a number of other instances.

The young shepherd Colin in the *January* eclogue of *The Shepherd's Calendar* rejects the advances of the older shepherd Hobbinol, "Albe my love he seek with daily suit: / His clownish gifts and curtsies I disdain" (56–57). Colin instead pursues the unresponsive Rosalind. Hobbinol's flirtation is presented simply as part of the poet-shepherd's experience; but since Colin is identified in the book as Spenser and

Hobbinol as Gabriel Harvey, the allusion seems to have a specific application as well, to be saying something about the relationship between Spenser and Harvey. Spenser clearly does not consider this libelous, and judging from their continued association, neither did Harvey. But it makes the volume's editor, E. K., nervous: in glossing the passage he duly cites the relevant classical precedents of Socrates and Alcibiades. These lead him to the conclusion that "paederistike [is] much to be preferred before gynerastike, that is the love which enflameth men with lust toward womankind." He adds at this point in his gloss on line 59 that he is not thereby condoning (or, presumably, implying that Harvey is guilty of) the "execrable and horrible sins of forbidden and unlawful fleshliness" celebrated by Lucian and Pietro Aretino.

The strategy here is significant, and to modern eyes puzzling. In order to disarm the allusion, E. K. need only have cited Virgil's second eclogue, which he has already recognized as one of Spenser's principal sources: here the poet imitateth Virgil. But instead he gives an argument from classical authority in defence of pederasty and against heterosexual love. This is entirely unnecessary as a strategy on Spenser's behalf, since Colin has rejected Hobbinol in favor of Rosalind. Nevertheless, E. K. wants to insist on the privileged status of homosexuality, not as an aspect of poetry, but of the highest moral philosophy—Socrates authorized it. To do this it is only necessary to deflect the prohibited aspects of homosexual behavior onto women on the one hand, and Italians on the other. It is important to observe that despite Colin's interest in Rosalind, there is no argument here in favor of the love of women, and that homosexual love is defined in opposition to heterosexuality, which is equated with lust.

Marlowe, in *Hero and Leander*, expresses a good deal more enthusiasm for the physical side of homoeroticism. He also, like the anti-theatrical polemicists, assumes the interchangeability of male and female, though this is a source of excitement rather than panic. When Leander is first described, he is praised primarily for his erotic effect on men. Cynthia, apparently alone among women, "wished his arms might be her sphere"; whereas Leander's hair "Would have allured the venturous youth of Greece / To hazard more than for the Golden Fleece." Leander could have replaced Ganymede as Jove's cupbearer; if Hippolytus had seen Leander, he would have abandoned his chastity and fallen in love with him; the rudest peasant and the barbarous Thracian soldier sought his favor. After this, it is not surprising that he attracts the attentions of Neptune, who mistakes him for Ganymede and is described in an extraordinarily explicit passage making passes at Leander as he swims naked to Sestos. The episode is notable for the total lack of anxiety it projects. It is comic, and enthusiastic.

In *Troilus and Cressida*, Patroclus urges Achilles to return to the battlefield:

> To this effect, Achilles, have I moved you.
> A woman impudent and mannish grown
> Is not more loathed than an effeminate man
> In time of action. I stand condemned for this.
> They think my little stomach to the war
> And your great love to me restrains you thus.
> Sweet, rouse yourself; and the weak wanton Cupid
> Shall from your neck unloose his amorous fold
> And, like a dew-drop from the lion's mane,
> Be shook to air.

The language is the language of love, but the terms might have been borrowed from any polemicist; and Thersites comes straight out with it: there is nothing platonic about the relationship between the two heroes—Patroclus is "Achilles' male varlet . . . his masculine whore." Thersites is not the most reliable of witnesses, but the play makes no attempt to represent Achilles and Patroclus as innocent of the abominable crime. Achilles is unmanned, however, by love itself, not by its object, which turns out at the crucial moment to be female as well as male. He is also in love with Priam's daughter Polyxena, and the love of women proves finally more antithetical to the claims of martial heroism than the love of men:

> My sweet Patroclus, I am thwarted quite
> From my great purpose in tomorrow's battle.
> Here is a letter from Queen Hecuba,
> A token from her daughter, my fair love,

> Both taxing me and gaging me to keep
> An oath that I have sworn. I will not break it.
> Fall Greeks, fail fame, honor or go or stay,
> My major vow lies here; this I'll obey.

To my knowledge the only dramatic instance of a homosexual relationship presented in the terms in which the culture formally conceived it—as antisocial, seditious, ultimately disastrous—is in Marlowe's *Edward II*. It would certainly be possible to account for its perspective, if not for its uniqueness, by viewing it in the context of Sedgwick's thesis about Renaissance homosexuality: that it was not viewed as threatening because it was not defined in opposition to, or as an impediment to, heterosexuality and marriage.[22] Edward's love for Gaveston is destructive because it *is* presented as anti-heterosexual; it renders him an unfit husband, as his passion renders him an unfit king. I am not happy with this explanation not because there is anything wrong with it, but because it is too straightforward to account for what seems to me a very devious and genuinely subversive play. Both politically and morally, the power-hungry nobles and the queen's adultery with Mortimer are as destabilizing as anything in Edward's relationship with his favorite, and the real complaint against Gaveston has nothing to do with his sexuality, but with the fact that he is being given preferments over other powerful and ambitious courtiers. For Marlowe to translate the whole range of power politics into sodomy certainly says something about his tastes and that of Elizabethan audiences, but it also has to be added that it was probably safer to represent the power structure in that way than it would have been to play it, so to speak, straight. Had Richard II been presented as a sodomite, would the authorities have found it necessary to censor the deposition scene? Maybe Edward's sexuality is a way of protecting the play, a way of keeping what it says about power intact. This is the work of Marlowe the government spy, at once an agent of the establishment and deeply subversive. And if we look forward, Edward's relation to Gaveston provides so clear a mirror of King James's behavior toward Carr, Buckingham, and the other favorites that it is startling to find that the play was reissued in 1612 and performed publicly in 1622. Its subject is advertised on the title page, as it had been in the original edition, as "the tragic fall of Mortimer." In fact, in 1621, in an inflammatory parliamentary speech, Sir Henry Yelverton had made the analogy between James's treatment of Buckingham and Edward's of his favorites explicit—the particular favorite cited was not Gaveston but his successor Hugh Spencer, but the point was not lost on James and Buckingham. James demanded a retraction on the grounds that the comparison represented him as a weak king, and Yelverton was forced to apologize and was heavily fined.[23] Had it been possible for a Jacobean audience to acknowledge sodomy as an English vice, the play, and the allusion, would have been treasonable.

≡≡≡≡

Homosexuality in this culture appears to have been less threatening than heterosexuality, and only in part because it had fewer consequences and was easier to desexualize. The reason always given for the prohibition of women from the stage was that their chastity would thereby be compromised, which is understood to mean that they would become whores. Behind the outrage of public modesty is a real fear of women's sexuality, and more specifically, of its power to evoke men's sexuality. This is dangerous because it is not subject to rational control, which is a way of saying that it is not subject to any other kind of authority either—what from one perspective was slavery to passion, from another was a declaration of independence. This bears on the question of what women found attractive about a theater we find misogynistic—the end of *The Merchant of Venice*, with Portia's and Nerissa's ring trick, plays on both the male fears and the female fantasies of a patriarchal society.

Shakespearean drama often confronts these anxieties; comedy looks for ways to control them, they constitute a subject for tragedy. Othello's and Iago's assumptions about Desdemona, and about women generally, include all the familiar claims of Renaissance treatises on women and the dangers of the stage; they are false in this case, but Desdemona's chastity does not save her or Othello from a tragic outcome. Moreover, critics with patriarchal leanings might argue, and have on occasion done so, that the real source of the tragedies of Desdemona and Juliet is their refusal to obey their fathers, their insistence on choosing their own husbands. In one respect, these plays exemplify a perfectly standard patriarchalist and anti-feminist line, and though Elizabethan audiences would certainly have responded to their tragic force, it is doubtful that any Elizabethan spectator would have found them subversive.

Greenblatt has related the transvestism of figures like Portia, Rosalind, and Viola to the teleology of masculinity implied by the medical and gynecological theories cited earlier. Such figures, in this reading, "pass through the state of being men in order to become women. Shakespearean women are in this sense the projected mirror images of masculine self-differentiation."[24] But even this clearly has its anxieties: Shakespeare shows on occasion an unwillingness to allow them to return to being women. Viola announces in the final moments of *Twelfth Night* that she cannot become a woman and the wife of Orsino until her woman's clothes have been recovered—a dress borrowed from Olivia or a new one purchased for the occasion apparently are not options—and that this will require the release of the sea captain who alone can find them, which in turn will neces-sitate the mollification of the enraged Malvolio, who has had the sea captain incarcerated: this all materializes out of nowhere in the last three minutes of the play. And Malvolio at the play's end offers no assistance but runs from the stage shouting "I'll be revenged on the whole pack of you." For Viola to become a woman requires, in short, a new play with Malvolio at its center. Rosalind, speaking the epilogue to *As You Like It*, reminds us that she is a boy, and that the drama has not represented an erotic and heterosexual reality at all: "If I were a woman, I would kiss as many of you as have beards that pleased me. . . ." This is the only place in Shakespeare where the hero-ine undoes her gender in this way (though Cleopatra at one moment approaches it). And yet Rosalind is surely among the most attractive and successful of Shakespeare's women: it must be to the point that Shakespeare does not want to leave her intact. I think it is also to the point that *Twelfth Night* includes the only overtly homosexual couple in Shakespeare except for Achilles and Patroclus. What the presence of Antonio and Sebastian acknowledges, in a play that has at its cen-ter a man wooing a man, is that men *do* fall in love with other men. "You are betrothèd," Sebastian tells Olivia, "to a man and maid," recalling the master-mistress of Shakespeare's passion in the sonnets. The same point is made by giving Rosalind the name Ganymede.

Finally, a brief observation about Olivia. She is referred to twice as the Countess Olivia, and Malvolio imagines himself becoming Count Malvolio by marrying her. In the English peerage, the only way for Olivia to be a countess would be as the wife or the widow of an earl. But Olivia is as yet unmarried. Her father, however, was a count, and Shakespeare seems to be using the Italian system, in which all the children of a nobleman inherit the title. But there is no system in which a man can become a count by marrying a countess. Malvolio will raise his status by marrying Olivia only if Olivia is also a man.

Notes

For references and valuable suggestions, I am indebted to A. R. Braunmuller, David Halperin, Ursula Heise, Karen Newman, David Riggs, Winfried Schleiner, and Marion Trousdale.

1   Most Spanish companies included both women and transvestite boys, and one or the other was prohibited from time to time. Female cross-dressing, however, seems to have been considered a more serious problem than transvestite boys, and was repeatedly banned (e.g., in 1600, 1608, 1615, and 1641), which suggests that the ban must have been repeatedly ignored. The first actresses appeared on Dutch stages in 1655, to predictably outraged clerical opinion. Holland is not a parallel case because it had had no public theater before this time, but the event is suggestive and probably points to contrasting Protestant and Catholic attitudes as well. See Simon Schama, *The Embarrassment of Riches* (New York, 1987), 408.

2   G. E. Bentley also notes the 1629 visit of a French company that included actresses. One reporter claims that the troupe was driven from the stage by public outrage at the first and only performance, but the records indicate that this was not the case, and that they performed at least twice more at public theaters in London. See G. E. Bentley, *The Jacobean and Caroline Stage* (Oxford, 1966), 1:25.

3   I am here summarizing the work of Ian Maclean, *The Renaissance Notion of Women* (Cambridge, 1980); Thomas Laqueur, "Orgasm, Generation, and the Politics of Reproductive Biology," *Representations* 14 (Spring 1986): 4–16; and Stephen Greenblatt, "Fiction and Friction," in *Reconstructing Individualism*, ed. Thomas C. Heller et al. (Stanford, 1986), 30–52.

4   Such an etiology is not unknown in nature. The sex of alligators is determined by the heat at which the eggs are incubated: if it is 90° or over, they are male, if 87° or under, they are female. On the question of whether at 88° or 89° they become androgynes, the authorities are silent.

5 Thomas Wright, *The Passions of the Mind in General*, ed. W. W. Newbold (New York, 1986), 237.

6 Jonas Barish, *The Antitheatrical Prejudice* (Berkeley, 1981), 92.

7 Ibid.

8 Laura Levine, "Men in Women's Clothing: Anti-theatricality and Effeminization from 1579 to 1642," *Criticism* (Spring 1986): 121–43. In what follows I am in part summarizing Levine's argument.

9 John Rainolds, *Th'Overthrow of Stage Plays* ([Middleburg], 1599), 11, 18.

10 William Prynne, *Histriomastix* (London, 1633), 209.

11 Philip Stubbes, *Anatomy of Abuses* (London, 1585), sig. L8v.

12 Greenblatt, "Fiction and Friction," 47.

13 Katharine Maus, "Horns of Dilemma: Jealousy, Gender and Spectatorship in English Renaissance Drama," *ELH* 54 (Fall 1987): 561–62.

14 After the enactment of the Canons of 1604, parental consent was required for the marriage of children up to the age of twenty-one.

15 *Works of Thomas Middleton*, ed. A. H. Bullen (Boston, 1886), 8:77.

16 Alan Bray, *Homosexuality in Renaissance England* (London, 1982), 54–55.

17 Ibid., 77.

18 Ibid., 75.

19 To my knowledge, the only instance of political capital being made of King James's homosexuality is in the scurrilous *Corona Regia* (1615), almost certainly by the German Catholic satirist Caspar Schoppe (Scoppius), but maliciously credited to James's supporter Isaac Casaubon and published with a false imprint. This makes much of James's conferring on his favorites the title of "*Magnus Cubicularius tuus*" (Knight of your Bedchamber), praises the king for so successfully mixing lust with religion, and compares him with the notorious Heliogabolus. James, outraged, offered a reward for the identification of the author, which was not claimed until 1639. I am indebted to Winfried Schleiner for this reference.

20 *Memoirs of the Life of Colonel Hutchinson*, ed. C. H. Firth (London, 1906), 69.

21 *Letters of King James VI & I*, ed. G. P. V. Akrigg (Berkeley, 1984), 431.

22 See Eve Kosofsky Sedgwick, *Between Men: English Literature and Male Homosocial Desire* (New York, 1985), 1–48.

23 The incident is discussed in Roger Lockyer, *Buckingham* (London, 1981), 101–3.

24 Greenblatt, "Fiction and Friction," 51.

John R. Leo

The Familialism of "Man" in American
Television Melodrama

I think it is possible to argue that the power of
speech should no longer be seen as the primary
model for all signification and communication,
but as a primitive technology that occupies in the
economy of sense-making the sort of position that
wood-burning does in the economy of energy. . . .
[T]he power of speech is now the electronic media
in general and television in particular. Its source
is no longer (if it ever was) the individual human
subject, but society. It is characterized by . . . the
exchange of a "subsistence wage" that is just sufficient for the sense-making economy to sustain
and reproduce itself and its social relations—the
"wages" of common sense.
—John Hartley [1]

By the mid-1980s North American broadcast television—the very instrument of
stereotypicality and legitimation, of centralized information and commercialized values
—was timidly offering more programming
with gay male characters (almost never lesbians) or themes, a phenomenon suggesting
perhaps less the mainstreaming of homosexual desire and more its rationalization as

an entertainment commodity within what Nick Browne has called the "political economy of the television supertext."[2] Television's strategies of recontainment, which allow "liberal gay discourse"[3] rare flow-slices of visibility but not serial amplification, deserve scrutiny as complex operations of power, including how the deployment of representational modes excludes the gay subject and occludes the gay object. At once a theft and an alibi, which would normalize gay relations by "uplifting" them into the fantasm of the nuclear family (the shopping unit whose true home is the mall), this televisual mapping is yet another patriarchal commodification of the "masculine." But even gestures generate (opposing) information in discursive vacuums. It is precisely within the heterogeneity of men's bodies and lives that we find the "others" who have always been there and are now transmitted back, like shelf products, in their stripped "generic" forms.

Following Roland Barthes in *S/Z*, let's provisionally say that a stereotype is an achieved transparency, a reduction of classes of people and events to a pure *denotation* ("the one which seems both to establish and close the reading").[4] The stereotype would think for us; it works as a realism, a conventionalized signification at first glance mirroring or extending directly from an unproblematic referent. It reads social space even while making meanings legible according to the outlines of its predispositions or those of an audience, who plug into its streamlined efficiency in varying ways. The stereotype assists and constructs perceptions, but even while it works as a device, as a mediation, as a condition of knowledge, it does so invisibly, seemingly "naturally." As a structure of signs, this apparently simplifying denotation works as a connotation, one which seems to designate persons and groups ahistorically and yet which assimilates new meanings over time. A stereotype works objectively (everything is an object), it works functionally (itself is a function), and it works willy-nilly (it is also desire). For better or worse, this is generally how stereotypicality manages its task of social construction, of information processing. At the very outset, then, we note this static and yet volatile nature of the stereotype, its roots in the representational activity of a society: its illusory status and its persuasive effects, its power of reduction and its inherent instability.

This understanding of stereotypicality underscores the difficulty in conceptualizing gender. My own assumption is "anti-essentialist" (not to be confused with "anti-referential"): that there is not an irreducible gay essence or core, some originary reference that is somehow "out there" on the other side of representation, which in turn can be invoked as the "truly gay," a master or unequivocal control referent or standard against which the false, the misleading or distorting stereotype can be measured. Talk about homosexual desire is already political and questions the conditions for (its) knowledge: the procedures, methods, codes, assumptions, and mental sets defining and constructing it as a critical object. By the same token, to talk about the gay stereotype requires that we locate *how* a discourse has situated its representations within the incontrovertible reality and variety of sexual difference, mixed audiences, and conflicting viewing strategies.[5]

Stereotypes collaborate with larger social narratives, specifically discourses whose juridic and authoritative natures also perform political and ideological work: discourses we can take to be the institutional languages and performatives infused across and within the social formation; sets of explicit and implicit rules authorizing both the positions of speaker and auditor; rules about who or what speaks and listens, and what may or may not be said. These "language games" (after Lyotard) are normative; they validate and embody the status quo and its most cherished realisms. Western versions are concrete manifestations of what Lyotard calls "master narratives," "Canonical Narratives" or "subject systems," what Foucault constellates as "knowledge/power," and what Fredric Jameson might call socialized "master codes" or "allegories," ones conferring legitimacy on or determining the interpretive conditions for social spaces and their organization.[6]

With these admittedly large reappropriations of quite divergent conceptions of stereotype and of discourse I wish to carry out two intertwined projects. One is to explore the telediscursive conditions for the production and reception of gay meanings for viewers, with particular reference to gay characterization and the melodramatic subtext in the made-for-TV film *Consenting Adult* (first broadcast on ABC in 1985 and 1987; sold to European TV syndication in 1987). The other is to elaborate, in the words of Abigail Solomon-Godeau, the "insight" that meanings "are not *only* hermetically contained within the 'endless chatter' of the circulation of signs . . . which in the absence of either recognition or challenge, by artist [producer] and spectator alike, will inevitably continue to be reproduced."[7] In short, my general goal is to help bring about the conditions for an oppositional reading of and within the "gay stereotype," not only to mark its positive but rather to prise its other, its history as a stereotype, already there. By locating muted "heterologies"[8] within the category of the homosexual, we advance historicist scholarship by publicizing what's bogus in the category itself and its heterosexist proppings.

Of course we must talk about several gay stereotypes since these are articulated by dominant discourses and nurtured by popular story-telling traditions. The gay subject, for example, has been textualized intensively by theology, jurisprudence, and medicine in the modern period, and it is this discourse proper on homosexual desire, which has separated the homosexual as a type of *person* ("invert") from the spectrum of permissible *experiences*, that gives rise to sexual classifications and their management of the sexual.[9] Thus while the discursive tropes helping to structure male interiority were being put into place—notions such as the "oedipal complex," the equation of all pleasure with heterosexuality if not with parenting, and antipathy toward any feminization of the masculine—the homosexual was invoked as the vanishing point of allowable male behavior and of representation. This deviancy was talked about and printed about, but as moral failing or case study. To be a homosexual was obscene, to represent one visually was pornographic.

This privatization—this *loss*—of sexual experience and even of limited community, and subsequent rigidification of sexual roles, serves the ideological program of familialism, or the mapping ("familializing") of conservative gender and family hierarchies onto the social formation.[10] To be a sissy, a "nellie" male, or an s/m leatherman, was by definition to be "queer": no longer of service to the true work of being a middle-class male, to be instead a failed male produced by failed parents (the sappy or missing father, the aggressive mother) or by a mutant body (unbalanced hormones). Visual representation tends to the synecdochic (genitalia and mouths define the graffiti) as does the verbal ("gay guys are mouth cunt").

If these earlier discourses and traditions, rooted in oral and printed media, historicize the social representation of the American gay male, he has a short history of any sort in mass media which, as Hartley argues, now replace speech in "the economy of sense-making." Appearances of gay characters on TV have been sparse until the 1980s and have tended to be confined to just a few genres—mainly melodrama and sitcoms—further typing a character quite unrealized in the first place. It was not until the Stonewall events provided the impetus for the national gay liberation movement that the electronic media took notice of gays in different regions, and then typified their acts and gestures of decolonization as either trends or sixties-styled countercultural groupings. By 1973 this unpredictably widespread movement in turn helped mobilize a coalition of doctors, psychologists, and clients which forced the American Psychiatric Association to declassify homosexual desire as an "illness." This was a crucial tactical step in the post-Stonewall history of gay representation by media, because a (literally) "recuperated" homosexuality—a "disorder," perhaps, or an "orientation," but no longer an "illness"—could now, cautiously, become TV life-style material: entertainment.

Pre-Stonewall representational hints of homosexual difference were on the small screen, but by displacement. Early gay analogues on TV in the 1950s, for example, include the utter artifice of Liberace ("the son every mother wishes for") and a swishing, camping Milton Berle wearing outlandish hats (a reminder of the pervasiveness of gays and gay references since the nineteenth century in the performance worlds of theater, vaudeville, and burlesque, TV's immediate ancestors for source material in its crucial early years), or just "fey" routines (Frank Nelson on Jack Benny's show or as Freddie Filmore on "I Love Lucy").[11] The *figure* of sexual difference was reduced to court jestering; (unspoken) homosexuality was not only not serious, it was also not the right stuff. Little from outside TV's idealized version of the family penetrated sitcoms, one exception being a "sensitive" and well-mannered male dancer on the "Honeymooners," who raises the red-blooded hackles of Ralph and Norton. Just as gays were imagined to be exterior to the nuclear family, more prodigal exile than aberrational part, so too were they dismissed from representative space in the media during the 1950s and 1960s, unless one were to count the televised fulminations against gays by McCarthy. It is hard, in this irreal but homophobic teleworld of Ozzie and Harriet, of Beaver and Howdy Doody, of male wrestling and Lucy and Desi, to imagine an established (serial) gay or lesbian character. But as David Marc has shown, during this period the televised family was patently out of it; its crises were all trivia, and its ethical dilemmas on the order of who really broke the window.[12]

More direct representation of homosexuality on TV occurs in the 1970s with occasional treatments on programs such as "All in the Family," "Maude," and the notoriously biased CBS Reports, "Gay Power, Gay Politics" (a "documentary" on San Francisco gays filled with errors and used—illegally—for fundraising by the right wing until stopped by CBS). With well-meaning and self-consciously liberal sitcoms, at least, the viewing impression is that the gay, like the camel, is a horse put together by a committee. When gays are admitted into a handful of these second-generation sitcoms the focus is on the adult or parental dilemma (but there are no children around in these episodes). Gays usually provide some comic relief even as they add a "sensitive theme programming" element to the plots. Disruption in these shows is comic, resolved always by the formulas of comedy and the prompting of the laugh track.[13]

Typical in these shows, usually an established series, is the isolated instance of gay-presence-as-disruption, a "problem" the presumably straight regulars can encounter, deal with, and perhaps be liberalized by. The dramatic problem is to represent a properly liberal reaction within the "normality" of social pluralism and consensus and emergent liberal gay discourse. The "problem" from the perspective of TV offices of standards and practices was how to present or format a gay character in any genre without alluding to his sexuality. In her history of a network's handling of homosexuality in a made-for-TV film[14] in the 1970s while it was consulting, for the first time, with gay organizations in both New York and Los Angeles, Kathryn Montgomery describes the hierarchy of criteria agreed to for packaging any viewing of homosexual desire on commercial TV:

[A]ll the decisions affecting the portrayal of gay life were influenced by the constraints which commercial television as a mass medium imposes upon the creation of its content. The fundamental goal of garnering the largest possible audience necessitated that (a) the program be placed in a familiar and successful television genre—the crime drama; (b) the story focus upon the heterosexual male lead character and his reactions to the gay characters rather than upon the homosexual characters themselves; and (c) the film avoid any overt display of affection which might be offensive to certain segments of the audience. These requirements served as a filter through which the issue of homosexuality was processed, resulting in a televised picture of gay life designed to be acceptable to the gay community and still palatable to a mass audience.

Even as these concessions were being struggled for, Montgomery's arguments imply that the networks negotiated them not because they were just or equitable. Rather, the broadcasters could avoid certain fights with gays and bad publicity (demonstrations and boycotts) by agreeing to a few programming changes; they thereby could increase their efficiency and optimize their performativity measured as profit.

It is illuminating in this context to note the taboos still operative within CBS during this same period, when TV was opening itself up to new programs and emphases and yet de-emphasizing sex to placate the right wing. Mere outspokenness on "Phyllis," for example, suffered "in the worsening network atmosphere of mid-70s censorship with the imposition of the Family Viewing Policy . . . [whose] primary victims were the adult comedies still scheduled before 9:00." Another observer gives more details, contrasting the earlier situations of give-and-take among the standards and practices people:

Now, suddenly, day into night. Phyllis has an important line, paying off a story she has told: "Of course, they were gay." That line has to come out, the network guy says. Offensive. "But don't you agree the line's proper in its context?" Oh yes, he agreed. . . . What would not be offensive, he had been authorized to say, would be a hand gesture that implied the word gay.[15]

Perhaps the hand gesture here would be a limp wrist.

Defined network policies of limited representation of gays and the Family Viewing Policy of mere implication share the same assumption that dramatic focus and resolution are to be reactive to a gay presence, and that gays are not to be solutions to the problem that, indeed, they pose. As John Ellis has shown persuasively, the network reasoning here is based on conceptions of its audience no different from familialism, albeit in its hyper-imaginary commodity form appropriate to an advertising medium. "TV viewers," he writes, "are assumed to be seeking diversion, to be watching in domestic surroundings, to be part of some family grouping. The TV viewer is given a certain position by these assumptions: the viewer is constituted as the normal citizen. . . . Normality is constituted as a constituent of the viewer's position by the intensive use of the familial and the domestic as point of reference for TV, both in direct address and in fiction; and by the constitution of the opposition 'inside'/'outside,' which insulates the viewer from events seen by TV."[16]

By the 1980s, however, gay sons and siblings are reincorporated inside the bourgeois family order of melodrama, albeit their homosexuality remains the crisis to be resolved according to the genre's formulas and codes (as in *Consenting Adult*, *An Early Frost*, and *Welcome Home, Bobby*). Or more exactly: the crisis to be resolved is the nuclear nest's repugnance and intransigence before an unrelentingly, unrepentantly gay son whose aberration in the post-Stonewall context is officially no longer a sickness and hence no longer treatable by the rationalism of science and psychiatry, the last great refuge, in a world of shot canonical narratives, for the middle class. Some of the constraints on gay representation described by Montgomery remain in place: he is sexless, an untouchable monad, not a subject within a community. This representational mode, however, is also interdiscursive: its incorporation of bits and pieces of older representations generates a subtextual level of signification frequently at odds with other dimensions of the storytelling's planes.

In the televisual world of narrative realism and sitcom, all is formula and stereotype in advance, albeit with new permutations and combinations, new denotations and connotations. In the 1980s some overtly gay topics and representations appear infrequently or indirectly on any network (mini)series, "Dynasty" being more longlasting rule than exception with its peek-a-boo handling of Steve Carrington's polysexuality. "Soap" was a short-lived critical and popular "recombinant" (or in Marc's phrase, "self-reflexive") exception vindicating itself in cable syndication. "Brothers," a series built around a family with a gay brother, is Showtime Cable, and "Benny Hill," like "Barney Miller," is all farce and disguise from the start.[17] "Hail to the Chief" and "Sara" had their brief play before millions in the 1985 season, but like "Brothers" are distinguished for having serial gay characters with full roles. By 1987 gay characters appeared in "serious" (nonreductive) roles in episodes from "Barney Miller," "St. Elsewhere," "Miami Vice," "Hotel," "Trapper John, M.D.," "L.A. Law," "Hooperman," and "The Golden Girls"; several of these programs won awards from the Alliance for Gay and Lesbian Artists in 1987 for their "responsible portrayal of gay and lesbian characters on screen [and] television."[18] Notwithstanding these exceptions, the near-banishment of homosexuality from everyday seriality effectively precludes its inclusion within TV normality, that is, from telediscourse and the forms of social familiarity it produces. Gay representation perforce must take the form of a disruption of the norm, which minimally is white and heterosexist, its presence being a "dilemma," a disruption of normal interiority, by definition the home, the stable world of middle-class manners and of heterosexual expectations.

═══

In the past few years several circumstances have combined to change what TV shows and finds profitable. Faltering ratings and alternative TV viewing habits have been ushered in by cable and VHS technology. The medium's programming needs, predicated on a principle of built-in obsolescence—styles, chromas, and topics get stale, syndication circulates older fare as a nostalgia commodity for which ad slots can be sold indefinitely—constantly require new treatments of existing genres, new oblivions and intensities. In industry jargon, what used to be censored as controversial is now welcomed as sensitive theme programming: programming open to new commodified topics, themes, and life-styles (homosexuality, male rape, alcoholic husbands, child abuse and incest, anorexia, bag ladies, conflicts among the deaf, an atomic bomb dropped on Kansas). Recent TV films (to pass over soaps and talk shows) such as *Consenting Adult, Love is Never Silent, Dress Grey, Burning Bed,* and *The Day After* are as symptomatic of discourses such as psychology by which new markets with new packages and formats for "experience" ("dysfunctional families") are cultivated, as they are of telediscourse which programs today's headlines the better to target specific spending groups and sell them as audiences ("life-styles") to advertisers.

Despite these reterritorializations and TV's efficiency (measurable as profits), it took producer Ray Aghayan nearly ten years to get Laura Z. Hobson's bestselling novel *Consenting Adult*—whose configurations are familiar and familial—to the small screen (ABC, 1985). Robert Calley never did get sufficient backing to adapt a play from the novel.[19] Through a maternal narrative filter Tessa Lynn tells the story of the traumatic fights, standoffs, and final reconciliations of the Lynn family as it came to terms, over a period of years, with the reactions and altered familial positions set in violent motion by the coming out and activist stance of her gay son, Jeff. Even after ABC agreed to do the movie, there were debates over lines and gestures in the script. It was only after the outpouring of public sympathy attending the death of Rock Hudson from AIDS that significant cuts were restored.[20]

Using Hollywood feature and soap editing styles, the melodrama combines discourse and stereotype within the genre of melodrama to put across, in seven segments, not so much Jeff's story—that would still be too "unpresentable," too much "advocacy"—but rather his mother's. The film's multiple story lines (Jeff's attempt to reconcile with his parents, his easygoing post-Stonewall compatibility with his sister Margie and brother-in-law Nate; Tess's conflicts with her husband Ken, who is impotent and dying from heart disease, and with her daughter, who resents mom's intrusions into everyone's lives; Ken's homophobia) and distribution of expository scenes (fights, outbursts, deferred emotional resolutions), plus the film's use of parallels and plot inversions, all contribute to competing centers for emotional investment and lines of interpretive decoding.

Melodrama on American commercial television is invariably built around conflicts within and threats from without to the idealized nuclear nest it represents. This imaginary family is at once the stage for its own "naturalness," a signifier of a taken-for-granted belonging-ness within the culture it simulates and validates, and also the locus for its naming of "strangeness," a signifier for being besieged by alien forces and "dangers." In Hartley's sense (citing Barthes), "middle-classness" (as distinct from race, youth, women, working class) is precisely that which is "ex-nominated" in representation: it "disap-pears" as a signifier and offers "what looks like a settled, positive, natural 'inside' for 'us' to access as our own selves."[21]

Consenting Adult and *An Early Frost* both demonstrate this generic condition. The macronarration for these films transcodes an "out-side" danger into an "inside" one: the abominable Other is a sibling-child at home wearing Weejuns. The homogeneous space of the bour-geois interior *irrupts* (from inside) and *produces* the heterologous: the homo travails with the hetero, the hetero with the homo. When gen-der relations are the specificities around which the melodrama must enact its simulations of familial and cultural crisis, the domestication of issues cannot help but read as a revision of discourses—here those sociosexual expectations which are patriarchal, heterosexist, and condemning of homosexual desire. Moreover, the genre's discursive hierarchies kept in place by the father (he dies in *Consenting Adult*), traditionally autonomous but relatively integrated at least in their dismissal of homosexuality from the family dinner table, perforce are pitted against each other. Jeff, for example, rejects his psychiatrist's attempt to "change" him into the image of what his parents wish, but on the basis that "I'm not sick." Religious discourse is simply not shown (psychiatry is, after all, an easier target for revision), and the juridical is moot. If a genre is a structure of expectations, and we expect acute conflict in a melodrama, then melodramas centered on homosexual desire flirt with the "ruin of representation" or of TV "realism" because they simply do not conform with majority notions of either desire or expectation. No wonder Ken, the angry but finally calm father/husband, dies from heart failure, although he leaves be-hind for Jeff a letter whose sentiment he just cannot face giving his son in person: "What father wants a homosexual for a son? . . . I do. . . . But I will not give up my son. You say you had no choice, then neither do I. . . . I love you. Dad." Nevertheless, Jeff's reconciliation with his father is symbolic but not literal; it is a melodramatic excess or fissure indicative of the discursive prohibitions operating within the dramatic.

As the delegate of liberal gay discourse in *Consenting Adult*, Jeff is mainly a signifying absence, in keeping with broadcast policy, and his entrances and exits are mainly keyed to keep attention on the parental anguish his transgression eventuates. His most dramatic scenes are at the boundaries: marking what cannot be shown about him but about which he can speak, or marking his parents' ignorance and resentment over which they have confrontations. He and Tess meet for lunch, for example, and while Jeff tells her about his physical attraction to men the camera zooms slowly to close-up: "Remember when you met dad? You wanted him. . . . I try to feel what [men] feel . . . but none of it happens. . . . I feel alive [when next to my swimmate]. I can't think of anything else. I dream about him. . . . I feel the same things for him I'm supposed to feel for girls." The reverse shot shows an upset and rejected Tess.

But it is Jeff's status as a *composite* stereotype which I want to comment on, for (like Victor Frankenstein's "Creature") he is put together from disarticulating bits and pieces of the historical discourse on homosexual desire, which become a narrative pastiche for middle-class "entertainment." It is simply the precondition for any discussion or representation of the gay subject that he has been medicalized and juridicalized against a background of the modern celebration of heterosexuality. If this were not the case, homosexuality would hardly be the stuff of TV melodrama. Jeff's psychiatrist, who in the film claims a "25% cure rate," is the figure for homosexuality as a disease and for scientism (and implicitly rationalism) as the repository for dreams of therapy and progress. He is the rejected surrogate of Krafft-Ebing, Ulrichs, Freud, and others from nineteenth- and twentieth-century science who would naturalize social relations and displace them into the disciplines of psychiatry, biology, and so on.

Jeff is shown as loving and caring of his father, who rejects him and not vice versa, a representation at odds with the popular notion that gay men are oedipal wrecks who hate their fathers. On the other hand, Ken is ill and dies, so he is thematized discursively as the "weak father." Jeff is closer emotionally with Tess, corresponds and meets with her secretly, a script formula whose discursive oedipal subtext reads that he is "close" to his "strong," "pushy," and "aggressive" mother. Jeff is a scholar-athlete, however, whose post-Stonewall "new masculinity" questions the sissy or nelly homosexual paradigm especially popular and tenacious since the lumping together of "decadents" of all sorts (the *flâneur*, dandy, artist) after about 1875 and whose symbolic concretization is Oscar Wilde. His college roommate throws him out after discovering Jeff is gay, but Jeff finds a lover in medical school. Jeff is "out": at first isolated and fearful, he can later tell people in a restaurant he is a "fag." Moreover, he has close friendships with women, and remains close with his brother-in-law and sister, a staging surely of babyboomer mainstreamed masculinity and other values suggesting the continuing erosion of rigid gender roles. Thus: Jeff is labeled, stigmatized, colonized, medicalized, blackmailed emotionally by his family to undergo therapy, rejected, hurt; his animality and sexuality are regulated (ostracized as "unpresentable"). He is also reincorporated, as the rebel body returned, back into the bourgeois family and its attendant obligations of fealty, kinship, and property.[22]

This is the form of *Consenting Adult*'s subtext: in Jameson's sense, the "story" which the film has tried to manage. At the same time, when we realize the role played in the dissemination of these narrative tropes we can more fully appreciate the roles of storytelling and social bonding in the organization of desire of real social subjects, and especially the role of the family. Jeff's characterization as young man who comes out/into his own homosexual desire is a sort of palimpsest (Jameson's example of allegorical writing and rewriting); it is at once the locus of multiple historical possibilities and of Foucauldian "power/knowledge," the emergence of "subjugated knowledges" or "resurrected languages" over against the patriarchal inscriptions on the gay body. These narrative layerings function as instances of the power of stories to undo their own organization, to offer, in other words, the basis for a genuine historical and oppositional reading of the film, and by extension the basis of a delegitimizing reading of hegemonic discourses.

Is this it for a gay viewer? we ask. Well, not quite. I want to suggest another reading of the idealized family of *Consenting Adult*, letting it be the metonym for the unselfconscious world of the middle-class melodrama and at the same time letting it stand for a *difference* in how some gays might view the imaginary of familialism.

The Lynn family is (after Jameson) a "fantasm" and also capital's ideological "axiomatic" of what the family *would* be: it is both dream and dreamworld and yet just empirical enough to represent actual possibility.[23] Remember the idealized family of the TV representation: a working father, a housewife, two children with the older daughter married and comfortable, a quite roomy upscale home in suburban Seattle (although the film was shot on location in Vancouver, B.C.) with terraced yard. Jeff, a star athlete at the University of Washington, is financially dependent on his father for tuition and expenses. When Jeff and Ken have their climactic fight, with the son asserting his right to love another man as a "consenting adult," Ken's harsh reply is: "I'm educating you . . . paying for your psychiatrist . . . [you're] not getting another penny!" Jeff walks out, to return for his (chastened) father's funeral. Even Tess's rejection yields to her love for her son. Seemingly, this is a family that has everything, including the power to heal itself. No matter what winds and waves storm against it, such as Ken's illness and untimely death from heart disease and the nearly catastrophic discovery that homosexuality is *inside* it, this family is all-powerful and overcoming. This is the simulated family, as Ellis has it, of viewer "expectation" (generic repetition) and/or "desire" (fantasy, libidinal investment).[24] Or is it?

Freely adapting Jameson's remarks on Balzac, the "metonymic and connotative registers" of melodramatic "realism" release (construct) an "object of desire," one assumed as much as it is invoked by the melodramatic texts and their tradition of idealized home life, in this instance a genealogical descent from TV's Ozzie-and-Harriet family matrix and one clearly associated with disposable income. The viewer's "consent" must be secured "before the narrative process can function properly," which is to say that the text may offer "a plausible desire that we do not ourselves share."[25] Ken's financial and emotional cutting off of his son opens up a gap for not only a gay but an antipatriarchal oppositional viewing of this film, one which identifies and resists the specificity of a father's world held together by rigid gender roles as the price for consumption, and poverty/expulsion/castration as the penalty for disobedience.

The gap opens further because the melodrama sets in motion another equally desirable goal—that of family unity and reconciliation within structures of difference—which is what the motivating quest of the drama is all about. The narrative apparatus for this film, then, depends on the desirability of two incommensurate goals or objects "mythologically" rendered compatible only by the father's death, an incommensurability which can be transcoded as the "turn" of the postmodern against the modern within the family itself. The master narratives essential to familialism are trashed.

Let me put it this way: in a more traditional narrative structure of a rebellious son whose paradigm would be the myth of the Prodigal Son and not Oedipus, the father's approval and the son's economic and sexual self-determination are always in potential or actual conflict, until the son seeks forgiveness or (in other narrative subsets) overcomes paternal alienation by marriage. In *Consenting Adult*, the counterinsurgency of same-gender sex and filial rejection of patrimony and economic tyranny is a double assault on the high altar of patriarchy and its say on gender relations and dispositions: this (corporeal) "unpresentable" is glossed over by the double agency of a mother's love and the son's reincorporation of his body back into healing (he will be a physician) and the middle class.

A consummate irony: this telediscursive son who rejected psychiatry, who refused the "soft terror" of control and normalization by medicine, turns his "madness" and immorality into electronic speech. Thus the utopian projection released by this partial conglomeration of gay stereotypes rebounds as a critique of the social. The TV family of melodrama gives a fantasized objectivity to social problems, and viewers experience themselves and social problems by consuming them in this spectacular form. However, glimpses of *other* sexualities and communities may be caught in these *histories* of pop representations, prompting us "to learn to desire differently."[26]

———

Several things are manifestly clear from these examples on what and how the TV stereotype is constituted and received. One is that what

goes into the making of a stereotype is not necessarily what is consumed. Another is that the model of the communication process one
uses for the analysis of the stereotype has its own operating assumptions. It is also clear that in cultural dynamics and communications,
encoding and decoding activities are asymmetrical operations in the
production of meanings.[27]

Dominant or preferred interpretations at one encoding level, however, may be opposed or undermined by variant encodings at another
narrative level *and* by diffused receptions. The history of film, for
example, shows us that gay men a generation ago identified with
"strong" female *film noir* stars such as Bette Davis and Joan Crawford,
who were tough fighters and sexually free agents up against tough
odds (including their "bad girl" reputations and cynical piety), just as
today all sorts of men watch "Dynasty"'s Alexis through camp eyes.
Stereotypes, as part of an informational flow with shifting narrative
functions, thereby assist in destabilizing what appears most perma-
nent in the social order: distinctions between the sexes, or between
"good" and "evil." One could argue, to take another example, that
the lawyer dying from AIDS in *An Early Frost* (NBC) is stereotypical
in the sense that he fits into an old pattern: the gay hero is symbolically punished and killed, although in this movie his death is forecast,
not shown. (Vito Russo and others use this argument in putting down
No Way Out, a thriller with a gay villain who also kills himself.) My
point is, however, that the dying lawyer's stereotype is determined by
its structural position in the melodrama. As a *queer* or *fag* this man
is an object of scorn and fear, but as a *son* and successful *lawyer* he
is invested with sympathy because he reproduces middle-class professional desires. It is a truism that the networks do not "advocate"
homosexuality, yet they do advocate tearjerkers. Cultural contempt
is modified by the culture's own ideological investment in familialism. One of the unintended effects of *An Early Frost* is to narrate how
the family is itself an ideological construct which in turn reproduces
discursive conflicts to the point of agonized contradiction.

It is this flux in the communication process that undermines,
restages, and redefines an always shifting discursive "common sense,"
according to Hartley, whose point of view echoes Lyotard's arguments on the collapse of the "master narratives" (Christianity, Marx-

ism, capitalism). "Narratives," Lyotard argues in *The Postmodern Condition*, are not only "master" in the sense of discursively dominant (although ruined and "collapsed" because they are (a) increasingly dispersed, incredible, and inapplicable and (b) therefore no longer socially "efficient" and magisterially determinant); narratives are also "micronarratives" which use information *differently* and to ends *other* than those of the decision-makers and managers of the postmodern society of information manipulation. He writes:

> In a sense the people are only that which actualizes the narratives; once again, they do this not only by recounting them, but also by listening to them and recounting themselves through them; in other words, by putting them into "play" in their institutions. . . . Narratives . . . determine criteria of competence and/or illustrate how they are to be applied. They thus define what has the right to be said and done in the culture in question, and since they are themselves a part of that culture, they are legitimated by the simple fact that they do what they do.[28]

In Lyotard's usage, which I am oversimplifying here, a stereotype would be a sort of abstracted embodiment of a "language game," a "phrase linkage" or "rule," one floating about institutions and (always regrouping) discourses, connecting them and operating their power. In this view a stereotype would be useful to the extent that it optimized an institution's performativity (profits) by achieving the aims of a specific narrative (positioning individuals within the social character roles allocated by a particular story or plot). For the same reason a stereotype could be changed, recombined with others, or otherwise made commensurable (useful, visible) as information. Gays, minorities of all sorts, and WASPs all constitute "clouds of sociality" ("language clouds") which are managed by decision-makers "according to input/output matrices, following a logic which implies that their elements are commensurable and that the whole is determinable." A possible end to which stereotypes are put, then, is the "organic" ("melting pot") view of society, one supporting a rationalist view of the socioeconomic system as inherently "centrist" and "centralized," in Ellis's useful terms.

Managers, Lyotard continues, "allocate our lives for the growth of power. In matters of social justice and of scientific truth alike, the legitimation of that power is based on its optimizing the system's performance—efficiency. The application of this criterion to all of our games necessarily entails a certain level of terror, whether soft or hard: be operational (that is, commensurable) or disappear."[29] The extent to which a narrative function, including the stereotype, is commensurable (that it carry out the assigned task of realism: "to preserve various consciousnesses from doubt," or give them "nostalgia" or aesthetic "suffering"), means that it is socially efficient in the derealized world of late capitalism. "Realism" is now problematized, and with it any notion of stereotypical representation:

> Industrial photography and cinema will be superior to painting and the novel whenever the objective is to stabilize the referent, to arrange it according to a point of view which endows it with a recognizable meaning, to reproduce the syntax and vocabulary which enable the addressee to decipher images and sequences quickly, and so to arrive easily at the consciousness of his own identity as well as the approval which he thereby receives from others—since such structures of images and sequences constitute a communication code among all of them. This is the way the effects of reality, or if one prefers, the fantasies of realism, multiply.[30]

To "stabilize the referent" means that a major function of cultural artifacts, including TV representation, is to repeat efficiently, quickly, and easily a point of view with "recognizable meaning," a homogeneity culturally produced and sustained which devalues difference. Or, if difference is to be reincorporated (made commensurable, mainstreamed) into the body politic, it is to be repeatedly narrated along new story lines building on shared "communication codes": the very business of TV. The "effects of reality" are indistinguishable from the (televised) "fantasies of realism," which, as Lyotard goes on to demonstrate, are functionally the "mixing" and recombining of story elements, images, and hints of an avant-garde (the unpresentable) into a pulsing, changing pastiche. *This* is the post-modern *condition*: pastiche, mishmash, a citation here and another there always in segments, TV's final commodity form, an endless production of reproduction for optimum profit.

Perhaps what we need is an acceleration of citations and pastiches, an overdetermination of TV "realisms" and stereotypes so as to inundate an unsuspecting body politic already awash with "entertainment" to the point of being swamped; perhaps we need to broadcast made-for-TV Bataille, Nietzsche, Kathy Acker, at least *Taxi zum Klo* (as was done during prime time by NOS Dutch Television in the spring of 1986).[31] The oppositional postmodern gesture would be to push language games to their limits, to partake of the *duplicity* of an exhausted "tasteful" (reactionary, modernist) intention in order to bring the unpresentable a little closer—to celebrate the commodification of the gay man as a middle-class hero of consumption—for the purpose of disarticulating not only the logic of modernity's constraints but also their power.

Notes

1 John Hartley, "Encouraging Signs: Television and the Power of Dirt, Speech, and Scandalous Categories," in *Interpreting Television: Current Research Perspectives*, ed. Willard D. Rowland, Jr., and Bruce Watkins (Beverly Hills, 1984), 138.

2 Nick Browne, "The Political Economy of the Television Supertext," *Quarterly Review of Film Studies* 9 (Summer 1984): 174–82; see Larry Gross, "The Cultivation of Intolerance: Television, Blacks, and Gays," in *Cultural Indicators: An International Symposium*, ed. Gabriele Melischek et al. (Vienna, 1984), 345–63, and his "Out of the Mainstream: Sexual Minorities and the Mass Media," in *Rethinking the Audience*, ed. Hans Borchers and Ellen Seiter (London, forthcoming).

3 Mark Finch, "Sex and Address in *Dynasty*," *Screen* 27 (November–December 1986): 24–42.

4 Roland Barthes, *S/Z*, trans. Richard Miller (New York, 1974), 8–9.

5 Richard Dyer, "Stereotyping," in *Gays and Film*, ed. Richard Dyer (New York, 1984), 27–39; Andy Medhurst, "'Victim': Text as Context," *Screen* 25 (July–October 1984): 22–35; and Frank Lentricchia, "Patriarchy Against Itself—The Young Manhood of Wallace Stevens," *Critical Inquiry* 13 (Summer 1987): 742–86.

6 Jean-François Lyotard, *The Postmodern Condition: A Report on Knowledge*, trans. Geoff Bennington and Brian Massumi (Minneapolis, 1984); Michel Foucault, "Powers and Strategies," in *Power/Knowledge: Selected Writings, 1972–1977*, trans. Colin Gordon et al., ed. Colin Gordon (New York, 1980); Fredric Jameson, *The Political Unconscious: Narrative as a Socially Symbolic Act* (Ithaca, 1981).

7 Abigail Solomon-Godeau, "Beyond the Simulation Principle," in *Utopia Post Utopia: Configurations of Nature and Culture in Recent Sculpture and Photography*, Exhibition Catalogue at the Institute for Contemporary Art (Boston, 1988), 97.

8 Michel de Certeau, "History: Science and Fiction," in *Heterologies: Discourse on the Other*, trans. Brian Massumi (Minneapolis, 1986), 199–221. See also Gad Horowitz and Michael Kaufman, "Male Sexuality: Toward a Theory of Liberation," in *Beyond Patriarchy: Essays by Men on Pleasure, Power, and Change*, ed. Michael Kaufman (Toronto, 1987), 103–17.

9 See two works by Jeffrey Weeks: *Coming Out: Homosexual Politics in Britain from the Nineteenth Century to the Present* (London, 1977), and "Discourse, Desire and Sexual Deviance: Some Problems in a History of Homosexuality," in *The Making of the Modern Homosexual*, ed. Kenneth Plummer (London, 1981). See also Gary Kinsman, "Men Loving Men: The Challenge of Gay Liberation," in Kaufman, ed., *Beyond Patriarchy*, 103–17; and Don Mager, "Gay Theories of Gender Role Deviance," *SubStance* 46 (1985): 32–48.

10 Michele Barrett and Mary McIntosh, *The Anti-Social Family* (London, 1982), discussed by Serafina Bathrick, "The *Mary Tyler Moore Show*: Women at Home and at Work," in *MTM: "Quality" Television*, ed. Jane Feuer, Paul Kerr, and Tise Vahimagi (London, 1984), 99–100. See also Jacques Donzelot, *The Policing of Families* (New York, 1979).

11 On gays and theater see Kaier Curtin, *We Can Always Call Them Bulgarians* (Boston, 1987); and on "fey" TV, Richard Laermer, "The Televised Gay: How We're Pictured on the Tube," *The Advocate*, 5 February 1985, 20–21, 23–25.

12 David Marc, *Demographic Vistas: Television in American Culture* (Philadelphia, 1984).

13 See Paul Attallah, "The Unworthy Discourse: Situation Comedy in Television," in Rowland and Watkins, eds., *Interpreting Television*, 222–49.

14 Kathryn Montgomery, "Gay Activists and the Networks," *Journal of Communication* 31 (Summer 1981): 49–57; and Braddlee and Michael Killoren, "In the Matter of Pacifica: Free Speech and Governmental Regulation" (Paper presented at the American Culture Association, New Orleans, March 1988).

15 "MTM Productions: A Guide," in Feuer, Kerr, and Vahimagi, eds., *MTM: "Quality" Television*, 214.

16 John Ellis, *Visible Fictions* (London, 1982), 169.

17 Attallah, "Unworthy Discourse," 239.

18 Deborah Caulfield, "Gay Alliance Awards: E for Effort, Emotion," *Los Angeles Times*, 23 March 1987, sec. 4.

19 Laura Z. Hobson, *Laura Z: A Life* (New York, 1986), 281–309.

20 Adam Block, " 'An Early Frost': The Story Behind NBC's AIDS Drama," *The Advocate*, 26 November 1985, 43–47.

21 Hartley, "Encouraging Signs," 129.

22 Francis Barker, *The Tremulous Private Body: Essays on Subjection* (New York, 1985).

23 Jameson, *Political Unconscious*, 153–57, 180–82.

24 Ellis, *Visible Fictions*, 6–7.

25 Jameson, *Political Unconscious*, 156.

26 Colin Mercer, "A Poverty of Desire: Pleasure and Popular Politics," in *Formations of Pleasure*, Formations Editorial Collective (London, 1983), 100.

27 Dick Hebdige, *Subculture: The Meaning of Style* (London, 1979); and two essays by Stuart Hall, "The Rediscovery of 'Ideology': Return of the Repressed in Media Studies," in *Culture, Society and the Media*, ed. Michael Gurevitch et al. (London, 1982), 56–90; and "Encoding/Decoding," in *Culture, Media, Language: Working Papers in Cultural Studies, 1972–1979*, ed. Stuart Hall et al. (London, 1980), 128–38.

28 Lyotard, *Postmodern Condition*, 23.

29 Ibid., xxiv.

30 Ibid., 74.

31 John R. Leo, "Postmodernity, Narrative, Sexual Politics: Reflections on Jean-François Lyotard," forthcoming in *Centennial Review*.

Eve Kosofsky Sedgwick

Across Gender, Across Sexuality:
Willa Cather and Others

I want to challenge the assumption that feminism
is or should be the privileged site of a theory of
sexuality. Feminism is the theory of gender oppression. . . . Gender affects the operation of the
sexual system, and the sexual system has had gen-
der-specific manifestations. But although sex and
gender are related, they are not the same thing.
—Gayle Rubin, "Thinking Sex"

Let's hypothesize, with Gayle Rubin, that
the question of gender and the question
of sexuality, inextricable from each other
though they are in that each can be expressed
only in the terms of the other, are nonetheless not the same question, that gender and
sexuality represent two analytic axes that
may productively be imagined as being as
distinct from each other as, say, gender and
class, or class and race.[1] Under this hypothe-
sis, just as we've learned to assume that no
issue of racial meaning fails to be embodied
through the specificity of a particular class
position—and no issue of class, for instance,
through the specificity of a particular gender

position—so we can assume that no issue of gender would fail to be embodied through the specificity of a particular sexuality, and vice versa; nonetheless, there could be use in keeping the analytic axes distinct.

Next, let's hypothesize that gay/lesbian and antihomophobic inquiry still has a lot to learn from asking the questions that feminist inquiry has learned to ask—but only so long as we don't demand to receive the same answers. Comparing feminist and gay theory as they currently stand, the newness and consequent relative underdevelopment of gay theory are most visible in two manifestations. First, we are by now very used to asking as feminists what we aren't yet used to asking as antihomophobic readers: how a variety of forms of oppression intertwine systemically with each other, and especially how the person who is disabled through one set of oppressions may *by the same positioning* be enabled through others. For instance, the understated demeanor of educated women in our society tends to mark both their deference to educated men and their expectation of deference from women and men of lower class. Again, a woman's use of a married name makes graphic her subordination as a woman and at the same time her privilege as a presumptive heterosexual. Or again, the distinctive vulnerability to rape of women of all races has become in this country a powerful tool for the racist enforcement by which white people, including women, are privileged at the expense of black people of both genders. That one is *either* oppressed *or* an oppressor, on the other hand, or, if one happens to be both, that the two are not likely to have much to do with each other, still seems to be a common assumption in at least male gay writing and activism, as it hasn't for a long time been in careful feminist work.

Indeed, it was the long, painful realization, *not* that all oppressions are congruent, but that they are *differently* structured and so must intersect in complex embodiments, that has been the first great heuristic breakthrough of feminist thought. This realization has as its corollary that the comparison of different axes of oppression is a crucial task, not for any purpose of ranking oppressions, but to the contrary because each oppression is likely to be in a uniquely indicative relation to certain distinctive nodes of cultural organization. The *special* centrality of homophobic oppression in the twentieth century has been in its inextricability from the question of knowledge and the processes of knowing in modern Western culture at large.

The second and perhaps even greater heuristic leap of feminism has been the recognition that categories of gender—and hence oppressions of gender—can have a structuring force for axes of cultural discrimination whose thematic subject isn't explicitly gendered at all. We have now learned as feminist readers that dichotomies in a given text—of culture as opposed to nature, for instance, public as opposed to private, mind as opposed to body, activity as opposed to passivity—are, under particular pressures of culture and history, likely places to look for implicit allegories of the relations of men to women; more, that to fail to analyze such nominally ungendered constructs in gender terms can itself be a gravely tendentious move in the gender politics of reading. This has given us ways to ask the question of gender about texts even where the culturally "marked" gender (female) is not present as either author or thematic. Coming of age at the same time as and in a synergistic relation to deconstruction, much feminist reading is moreover richly involved with the deconstructive understanding that categories presented in a culture as symmetrical binary oppositions— male/female, as well as culture/ nature, etc.—actually subsist in a more unsettling and dynamic tacit relation according to which, first, term B is not symmetrical with but subordinated to term A; but, second, the ontologically valorized term A actually depends for its meaning on the simultaneous subsumption and exclusion of term B; hence, third, the question of priority between the supposed central and the supposed marginal category of each dyad is irresolvably unstable.

The dichotomy heterosexual/homosexual, as it has emerged through the last century of Western discourse, would seem to lend itself peculiarly neatly to a set of analytic moves learned from this deconstructive moment in feminist theory. One has perhaps only to remind oneself that the "deviant" category "homosexual" antedates the supposedly normative "heterosexual": conceptually by something over a decade, and lexically, in American English, by at least two years.[2] In fact, heterosexual/homosexual fits the deconstructive template much more neatly than the dichotomy male/female does, and hence, importantly differently. The most dramatic difference between gender and sexual orientation—that virtually all people are publicly and unalterably assigned to one or the other gender, and from birth—seems if anything to mean that it is rather sexual orientation, with its far greater potential for rearrangement, ambiguity, and representational doubleness, that would offer the more apt deconstructive object. An essentialism of sexual object choice is far less easy to maintain, far more visibly incoherent, more visibly stressed and challenged at every point in the culture, than any essentialism of gender. Indeed the unbudging conceptual deadlock over the last hundred years between minoritizing views of homosexuality as the fixed trait of a distinct small percentage of the population, and universalizing views of it as a widely diffused potential in whole populations whom only its pointed repression renders heterosexual, answers the deconstructive analysis of the instability of binary oppositions with a congruence that may prove telling on both sides. And our developing understanding of the centrality of homosocial bonds to patriarchal heterosexist culture suggests ways of extending such an analysis from the individual to the systemic level.

A definitional and methodological caution concerning the relation of my current subject, gay/lesbian and antihomophobic theory, to the project alluded to by Gayle Rubin in the sentences I've used as an epigraph, a theory of sexuality. The two can after all scarcely be coextensive. And this is true not because "gay/lesbian and antihomophobic theory" would fail to cover heterosexual as well as same-sex object choice (any more than "feminist theory" would fail to cover men as well as women), but rather because sexuality extends along so many dimensions that aren't well-described in terms of the gender of object choice at all. Some of these dimensions are habitually condensed under the rubrics of object choice, so that certain discriminations of (for instance) *act*, or of (for another instance) *erotic localization*, come into play however implicitly and however incoherently when categories of object choice are mobilized. For example, one used to hear a lot about a high developmental stage called "heterosexual genitality"; or again, a certain anal-erotic salience of male homosexuality is if anything increasingly strong under the glare of heterosexist AIDS-phobia; while several different historical influences have led to the degenitalization and bodily diffusion of many popular, and indeed many lesbian, understandings of lesbian sexuality. Other dimensions of sexuality, however, distinguish object choice quite differently (for example, human/animal, adult/child, singular/plural, autoerotic/alloerotic) or are not even about object choice (e.g., orgasmic/nonorgasmic, noncommercial/commercial, using bodies only/using manufactured objects, in private/in public, spontaneous/scripted). Some of these other dimensions of sexuality have had high diacritical importance in different historical contexts (e.g., human/animal, autoerotic/alloerotic). Others, like adult/child object choice, visibly do have such importance today, but without being very fully subsumed under the homo/heterosexual binary. Still others, including a host of them I haven't mentioned or couldn't think of, subsist in this culture as nondiacritical differences, differences that seem to make little difference beyond themselves—except that the hyperintensive structuring of sexuality in our culture sets several of them at the exact border between legal and illegal. What I mean, at any rate, to emphasize is that the implicit condensation of "sexual theory" into "gay/lesbian and anti-homophobic theory," which corresponds roughly to our by now unquestioned reading of the ubiquitous "sexual orientation" to mean "gender of object choice," is at the very least damagingly skewed by its present historical placement.

Even insofar as the question of sexuality can be condensed as the question of homo/heterosexuality, however, its conceptualization is anything but simple. In recent work, I have been arguing that our culture's crystallization of gay identities over the past hundred years has persistently been structured by two conceptual impasses or incoherences, one concerning *gender* definition and the other concerning *sexual* definition.

	Separatist	Integrative
Homo/hetero *sexual* definition	*Minoritizing*, e.g., gay identity, "essentialist," third-sex models, civil rights models	*Universalizing*, e.g., bisexual potential, "social constructionist," "sodomy" models, "lesbian continuum"
Gender definition	*Gender separatist*, e.g., homosocial continuum, lesbian separatist, manhood-initiation models	*Inversion/liminality/transitivity*, e.g., cross-sex, androgyny, gay/lesbian solidarity models

With regard to gender, two quite opposite possibilities for defining the person who desires someone of their own gender have prevailed, often at the same time. One of these, the gender-integrative possibility manifest in the turn-of-the-century topos of inversion ("a woman's soul trapped in a man's body" or vice versa), but longer-lived in homophobic folklore and "common sense," in certain influential formulations of psychoanalysis and psychiatry, and also in many vibrant aspects of current gay and lesbian culture, points to an essential femininity in gay men and/or an essential masculinity in lesbians. While this topos of inversion or liminality places gay people exactly at the threshold between genders, its persistence has been yoked, at the same time, to that of its contradictory counterpart, the topos of gender separatism. Under this latter view, far from its being of the essence of desire (including same-sex desire) to cross boundaries of gender, it is instead the most natural thing in the world that people of the same gender, people grouped together under the single most determinative diacritical mark of social organization, people whose social needs and knowledges may have so much in common, should band together also on the axis of sexual desire. As the gender-separatist substitution of the concept "woman-identified woman" for the gender-liminal stereotype of the mannish lesbian suggests, as indeed does the concept of the continuum of male or female homosocial desire, this topos tends to reassimilate identification with desire. Inversion models, by contrast, depend conceptually on the distinctness of identification from desire. Gender separatist models would thus place the woman-loving woman and the man-loving man each at the "natural" defining center of their own gender, rather than, as gender-integrative models would, at the threshold between genders. The immanence of each of these models in the history of gay theory is clear from the early split in the German homosexual rights movement between Magnus Hirschfeld, who posited, in Donald Mager's paraphrase, "an exact equation . . . between cross-gender behaviors and homosexual desire," and Benedict Friedländer, who concluded to the contrary "that homosexuality was the highest, most perfect evolutionary stage of gender differentiation. Men who needed women were seen as less manly than those who could transcend the procreational imperative in favor of this higher 'masculinity.' "[3]

Along with the incoherence about *gender* definition, a deadlock or incoherence of definition prevails, as well, between separatist and integrative conceptualizations of homo/hetero*sexual* definition. Over the span of a century, definitions of homosexuality as a universal human potential have conflicted with definitions of it as the trait of a distinct and fixed minority. The most current form in which this conflict is visible is in the debate between "social constructionist" and "essentialist" understandings of homo/heterosexual identity. The conflict has a long history, however. Historical narratives since Foucault have seemed to show universalizing paradigms, such as the proscription of particular *acts* called "sodomy" (acts that might be performed by anybody), as being displaced after the late nineteenth century by the definition of particular kinds of *persons*, specifically "homosexuals." But the truth seems to be that since the late nineteenth century the two understandings, contradictory though they are, have coexisted, creating in the space of their contradiction enormous potentials of discursive power. We have just at the moment of this writing (March 1988) a perfect example of this potent incoherence in the anomalous legal situation of gay people and acts in this country: while the Supreme Court in *Bowers v. Hardwick* has notoriously left the individual states free to prohibit any *acts* that they wish to define as "sodomy," by whomsoever performed, with no fear at all of impinging on any rights, and particularly privacy rights, safeguarded by the Constitution—at the same time a panel of the Ninth Circuit Court of Appeals ruled last month (in *Sergeant Perry J. Watkins v. United States Army*) that homosexual *persons*, as a particular kind of person, *are* entitled to Constitutional protections under the Equal Protection clause. To be gay in this system is to come under the radically overlapping aegises of a universalizing discourse of acts and at the same time of a minoritizing discourse of persons. Just at the moment, at least in the institutions of law, the former aegis prohibits what the latter protects. But in the concurrent public health constructions around AIDS, for instance, it is far from clear that a minoritizing discourse of persons ("risk groups") is not even more oppressive than the competing, universalizing discourse of acts ("safer sex"). In the double binds implicit in the space overlapped by both, the stakes in matters of definitional control are extremely high.[4]

One thing that does emerge with clarity from this complex and contradictory map of sexual and gender definition is that the possible grounds to be found there for alliance and cross-identification among various groups will also be plural. To take the issue of gender definition alone: under a gender separatist topos, lesbians might look for identifications and alliances among women in general including straight women (as in Adrienne Rich's "lesbian continuum" model); and gay men, as in Friedländer's model—or more recent "male liberation" models—of masculinity, might look for them among men in general including straight men. Under a topos of gender inversion or liminality, on the other hand, gay men might look to identify with straight women (on grounds that they are also "feminine" or also desire men), or with lesbians (on grounds that they similarly occupy a liminal position); while lesbians might analogously look to identify with gay men or, though this latter identification has not been strong since second-wave feminism, with straight men. Note, however, that this schematization over "the issue of gender definition alone" also impinges on the issue of homo/heterosexual definition, and in an unexpectedly chiasmic way. Gender-*separatist* models like Rich's or Friedländer's seem to tend toward *universalizing* understandings of homo/heterosexual potential. To the degree that gender-*integrative* inversion or liminality models suggest an alliance or identity between lesbians and gay men, on the other hand, they tend toward gay-*separatist*, minoritizing models of specifically gay identity and politics. These crossings are quite contingent, however, as suggested by Freud's universalizing understanding of sexual definition which seems to go with an integrative, inversion model of gender definition. And more broadly, the routes to be taken across this misleadingly symmetrical map are fractured in a particular historical situation by the profound asymmetries of gender oppression and heterosexist oppression.

For a particular gay or lesbian subject, then, to choose a figure in a different position with whom to identify even partially always has the potential of being revelatory in *some* way about *some* aspect of the positioning of the subject her- or himself: not through a vague invocation of the commonality of all people of all genders and sexualities, though that may also be at work, but through the complex and conflictual specificities of what different positionings may have in common under the contradictory definitional aegises of our century.

═════

Willa Cather's 1905 short story, "Paul's Case: A Study in Temperament," was her own lifelong favorite among her stories, the one she republished most and the only one she allowed to be anthologized by others. The *omphalos* of her continuing attachment to this story is oddly difficult to locate; but (if it's permissible to complicate the navel metaphor in this way) the knotted-up surgical scar of her *de*tachment from the story's main character is almost its first legible sign. "It was Paul's afternoon to appear before the faculty of the Pittsburgh High School to account for his various misdemeanors," the story begins; with a "rancour and aggrievedness" for which they themselves feel shamed by their inability to account, the teachers of this tense, unlovely, effeminate, histrionic boy "fell upon him without mercy, his English teacher leading the pack."[5]

> Once, when he had been making a synopsis of a paragraph at the blackboard, his English teacher had stepped to his side and attempted to guide his hand. Paul had started back with a shudder and thrust his hands violently behind him. The astonished woman could scarcely have been more hurt and embarrassed had he struck at her. The insult was so involuntary and definitely

personal as to be unforgettable. In one way and another, he had made all his teachers, men and women alike, conscious of the same feeling of physical aversion.

The equivocalness of "the same feeling of physical aversion"—does the aversion live in his body, or in theirs; or is the aversiveness tied up with a certain threat of de-differentiation between them?—seems fulfilled when it is the teachers, and not the object of their discipline, who "left the building dissatisfied and unhappy; humiliated to have felt so vindictive toward a mere boy, to have uttered this feeling in cutting terms, and to have set each other on, as it were, in the grewsome game of intemperate reproach." And that evening, when the English teacher arrives at a concert for which the boy is officiously acting as usher, it is she who betrays "some embarrassment when she handed Paul the tickets, and a *hauteur* which subsequently made her feel very foolish."

The Pittsburgh High School English teacher evaporates as a character from "Paul's Case" shortly thereafter—"Paul forgot even the nastiness of his teacher's being there." There is nothing in the story to suggest where her unushered homeward steps will take her, though they would have taken one Pittsburgh high school English teacher any evening in 1905 back to a bedroom shared with a sumptuously beautiful young woman, Isabelle McClung, who has defied her parents to the extent of bringing her imposing lover, Willa Cather, into the family home to live. While this English teacher doesn't require to be identified with that English teacher, it is also less easy than it might be to differentiate firmly their attitudes toward what Katherine Anne Porter confidently labels as "a real 'case' in the clinical sense of the word," that is to say, "boys like Paul."[6]

Paul's teachers feel humiliated because they have found themselves momentarily unified in a ritual of scapegoating, without being at all clear what it is in the scapegoat that deserves torment or even what provokes this sudden communal construction. Cather herself had some history of being an effeminophobic bully; perhaps also of feeling shamed by being one. Ten years before "Paul's Case," for instance, in 1895, the year when a new homophobic politics of indignity had its watershed international premiere in the trials of Oscar Wilde,

Cather published two columns on Wilde. In each of these, she harnesses her own prose eagerly to the accelerating rhetoric of the public auto-da-fé. Wilde is not just some random sinner—certainly not the object of any injustice—but something more, a signal criminal of Luciferian stature, the "ghastly eruption that makes [society] hide its face in shame."[7] Wilde "is in prison now, most deservedly so. Upon his head is heaped the deepest infamy and the darkest shame of his generation. Civilization shudders at his name, and there is absolutely no spot on earth where this man can live. Cain's curse was light compared with his." Joining so perfervidly in the public scapegoating of Wilde, Cather also seems, however, to assert a right, earned by the very excess of her revilement, to define for herself, and differently from the way the society or for that matter the courts had defined it, the "true" nature of Wilde's sin and hence the true justification for his punishment of two years' imprisonment with hard labor. Wilde's disgrace is, in Cather's account, no isolated incident but "the beginning of a national expiation" for "the sin which insults the dignity of man, and of God in whose image he was made," "the potentiality of all sin, the begetter of all evil." And that sin? "—Insincerity." "Art that is artificial and insincere" is the true "sin against the holy spirit," "for which there is no forgiveness in Heaven, no forgetting in Hell." The odd oversight of the framers of the Criminal Law Amendment Act and the 1885 Labouchère amendment to it, in omitting to include by name the unspeakable crimes of artificiality and insincerity, doesn't slow Cather a bit in this determined act of redefinition. Reactivating the ancient, barely latent cognitive antithesis between homosexual acts and *the natural*, Cather strongly reinforces the assaultive received association between Wilde's sexuality and a reprobated, putatively feminine love of artifice. At the same time, though, distinguishing however slightly and invidiously the one crime from the other ("The sins of the body are very small compared with that"), she also holds open a small shy gap of nonidentification between the two in which some nascent germ of gay-affirmative detachment, of critique, or even of outlaw love might shelter to await her own less terroristic or terrorized season.

Had that season arrived with the writing a decade later of "Paul's Case"? In the early, Pittsburgh part of the story, it seems, quite to the contrary, that the identification between Paul's pathology on the one hand and his insincerity and artificiality on the other is so seamless that the former is to be fully evoked by the latter, through a mercilessly specular, fixated point of view that takes his theatrical self-presentation spitefully at its word. "His eyes were remarkable for a certain hysterical brilliancy, and he continually used them in a conscious, theatrical sort of way, peculiarly offensive in a boy." Paul's glance is a jerkily unsteady one—"Paul was always smiling, always glancing about him, seeming to feel that people might be watching him and trying to detect something"—but the gaze of the narrative at him is so unresting as to give point to his desperate way of regarding the world; one English teacher, at least, is eternally there to describe him "looking wildly behind him now and then to see whether some of his teachers were not there to witness his light-heartedness." Like Cather's Wilde a decade earlier, it seems as if Paul is to be hounded to exhaustion or death for a crime that hovers indeterminately between sex/gender irregularity and spoilt sensibility or bad art. The invidious need of a passionate young lesbian to place, and at a distance, the lurid, contagious scandal of male homosexuality: it is as if that were not quite to be disentangled from the invidious need of a hungry young talent to distinguish itself once and for all from the "hysterical" artifice of the hapless youth who needs talent but hasn't it.

If the early parts of "Paul's Case" seem written from the unloving compulsions of the English teacher, however, the latter part of the story, after Paul has stolen a thousand dollars from his father's employer and run away to New York, opens out to what seems to me an amazing tenderness of affirmation. How common is it, in a fictional tradition ruled by *le mensonge romantique*, for a powerfully desiring character to get the thing that he desires, and to learn immediately that he was right—that what he wanted really is the thing that would make him happy? And especially in the specific tradition of, shall we say, *Madame Bovary*, the fictional lineage whose geography consists solely of *the provinces* and *the capital*, and whose motive for desire is an acculturated stimulus that is explicitly said to be at once entire artifice and yet less than art? But this is what happens to the furtive, narrow-chested, nerve-twanging Paul in snowy New York.

Furnished in one single expert shopping spree with suits, shoes, hat, scarfpin, brushes, handsome luggage, installed in a suite in the Waldorf, catered to with violets and jonquils, bathed, warmed, rested, and dressed, the opera in prospect and the popping of champagne corks to waltz music, Paul looks in the mirror the next day: "Everything was quite perfect; he was exactly the kind of boy he had always wanted to be." And it seems to be true. Even when, days later, running out of money and time he throws himself in front of a train and is crushed to atoms, nothing has undermined the preciousness for Paul of, not art, but the chrism of a feminized or homosexualized culture and artifice. "He felt now that his surroundings explained him"; the lights forgivingly, expensively lowered, himself at last the seeing consciousness of the story, even the past of his life and his body are, as in a coming out, reknit with the new, authoritative fingers of his own eyes. "He realized well enough that he had always been tormented by . . . a sort of apprehensive dread that, of late years, as the meshes of the lies he had told closed about him, had been pulling the muscles of his body tighter and tighter. . . ." This offering of Paul's proprioception is a new gift to the reader. "There had always been the shadowed corner, the dark place into which he dared not look, but from which something seemed always to be watching him." But now —"these were his people, he told himself." "It would be impossible for anyone to humiliate him." If Cather, in this story, does something to cleanse her own sexual body of the carrion stench of Wilde's victimization, it is thus (unexpectedly) by identifying with what seems to be Paul's sexuality not in spite of but *through* its saving reabsorption in a gender-liminal (and very specifically classed) artifice that represents at once a particular subculture and culture itself.

Cather's implicit reading here of the gendering of sex picks out one possible path through the mazed junction at which long-residual issues of gender and class definition intersected new turn-of-the-century mappings of sexual choice and identification. In what I am reading as Cather's move in "Paul's Case," the mannish lesbian author's coming together with the effeminate boy on the ground of a certain distinctive position of gender liminality is also a move toward a minority gay identity whose more effectual cleavage, whose more determining separatism, would be that of homo/hetero*sexual* choice rather than that of male/female *gender*. The playing out of this story through the intertwinings of such gender-polarized terms as culture, artifice, and the punitive gaze, however, means that the thick semantics of gender asymmetry will cling to the syntax however airy of gender crossing and recrossing—clogging or rendering liable to slippage the gears of reader or authorial relation with a special insistence of viscosity.

Such formulations as these might push us toward some new hypotheses and new clusterings in the rich tradition of cross-gender inventions of homosexuality of the past century whose distinguished constituency might include—along with Cather—James, Proust, Yourcenar, Compton-Burnett, Renault, and more recent writers in sometimes less "literary" forms such as Gayle Rubin, Esther Newton, Susan Sontag, Judy Grahn, Joanna Russ—or, I might add, Prince in his astonishingly Proustian recent hit single "If I Was Your Girlfriend." We could ask, for instance, about a text like James's *The Bostonians*, whether certain vindictive wrenchings of it out of "shape," warpings in its illusionistic surface of authorial control and address, might not represent less a static parti pris *against* women's desire for women than a dangerously unresolved question *about* it. How far, the novel asks, or more powerfully resists asking for fear of either the answer or no answer or too many answers—how far are these two things parallel or comparable: the ventriloquistic, half-contemptuous, hot desire of Olive Chancellor for a girl like Verena Tarrant; the ventriloquistic, half-contemptuous, hot desire of Henry James for a boy like Basil Ransome? To the degree that they aren't parallel, the intimate access of the authorial consciousness to the characters' must be dangerously compromised; to the degree that they are, so must its panoptic framing authority of distance and diagnostic privilege. Whether (in those waning decades of an intensive American homosociality) men's desire for men represents most the central and naturalizing maleness of its communicants, and women's for women an ultrafemininity unnatural only for its overtypifying concentration; or whether (in those inaugural years of medical, psychiatric, and legal discourses, both pro- and anti-gay, that variously distinguished "homosexuals" male and female as a singular minority) a same-sex desire necessarily invoked, as well, a *cross*-gender liminality; the crisscrossed reading of such desires so ruptures the authorial surface of James's writing that what shoves through it here is the fist not of a male-erotic *écriture* but less daringly of a woman-hating and feminist-baiting violence of panic.

A more truly sexy moment, in Proust, gives the thrill of authorial availability through these eruptive diagonals of definition. After the flight and death of his probably lesbian mistress Albertine, the narrator of *A la recherche*, his jealousy only the more inflamed by its posthumousness, dispatches on an errand of detection and reconstruction along the trail of her elopement a functionary named Aimé, a headwaiter who has himself already been both a procurer and an object of desire both within and across gender through several volumes of this novel. Aimé sends back an account of Albertine which the narrator reproduces thus, its peculiarity being that Aimé, half-educated, "when he meant to put inverted commas . . . put brackets, and when he meant to put something in brackets . . . put it in inverted commas":[8]

> "The young laundry-girl confessed to me that she enjoyed playing around with her girlfriends and that seeing Mlle Albertine was always rubbing up against her in her bathing-wrap she made her take it off and used to caress her with her tongue along the throat and arms. . . . After that she told me nothing more, but being always at your service and ready to do anything to oblige you, I took the young laundry-girl to bed with me. She asked me if I would like her to do to me what she used to do to Mlle Albertine when she took off her bathing-dress. And she said to me: (If you could have seen how she used to wriggle, that young lady, she said to me (oh, it's too heavenly) and she got so excited that she could not keep from biting me.) I could still see the marks on the laundry-girl's arms."[9]

The deroutinization of the subordinating work of punctuation here strips away the insulation of the text against every juxtaposition of sexualities. Albertine to the laundry-girl, the laundry-girl to Aimé, Aimé to the male narrator, the narrator to the reader: the insubordinated address of pain and ecstasy is anchored only at the last moment by its cryptic laundry-mark, residue of a rinsing and ravenous illegible rapture.

This highly chiasmic organization of homo/heterosexual definition in Proust, which prompts Leo Bersani to formulate "the ontological necessity of homosexuality [in the other sex] in a kind of universal *hetero*sexual relation of all human subjects to their own desires," [10] confirms that insofar as a growing minority gay identity does or did depend on a model of gender liminality, it tends to invest with meaning transpositions between *male* and *female* homosexuality, but also between the bonds of *homo-* and *hetero*sexuality. The Proustian example suggests that this choreography of crossings, identification, and momentary symmetries, this hummingbird ballet of within and without the parenthesis, represents a utopian possibility somewhere to one side of the stresses of gender or of other exploitations; I think there is evidence, however, that the truth of this choreography of cross-translation is at once less blithe and more interesting.

Back, for one final example, to Willa Cather: to her beautiful and difficult novel *The Professor's House*, whose eponymous domesticity (the house itself, that is to say, not the Professor) is biographically thought to allude to the enabling provision for Cather's own writing of a room of her own, first by Isabelle McClung and then perhaps by her more domesticated and serviceable companion/lover of decades, Edith Lewis. Though the love that sustains these necessary facilitations has been a lesbian one, its two crystallizations in the novel are both cross-translations: one across gender, into the gorgeous homosocial romance of two men on a mesa in New Mexico; the other across sexuality as well as gender, into the conventional but enabling heterosexual marriage of a historian of the Spanish in the New World. As with the insubordinating parentheses in Proust, the male-homosocial romance represents at the same time the *inside* lining of the heterosexual bond (since the two segments of the domestic story flank their own history in the flashback interpolation of the mesa story) and equally its *exterior* landscape (since the Blue Mesa romance of Tom *Out*land, true to his name, is also figured in the "single square window, swinging outward on hinges" that vents from the Professor's attic study the asphyxiating gas of his stove, and admits to it the "long, blue, hazy smear"—the view of Lake Michigan "like an open door that nobody could shut"—that makes the empowering distance for his intellectual achievements and desires).[11] The room of one's own, in short, as a room with a view: in this text the crossing of the upstairs/downstairs vertical axis of heterosexual domesticity *by* the space-clearing dash of a male-male romance may somehow refract and decompress the conditions of a lesbian love and creativity.

What become visible in this double refraction are the shadows of the brutal suppressions by which a lesbian love did not in Willa Cather's time and culture freely become visible as itself. Still, we can look for affordances offered by that love to these particular refractions. On the one hand, there is the distinctive sensuality attributed to the male-homosocial romance, its extravagant loyalties aerated by extroversion, eye-hunger, and inexpressiveness. On the other hand, there is the canny and manipulative relation to permeable privacies, of a tradition of heterosexual marriage in which marriage is inveterately reconstituted in relation to its others, in the age-old economy of the muse represented in this book by the memory of the dead boy Tom Outland. Each of these refractions seems moreover to be a way of telling the same story: the story of how expensive and wasteful a thing creative energy is, and how intimately rooted in a plot of betrayal or exploitation: Tom Outland's conscious and empowering betrayal of his beloved friend on the mesa, the Professor's self-deceived expropriation of the labor, vitality, and money of his wife and daughters. Certainly there is no reason why the right artist at the right moment cannot embody these truths that seem to be, among other things, lesbian truths, directly in the plots of lesbian desire, nurturance, betrayal, exploitation, creativity from which they here seem to have sprung. Then why *not* here? Among the reasons Cather may have had for not doing so must have been, besides the danger to herself and her own enabling privacy, the danger also from this particular steely and un-utopic plot to the early and still-fragile development of *any* lesbian plot as a public possibility for carrying value and sustaining narrative.

She may also, however, have liked the advantage there was to be taken of these other, refracted plots as the most apt carriers, brewed in the acid nuance of centuries, for the exposition precisely of exploitation and betrayal. Anyone who knows how to read anything is experienced in reading, for instance, the story of a husband; we have all read that one all our lives, however resentfully or maybe all the better because resentfully. Our skills are honed to hear its finest vibrations and hollownesses: the constitutive one-sidedness of the story, the self-pity masquerading as toughness, self-ignorance as clearsightedness, abject exactions as rugged independence. We hear this and yet, in our immemorial heterosexist intimacy with this plot, we are also practiced in how not to stop listening there. We are experienced at looking in this place, even, for unrecognized pockets of value and vitality that can hit out in unpredictable directions.

The Professor's House ends with the exaction of such a reading, I think. Alone in his study while his family has summered in Europe, the Professor now feels he has taken the manful measure of the hard truths of life itself, the ones most alien, he insists, to the venal and feminized values of the familial (read female) life that had supported and must return to envelop him.

> He had never learned to live without delight. And he would have to learn to. . . .
>
> . . . He doubted whether his family would ever realize that he was not the same man they had said good-bye to; they would be too happily preoccupied with their own affairs. If his apathy hurt them, they could not possibly be so much hurt as he had been already. At least, he felt the ground under his feet. He thought he knew where he was, and that he could face with fortitude the *Berengaria* and the future.[12]

"Face with fortitude the *Berengaria* and the future," the novel's last words. Conceivably it is the very coarseness and obviousness of the gender asymmetry of heterosexual marriage that licenses, here, a certain sadism of suspicious reading, that forces us not to take this straight as the zero-degree of revelation in Willa Cather's novel. It might impel us to want to lay our ear against the tight-stretched drum of that stirring nonsense word, the she-vessel's name *Berengaria*. (A nonsense word insofar as it is a proper noun, it has for the same reason its own attachments: Berengaria was the wife of Richard the Lion-Hearted, who was known for preferring to her intimacy that of men including, legendarily, his young minstrel.) *Berengaria*—a very mother-lode of anagrammatic *energia;* within language, a force of nature, a force of cleavage. Underneath the regimented grammatic f-f-fortitudes of the heterosexist orderings of marriage, there are audible in this alphabet the more purely semantic germs of any vital possibility: *Berengaria*, ship of women: the {green} {aria}, the {eager} {brain}, the {bearing} and the {bairn}, the {raring} {engine}, the {bargain} {binge}, the {ban} and {bar}, the {garbage}, the {barrage} of {anger}, the {bare} {grin}, the {rage} to {err}, the {rare} {grab} for {being}, the {begin} and {rebegin} {again}.

Notes

The people who sparked my interest in "Paul's Case" were an English teacher, Rita Kosofsky, and a graduate student, Eric Peterson (whose English teacher I was), on whose work on "Paul's Case" this reading tries to build. This essay is part of my forthcoming book, *Epistemology of the Closet*, to be published by the University of California Press in early 1990.

1 Gayle Rubin, "Thinking Sex: Notes for a Radical Theory of the Politics of Sexuality," in *Pleasure and Danger: Exploring Female Sexuality*, ed. Carole S. Vance (Boston, 1984), 307–8.

2 Jonathan Ned Katz, *Gay/Lesbian Almanac: A New Documentary* (New York, 1983), 145–50.

3 Donald Mager, "Gay Theories of Gender Role Deviance," *SubStance* 46 (1985): 35–36. His sources here are John Lauritsen and David Thorstad, *The Early Homosexual Rights Movement* (New York, 1974), and James D. Steakley, *The Homosexual Emancipation Movement in Germany* (New York, 1975).

4 This argument is given more fully in "Epistemology of the Closet I," *Raritan* 4 (Spring 1988): 39–69.

5 All quotations from "Paul's Case" are from Willa Cather, *Five Stories* (New York, 1956), 149–74.

6 Katherine Anne Porter, "A Note," in Willa Cather, *The Troll Garden* (New York, 1971), 150–51.

7 *The Kingdom of Art: Willa Cather's First Principles and Critical Statements 1893–1896*, ed. Bernice Slote (Lincoln, Neb., 1966), 390. See also 389–93.

8   Marcel Proust, *Remembrance of Things Past*, trans. C. K. Scott-Moncrieff, Terence Kilmartin, and Andreas Mayor (New York, 1982), 3: 525.

9   Ibid., 535.

10 Leo Bersani, "The Culture of Redemption: Marcel Proust and Melanie Klein," *Critical Inquiry* 12 (Winter 1986): 416.

11 Willa Cather, *The Professor's House* (New York, 1973), 16, 28, 30.

12 Ibid., 282–83.

Joseph A. Boone

Mappings of Male Desire in Durrell's
Alexandria Quartet

It is hard to recapture the intense excitement
that greeted the publication of Lawrence Durrell's *Alexandria Quartet* in the late 1950s—
my parents' generation keenly awaited each
successive volume with a sense of participating in the making of a masterpiece. The
success of the *Quartet* could be measured
not only in its popular reception and generally glowing reviews, but also, on an institutional level, in the literally hundreds of
scholarly articles it spawned in the following
decade: the Durrell entries in the MLA Bibliography for this period vie in number with
those accorded long-time favorites like Lawrence, Joyce, and Faulkner. Simultaneously,
the *Quartet* found its way onto Ivy League
syllabi; while Albert J. Guerard sang Durrell's praises at Harvard, Walton Litz made
the *Quartet* a highlight of his modern fiction course at Princeton. This masterpiece, it
seemed clear, was going to be around for a
long while.

Durrell's critical stock, ironically, couldn't
be lower today; his blend of existential soul-

searching and lush romanticism stands at a far remove from current postmodern critical sensibilities. And indeed, at worst, a synopsis of the *Quartet*'s multilayered plots sounds ominously similar to television's "Dynasty" series: a panorama of ever-shifting sexual alignments glossed over with a pretense to sophistication—or, as one early detractor put it, "Melodramatic erotica . . . made respectable by epigrammatic catchphrases."[1] I'd like to suggest, however, that if we employ some of the insights that have marked literary criticism—particularly narrative and gender theory—since Durrell's eclipse, we will find a text very much worth our attention, not so much for its successes as for the way it insistently dramatizes the sexual politics of the colonial narrative, especially as filtered through the eyes of its desiring male—and ostensibly heterosexual—narrator, Darley, a blocked writer and confused sexual subject for whom issues of erotic perception, masculine subjectivity, and narrative authority are inextricably linked.

The "investigation of modern love" that is Durrell's declared subject matter pivots upon his narrator's negotiation of the labyrinthine mazes of Egyptian—and specifically Alexandrian—sensuality.[2] In the process, Egypt becomes much more than an exotic backdrop to the *Quartet*; rather, its geopolitical reality is transformed into a kind of psychic playground upon which Durrell can project titillating visions of sexual otherness and polymorphous freeplay. Not coincidentally, engaging with libidinous fantasy on this symbolic terrain frees Darley to emerge as mature novelist and successful lover at the end of the fourth volume. But Darley's (and Durrell's) response to the lure of foreign otherness is double-edged: such figurations of Oriental sexuality, for all their attraction, are also terrifying, not the least because they give vent to possibilities unthinkable within a Western construction of the masculine—hence posing a threat to the very constitution of white male subjectivity. And, tellingly, within the psychodramatic landscape of the *Quartet* that unthinkability is time and again coded as the specter of homosexuality. The possibility—and fear—of being "unmanned" by homoerotic impulses gives the *Quartet* its deconstructive twist, in that the four novels map out a geography of male desire in which Darley's quest for identity depends upon a continual negotiation of the one taboo that undermines its goals of "heterosexual" fulfillment and a "written" text. If the Near East seems to hold the promise of literary inspiration and (dreams of) sexual liberation for Durrell, these discursive manifestations of homosexuality suggest another story, one that can tell us much about the sexual anxieties motoring the enterprise of male-authored colonial narrative and its relation to phallocentric discourse.

In 1935 the yet unknown Durrell wrote a gushing fan letter to the current *bête noir* of literary letters, Henry Miller, whose infamously graphic *Tropic of Cancer* Durrell proclaimed to be "the only really man-size piece of work which this century can . . . boast of." Miller, his "man-size" ego no doubt flattered by such praise, quickly wrote back, touting Durrell's views a mirror of his own ("it's the kind of letter I would have written myself"): thus began a series of narcissistically enabling epistolary exchanges that would bond the two writers, man to man, in a life-long correspondence.[3] The terms of Durrell's adulation, of course, also reveal the young writer's desire to produce his own "man-size piece of work"—a goal which in terms of sheer bulk, if not in terms of outright sexual explicitness, he accomplished twenty-odd years later with the publication of the *Alexandria Quartet*. It is not surprising, then, to find an echo of this early ambition espoused by the *Quartet*'s one successful writer-figure, the larger-than-life Pursewarden, who announces that he wants to write a novel "characterised by a *total lack of codpiece!*"[4] But precisely how, under Miller's inspiration, did Durrell learn to divest himself of *his* "codpiece," to let it all hang out, as it were, in order to display a "piece of work" that, as he says of *Tropic*, "goes straight up among those books . . . which men have built out of their own guts"?

With this phallic imagery towering before us, we might turn to another of the young Durrell's epistolary homages to his literary master: "in telling anyone about myself these days," he proudly boasts, "I always say I'm the first writer to be fertilized by H. M."[5] If, as one critic puts it, "Miller's seed obviously fell on fallow soil," we may reasonably wonder what it meant for Durrell to find himself assuming a procreative role so diametrically opposed to his man-size ambitions.[6] "Creative" intercourse this may only be, but the fact, nonetheless, is that Durrell's wording places him in a specifically "feminine" relation to his mentor, one in which the fledgling novelist's proud task is the sexual one of serving as womb (or "fallow soil") to Miller's "seed." Language, one is tempted to deduce, subtly contaminates the hitherto platonic terms of this manly friendship.[7]

Even more fascinating, in the light of language's destabilizing potential, is the metaphor that Durrell uses when writing Miller from Alexandria, seven years later, to describe Eve Cohen, his future wife and original inspiration for the *Quartet*'s archetypal woman-temptress, Justine. Attempting to capture the essence of this "strange, smashing, dark-eyed woman" for Miller, Durrell declares that his enticing new acquaintance "is *Tropic of Capricorn* walking." From Durrell's point of view, it would appear that Miller's man-size oeuvre—*Capricorn* having superseded *Cancer*—has grown altogether feminine legs. And with this figurative metamorphosis of one text (Miller's) into a woman (Eve) who becomes the basis for another text (Durrell's), the younger partner in this literary collaboration adroitly reverses the sexual dynamic inscribed in the earlier letter; it is now Durrell who assumes the male role and Miller, via the agency of this female incarnation of his *Tropic*, who is inseminated. For Eve becomes, quite literally, Durrell's means of access to an "inside" of Egyptian sexuality that he penetrates not only as lover but as voyeur and, ultimately, writer: "She sits for hours on the bed and tells me all about the sex life of Arabs," Durrell writes to Miller, proceeding to list what sounds like a précis of the various exotica forming the backdrop of the *Quartet*: "perversions, circumcision, hashish, sweetmeats, removal of the clitoris, cruelty, murder. . . . [S]he has seen *the inside* of Egypt to the last rotten dung-blown flap of obscenity."[8]

Durrell fertilized by H. M., Miller's *Tropic* penetrated by Durrell: such metaphorically (t)horny intersections should inspire us to look, once again, at the sexual negotiations that make up the lush romanticism of the *Alexandria Quartet*. On one level, the Durrell-Miller relation resembles the homosocial pattern of male bonding outlined by Eve Kosofsky Sedgwick.[9] Hence, when Durrell, reminiscing about the closing of the French brothels, laments the loss of some "marvellous encounters," he is *not* talking about encounters with their female clientele but, rather, those with the other male patrons, particularly his fellow artists: "I spent some fabulous hours with Henry

Miller at the Sphinx," he remembers—hours "spent," we are surely meant to assume, in verbal rather than, as the archaic expression goes, the "criminal conversation" more commonly associated with *maisons closes*.[10] Such homosocial behavior, as Sedgwick points out, is neither antithetical to patriarchal formations (such as brothels) nor to male heterosexual (and often homophobic) norms. And of the sexual orientation of this "priest of heterosexual love,"[11] there is "no homosexual component at all," his friend and critic G. S. Fraser hurries to assure us: "Durrell is an extraordinarily purely masculine creature. . . . He has had three marriages . . . in each case to an extremely attractive woman."[12] Fraser's defense of Durrell, mediated by the evidence of Durrell's wives, indeed provides an apt illustration of Sedgwick's homosocial theory at work: Fraser avoids his own contamination, in speaking of such unsavory matters as homosexual tendencies in writers, while also asserting Durrell's monolithic heterosexuality.

On another level, however, the premise of homosocial bonding, pervasive as it is in the world of the *Alexandria Quartet*, doesn't seem to me the only way to get at the curiously elliptical negotiations of "other" sexualities that not only keep rearing their heads in the Miller-Durrell correspondence, but that also determine the paths whereby the whole problematic of masculine (hetero)sexual identification, with all its attendant uncertainties, is continually brought to bear on the act of writing in the *Quartet*.[13] Durrell-as-writer obviously holds to an at least partially phallocentric creed—as his desire to emulate Miller's man-size work attests—but the fact is that the very means of his craft with which he has chosen to experiment in the *Quartet*—language, structure, point of view—work to evoke a flux of libidinous desire which, once freed *into* his text, threatens to overwhelm the coherence of its representations of masculine heterosexual competence. What ensues is a profound case of authorial anxiety in which the "imaginary geography"[14] of Durrell's eroticized Egyptian landscape helps to throw the modernist and masculinist tenets of his text into disarray.

≡

In the four interlocking volumes of the *Quartet*, issues of sexuality and writing are never far apart: "loving is only a sort of skin language, sex a terminology merely," Darley writes; the novelist Pursewarden dreams of a novel that will "have the curvature of an embrace, the wordlessness of a lover's code."[15] Thus *Justine*, the first volume of the *Quartet*, begins with Darley's retrospective and highly subjective attempt to come to grips with his narcissistic love affair with the Egyptian-Jewish beauty Justine Hosani by recording events not in chronological sequence but impressionistically, "in the order in which they first became significant for me." The blinders imposed by his romantic solipsism become painfully clear in *Balthazar*, where Darley is forced to relive the "truth" of the sensations he has recorded in *Justine* from a completely different vantage point, that of the Alexandrian doctor Balthazar, whose "corrected" version of the *Justine* manuscript reveals that Justine has possibly engineered the whole affair to conceal her more important liaison with none other than Pursewarden, Darley's mentor. As if to underline further the instability of sexual and narrative perception, *Mountolive* relegates Darley to the background of its action; the now omnisciently narrated action reveals *all* the love plots of the first and second volumes to have been "false," screens for a greater political plot (involving the attempt of Justine and her husband Nessim to rouse Coptic support for the overthrow of Palestine). Only in the final volume of this quartet, *Clea*, does time move forward, as Darley's first-person narration resumes, recording his return to Alexandria and successful love affair with Clea, another expatriate European artist.

In employing multiple points of view to dramatize the instability of truth and the relativity of known reality, Durrell gestures toward the legacy of literary modernism, whose tenets, he intimates, his formal experiments in the *Quartet* have revivified for a post-Einsteinian nuclear age.[16] Durrell also shares with his modernist forebears the desire to find a way of representing the spatiality of consciousness in narrative form, of capturing the flux of "inner" reality and the drift of subconscious desire. "*I would set my own book free to dream*," he has one of the *Quartet*'s writers say, and he comes closest to achieving this aim in *Balthazar*, where he uses the surreal nightworld of Alexandria to create a series of psychodramatic set pieces emblematic of mental states. If the technique sounds familiar, it is because Joyce does much the same thing with Dublin's Nighttown in the Circe section of *Ulysses*. But the stakes are quite different, as the following passage illustrates. In this episode, Narouz, one of Darley's many alter egos, wanders through Alexandria's prostitute district the night of a Moslem religious festival:

> From the outer perimeter of darkness came . . . the hoarse rumble of the approaching procession with its sudden bursts of wild music. . . . From the throat of a narrow alley . . . burst a long tilting gallery of human beings headed by the leaping acrobats and dwarfs of Alexandria, and followed at a dancing measure by the long grotesque cavalcade of gonfalons, rising and falling in a tide of mystical light, treading the peristaltic measures of the wild music—nibbled out everywhere by the tattling flutes and the pang of drums [and] the long shivering orgasm of tambourines struck by dervishes in their habits as they moved towards the site of the festival. . . . The night accommodated them all —a prostitute singing in the harsh clipped accents of the land to the gulp and spank of a fingerdrum, the cries of children, . . . the cock-shies and snake-charmers, the freaks (Zubeida the bearded woman and the calf with five legs), the great canvas theatre outside which the muscle-dancers stood, naked except for loin-cloths, to advertise their skill, and motionless, save for the incredible rippling of their bodies—the flickering and toiling of pectoral, abdominal and dorsal muscles, deceptive as summer lightning.
>
> Narouz was rapt and looked about him with the air of a drunkard, revelling in it all. . . .[17]

As in Joyce's Circe, this carnivalesque spectacle, with its pulsating rhythms and cacophony of elements, attempts to represent in externalized form an unleashing of the unconscious, a "setting free [of] the polymorphous desires of the city." On this level, Durrell's modernist and psychological intentions seem to work hand in hand: his multidimensional, dispersive, polyphonic text approximates the fragmented, anarchic, psychic terrain of the component instincts sketched out, for instance, by Freud in the *Three Essays on the Theory of Sexuality*. But this equation brings us to a more troubling facet of the passage: the fact that its representation of the polymorphous perverse, of the "dark tides of Eros," has been literally displaced onto a foreign geography, that of Egypt.[18] As such, *The Alexandria Quartet* participates in the enterprise of colonial narrative, its modernist polemics and its sexual politics inextricably bound to its representation of Egyptian sexuality as an alluring but dangerously foreign other.

Edward Said's *Orientalism* has been invaluable in its uncovering of the discursive paths whereby countries like Egypt have come to represent "one of [the West's] deepest and most recurring images of the Other." The "threatening excess" of this otherness, Said suggests, has most often been gendered as "feminine" and sexually available so that it can be penetrated, cataloged, and therefore contained by the "superior" rationality of the Western mind. The upshot of these representations is an "almost uniform association between the Orient and sex." Said takes Gustave Flaubert's 1849–50 journey to Egypt as paradigmatic of the Western writer's tendency to idealize the East as "a place where one could look for [a degree of] sexual experience unobtainable in Europe" and enjoy "a different type of sexuality, perhaps more libertine and less guilt-ridden." An overview of Flaubert's experience provides a useful context for evaluating Durrell's comparable fascination with Egyptian sensuality one hundred years later.[19]

First, however, we need to interrogate more precisely the nature of the "unavailable" sexual experience to which Said is referring. In Flaubert's case, Said locates such desire in the writer's affair with the celebrated Egyptian female courtesan and dancer, Kuchuk Hanem. Seeing in Kuchuk's "luxuriant and seemingly unbounded sexuality" a symbol of Oriental fecundity, the young writer-to-be uses his diary to transform her material presence, her fleshly being, into a sheerly poetic occasion, making her "dumb and irreducible sexuality" the stage for the exercise of his own creative musings and observations. Such appropriation, Said argues, is typical of the Westerner's experience of the East; the latter's exoticism is deliberately experienced as a titillating spectacle, a "living tableau of queerness" that the traveler can enjoy voyeuristically but nonetheless stand apart from, thus theoretically remaining untouched by its difference.

Yet what Said forgets to mention in analyzing the West's sexualized response to the Orient is precisely what his unfortunate wording—

"living tableau of queerness"—perhaps subconsciously betrays. For, in Flaubert's case, it is not the female Kuchuk but a homosexual *male* dancer who first catches the traveler's eye. Said's oversight, it would seem, is of a piece with the apologetic disclaimer that immediately follows his account of Flaubert's association of Egypt and sexuality: "Why the Orient seems still to suggest not only fecundity but sexual promise (and threat) . . . is not the province of my analysis here, alas, despite its frequently noted appearance."[20] And what is it that Flaubert (quite literally) sees but that Said feels it necessary, "alas," to repress? As Flaubert puts it in a letter home to Louis Bouilhet, his closest friend:

> But we have seen male dancers. Oh! Oh! Oh! . . . [I]magine two rascals, quite ugly but charming in their corruption, in their obscene leerings and the femininity of their movements, dressed as women, their eyes painted with antimony. . . . [D]uring the dance, the impressario . . . plays around them, kissing them on the belly, the arse, and the small of the back, and making obscene remarks in an effort to put additional spice into *a thing that is already quite clear in itself.* . . . I'll have this marvellous Hasan el-Belbeissi come again. He'll dance the Bee for me, in particular. Done by such a bardash as he, it can scarcely be a thing for babes.[21]

Given the fact that a "bardash" is, in modern terminology, a homosexual, we might cast a second glance at that display of nakedly rippling male flesh, otherwise "motionless" amidst the swirl of the celebrants, evoked by Durrell in *Balthazar*, and note that the dazed Narouz, his footsteps leading him through a corridor of "brilliantly lighted circumcision booths," comes to a halt before a riveting spectacle: a "magnificent-looking male prostitute, whose oiled curls hung down his back and whose eyes and lips were heavily painted" as his breast is being tattooed. The miniature quest on which Durrell has sent Narouz uncovers Hasan's twentieth-century incarnation.[22]

It hardly needs to be stressed that that which is erotically alluring in these Western male representations of Egyptian sexuality is *not only*, or *necessarily*, female, however "feminized" these objects may appear. We need merely return to Flaubert's account to confirm this intuition. On the one hand, Flaubert's immediate defense against the "charming corruption" of Hasan and his fellow dancers is to assume the outsider's position of artist-observer, noting that their dance "is too beautiful to be exciting" and that their "ugliness" only "adds . . . to the thing as art." On the other hand, as the excited "Oh! Oh! Oh!" and the wish to have Hasan "come again" to perform "a thing that is already quite clear in itself" indicate, the sexuality of the bardash is less easily turned into a purely aesthetic experience than Flaubert's language first suggests. Indeed, as he continues in his letter to Bouilhet, "Speaking of bardashes, . . . [h]ere it is quite accepted. One admits one's sodomy, and it is spoken of at table in the hotel. Sometimes you do a bit of denying, and then everybody teases you and you end up confessing"; whereupon, this womanizer and compulsive habitué of brothels drolly adds,

> we have considered it our duty to indulge in this form of ejaculation. . . . It's at the baths that such things take place. You reserve the bath for yourself . . . and you skewer your lad in one of the rooms. Be informed, furthermore, that all the bath-boys are bardashes.

What is remarkable here, as Flaubert goes on to narrate an abortive attempt to be serviced by one of these "quite nice young boys," is the sheer *ease* of his transition from hetero- to homosexual banter: when in Egypt, do as the Egyptians . . . seems the prevailing attitude. This is not to suggest that Flaubert suddenly renounced his heterosexual propensities—to the contrary, his written record enumerates many such encounters with great relish and exacting anatomical detail—but to point to an unexpected opening in his perception of the conceivable and doable. The behavior of his traveling companion, Maxime Du Camp, might be taken as a paradigmatic example: "Max, the old lecher," is excited by native women at one moment, Flaubert reports of the morning they arrive in Egypt, but the next is "just as excited by little negro boys. By whom is he *not* excited? Or, rather, by *what*?" Nor does Flaubert remain immune to these unexpected sources of titillation, as references scattered throughout his papers reveal; he amusedly records the flagrant displays of male sexuality that mark his journey down the Nile, lavishes a page of erotic description on one of his crew's youthful rowers (on whom he appears to have developed a crush), and cavalierly confesses that he has consummated his "business at the baths" with an ugly "young rascal": "It made me laugh, that's all. But I'll be at it again. To be done well, an experiment must be repeated." [23]

This fluid movement across sexual boundaries turns out to be considerably more terrifying to Durrell's Darley, but the *possibility* of such effortless transgression remains very real for him, a situation heightened by the continually blurring boundaries of Alexandria itself, a polyglot universe comprised, Darley writes at the beginning of the *Quartet*, of "five races, five languages, a dozen creeds . . . [and] more than five sexes, [with] only demotic Greek . . . to distinguish among them." [24] This heterogeneity is also precisely what attracts Durrell—and before him Flaubert—to Egypt as a symbolically feminized terrain onto which he can project Western male fantasies of sexual otherness and polymorphous freeplay, that unbridled eroticism supposedly unavailable in European society. "The sexual provender which lies to hand is staggering in its variety and profusion," Darley notes in a voice at once envious and slightly frightened. And although Durrell adds that "for the artist in [one]self . . . some confusions of sensibility [are] valuable," [25] the defamiliarizing experience of Alexandria's "variety and profusion" is as contradictory for Darley as it is instructive; for the fact is that his quest for sexual identity cannot escape a continual negotiation of the homoerotic, in the guise of foreign otherness, that threatens the status of the personal and public texts he wishes to produce. To make sense of the "confusions of sensibility" that ensue from this homosexual subtext, we need to turn, however briefly, to the overt heterosexuality of the *Quartet*'s love plots and investigate Darley's textual affair with Alexandria the city and his sexual affair with Justine, its representative denizen.

=====

The mysteriously strange, always protean world of Alexandria holds a tantalizing allure for Darley, a seductive appeal that he attempts to fend off by assuming, like Flaubert, the role of curious but detached artist-spectator. This pose of uninvolvement, however, swiftly breaks down when he meets and falls "blindly and passionately in love" with Justine—or rather, with "one of the many selves she possessed and inhabited," for Justine is the embodiment of Alexandria's protean variety. To Darley's Westernizing imagination, this protean quality makes Justine the eternal feminine, ever evading capture yet hopelessly yearning to be possessed by the right man; simultaneously, this quality renders her a variant of the archetypal Oriental woman, a "voluptuar[y] . . . of pain" in whom a vast array of apparent contraries meet: sensuality and asceticism, mystery and knowledge, fecundity and sterility, pain and pleasure.[26] So too Alexandria is a combination of clashing elements, its divided origins reflected in its mythic history, variously marked by Alexander's library, Cleopatra's court, and Plotinus's philosophy. A city without one unifying origin or truth, Alexandria becomes the equivalent not only of Justine but of the *Quartet* itself, whose ever-shifting points of view also reveal that there is no single interpretation or representation that will capture its multiple realities.

Neither one thing nor the other, Alexandria functions as a passage, a threshold between different cultures and ways of being; it remains a promiscuous "whore among cities." Similarly, within Darley's imaginative geography of desire, Justine becomes a sexualized site on his route to manhood—or, in Pursewarden's rudely deflationary, and characteristically misogynistic, rhetoric, "a tiresome old sexual turnstile through which presumably we [men] must all pass." The degree to which Justine serves as a stationary marker in Darley's quest for self-knowledge also raises the (appropriately Egyptian) specter of the Sphinx who confronts the questing Oedipus with the riddle of woman.[27] Both enigma and riddle, Justine becomes the text's overdetermined symbol for the instability of truth and language in an existential world—that belated and bitter knowledge awaiting all the *Quartet*'s male seekers. As such, Durrell's representation of Justine forms a classic illustration of the phenomenon Alice Jardine labels "gynesis," the philosophical setting-into-motion of the concept of woman as a symbol of the postmodern crisis.[28] Darley colludes in this process by making Justine's "enigma" the *raison d'être* of his own text, but his words betray what is at stake for him, for all men, in this maneuver:

> There was no question of true or false. Nymph? Goddess? Vampire? Yes, she was all of these and none of them. She was, like every woman, everything that the mind of man (let us define "man" as a poet . . .) *wished to imagine.* . . . I began to realize with awe the enormous reflexive power of woman.[29]

This conceptualizing of woman as man's mirror/other points to an even more suspect feature of Darley's desires: namely, the degree to which his projections onto Justine are narcissistic, mirroring, as Luce Irigaray would say, the masculine back upon itself. And such male worship of sameness begins to suggest the presence of a homoerotic underside to Darley's passion for Justine, and, indeed, to Durrell's plotting of male heterosexual desire.[30] Hence Alexandria—elsewhere feminized as "princess and whore"—is also figured as "a city of incest," in which the "lover mirrors himself [as] Narcissus." Not only does Darley meet and fall in love with Justine through her reflection in a mirror; mirrors become the text's metaphor for its own destabilizing, multidimensional refractions of point of view. Darley begins *Justine* by warning that the "symbolic lovers of the free Hellenic world are replaced here by something different, something subtly androgynous, inverted upon itself," his use of the word androgyny indicating a likeness that is narcissistic in its intimacy; and when Darley speaks of those lovers who emerge from Alexandria's "great wine-press of love . . . deeply wounded in their sex," he subconsciously attests to the degree to which Alexandria's mirror inversions have undermined the security of his authority as removed, all-seeing observer. The staged spectacle of Egyptian sexuality has become a reflecting glass, "inverted upon itself," for in a world of fluid boundaries, he who gazes ultimately finds himself penetrated in turn by his reflection in the Other.[31]

Moreover, as the unsuccessful outcome of Darley's affair with Justine indicates, he has reason to feel "wounded in [his] sex," unsure of his "masculine" status, and by extension, his heterosexual competency. A curious impotence has dogged this would-be writer and dazed voyeur ever since his arrival in Alexandria, leading him to experience a failure in all domains of feeling: "to write; even to make love." His first Egyptian lover, the nightclub dancer Melissa, will confess that "he never excited me like other men did." And when Justine sweeps Darley across the borderline of voyeuristic detachment into the anarchy of her interior world, Darley assigns to himself the grammatical position of passive object of her desire: "She had achieved me." It comes as no surprise that this "timid and scholarly lover with chalk on his sleeve," having left Alexandria for an island retreat where he can lick his wounds in solitude, acquiesces with hardly a word of protest to Balthazar's charge (in the latter's heavily annotated and edited draft of the *Justine* manuscript) that the most important love of Darley's life has been a total sham. The fact that Balthazar argues that Justine has used Darley as a "decoy" to conceal her affair with Pursewarden—already Darley's rival as a successful novelist—only underlines Darley's present authorial and psychic impasse. His entire framework of reality thus radically transformed, he must begin the work of "learn[ing] to see it all with new eyes," accustoming himself "to the truths which Balthazar has added," among which he seems to accept as a given the revelation of his "unmanning" at Justine's hands.[32]

As Darley begins this process of reevaluation, a series of memories and events repressed from *Justine* spontaneously rise to the surface of his recording consciousness, making up the reader's text of *Balthazar*. And, tellingly, what each of these hitherto repressed "events" obsessively reveals are less instances of Justine's infidelity (which we might expect from a deceived lover), than instances of Darley's own profound uncertainty about his status as a man and about the nature of male sexuality in general. For the simple fact is that each of these "returns of the repressed" engenders anxieties that cannot be extricated from the pulsations of homoerotic desire.

≡≡≡

It is no coincidence that *Balthazar* is named after the character whose text—nicknamed the Interlinear—threatens the sexual and narrative authority that Darley has attempted to establish over his passion by writing *Justine*. Unexpectedly appearing on Darley's island "like some goat-like apparition from the Underworld," sporting "dark Assyrian ringlets and the beard of Pan," Balthazar is the perfect guide to lead

Darley to the polymorphous realm of forbidden desire. Not insignifi-
cantly, he is also a lover of his own sex, as Darley should well know,
since he is "often" prone, he casually notes, to walk in unannounced
on Balthazar in bed with various sailors. If Balthazar is the first of a
series of homosexuals to flood the psychodramatically charged landscape of *Balthazar*, he is also the only man whose "inversion" Darley
claims to admire, since, in Darley's view, it doesn't compromise "his
innate masculinity of mind." Darley's phrasing is worth note: the pro-
noun "his" obviously refers to Balthazar, but like so much else that is
objectified as a third-person observation in this volume, the following
description could apply equally to its speaker; "innate masculinity of
mind" is precisely that which Darley wishes to claim for himself, as
well as that which Balthazar's text has thrown into question. "And
so, slowly, reluctantly," Darley writes at the end of the first chapter
of *Balthazar*, "I have been driven back to my starting-point. . . . I
must set it all down, in cold black and white. . . . [T]he key I am
trying to turn is in myself."[33]

Darley's words prove more prophetic than he knows, for the seemingly objective "facts" that he goes on to record in *Balthazar* are
indeed often hidden "keys" to himself. Nothing could make this
clearer than the series of four triggering events whereby the repressed
surfaces to rewrite the story of *Justine*: a recollected photograph,
the memory of a kiss, a religious festival, Carnival. As soon as Balthazar leaves, Darley turns in chapter 2 to a photograph taken outside
Mnemjian's barbershop, the hub of the *Quartet*'s male homosocial
world. Examining this random "text" for clues to that which he has
hitherto failed to see, Darley fixes on two figures, Toto de Brunel
and John Keats—characters who have gone totally unmentioned in
Justine.[34] First, he takes up the case of Toto, an aged and effeminate homosexual whose marginal position in the photograph is tellingly the reverse of Darley's own: "And in one corner there I am,
in my shabby raincoat—the perfected image of a schoolteacher. In
the other corner sits poor little Toto de Brunel . . . the darling of old
society women too proud to pay for gigolos." As we might suspect
from Darley's condescending tone—which contrasts markedly with
his *professed* tolerance for Balthazar's sexual practices—Toto has become a projection of the speaker's own inadequacies and uncertain

self-image. For in serving as the "lapdog" of rich society women, Toto's position uncomfortably reminds Darley of the passive role he has unconsciously assumed as Justine's decoy. The fear of having been emasculated by this experience only intensifies his virulent put-down of Toto as a woman-identified man: "There was . . . nothing to be done with him for he was a woman." [35]

Having thus trashed "poor little Toto," Darley moves on to "poor John Keats," the newspaper correspondent who has snapped this photograph. As the recording "eye" behind the camera lens, Keats symbolically occupies the position of the invisible but all-knowing author, until Darley quickly moves in to let us know better: "Once he had wanted to be a writer but took the wrong turning." Yet the more Darley ridicules Keats's counterproductive "mania to perpetuate, to record, to photograph everything," the more these traits begin to sound suspiciously like Darley's own; he, after all, is the blocked writer whose failure to produce a novel is tied to his disabling belief that he can contain everything within one frame of reference—which Balthazar's Interlinear, as a corrective to *Justine*, has already begun to disprove.

As the inaugural event in Darley's imaginative re-envisioning of the past, then, it is no accident that his memory exhumes two figures who, respectively, illustrate the impasse of sexual and narrative authority that has precipitated his own identity crisis. Both Toto and Keats, furthermore, individually illustrate the inextricability of the sexual and literary. Toto's sexual perversion is reflected in his comic perversion of language, for he speaks in "a Toto tongue of his own," composed of three languages, whose destabilizing logic subverts the status quo by undermining the assumed relation between signifier and signified: "whenever at a loss for a word he would put in one whose meaning he did not know and the grotesque substitution was often delightful. . . . In it, he almost reached poetry." A more orthodox yoking of sexual potency and the power of the word occurs in Keats's case. For in *Clea*, this nondescript journalist undergoes a radical transformation, returning from the war front not only a true writer but a masculine sex symbol: so Darley learns when he finds his double taking a shower in his bathroom, Keats's body now the bronzed, athletic physique of a "Greek god!" Yet as this telltale exclamation suggests, even this now positive projection of Darley's dual goals of writerly and masculine authority is not without a homoerotic undertone that destabilizes its apparent signification, and this slippage turns us back to the anxieties that keep surfacing to plague Darley throughout *Balthazar.*

The last figure whom Darley recalls in Keats's photograph, Scobie, brings to the plane of consciousness more thoughts of sexual and linguistic perversion. Nothing could be more authentic, Darley assures us, than this colorful ex-sailor and befuddled employee of the Egyptian secret police, who has "the comprehensibility of a diagram—plain as a national anthem." Yet, curiously, Darley's train of thought reveals that this old friend's signifying capacities are not so apparent after all: he immediately recalls the day Scobie confesses to him that he has "Tendencies" for which he is not "fully Answerable"—namely, that he is a "Peddyrast." In exile from a puritanical England which has not appreciated his zeal as a scoutmaster, Scobie has found a paradise for his proclivities in the colonized Orient: "Looking from east to west over this fertile Delta what do I see?" Scobie rhapsodizes in words that recall Maxime du Camp's excitement upon landing in Egypt with Flaubert, "Mile upon mile of angelic little black bottoms."[36] Nothing could better uncover the ambiguous sexual politics of Durrell's colonial narrative than Scobie's wording: beneath the sexual allure of the Orient's "fertile Delta"—age-old symbol for *female* fecundity—there lurks a hidden penchant for *boys*' "black bottoms."[37] Scobie's transgressive tastes, however, do not stop with boys; with the lyrics of a popular jazz melody, "Old Tiresias," drifting in the background, the old man confesses that he doesn't mind "slip[ping into] female duds . . . when the Fleet's in." The frighteningly swift and altogether convincing transformation of Scobie into "a veritable Tuppenny Upright" that follows exposes Darley to another slippage in signification that, by analogy, raises the haunting possibility of his own metaphoric undoing. Moreover, as in Toto's case, this destabilization in sexual meaning is marked by a subversion of linguistic content; Scobie speaks in so arcane a dialect that his verbal perversions necessitate a glossary at the end of the volume.

The manner in which being metaphorically "unmanned" or female-identified may vitiate one's artistic powers becomes the subject of

Darley's thoughts even more explicitly in the next chapter, as Balthazar's reconstructed text forces him to travel back in memory to the inception of Justine's lesbian affair with the artist Clea. This is another known "event" that is all but absent from *Justine*, since it runs counter to Darley's romanticizing vision of his and Justine's heterosexual passion. "Distasteful" as Darley claims to find "this subject-matter," he now dwells on the affair at length, and for reasons not merely voyeuristic. First, because the women's lovemaking literally "interrupt[s]" Clea's artistry, her kisses "[falling] where the painter's wet brush should have fallen," this tableau serves as a cautionary fable for one whose own creative productivity has been blocked by his love for Justine. Second, Clea's break with Justine provides Darley with a model for avoiding inappropriate desires—the homosexuality that he denigrates as "the consuming shape of a sterile love"—and this model is particularly relevant given that Clea becomes Darley's ideal female love object in the final volume of the *Quartet*. Hence Darley subconsciously depicts Clea's experience as the complementary inverse of his own: her naive brush with lesbianism proves "that relationships like these did not answer the needs of her nature," that "she was a woman at last and belonged to men." This investment in maintaining Clea's "innocence" attests to the strength of Darley's pressing need to establish his own "innocence," his untainted masculine integrity, in the midst of the sexual "perversions" that increasingly surround him, threatening the presumed "needs of [his own] nature."[38]

Given the welling-up of all the forbidden desires represented by Balthazar, Toto, Scobie, and company, it is fascinating to turn to the next "repressed" event reported for the first time in *Balthazar*. This involves chapter 7's long account of the orgiastic *mulid* (or religious festival) of Sitna Mariam, whose dreamlike atmosphere I have already cited. It only takes a few jotted words in Balthazar's Interlinear—"So Narouz decided to *act*"—to "detonate" in Darley's "imagination" his version of Narouz's movements through the night-time festival, which reads as if it were an excerpt from a third-person omniscient narration. What this attempt at narrative distancing fails to conceal, however, is that the sensations attributed to Narouz, the "desires engendered in the forests of the mind," are actually projections, once again, of Darley's own psyche.[39]

But why does Darley choose Narouz to "stand in" as actor in his own imaginative fantasy? Because, it turns out, Narouz in many ways embodies Darley's ideal of masculinity. Clad in loose peasant clothes that "expos[e] arms and hands of great power covered by curly dark hair," possessed of a powerful body that emanates "a sensation of overwhelming strength," Narouz epitomizes a kind of untamed, sensual virility. This is a man who can easily, not to say sadistically, dismember animals with one crack of his whip, and who, D. H. Lawrence-like, experiences delirious orgasm when breaking in a wild horse. Narouz's unrequited love for Clea reinforces his function as Darley's heterosexual role model, outlining the proper route for the latter's wayward drives. From Darley's narrating perspective, then, Narouz looms, in perhaps too many senses of the word, as a man's man—so much so, in fact, that an ambiguously homoerotic element begins to infiltrate the narrator's appreciative descriptions of one who, after all, is supposed to be his guide to heterosexual fulfillment. Not only might Darley's lingering evocation of Narouz's orgasm on horseback sound slightly suspect, but the muted feminization of his subject that infiltrates his description of Narouz's "splendid" eyes, "of a blueness and innocence that made them almost like Clea's," along with the "deep and thrilling . . . magic of a woman's contralto" that he reads into his voice, points—as in Flaubert—to an erotic intensity just barely contained by the appeal to sexual difference. Masculine heterosexuality, once again, is contaminated by its proximity to the homoerotic. The one flaw in Narouz's appearance, the harelip that he considers his "dark star," might seem to run counter to this coded language of attraction, until we remember that Flaubert also emphasizes the facial "ugliness" of his (male) objects of desire: in the colonial narrative, a degree of ugliness, as Sander L. Gilman has argued in regard to representations of Africa, becomes a signifier, paradoxically, of sexual availability.[40]

That there is more going on here than first meets the eye is confirmed in Darley's evocation of Narouz's night odyssey through the festival grounds. Narouz's movements culminate, finally, in his feverish intercourse with an aged, fat prostitute, in whose voice and body he imagines Clea's presence. "A voice spoke out of the shadows at his side—a voice whose sweetness and depth could belong to one person only: Clea. . . . The voice was the voice of the woman he loved but it came from a hideous form, seated in half-shadow—the grease-folded body of a Moslem woman. . . . Blind now to everything but the cadences of the voice he followed her like an addict."[41] Having entered a mutable and sightless realm where sexuality takes all forms, Narouz in effect creates his own desired love object out of this amorphous and anonymous body, embuing the prostitute with his disembodied desires for Clea. When we remember that Narouz's perceptions are being hypothesized by the narrating Darley, this moment becomes absolutely crucial in illuminating the stakes involved in this text's constitution of male sexual identity. For what this encounter reveals about the nature of sexual attraction is the fact that *all* desire is unfixed, or, to put it in Freud's terms, that there is no *necessary* link between sexual instinct and object choice: the only "natural" objects of our desires are those that our fantasies construct. In practical terms, Narouz's example teaches Darley the freedom of choice that is his: he too can put his love for Justine aside and redirect his desire to a more "appropriate" object choice. What Balthazar has said in praise of homosexual relations—"Sex has left the body and entered the imagination now"—turns out to be true of all negotiations of desire.[42]

And Darley should know something about the constructed nature of sexual fantasy, because—in yet another of this text's revelations of repressed knowledge—it turns out that he has not only been a participant in this festival, he has witnessed Narouz's copulation with the prostitute firsthand: "my memory revives *something which it had forgotten;* memories of a dirty booth with a man and woman lying together in a bed and *myself looking down at them,* half-drunk, waiting my turn." Waiting his turn, that is, to do the same as Narouz, and spend the image of his lost love for Justine on this nameless body; which also means waiting his turn to take Narouz's place, to *become* his eroticized masculine ideal, a "real" man. Unless, of course, Darley means to take the place of the prostitute, to be *with* rather than become his ideal—a possibility which returns us to the sexual ambiguities that have plagued Darley's quest for manhood throughout.[43] Darley's voyeuristic tendencies, one recalls, are especially acute when it comes to spectacles of male sensuality: visiting

Balthazar in bed with his boyfriends; walking in on Keats's newly godlike body under the shower; and, now, interrupting Narouz's orgasm. Given these recurrences, it no longer suffices to explain (away) Darley's obsessive thoughts of homosexual taint solely as an internalized reaction to his "failure" as Justine's lover; it becomes more and more clear that he also actively searches out that which he fears because it speaks to his unspoken desires.

Thus it is ironically but psychologically appropriate that the welter of polymorphous desires unleashed by Darley's vivid recreation of the *mulid* of Sitna Mariam is immediately set against an account of Scobie's murder (which occurs earlier in narrative time) at the beginning of chapter 8. Cruising the docks in his female clothes, the genial old "Peddyrast" is brutally kicked to death in an evident case of fag-bashing. In so manipulating the sequential order of his text, Darley subconsciously uses his narrative authority to serve warning on his analogous potential for perversity: not only do Scobie's "Tendencies" catch up with the old sailor, but the latent desires that Darley's account of Narouz have expressed have also been, if not literally punished, at least overwritten. This report of homophobic violence prefigures the psychodramatic climax of *Balthazar*—the Carnival ball during which the effeminate Toto de Brunel is discovered brutally murdered, his head run through with a hatpin—yet another of the events deliberately suppressed from *Justine*'s text, as Darley himself admits. "Why have I never [before] mentioned this [incident]? . . . I was even there at the time, and yet somehow the whole incident . . . escaped me in the press of other matters. . . . Nevertheless, it is strange that I should not have mentioned it, even in passing."[44]

Even more so than the mad jumble of color, sounds, and human grotesques characterizing the festival of Sitna Mariam, Alexandria's celebration of Carnival assumes the contours of a Freudian dream-work. "The dark tides of Eros . . . burst out . . . like something long dammed up and raise the forms of strange primeval creatures—the perversions," Darley says, noting how "the polymorphous desires of the city" well up "like patches of meaning in an obscure text." The "ruling spirit" of this three-day-long debauch, Darley continues, is "utter anonymity," in which the black costumes and dominos donned by the participants become "the outward symbols of our own secret minds," "shroud[ing] identity and sex," blurring the boundaries "between man and woman, wife and lover, friend and enemy." In this world of dissolving boundaries, of unmoored sexuality and identity, Darley finds an exhilarating freedom implicitly related to the taboo subject that has haunted him throughout *Balthazar*:

> One feels free in this disguise to do *whatever one likes* without prohibition. . . . [W]e are delivered from the thrall of personality, from the bondage of ourselves. . . . You cannot tell whether you are dancing with a man or a woman. . . . Yes, who can help but love carnival when . . . all crimes [are] expiated or committed, *all illicit desires sated* . . . without the penalties which conscience or society exact?[45]

To do whatever one likes, for Darley, seems intimately connected to the pleasure of, just perhaps, finding oneself dancing with a member of the same sex. But if Carnival, through its exteriorization of internal desire, seems to make possible the unthinkable by temporarily escaping the socially repressive law of prohibition, penalties, and conscience, the festival is also, simultaneously, the siting for a much more ambiguous reenforcement of repression: it is against this ambisexual backdrop that the costumed Toto, Darley's negative alter ego, meets his doom. The satiation of "illicit desires" also exacts its price.

Significantly, Toto is mistaken for Justine when he is killed; on the way to the Cervoni ball, Justine has given him her well-known intaglio ring to wear, so that she can slip away from the ball unobserved, granting him in the meantime "a miracle long desired: . . . to be turned from a man into a woman."[46] The unintended result of this substitution assumes several levels of meaning: metaphorically, it enacts the death of the feminized or "unmanned" man that Darley has feared becoming, while, literally, it marks the death of a scapegoat for Justine herself, the negative love object who has engendered his self-doubts. But the death of Toto also symbolizes the scapegoating of Darley's homosexual impulses. For just as significant as the fact that Toto dies wearing Justine's ring is the fact that she has marked his black sleeve with white chalk so that she may identify him among the other costumed revelers. Crucially this signifying mark echoes an image that the narrating Darley has already generated to identify *himself* as "this timid and scholarly lover with chalk on his sleeve." Toto is not only Darley's negative foil, not only a scapegoat for Justine, but a double or mirror—in this world of incestuously multiplying mirrors—of Darley himself.

And who is it that kills Toto? None other, of course, than Narouz, the male principle incarnate. In the act of narrating Toto's death, therefore, Darley allows his hypermasculine double (Narouz) to assert itself by slaying his feminine self-image (Toto) and with it the specter of his guilty homoerotic desires. This purgation allows Darley to begin to reorient himself as a sexual being and an artist, as the rest of the *Quartet* demonstrates. The primary male heterosexual task, Durrell would appear to be saying, is to create a love object appropriate to one's desired self-image. But such a goal involves several paradoxes. For that which Darley is exorcising is any expression of the polymorphous play, the slippages in signification, that Carnival (like the tent-city episode preceding it) has revealed to be the underlying "truth" of all sexual desire. Without Carnival's reign of anarchy, this knowledge would never have occurred to Darley, nor would this symbolic exorcism have been possible. Moreover, to the degree that Darley's male ideal, Narouz, is responsible for slaying his effeminate self, Darley's narration achieves a perversely metaphoric union with the covert object of his desire in spite of himself: Toto/Darley gets "pinned" by Narouz after all. In "hunting from room to room . . . for an identifiable object to direct our love," as Darley says of the Carnival revelers, we find that there are no "destined" objects except those we construct—or those we choose to kill.

The quintessential Carnival story of unmasked true love, interestingly enough, turns out to be all about the (quite literal) construction of one's desired sexual object, and as such it sheds light on Durrell's resolution to his protagonist's anxieties in the final book of the *Quartet*. It is at Carnival that the doctor Amaril falls "madly in love" with a masked lady who disappears without leaving her name; the next year, Amaril meets her again, and after a frenzied pursuit, strips her of her mask, only to learn she has no nose. Undeterred by this revelation, Amaril uses his surgical skills to reconstruct a nose for his beloved—in effect, to replace her lack with his own phallic projections. As Clea, who tells this fable, notes, "You see, he [was] after all building a woman of his own fancy. . . . Only Pygmalion had such a chance before!" Once Amaril has successfully "authored" this "lovely nose," he bestows on his bride a very special wedding present: a doll's surgery, where she can repair children's wounded dolls, static Galateas like herself, the rest of her life. " 'It is the only way,' says Amaril, 'to hold a really stupid woman you adore. Give her something of her own to do.' " [47]

It is most fitting that Clea narrates this story: not only has she helped Amaril engineer Semira's transformation by sketching models for the new nose, but Semira's fate will become Clea's own. As I've already mentioned, *Clea* details Darley's return to Alexandria and the self-confidence that he gains as he lays to rest Justine's dangerously Oriental allure and then redirects his sexual energies toward the serenely virginal, blond beauty of Clea. To become a part of this text's economy of male desire, however, Clea must first be remade by man in his image, no matter how perfect she may appear to be, and this symbolic act of rebirth forms the *Quartet*'s symbolically charged climax. Darley and Clea have been swimming underwater when Clea's hand is accidentally harpooned to a submerged wreck. Unable to free the harpoon, Darley is forced to hack Clea's arm off with a knife, and then, on shore, pump her nearly drowned body back to life (she gasps for air like "a newly born child") in a grotesque "simulacrum of the sexual act—life saving, life-giving." [48] Not surprisingly, even Durrell's most ardent supporters have had problems justifying the heavy-handed construction of this scene. Rather than "justify" Durrell's execution, I would suggest its *inevitability*, given his unfolding theme. The acute strain that the text evinces at this juncture has everything to do with the difficulty (and desperation) involved in the attempt of his male subject, Darley, to construct a properly heterosexual object of desire.

Durrell's symbolism, indeed, is painfully obvious; not only is Clea pinioned by one phallic object and castrated by another, not only does a simulated sex act by a man bring her back to life, but it is her painter's arm—her means of independent creative productivity—that she loses: the "necessary sacrifice of a useless member," according to one critic.[49] In turn, Darley's role in reanimating Clea transforms him into a Pygmalion-like "life-giver" whose powers of creation, in "reversing the sexuality of birth," thereby subsume the threat that women's reproductive powers—like Egypt's emblematic fecundity—have traditionally posed to the questing male.[50] This series of identifications is cinched by the fact that it is none other than Amaril who treats the wounded Clea, replacing her missing hand with a mechanical one that, damningly, paints even better than her original: her creativity is rendered a product of male instrumentality. Simultaneously, Clea reveals that Amaril was the unnamed lover to whom she has earlier lost her virginity, thus "turn[ing]" her "into a woman" emotionally and sexually ready for Darley's advances. "I suppose I was even a bit eager to be wounded," she says of her sexual initiation, and wounded she indeed becomes in this final bit of psychodrama.[51] Durrell's narrative, in effect, has (forcibly) fashioned an object that answers to Darley's desired self-image as a heterosexually competent man: via the agency of Greek myth, a perfect (and perfectly Western) mate is born from his foray into the dangerously torrid zone of mid-Eastern sexuality.

But in order to construct his female counterpart, Darley must first refashion his own self-image, a process which returns us to the sexual ambiguities that have marked his negotiations of masculine subjectivity throughout the *Quartet*. Just as Darley's internalized doubts have been expressed through externalized self-projections, so too a double figure becomes the measure of his potential for self-fashioning: in this case, the hack journalist Johnny Keats, recently returned to Alexandria from the front (World War II has commenced) newly metamorphosed: "And . . . you know what? The most unaccountable and baffling thing. [War] has made a man of me, as the saying goes. More, a writer! . . . I have begun it at last, that bloody joyful book of mine." If Keats can undergo such a sea-change, there would seem to be hope for Darley yet. Keats's doubling function also explains his pronouncement that he considers himself a competitor for Clea: manhood, writing, and wooing Clea seem one and the same in the world created by this text. But the actual moment of re-encounter between Darley and his double unleashes an extraneous erotic energy that belies the assumed coherency of this formula. This scene, briefly noted earlier, occurs when Darley returns to his old apartment to find Keats in the shower: "Under the shower stood a Greek god! I was so surprised at the transformation that I sat down abruptly on the lavatory and studied this . . . apparition. Keats was burnt almost black, and his hair had bleached white. Though slimmer, he looked in first-class physical condition." While Keats dries himself, the two men make conversation:

> "God, this water is a treat. I've been revelling."
> "You look in tremendous shape."
> "I am. I am." He smacked himself exuberantly on the buttocks.
> . . . "You look in quite good shape, too," he said, and his blue eyes twinkled with a new mischievous light.[52]

Taken out of context, this exchange might seem more the prelude to a soft-porn scene in a gay novel by Gordon Merrick than the encounter of a straight hero with his role model. For under Darley's intense gaze, Keats becomes as much an object of consumption, a living spectacle, as the dancer Hasan el-Belbeissi has been for Flaubert (whose reaction is equally surprised but delighted, his prefatory "Oh! Oh! Oh!" mirrored in Darley's "Greek god!" exclamation). But there is a significant difference between these two eroticized objects: this new-born Adonis is as unmistakably English as the Pygmalion-like artist whose vision metaphorically creates him. Just as Justine's dark exoticism has been replaced with Clea's rational clarity, the swarthy foreignness of Darley's former male ideal Narouz—murdered at the climax of *Mountolive*—is overwritten by a newly fantasized masculine self-image whose Aryan good looks perfectly complement Clea's own. Yet even the retreat from Oriental sexuality implicit in this pair of substitutions cannot completely eradicate the homoerotic possibility—or threat—that Egypt has already unlocked in the narrator's psyche. It is thus inevitable that Keats dies in battle almost immediately after this encounter; not only does his death free Darley to become the new Keats, as it were, it also insures that those lingering glances in the bathroom go no further. In death, Keats joins those other silenced signifiers of homoerotic taboo—Toto, Scobie, and Narouz. Within the world of Durrell's imaginary, the price of masculine subjectivity is that of killing off the very desires that make such a construction a pressing, immediate necessity.

Given the impact of this restructuring imperative on the psychodramatic level of character, it is reasonable to wonder what effects it has on the narrative's formal trajectories of desire. *Clea* includes a vignette that offers a metaphoric answer. In Darley's last walk about town on the eve of his final departure from Alexandria, he comes across a religious procession that echoes the Sitna Mariam and Carnival scenes in *Balthazar*. But the erotic and ecstatic energies of those events have been subtly homogenized, routed into one linear trajectory, in this reprise: "And to all this queer discontinuous and yet somehow congruent mass of humanity the music lent a sort of homogeneity; it bound it and confined it. . . . [C]ircling, proceeding, halting, the long dancing lines moved on towards the tomb, bursting through the great portals . . . like a tide at full."[53] This channeling of the many tributaries of desire into one massive tide not only uncannily recalls Freud's description of the way sexual instincts are brought into the service of a single drive but also inscribes the physiological process of male orgasm. And with this climactic ejaculation, the hitherto dispersive energies of this multilayered text are "bound and confined" within a specifically phallocentric model of narrative that has little to do with the polymorphous freeplay Durrell has hitherto promoted. Ironically, the goal, the aim of the processional, is Scobie's former lodging: this lecherous old Tiresias has been resurrected by the Moslem population of his quarter as El Scob, a fertility god to whom barren women pray. With this rewriting of the very type of male sexual ambiguity into an emblem of heterosexual productivity, the narrative's homogenizing of its deviant impulses would seem to have finally cleared the way for Darley, now the writer par excellence, to produce, at long last, his "man-size" masterpiece.

So how does the artist feel, proverbial pen in hand and facing the blank page? "[L]ike some timid girl, scared of the birth of her first child."[54] Perhaps this return of the feminine whereby Darley identifies himself as a "her" is only a joke, or a slip of the tongue, or an assertion of mastery over his former anxieties; nonetheless, this age-old conflation of masculine artistic productivity and female reproductivity betrays the shadow of a fear that lingers to disturb Darley's newborn confidence. Perhaps he should join the barren wives who pray to El Scob for succor.

―――――

This welter of contradictions brings us back to the male writer's problematic relation to phallocentric discourse, in this case exacerbated and illuminated by the sexual and representational politics of the colonial narrative. For Durrell is attracted to Alexandria as the locus of his narrative precisely because its exotic, foreign otherness allows him to indulge in fantasies of, as Said puts it, "a different type of sexuality"—certainly one more open, in Flaubert's noun, to "experiment." Likewise, the polyphonic execution of this work evokes a geography of the instincts at least temporarily freed from constrictions of time and space and, to the writing Western consciousness, from sexual/moral orthodoxy. But such representations of foreign sensuality and freeplay, for all their appeal, simultaneously prove unnerving because they expose the contradictions and incoherencies underlying Western culture's plots of masculine maturation and articulation. Hence Darley's compulsion to code the "possible" as "homosexual," the absolute antithesis of Western manhood, and hence his impulse to *colonize* these fantasies by equating them with the "feminine," thereby categorizing their difference within familiar hierarchical terms that allow him to pretend to have control over their subversive attraction.

But this desire to control, to pin down as one thing and not the other, is also what the *Quartet*, with its paean to the relativity of all truths and its repeated illustrations of the slipperiness of all signification, works to counter. For if the multiple, overlapping perspectives engendered by the *Quartet*'s refracting linguistic and formal structures are meant to suggest the subjectivity of all viewpoints, so too its evocations of the Alexandrian nightworld of the festival and Carnival are meant to suggest that the only truth of sexuality and sexual identification is its similarly fluid and individually constructed nature. The irony, then, is that Darley's discovery of the arbitrariness of sexual choice, and the role that imagination plays in creating any object of desire, makes all the more urgent his formulation of a choice toward sexual fixity, toward an absolutism of heterosexual identification and, as it were, "straightforward" artistic productivity. Thus *Clea* ends with an exchange of letters between Darley and Clea, letters tremulous with the anticipation of a not-too-distant reunion on safe European soil, followed, on the last page, with the narrator's declaration that he has just penned the first words of his long-deferred novel: "Once upon a time. . . ." At this moment, with Clea practically in his arms, Darley has become the apotheosis of the Western writer, and the East his safely colonized other, whose perversities he can survey from the authorizing distance of myth and fairy tale.

The catch, though, is that Clea really *isn't* in Darley's arms. Despite the fact Darley has begun to write, his romantic desires remain in a state of suspension; the concluding exchange of letters gives an illusion of romantic closure where none exists. And with this image of Clea writing from Paris and Darley writing from his island retreat, I inevitably call to mind two other writing couples for whom correspondence whets rather than consummates desire: Miller in Paris, Durrell on one of his Mediterranean islands; Flaubert in Egypt, Bouilhet back home in France.[55] I return to this latter pair and Flaubert's epistolary comment after describing sex with the exotic dancer Kuchuk Hanem:

> In my absorption in all those things, *mon pauvre vieux*, you never ceased to be present. The thought of you was like a constant vesicant, inflaming my mind and making its juices flow by adding to the stimulation. I was sorry (the word is weak) that you were not there—I enjoyed it all for myself and for you—the excitement was for both of us, and you came in for a good share, you may be sure.[56]

In this example of male homosocial desire at its most crystalline, Kuchuk's sexualized body primarily serves to bond the two correspondents: as she stimulates Flaubert's bodily parts, his mind is inflamed by thoughts of Bouilhet. This latter is the ultimate in safe sex, since minds, however "juiced" to overflowing, aren't the same as real bodies. But what happens when the female intermediary is removed from the fantasized tableau? We get a glimpse of such a possibility in the conclusion of the letter in which Flaubert tells Bouilhet all about the sodomitical practices of his fellow Egyptians:

> Dear fellow how I'd love to hug you—I'll be glad to see your face again. . . . At night when you are in your room and the lines don't come, and you're thinking of me, and bored, with your elbows on the table, take a sheet of paper and write me everything—I devoured your letter and have reread it more than once. At this moment I have a vision of you in your shirt before the fire, feeling too warm, and contemplating your prick.[57]

Whatever one may want to argue about Flaubert's tone or his "true" sexual preference, this letter inscribes the body of a homosexual rather than merely homosocial desire—mental vesicants have been replaced by warm pricks. Nonetheless, the framework in which Flaubert encases this masturbatory scenario presupposes a relation of writing to sexuality as potentially disabling as that which generates Darley's crisis of masculinity in the *Quartet*. For Flaubert must first represent the homoerotic revery as that which takes place when "the lines don't come," when Bouilhet is "bored" with his poetry and abdicates pen for prick: so too the homoerotics of the *Quartet* literally take place between the lines, precisely because the exotic otherness of sexual "perversion" is figured as the threat of erasure, the negation of artistic vitality or "sap." Thus in his journal Flaubert will use non-reproductive sexual play as a metaphor to express his despair at not having yet achieved his writing goals: "Where is the heart, the verve, the sap? . . . We're good at sucking, we play a lot of tongue-games, we pet for hours: but—the real thing! To ejaculate, beget the child!"[58] Against this phallocentric model of narrative creation, in which the pen is the penis only if the desire is heterosexually productive, the substance of the narrative that Flaubert relays to Bouilhet *simultaneously* speaks another story, however. For the erotic tableau he unfolds is, first of all, *of* writing—"take a sheet of paper *and write*,"—and, second, on Flaubert's part, it has taken the *form* of writing: "At this moment," he *writes*, "I have a vision of you." That which takes place between the lines, as in Durrell's case, or when the lines don't come, as in Flaubert's, writes itself into the text nonetheless, engendering a discourse of "foreign otherness" that is always already inscribed in its denial. In the case of the *Alexandria Quartet*, the sheer effort of Darley's attempt to construct a nonperverse, "productive" model of sexuality and narrativity, underlining the extremity of the masculine anxiety that at once drives and undercuts his story, ends up only clearing space for the play of the desires it (in both senses of the term) writes out. Meanwhile Darley corresponds expectantly with Clea in Paris, and Clea replies in kind, serenely awaiting a consummation that never comes; and in the gap between these two lovers, one the constructed mirror-projection of the other, exists an other "other" that will not disappear from this text's mappings and remappings of the problematic terrain of male desire.

Notes

I would like to express my gratitude to Laura Claridge and Elizabeth Langland for generously allowing this essay, which was written for their exciting new collection, *Escaping Patriarchy: Male Writing and Feminist Inquiry* (1989), to appear first in this issue.

1   R. T. Chapman, "Dead, or Just Pretending?: Reality in the *Alexandria Quartet*," *Centennial Review* 16 (Fall 1972): 412.

2   "The central topic of the book is an investigation of modern love," Durrell states in an explanatory note at the beginning of *Balthazar* (New York, 1961). The series was first published by E. P. Dutton: *Justine* (1957), *Balthazar* (1958), *Mountolive* (1959), and *Clea* (1960). I will be citing the Pocket edition of the *Quartet* (New York, 1961) throughout.

3   *Lawrence Durrell—Henry Miller: A Private Correspondence*, ed. George Wickes (New York, 1963), 4–5. Durrell repeats the phrase "man-size" twice in his letter.

4   Durrell, *Clea*, 130.

5   Wickes, ed., *Private Correspondence*, 90.

6   Morton P. Levitt, "Art and Correspondences: Durrell, Miller, and *The Alexandria Quartet*," *Modern Fiction Studies* 13 (Autumn 1967): 302.

7   Wickes, ed., *Private Correspondence*, 89–90. Durrell has been mocking the English tendency to self-deprecation, which, he jokes, he can do as well as anyone, and then gives this example: "I part my hair in the middle, adjust the horn-rimmed lenses and settle like a Catholic homosexual at the master's feet" (89); he seems to remain blissfully unaware of the parallels that might be drawn between this image and his expression of literary discipleship which follows.

8   Ibid., 189–90; emphasis mine.

9   See Eve Kosofsky Sedgwick, *Between Men: English Literature and Male Homosocial Desire* (New York, 1985).

10   Lawrence Durrell, *The Big Supposer: A Dialogue with Marc Alyn*, trans. Francine Barker (New York, 1974), 130. As Jane L. Pinchin pithily comments in "Durrell's Fatal Cleopatra," *Modern Fiction Studies* 28 (Summer 1982), apropos this world of male camaraderie, "Prostitutes, for Durrell . . . are places men go to play with one another" (231).

11   Jane L. Pinchin, *Alexandria Still: Forster, Durrell, and Cavafy* (Princeton, 1977), 174.

12   G. S. Fraser, *Lawrence Durrell: A Study* (London, 1968), 19.

13   See Pinchin's comments in "Fatal Cleopatra," an acute exegesis of the way in which women become pawns in what is an essentially homosocial world of male bonding; writing in 1982 before Sedgwick coined the term "homosocial," Pinchin comes to conclusions very similar to those advanced in *Between Men*.

14   I borrow this term from Edward Said, *Orientalism* (New York, 1978), where it appears in the title of sec. 2, chap. 1.

15   Durrell, *Justine*, 177; *Balthazar*, 235.

16   The impress of modernist aesthetic is most directly felt in Durrell's first major novel, *The Black Book* (1938; reprint New York, 1962); see also his *A Key to Modern British Poetry* (Norman, Ok., 1952). In the prefatory note to *Balthazar* he makes explicit his innovative agenda.

17   Durrell, *Balthazar*, 147, 149.

18   Ibid., 196, 185.

19   Said, *Orientalism*, 1, 56, 188, 190. Durrell's position vis-à-vis colonialism is relevant here: although he claims "I don't give a damn about British Empire," he allows himself to be labeled a "colonialist," having been born and raised in India in a family whose Anglo-Indian roots go back three generations. See Joan Goulianos, "A Conversation with Lawrence Durrell about Art, Analysis, and Politics," *Modern Fiction Studies* 17 (Summer 1971): 164–65.

20   Said, *Orientalism*, 103, 187–88.

21   *Flaubert in Egypt: A Sensibility on Tour*, ed. and trans. Francis Steegmuller (Chicago, 1979), 83–84; emphasis mine.

22   Durrell, *Balthazar*, 149–50.

23   See Steegmuller, ed., *Flaubert in Egypt*, 203–4, as well as 62–63, 85–86, 89, 127, 133–34, 146, 150, for Flaubert's accounts of repeated "experiments." Of Flaubert's declaration that he has "consummated that business at the baths," Steegmuller notes the elaborate extremes to which Jean-Paul Sartre has gone in his study of Flaubert, *L'idiot de la famille*, to prove all this homosexual jesting is merely that— locker-room banter. As Steegmuller notes with delicious understatement: "Other writers differ from Sartre on this question" (204).

24   Alexandria is not just or simply the Other, because its historical position as conduit between East and West renders it at once familiar and foreign to its Western visitors. This fact radically complicates the Orientalist's goal (and makes a simplistic application of Said's formula impossible), for it means that Alexandria can never be totally differentiated and appropriated, since it is also a part of the West-

ern consciousness. Hence the impossibility of Darley's attempt to render the city's exoticism a theatrical spectacle.

25 Durrell, *Justine*, 4; *Balthazar*, 46.

26 Durrell, *Balthazar*, 121; *Justine*, 35. Durrell's evocation of Justine is similar to Said's description of Western visions of the Orient as "passive, seminal, feminine, even silent and supine" (*Orientalism*, 138).

27 Durrell, *Balthazar*, 13, 105. Here my terminology evokes Teresa de Lauretis's description of narrative desire as an oedipal and male-gendered activity in *Alice Doesn't: Feminism, Semiotics, Cinema* (Bloomington, 1984), 109, in which woman is doomed to serve as a marker or obstacle, like the Sphinx, in a story of heroic quest that is never her own.

28 Alice Jardine, *Gynesis: Configurations of Woman and Modernity* (Ithaca, 1985), 33–34, 42. For more on Durrell's existentialism, see Chet Taylor, "Dissonance and Digression: The Ill-Fitting Fusion of Philosophy and Form in Lawrence Durrell's *Alexandria Quartet*," *Modern Fiction Studies* 17 (Summer 1971): 167–79.

29 Durrell, *Clea*, 47–48; emphasis mine.

30 On this specular logic of the same, see Luce Irigaray, *Speculum de l'autre femme* (Paris, 1974). Punning on the French *homme* (man) and Latin *homo* (same), she labels patriarchy's economy of desire as *hom(m)osexualité*; in Durrell, what might be called the "hom(m)oerotic" desires generated by masculine specularization ironically open the floodgates to a "homoerotics" of desire in the usual sense of the term.

31 Durrell, *Clea*, 54; *Justine*, 82, 4.

32 Durrell, *Justine*, 11, 21; *Clea*, 214; *Balthazar*, 121, 12.

33 Durrell, *Balthazar*, 8, 13; *Justine*, 78.

34 I am greatly indebted to David Wingrove, whose superb seminar paper, "Dance of the Black Dominos: Narrative and Sex-Roles in Durrell's *Balthazar*," inspired me to return to Durrell in the first place, for making this connection, as well as for his comments on the roles that Scobie, Clea, and Narouz play in bringing Darley's repressions to the surface of the narration.

35 Durrell, *Balthazar*, 15–16.

36 Ibid., 19, 23, 32–33; *Justine*, 108.

37 Much less humorously, Scobie's perspective captures the unthinking mentality that allowed for the Western appropriation and exploitation of racially other, "inferior" bodies, male or female. As Sedgwick notes in reference to Sir Richard Burton's implicit linking of pederastic habits with racial inferiority, "the foreign siting, in imperialist literature," makes "the image of [sodomy] more articulately available" (*Between Men*, 193). See Wickes, ed., *Private Correspondence*, 90, 195, 196, where Durrell suggests to Miller that the underlying inspiration of the *Quartet* as a heterosexist fantasy of girls as meat-to-be-devoured is the fear of sodomy as an ultimate kind of indulgence in passive pleasure (like drugs, food) that spells death to the self: "One could not continue to live here without practising a sort of death—hashish or boys or food." This overwriting of "boys" by "girls" as objects

to be consumed parallels, in reverse, Scobie's overwriting of female sexuality with pederastic pleasures.

38 Durrell, *Balthazar*, 41–42, 46.

39 Ibid., 157.

40 Ibid., 58–59. See Sander L. Gilman, "Black Bodies, White Bodies: Toward an Iconography of Female Sexuality in Late Nineteenth-Century Art, Medicine, and Literature," *Critical Inquiry* 12 (Autumn 1985): 212, 221, 229. In addition to Flaubert's references (Steegmuller, ed., *Flaubert in Egypt*, 85, 203), the conflation of "ugly" visage and desirability occurs in Maxime du Camp's description of the "former bardash" Khalil, one of the crew members, who is "rather ugly, with a shifty look," but does, "in fact, have a charming behind" (*Flaubert in Egypt*, 225).

41 Durrell, *Balthazar*, 158–59.

42 Sigmund Freud, *Three Essays on the Theory of Sexuality*, trans. James Strachey (New York, 1962), 13–14, 37–38. See Durrell, *Justine*, 82.

43 Durrell, *Balthazar*, 160; emphasis mine. On hindsight one realizes that this scene has been briefly represented in *Justine*, where Darley describes entering a prostitute's lighted booth "to wait my turn" (166)—the same phrase used in *Balthazar*.

44 Durrell, *Balthazar*, 182.

45 Ibid., 185; emphasis mine. See also 182, 186, 196.

46 Ibid., 195.

47 Durrell, *Mountolive*, 133, 137; *Clea*, 81.

48 Durrell, *Clea*, 244–45.

49 Alan Warren Friedman, *Lawrence Durrell and the Alexandria Quartet: Art for Love's Sake* (Norman, Ok., 1970), 148. Upon this "necessary sacrifice," Friedman continues, Darley "sheds his unmanly timidity" (149).

50 Pinchin, "Fatal Cleopatra," 235, citing Theodore Reik.

51 Durrell, *Clea*, 249, 101. To view Clea as sexually incomplete until her seduction by a man of course elides the sexual experience she has earlier shared with Justine: only from a heterosexual viewpoint is she a "virgin" at the time of Amaril's seduction. As Pinchin wittily puts it, "Amaril and Darley, male doctor and writer . . . make a good woman of Clea . . . [by] curing her of her homosexuality and her virginity" ("Fatal Cleopatra," 235).

52 Durrell, *Clea*, 173, 170.

53 Ibid., 262.

54 Ibid., 275.

55 I borrow the phrase "writing couples" from Alice Jardine, "Death Sentences: Writing Couples and Ideology," in *The Female Body in Western Culture: Contemporary Perspectives*, ed. Susan Suleiman (Cambridge, Mass., 1985), 84–96.

56 Steegmuller, ed., *Flaubert in Egypt*, 130.

57 Ibid., 86–87.

58 Ibid., 199.

Jonathan Goldberg

Colin to Hobbinol: Spenser's Familiar Letters

The *Januarye* eclogue of Spenser's *Shepheardes Calender* is filled with Colin Clout's insistent complaint about the unresponsiveness of Rosalind. Not far from the close of this lament, the text exhibits an exorbitancy beyond its compulsive repetitiveness:

> It is not *Hobbinol*, wherefore I plaine,
> Albee my love he seeke with dayly suit:
> His clownish gifts and curtsies I disdaine,
> His kiddes, his cracknelles, and his early
>   fruit.
> Ah foolish *Hobbinol*, thy gyfts bene
>   vayne:
> *Colin* them gives to *Rosalind* againe.[1]

A gloss for the third of these lines, provided by the marginal figure of E. K., seeks to establish the propriety of the entrance of Hobbinol onto the scene of Colin's complaint: "His clownish gyfts . . . imitateth Virgils verse, Rusticus es Corydon, nec munera curat Alexis."[2] E. K. invites the reader to open Virgil's second eclogue to line fifty-six, in which the shepherd Corydon addresses himself and scores the folly of his suit: his gifts have not won Alexis. "Ah foolish *Hobbinol*": the line translates and transfers "rusticus es, Corydon" to Hobbinol, doubling the allusion, provoking exorbitant questions—not only the question of what Hobbinol's love for Colin Clout is doing in this text, with its monomaniacal lament for Rosalind, but also this one: if Colin is Alexis to Hobbinol's Corydon, is Colin thereby cast as Corydon in relationship to Rosalind's Alexis? How far does the allusion to Virgil's eclogue go? Where does the literary allusion place the erotics of Spenser's text?

The questions begin to answer themselves, but only insofar as they point to an excessive economy, literary and erotic at once, of translation and transference. "It is not *Hobbinol*, wherefore I plaine"; Colin is not Corydon complaining about Alexis—*his* Alexis is Rosalind. The allusion establishes the genre of the *Januarye* eclogue through its Virgilian antecedent, and Colin's complaint transfers Corydon's, rewriting Virgil in a series of reversals. The iciness of January replaces the scorching heat of Virgil's second eclogue. Corydon burns: "Formosum pastor Corydon ardebat Alexim."[3] Colin freezes: "Such rage as winters, reigneth in my heart, / My life bloud friesing with unkindly cold." Genre revision is also gender revision; Rosalind, the woman from "the neighbour towne" who scorns Colin's rustic music, takes the part of Alexis, the urbane favorite of his master who cannot be persuaded of the pleasures of the countryside. E. K. gratuitously suggests the translation in a further gloss: "Neighbour towne . . . the next towne: expressing the Latine Vicina,"[4] a note that refers to no original Latin "vicina"; it suggests the "vicinity" of the *Januarye* eclogue nonetheless, for Spenser's poem translates Virgil's eclogue back to its model, the eleventh idyll of Theocritus, Polyphemos's lament for Galatea. The reversals of genre and gender are true to a doubled source.

"Ah foolish *Hobbinol*, thy gyfts bene vayne: / *Colin* them gives to *Rosalind* againe." The analogical structure of this exchange of gifts (Hobbinol is to Colin as Colin is to Rosalind) repeats the generic transformation of the second eclogue, a doubling (giving again) that splits the same, rerouting Corydon's catalog of gifts for Alexis. The same gifts pass from Hobbinol to Colin and from Colin to Rosalind; the same "vayne" effect is achieved in each case—it passes through several hands and is yet refused. Although it is the same, it is no one's and never proper, a text circulating from hand to hand, always out of hand, never arriving. Yet this circulation within the same also opens difference, sexual difference most notably. For the circular structure further suggests that if Colin is Alexis to Hobbinol's Corydon, and Corydon to Rosalind's Alexis, he plays Rosalind to Hobbinol's frustrated suit. The homologies of this circulation place Colin at a split center, doubling himself; Janus-faced, he looks two ways.

Mirror tricks of genre and gender: true, again, to the source. Colin looks at the "barrein ground" and sees "a myrrhour"; Corydon looks at the sea and sees himself, in an ideal projection, as Daphnis, as the image does not deceive ("si numquam fallit imago"). Corydon offers Alexis the chestnuts that pleased Amaryllis when she was his beloved; Colin passes Hobbinol's gifts on to Rosalind. Duplicating images, the same becomes different. In Virgil's poem, Corydon has loved Amaryllis and now loves Alexis to his sorrow; he might better, he says, have borne the disdain of Amaryllis, or have accepted Menalcas, unattractive as he is. In Virgil's Rome, such alternatives were possible—the love of boys and the love of women were not opposing categories.[5] And in Elizabethan England? "A Shepheards boye (no better do him call)": so is Colin Clout introduced. Can this boy thus play the woman's part? Another Rosalind, Shakespeare's, playing the part of Ganymede in *As You Like It*, might reply, affirming the identification: "for every passion something and for no passion truly anything, as boys and women are for the most part cattle of this color."

Such a reading is policed from the margin in E. K.'s gloss on Hobbinol: "In thys place seemeth to be some savour of disorderly love, which the learned call pæderastice: but it is gathered beside his meaning."[6] E. K., whose earlier translation of neighborhood had granted proximity to vicinity, rules "disorderly love" out of "thys place" and "beside his meaning." Beside: extraneous or parallel? The question, once again, is of the economies of exchange, of genre and gender. For, even as E. K.'s citation of Virgil suggests, the *Januarye* eclogue operates through displacement and replacement. Its "place" is translation, the mirrored spacing of a proximity; "thys place" is always "beside his meaning." The exorbitancy of allusion guarantees such proximity. And thus E. K.'s gloss registers its refusal of "disorderly love" by ordering it through an act of learned translation; this love properly speaks Greek (pæderastice) even as the poem's "neighborhood" is translated Latin. What is "gathered beside" is an exorbitancy written within the economies of exchange, the circulation of the gift and text: "for every passion something and for no passion truly anything," as Shakespeare's Rosalind puts it, the exorbitancy—something and nothing at once—of literature.

Even as E. K. rules out a reading, he rules it into the textual economies of the *Shepheardes Calender*; E. K.'s gloss continues with classical citations of a *proper* pederasty, the example of Socrates, to arrive at this conclusion: "And so is pæderastice much to be præferred before gynerastice, that is the love whiche enflameth men with lust toward woman kind."[7] Does this classicism—from Virgil's second eclogue to a platonized and delibidinized Socrates—secure the literary propriety of the text? Consider Erasmus's account of the second eclogue in *De Ratione Studii*, where Virgil's poem is chosen to illustrate pedagogic method. The poem, Erasmus says, will allow the teacher to discourse on friendship: " 'The essence of friendship,' the Master would begin, 'lies in similarity.' "[8] Pairs of friends like Castor and Pollux are to be adduced, and then the poem may be read: "Now it is as a parable of unstable friendship that the Master should treat this Eclogue. Alexis is of the town, Corydon a countryman; Corydon a shepherd; Alexis a man of society. Alexis cultivated, young, graceful; Corydon rude, crippled, his youth far behind him. Hence the impossibility of a true friendship."[9] For Erasmus, Virgil's poem savors of disorderly love, "unstable friendship," differences that refuse the homeostasis of "similarity," identifications within the self-same and proper. From an Erasmian perspective, E. K.'s glosses—the poet "imitateth Virgils verse," the learned disquisition on a proper pederasty —would be excessive; rather than placing Spenser's poem within the confines of classical purity, they overstep those limits.

Yet the "place" of that textual exorbitance, as we have remarked already, is within similitude, and even the Erasmian text offers a mirror. Among the exemplars of friendship adduced by Erasmus is "the beautiful myth of Narcissus." "What has more likeness to ourselves than our own reflection?" Erasmus goes on to ask. His text, too, succumbs to the mirror effects of the *Januarye* eclogue, displays the same logic as the marginal (and exorbitant) glosses of E. K. and their double-edged reflections that attempt to "place" the poem within its sexual and textual economies, a place that escapes those confines by passing through the mirror. The excessive logic of the mirror of Narcissus may overcome the moral economies in which Erasmus would place Virgil's second eclogue—or those that regulate a reading of the *Januarye* eclogue: "The Mirror Stage of Colin Clout."

Thus Harry Berger, Jr., titles his complaint against the *Januarye* eclogue for its "self-indulgent" displays of "narcissistic metamorphosis": "Perhaps, to speculate idly, this confusion of literary and erotic motives informed the poetry addressed to Rosalind and affected her adverse reactions: perhaps she questioned the poet-lover's sincerity as well as his taste."[10] Whether she did or not, Berger does. His "speculations" pass through the mirror as he assumes the place of Rosalind, disdaining Colin Clout's narcissistic literary love; or when he occupies the place in which he muses, "why love a lass rather than someone or something more tractable—e.g., Hobbinoll or the 'refyned forme' of the woman as Idea—and more susceptible to the allure of Epanorthosis and Paronomasia?" Berger reacts excessively to Colin's line "I love thilke lasse, (alas why doe I love?)" and to E. K.'s gloss, "a prety Epanorthosis in these two verses, and withall a Paronomasia or playing with the word." Mere rhetoric, Berger charges; rhetoric, E. K. defends. Berger "speculates" within the exorbitancy of identifications within the mirror—voicing, variously, vicariously, the positions of Rosalind, of Colin, of E. K., and Hobbinol. "How real—how genuine or authentic—are the love and grief that can be proportioned to the demands of poetry and displayed in the mirror of art?"[11] One answer suggests itself as the text places Berger's ethical stance, capturing it within the mirror. What, we may ask again, is the "place" of the *Januarye* eclogue within the "real"?

Alan Bray addresses the question, taking up the nineteenth-century misapprehension that the imitation of classical literature in the Renaissance functioned (as it did for the Victorians) as a sign "implying a tolerant attitude to homosexuality."[12] "Apparently homosexual themes in Renaissance literature need to be treated with extreme caution," Bray argues. Perhaps, he suggests, the extraordinary case of Christopher Marlowe (his supposed saying that St. John was "Our Saviour Christ's Alexis") does represent Marlowe's homosexual appropriation of Virgil's second eclogue, but more often classical imitations (as when Richard Barnfield writes to his Ganymede) are "literary exercises" and nothing more—except to those readers who wanted to find in such poems justifications for their sexual tastes.[13] They prove, Bray contends, nothing about their authors. Bray, then, would appear to agree with Berger; there is nothing real in the *Januarye* eclogue, it tells us nothing about Spenser himself, or his loves; it is all rhetorical play, exercises in a literariness at a remove from history.

What is shaky in Bray's argument is implicit in the title of the chapter in which he discusses these questions, "Society and the Individual," for those terms have already assumed an opposition that is, arguably, a post-Renaissance, post-Cartesian development, and whose use by Bray has the unfortunate effect of making an ideological argument by assuming as universal a quite particular historical (and liberal, bourgeois) construction of the "individual" subject.[14] This is something that Bray knows quite well since it helps him to explain the emergence of homosexual "individuals" in the early eighteenth century, and he cautions that the terms are not to be found in the Renaissance: "To talk of an individual in this period as being or not being 'a homosexual' is an anachronism and ruinously misleading"—misleading, as I have argued elsewhere, even in the case of Christopher Marlowe.[15]

When Bray decides that Barnfield's commonplace book, "never intended for publication and . . . both robustly pornographic and entirely heterosexual," offers the real truth about its author's sexual orientation, savoring of the "personal experience" lacking in his literary exercises addressed to Ganymede and other Arcadian shepherds, he anachronistically assumes the opposition of homosexual and heterosexual, and he assumes that Barnfield must have been one or the other. The characterization of those entries as "robustly pornographic" (as opposed to the "delicate sensibility" of the poems) as well as the categories of "entirely heterosexual" and "personal experience" needs to be scrutinized for what Eve Kosofsky Sedgwick might call their "inadvertent reification."[16] For Bray, the secret status of the commonplace book assures the truth of Barnfield's heterosexuality; but this, too, is anachronistic. It assumes a modern "deployment of sexuality" (in Foucault's term) [17] to be in place, in which one can be sure that the deepest secret of the self is its sexuality, especially if, as in the case of Barnfield, it assumes the excessive form that Bray calls pornographic. Yet to read the evidence about Barnfield this way rewrites him as a modern subject. It dismisses what might be called the "open secret" of Barnfield's published poems without asking how they assumed a "place" in the Elizabethan world. [18] For the answer to that question cannot be the one that Bray assumes: that its classical literariness necessarily assured that it would go unremarked (Erasmus suggests otherwise); nor that it could be read homosexually by those inclined in that direction. For, as Bray himself argues, one could not identify oneself as being so inclined. Or, to put the point—*Bray's point*—more radically, there were no homosexuals in Renaissance England.

Such, too, was the case in Virgil's Rome; if homosexuality is a term that signifies only in relationship to the binary opposition homosexual/heterosexual, then the second eclogue does not operate within that system. Within the Roman sexual system, as Veyne has argued (following Foucault), what mattered was not the gender of the love object but his/her class and age; sexuality was congruent with power differences. So long as a man was the penetrator, he was a man; slave boys and women were the appropriate objects of his desire. Virgil's poem is not necessarily circumscribed by this system—Alexis is not a slave, but his master's favorite; Corydon, who may well be older, also appears to be of a lower class than Alexis, and his love seems to exceed the Roman norm of a passionless sexuality. Virgil's poem, translating the grotesquerie of Polyphemos's love for Galatea, opens itself toward the Erasmian dismissal of its disorderliness even as it uses that safeguard to extend the limits of acceptability, an extension that may also return his poem to the orbit of the erotic system of ancient Greece, which, although similar to the Roman system, had not viewed slave boys as the preferred sexual objects. Rather, as Foucault has claimed, the entire ethical system of Greek pederasty was directed at questions having to do with free-born boys. [19]

Bray argues that differentials of class and age in a number of institutional sites—the family, the school, the apprentice system—also operate to define sexual spheres in Renaissance England in which homosexual acts could and did take place. Such acts do not prove their actors homosexual; likewise, texts like the *Januarye* eclogue (or Barnfield's classical pastorals) will never tell us whether their authors slept with boys. But they may, in the very exorbitancy that I have been reading, tell us about the "place" of homosexuality in Renaissance England; not least if, as Bray contends, it had no place, was not a site of recognition of sexual identity. Bray posits a *disconnection* between the stigmatization of homosexual acts (within the larger category of sodomy) and their enactment in places in which they went unseen and seen. This is, in effect, to describe the place of homosexuality as an open secret. If sodomy is the term most proximate to homosexuality in the period, it functions neither solely to designate sex between men, nor is it only (perhaps not even primarily) a sexual term. Designating a range of interlinked social and religious transgressions, it also leaves untouched, Bray argues, the ordinary social channels that permitted homosexual acts to be disseminated through all the differentials of power that mark the hierarchies of Renaissance society. "The individual could simply avoid making the connection; he could keep at two opposite poles the social pressures bearing down on him and his own discordant sexual behavior, and avoid recognising it for what it was." [20] But what *was* it? Bray's sentences, brilliant in suggesting the dehiscence that opens the place of homosexuality, has already foreclosed it by assuming an identity for that "it" which, as his argument suggests, cannot succumb to the later scheme in which "homosexuality" is a recognized and recognizable category.

The reading of *Januarye* that I have been offering may appear to have been an exercise in deconstructive undecidability, merely rhetorical play. I would contend, however, that it offers a way to read the (no) place of homosexuality in Renaissance culture—that the mirror effects of *Januarye* secure a place for homosexuality through such tactics of resemblance. How to move from the text, and these textual effects, into the world are in fact suggested by the *Shepheardes Calender*, not least by E. K.'s tactics of reading. For his gloss, on the margins, also opens up a relationship between the text and the world, opens it and covers it over as does his gloss on "pæderastice." That double play has the structure of the open secret. Who is Colin Clout? "Under which name this Poete secretly shadoweth himself." Hobbinol?: "a fained country name, whereby, it being so commune and usuall, seemeth to be hidden the person of some his very speciall and most familiar freend, whom he entirely and extraordinarily beloved, as peradventure shall be more largely declared hereafter." "Rosalinde . . . is also a feigned name, which being wel ordered, wil bewray the very name of hys love and mistresse, whom by that name he coloureth."[21] E. K.'s directions for reading cannot be taken very straightforwardly (nor, for that matter, can "E. K.," whose initials remain to be deciphered). If Spenser "is" Colin Clout, for example, he is also figured as Immerito in the *Shepheardes Calender* and no "proper" name is ever delivered for the doubly named author of a yet anonymous text.[22] E. K.'s directions for reading Rosalind treat her name as an anagram—as if the name were itself disordered (or the name of disorderly love), and as if to find her would be the same as performing a play on the letter. In this teasing play between revelation and reveiling, the *Calender* dangles its secrets—the secret of an authorship maintained through a disappearing act in disseminative naming; of an Eros that may never pass beyond the letter, and which yet opens a way (within a certain psychoanalytic framework, *the* way).[23] The open secret of this text is not homosexuality, as might well be the case if this were a Victorian imitation of a classical poem. Instead, it has no name, "being so commune and usuall" and, at the same time, "very speciall and most familiar." Or, if it does have one, it could be called (following Sedgwick) homosociality. In this text, the name of the open secret is Hobbinol.

Spenser's name remains veiled in the *Calender*. E. K. and Rosalind have never been deciphered. But E. K.'s promise to declare hereafter the identity of Hobbinol is delivered in a gloss to *September*. "Colin cloute . . . Nowe I thinke no man doubteth but by Colin is ever meante the Authour selfe. Whose especiall good freend Hobbinoll sayth he is, or more rightly Mayster Gabriel Harvey: of whose speciall commendation, aswell in Poetrye as Rhetorike and other choyce learning, we have lately had a sufficient tryall in diverse his workes." That revelation is prepared for from the start. E. K.'s dedicatory epistle to the *Calender* is addressed to Harvey, introducing the new poet to someone who scarcely needs such an introduction, "his verie special and singular good frend," and that description is immediately applied to Hobbinol, as we have seen, in the gloss to *Januarye*: "his very speciall and most familiar freend."[24] Hobbinol, moreover, is a name that Harvey takes for himself at the close of the third of the *Three Proper, and wittie, familiar Letters* that he exchanged with "Immerito" in a volume that appeared in 1580, a year after the publication of the *Calender*, another anonymous production in which Harvey's name is the open secret as soon as one gets past the title page and to the first letter addressed by Immerito to his "long approoved and singular good friende, Master *G. H.*" And, if there were any doubt about who "Maister G. H. Fellow of Trinitie Hall in Cambridge" is, as he is addressed in the first of the *Two Other very commendable Letters* that accompanied the first three, a poem of Immerito's enclosed in that letter twice names "Harvey" explicitly, puns on his angelic first name, Gabriel, and ends by bidding farewell to *"Mi amabilissime / Harveie, meo cordi, meorum omnium longè charissime"*: "My sweetest Harvey, to me of all my friends by far the dearest."[25]

Within the *Shepheardes Calender*, Hobbinol is the shepherd suffering from unrequited love for Colin, and that fiction is maintained from *Januarye* to *Aprill*, where, in response to Thenot's question about the causes of his sorrow—lambs stolen by wolves? bagpipe broken? abandoned by a "lasse"? weeping like the showers of April?—Hobbinol replies "Nor thys, nor that, so muche doeth make me mourne, / But for the ladde, whome long I lovd so deare"; to *June*, where Colin tells Hobbinol that his paradise is not for him; to *September*, and the line that E. K. glosses: "Colin he whilome my ioye." But in the gloss, and in the surrounding apparatus that extends from the poem to other texts and into the world, Hobbinol is Gabriel Harvey, and the poet's special friendship for him is repeatedly announced. Indeed, in the farewell poem to Harvey (written when Immerito plans to leave England on a voyage to the continent), Immerito's veil is almost dropped as well when he ventriloquizes Harvey's lament for his absent friend: "Would Heaven my Edmund were here. / He would have written me news, nor himself have been silent / Regarding his love, and often, in his heart and with words / Of the kindest, would bless me."[26] The relationship between Hobbinol, in the eclogues of the *Cal-ender*, and Harvey, in the margins, functions like the reverse mirror of *Januarye*, identifying (Hobbinol is Harvey), doubling (Harvey is Hobbinol), and reversing (the rejected lover is the special friend) all at the same time. This mirror extends into the world, Harvey taking Hobbinol for his own name in a letter to Immerito. What the eclogues structure as denial and refusal, the surrounding context figures as the acceptance of a special friendship. How is this (non)relationship to be read?

One answer lies within the eclogues themselves, and Hobbinol's role within the pastoral fiction; there he secures a literariness asso-ciated with that transformative place, and Colin's refusal of his ad-vances also signals his frustrated attempts to pass beyond pastoral. From the start, Colin has broken the pipes of Pan, moved toward the urban Rosalind, to his devastation; and as late as *Colin Clouts Come Home Again* (1595), his return to pastoral is a return to Hobbinol, as "The shepheards boy (best knowen by that name)" re-encounters the one who "lov'd this shepheard dearest in degree." As late as that poem or the sixth book of *The Faerie Queene*, Rosalind still names what cannot be had. And those returns to pastoral and to Hobbinol remain returns to a refusal of Hobbinol. Colin continues to look elsewhere. This is how Hobbinol explains his plight to Thenot in *Aprill:* "the ladde, whome long I lovd so deare / Now loves a lasse," and that love has made the writing of pastoral poetry impossible. "Lo *Colin*, here the place": so Hobbinol in *June* speaks to Colin, luring him to a "Para-dise" that Colin rejects as no longer possible. Hobbinol, throughout the *Calender*, is associated with "the place"—the literary, erotic, and sociohistorical place—from which Colin affirms his displacement.

This refusal reads doubly, however; within a duplicity that can be found in the *Calender*, one can begin to move toward the world which it mirrors in reverse. For however much Colin denies, he is a figure in a pastoral poem; the place from which Colin affirms his displacement is the place in which he affirms it. The poet embraces what his figure refuses. The denials are productive. They produce the poems as that double place from which aspirations—toward Rosalind, toward kinds of poetry other than pastoral—can be launched and denied at the same time. Rosalind refuses Colin; in *June*, he reports that she has instead taken Menalcas, the dark young man whom Virgil's Corydon scorned. Even as the poems glance beyond the confines of pastoral, they are returned within its limits, still turning on Virgilian tropes. But it is also within the confines of Virgilian pastoral that it be exorbitant, that it establish relationships with the world; it establishes them by denying them, and Hobbinol is within the eclogues the figure for that denial.

It has become commonplace in certain critical practices that are called "new historicist" to argue that "love is not love" or that pastoral otium is really negotium.[27] This essay shares with such work the desire to read texts into the world. But in describing the trick mirror that the *Shepheardes Calender* holds up to the world, in pursuing the reversed identification of Hobbinol and Harvey, it seems to me important not to allegorize and thematize the text so entirely that its sole function is to read the world at the expense of the text, to decide beforehand that the world is real and that the only reality that a text might have would be its ability to translate the world in terms that need to be translated back into the social, historical, or political. The literary and erotic translations performed in the *Calender* extend into the world, as the Hobbinol-Harvey identification would seem to guarantee. But it cannot be read as a simple act of translation. The name "Hobbinol" is carried beyond the confines of the *Shepheardes Calender*, even as the name "Harvey" appears on its borders. And the double structure within pastoral also extends into the "real" world. We can see it as congruent with the dehiscence that Bray describes, articulating the site of a (non)relationship and a (non)recognition. We can see it, too, in the fact of double nomination, Harvey/Hobbinol, Immerito/Colin, and the space of (non)identification that it opens. These are structures of identification in a mirror, a productive site of replication.

If we look at the moment in *September* when the veil is dropped, and Harvey's name delivered, we find it in a gloss on Hobbinol's request that Diggon tell the tale of Roffynn; Hobbinol would hear the story since "Colin clout I wene be his selfe boye"—i.e., Colin is Roffynn's boy and not, as Hobbinol goes on to say, as he once was, his own: "(Ah for Colin he whilome my ioye)." *September* is a particularly dark eclogue, glancing in Roffynn's tale and elsewhere at matters of state and church, but this particular identification is not all that hard to decipher. We can find "Roffynn" on the flyleaf to Harvey's copy of Jerome Turler's *The Traveiler*, as he records it as a gift from Spenser: "ex dono Edmundi Spenserii, Episcopi Roffensis Secretarii. 1578."[28] Roffynn anglicizes the Latin name of John Young, Bishop of Rochester, whose secretary Spenser became in the spring of 1578. If, elsewhere in the *Calender*, and throughout Spenser's poems, Hobbinol appears as the rival for Rosalind, here he is in a similar position with Roffynn; as Colin moves beyond the pastoral world, Hobbinol stays behind, representing what must be refused in order to advance. But advancement also occurs through what is represented by Hobbinol: a mode of high literariness that gives one credentials within the world—in this instance, the classicizing pastoral of the *Calender*—within the exorbitancy of humanistic pedagogy. The secrets of the *Calender* are the open secrets of a secretariat, and of aspirations that must veil themselves in this humble form.

Harvey's role in this worldliness is insisted upon as E. K. continues his gloss, identifying Harvey in the *September* eclogue; he lists his recent publications "aswell in Poetrye as Rhetorike" and details Harvey's presentation of a copy of "his late Gratulationum Valdinensium" to Queen Elizabeth "at the worshipfull Maister Capells in Hertfordshire."[29] Harvey's attempts to use his rhetorico-literary skills to secure him a place in the world are perhaps the most spectacular examples of the failure of the promises of humanistic pedagogy in the Elizabethan period. Uncannily, Spenser uses Hobbinol/Harvey as the name that secures failure by denying the very tools by which success can be achieved. Yet Harvey, probably not more than a couple of years Spenser's senior but, more importantly, already a Fellow at Pembroke when Spenser entered as sizar, a poor boy, in 1569, also functions as mentor and guide. The intimacy with his special friend writes the aspirations within the rhetorico-literary even as the name Hobbinol insists that such aspirers know their place: boys, secretaries to the great and powerful.

The trick mirrors of *Januarye* negotiate the place of the literary within the sociopolitics and the homoerotics of a textual economy that extends into the world and writes the world as much as the world writes the text. The veils of the *Calender* can be drawn only when they open upon an acceptable version of aspiration within the homosocial sphere, aspiration, that is, that knows its place—"A Shepeheards boye (no better doe him call)." Immerito, the worthless one, attaches himself to his special friend Gabriel Harvey, hailing him as in his farewell poem as "a poet transcendent" ("egregium . . . Poetam") addressed by "the lowliest poet" ("malus . . . Poeta"). The point of homeostasis in this differentiated and hierarchized relationship with angel Gabriel is their friendship; to this friend, the first line of the farewell poem insists, he is not unfriendly ("non inimicus Amicum"); no disorderly love, it secures the status quo. Within this mirror relation, Harvey/Hobbinol functions as an alter ego, so much so that E. K. can close his dedicatory epistle by urging Harvey to imitate the new poet and publish: "Now I trust M. Harvey, that upon sight of your speciall frends and fellow Poets doings, or els for envie of so many unworthy Quidams, which catch at the garlond, which to you alone is dewe, you will be perswaded to pluck out of the hateful darknesse, those so many excellent English poemes of yours, which lye hid, and bring them forth to eternall light."[30] And the letters exchanged between Immerito and G. H. continue this theme, referring again and again to their secret poems, and urging each other to make them public. This is a structure of emulation recommended by Erasmus and his followers as necessary to pedagogic success; the title page of the *Three Proper, and wittie, familiar Letters* proclaims the writers as "*two Universitie men.*"

Yet in the poem of farewell to Harvey, Edmund urges him to venture even further, beyond such pedagogic, humanistic, pastoral economies, toward the love that Harvey despises, what G. H. designates in the last of the letters as Immerito's "womanly humor": "A magnanimous spirit, I know, spurs you up to the summits / Of honor and inspires your poems with emotions more solemn / Than lighthearted love."[31] For the point seems to be that Harvey's misogyny (displayed at length in the three letters, as when he paraphrases "Arte Amandi" as "Arte Meretricandi," or offers two accounts of earthquakes, one for women, another for men) is not requisite for their attachment, nor does the poet's desire for Rosalind mean the end of their extraordinary friendship. So, Immerito's final letter closes, urging Harvey to believe in "the eternall Memorie of our everlasting friendship, the inviolable Memorie of our unspotted friendshippe, the sacred Memorie of our vowed friendship. . . . Farewell most hartily, mine owne good *Master H.* and love me, as I love you, and thinke upon poore *Immerito*, as he thinketh uppon you."[32] This mirroring reciprocity defines a proper "unspotted" relationship between men, not the path of Harvey's aspirations (figured in the *Calender* as Hobbinol's rootedness), and one secured through the negations written as Rosalind's refusals and transferred from Colin to Hobbinol, from Immerito to G. H. Letters of farewell, again and again. Harvey/Hobbinol confined to the margins—where the "real" enters the poem—and Harvey, in life, never making his way, confined to *his* marginalia.

The love of women does not interrupt this love. Thus the *Shepheardes Calender* closes by dispatching Hobbinol as go-between to Rosalind: "Adieu good *Hobbinol*, that was so true, / Tell *Rosalind*, her *Colin* bids her adieu." These poems of farewell to Harvey/Hobbinol also write him into Colin/Immerito/Spenser's position, structures of denial that ramify out into the world. Here, as they establish a relationship of nonrelationship *between men*, they do so as Hobbinol is asked in *December* to voice the farewell to Rosalind that he has so often received from Colin. In these (un)productive circles, the woman is drawn into the circuit of letters passing between men (Rosalind's name is never realized beyond such anagrammatization); the woman is infolded as that furthering negation that opens a movement toward the real.

So, too, in response to Immerito's question in the first of the *Three Proper, and wittie, familiar Letters*, asking why G. H. had not responded to his beloved's letters, G. H. responds—as Hobbinol—promising to reply in letters that are worthy of her: "By your own Venus, she is another dear little Rosalind; and not another but the same Hobbinol (with your kind permission as before) loves her deeply. O my Mistress Immerito, my most beautiful Collina Clout, countless greetings to you and farewell."[33] The *same* Hobbinol/Harvey (one and two at once) writes to Mrs. Immerito (the beloved Immerito has married), who is *not* Rosalind, within the folds of this letter to Immerito. But it is also within the letter that Immerito tells G. H. to remember their special friendship and love—"Continue with usuall writings," although he wishes for "a Reciprocall farewell from your owne sweete mouth." And G. H. hopes to comply, wishing that "I may personally performe your request, and bestowe the sweetest Farewell, upon your sweetmouthed Mastershippe."[34]

These *proper familiar* letters exchanged between friends openly declare their secrets of translation and transference from the start, beginning with a *literal* scene of translation in the very first letter from Immerito to G. H. Immerito offers samples of his skills in translation, his efforts (under the tutelage of G. H.) to classicize his English verses and make their meters Latin: "Seeme they comparable to those two," he asks, "which I translated you *ex tempore* in bed, the last time we lay togither in Westminster?"[35]

Spenser slept with Harvey, and it is no secret. Indeed this is the open secret of a *proper* and *familiar* scene, exhibiting the very structure E. K. read in the name of Hobbinol in *Januarye*, "so commune and usuall," "very speciall and most familiar," for men habitually shared beds in the Elizabethan age. A secret written elsewhere too, for there is nothing to hide. So Roger Ascham, pausing to memorialize his student John Whitney, now dead, and to bid him farewell, recalls, in his book on double translation, the scene of instruction: "John Whitney, a young gentlemen, was my bedfellow, who, willing by good nature and provoked by mine advice, began to learn the Latin tongue."[36] The text chosen for this double translation "out of Latin into English and out of English into Latin again" was "Tully *De amicitia.*" A proper choice. The scene fulfills the dictates of Erasmian pedagogy to the letter, as the teacher incites the pupil to learn—by loving imitation within the specular relationship of similarity and simulation. The child "must be beguiled and not driven to learning," Erasmus writes in *De Pueris Instituendis*, and he continues: "For a boy is often drawn to a subject first for his master's sake, and afterwards for its own. Learning, like many other things, wins our liking for the reason that it is offered to us by one we love."[37]

To that bedroom scene Harvey brings another. Judging some other efforts at translation, he recommends the use of models for imitation: "some *Gentlewooman*, I coulde name in England . . . might as well have brought forth all goodly faire children" [as a poet might produce excellent poems] "had they at the tyme of their *Conception*, had in sight, the amiable and gallant beautifull Pictures of *Adonis*,

Cupido, Ganymedes, or the like, which no doubt would have wrought such deepe impression in their fantasies, and imaginations, as their children, and perhappes their Childrens children too, myght have thanked them."[38] "Nature has made the first years of our life prone to imitation," Erasmus writes; pedagogy is founded in simulation.[39] But for Harvey, all conception is specular, for men and women alike are produced in the mirror, after the images of desire—Adonis, Cupid, Ganymede.

This is not only Harvey's fantasy; it is one shared by his culture. Consider the lines that open Shakespeare's first and third sonnets in the 1609 edition: "From fairest creatures we desire increase / That thereby beauties *Rose* might never die"; "Looke in thy glasse and tell the face thou vewest, / Now is the time that face should forme an other." This is, indeed, the mirror stage, and not only of Colin Clout. For, as Lacan writes in his essay on the role of the mirror stage in the formation of the "I," that initiation into an alienated and split subjectivity has a biological support instanced, for example, by the necessity for the maturation of the gonad of the pigeon that it see another member of its species—of either sex—or even that it see itself in a mirror: "Facts which inscribe themselves into an order of homeomorphic identification which would fold within itself the question of the notion of beauty as formative and as erogenic."[40]

The homeomorphic structures identified in this essay ramify within an order that Lacan calls "orthopedic," the (non)support of an ideal projection—for which Lacan finds the "ancient term *imago*" apt, and Spenser, the Virgilian *imago*—in which subjectivity is founded. The Lacanian insistence on the prematurity of human arrival, and its destiny within an imaginary scene, has its Erasmian correspondent: "Man, lacking instinct, can do little or nothing of innate power; scarce can he eat, or walk, or speak, unless he be guided thereto"; "a man ignorant of Letters is no man at all."[41] Imitation of the letter founds the human within a pedagogic apparatus, the "virage du *je* spéculaire en *je* social," turning the specular I into the social I.[42] Such destiny, as Derrida argues, is a destinerrance, a straying within a letter whose arrival is never guaranteed.[43] Within that spacing, which, for Elizabethans like Spenser and Harvey, takes the historically specific situation of the apparatuses of a homosocial pedagogy, the Spenserian career—in life, in letters—is launched. In it, Hobbi-nol/Harvey serves—in life, in letters—as a marginal site, the "place" of the exorbitant *méconnaissance* that guarantees that institution.

Notes

1   All citations are from *The Poetical Works of Edmund Spenser*, ed. J. C. Smith and E. De Selincourt (London, 1912). Here and elsewhere, inconsistencies in spelling in my text mirror those in the texts cited.

2   Ibid., 422.

3   "A shepherd, Corydon, burned with love for handsome Alexis." Citations of Virgil are from *The Eclogues and Georgics of Virgil*, trans. C. Day Lewis (Garden City, N.Y., 1964).

4   Spenser, *Poetical Works*, 422.

5   See Paul Veyne, "Homosexuality in Ancient Rome," in *Western Sexuality*, ed. Philippe Ariès and André Béjin (Oxford, 1985), 26. For a brilliant historical sur-vey, see David M. Halperin, "One Hundred Years of Homosexuality," *Diacritics* 16 (1986): 34–45.

6   Spenser, *Poetical Works*, 422–23.

7   Ibid., 423.

8   William Harrison Woodward, *Desiderius Erasmus Concerning the Aim and Method of Education* (New York, 1964), 174.

9   Ibid., 175.

10   Harry Berger, Jr., "The Mirror Stage of Colin Clout: A New Reading of Spenser's *Januarye* Eclogue," *Helios* 10 (1983): 151, 154.

11   Ibid., 156, 158.

12   Alan Bray, *Homosexuality in Renaissance England* (London, 1982), 59. Nothing in my critique of Bray is meant to devalue his book; the problem of literary evidence troubles many distinguished historians, and Bray remains the best guide to the question of homosexuality in Renaissance England.

13   Ibid., 65, 61.

14   My critique here follows Eve Kosofsky Sedgwick, *Between Men: English Literature and Male Homosocial Desire* (New York, 1985), 83–90.

15   Bray, *Homosexuality in Renaissance England*, 16; Jonathan Goldberg, "Sodomy and Society: The Case of Christopher Marlowe," *Southwest Review* 69 (1985): 371–78.

16   Bray, *Homosexuality in Renaissance England*, 61; see Sedgwick, *Between Men*, 86.

17   Michel Foucault, *The History of Sexuality*, trans. Robert Hurley (New York, 1980), pt. 4.

18   For the role of "open secrets" to secure the secret subjectivity of the modern subject, see D. A. Miller, "Secret Subjects, Open Secrets," in *The Novel and the Police* (Berkeley and Los Angeles, 1988), 192–220.

19   See Michel Foucault, *The Use of Pleasure*, trans. Robert Hurley (New York, 1986),

187ff. In Virgil's second eclogue, much depends on the final lines of the poem, whether Corydon continues to address himself or is being addressed—something that remains undecidable and thus keeps open the question of the perspective taken on his "dementia."

20 Bray, *Homosexuality in Renaissance England*, 67.

21 Spenser, *Poetical Works*, 422–23.

22 For further discussion of these issues, see my "Consuming Texts: Spenser and the Poet's Economy," in *Voice Terminal Echo: Postmodernism and English Renaissance Texts* (New York and London, 1986).

23 I have in mind the Lacanian framework, in which the refusal ever to embody Rosalind as a "real" woman would testify to the structure of desire shaped by an Other that is, by definition, inaccessible. This leads, within the Lacanian schema, to the postulate that there is no woman per se; and this leads, within an argument like Sedgwick's, to a realization of the homosocial structure between men that covers over the place of woman. Thus Berger's ethical complaint—that Colin is in love with a projected idea of woman—can be supported by the recognition of psychic and social structures that make the place of woman insupportable. Yet this structure obtains not only in the case of Rosalind, but also underwrites the place of Colin Clout—and that place writes itself into the real, although never in the same way for each gender.

24 Spenser, *Poetical Works*, 455, 415, 422.

25 Spenser, *Poetical Works*, 632, 611, 635, 638; translation of the Latin poem is included in *Spenser's Prose Works*, ed. Rudolf Gottfried (Baltimore, 1949), 258.

26 Spenser, *Prose Works*, 258; for the Latin text see Spenser, *Poetical Works*, 638.

27 The first phrase is Sidney's and is invoked by Arthur Marotti, "'Love is not love': Elizabethan Sonnet Sequences and the Social Order," *ELH* 49 (1982): 396–428, and is the guiding thesis as well in Marotti's *John Donne: Coterie Poet* (Madison, 1986). The translation of pastoral otium into negotium is the theme in a number of essays by Louis Montrose; see, for example, "Of Gentlemen and Shepherds: The Politics of Elizabethan Pastoral Form," *ELH* 50 (1983): 415–59. My argument attempts to modify the point made repeatedly in such work, that love must be translated into something "real"—ambition—or that pastoral functions as a cover for a place in the world and negotiates the desire for it.

28 Cited in Virginia Stern, *Gabriel Harvey: His Life, Marginalia, and Library* (Oxford, 1979), 237; for information on Spenser's secretaryship to Young, see 48–49. Harvey's parasitic relationship to texts, living in his marginalia, I take to describe a modus vivendi, an argument I make in part thanks to work in progress by Jennifer Summit.

29 Spenser, *Poetical Works*, 455.

30 Ibid., 419.

31 Spenser, *Poetical Works*, 641; Spenser, *Prose Works*, 256. For the Latin text, see Spenser, *Poetical Works*, 637.

32 Spenser, *Poetical Works*, 641, 638.

33 For the Latin text, see Spenser, *Poetical Works*, 632. My translation depends on the one offered in Frederic Ives Carpenter, *A Reference Guide to Edmund Spenser* (Chicago, 1923), 58.

34 Spenser, *Poetical Works*, 638, 636, 641.

35 Ibid., 611.

36 Roger Ascham, *The Schoolmaster*, ed. Lawrence V. Ryan (Ithaca, 1967), 80. The secret of the shared bed is more usually declared in patronage and servant-master relations where, as Bray argues in "Dreams, Fantasies, and Fears: Defining Sexuality in Elizabethan England" (a paper distributed at the International Scientific Conference on Gay and Lesbian Studies, Free University, Amsterdam, 15–18 December 1987), shared beds (or tables) suggest intimate power and influence. Thus Archbishop Laud recorded in his diary on 21 August 1625 a dream of sleeping with Buckingham. When these relations were politically suspect, such intimacies could fall under the shadow of sodomy. In another paper, "Pederasty in Elizabethan London," from the same conference, Robert M. Wren starts with the *Januarye* eclogue and extends Bray's argument to the theaters and schools—pointing as well to shared beds in such plays as Middleton's *Michaelmas Term*, Chapman's *Sir Giles Goosecap*, and Shakespeare's *Henry V* and *Othello*, suggesting too that medical manuals may have encouraged masturbation in a widespread and culturally countenanced pederasty.

37 Woodward, *Erasmus Concerning . . . Education*, 203.

38 Spenser, *Poetical Works*, 626.

39 Woodward, *Erasmus Concerning . . . Education*, 189.

40 Jacques Lacan, *Écrits I* (Paris, 1966), 92: "Faits qui s'inscrivent dans un ordre d'identification homéomorphique qu'envelopperait la question du sens de la beauté comme formative et comme érogène." In *Ecrits: A Selection*, trans. Alan Sheridan (New York, 1977), the passage reads: "Such facts are inscribed in an order of homeomorphic identification that would itself fall within the larger question of the meaning of beauty as both formative and erogenic" (3).

41 Woodward, *Erasmus Concerning . . . Education*, 184, 181.

42 See Lacan, *Écrits I*, 94, 90, 95.

43 See Jacques Derrida, *The Post Card from Socrates to Freud and Beyond*, trans. Alan Bass (Chicago, 1987).

Joseph A. Porter

Marlowe, Shakespeare, and the Canonization of Heterosexuality

Relations between Marlowe and Shakespeare, particularly as manifested in the character of Mercutio in *Romeo and Juliet*, serve as an index of the Western canonization of heterosexuality at the expense of homosexuality through the past four centuries. That exceedingly complex history, only recently starting to be told, continues to unfold in the present, with the ongoing denial, containment, and suppression of homosexuality countered by powerful recent movements toward undoing the orthodox hierarchy that privileges heterosexuality. Our evolving views of relations between the two playwrights, and our processing of the figure of Mercutio, continue to show where we stand in the battle of the sexualities, whether for maintenance of orthodoxy, or for its affirmative-action inversion in a privileging of homosexuality, or (as here) for peaceful coexistence and the elimination of hierarchy as a stage toward our freeing ourselves from the very categories of homosexuality and heterosexuality.[1]

Bearing in mind that "sexuality," like "homosexuality" and "hetero-sexuality," dates only from the early nineteenth century, and that these terms are variously problematic, as Eve Kosofsky Sedgwick, Jonathan Goldberg, Alan Bray, and others are currently helping us see, Marlowe's sexual stance might be described as intermittently misogynistic, aggressively sensual, and flagrantly homoerotic. I list the three characteristics in increasing degree of provocativeness or subversiveness. The misogyny shows in moments like Tamburlaine's off-the-cuff totalizing remark that "women must be flattered," and also in a stinginess notable even for the time with female dramatic roles. Marlowe's urgent sensuality, more often present than his misogyny and nearly always incipient, shows in many ways, including the apparent readiness of his imagination to eroticize, and perhaps above all in the sheer corporeality of his imagined world. In that world the human body of either gender is the most insistently corporeal of objects: it realizes with peculiar provocativeness the renascent and newly problematic (because newly secular) appreciation of the body that had come up from the Italy of Botticelli and Michelangelo to an England comparatively starved for pictures and statues of nudes.

The most provocative and subversive component of Marlowe's sexuality, however, is the preference flaunted in the vivid homoeroticism of *Hero and Leander*, in the love of Edward and Gaveston in *Edward II*, and at other points in his work such as the opening scene of *Dido, Queen of Carthage* with Jupiter dandling Ganymede on his knee. Marlowe may also have expressed his sexual preference in the claim "That all they that love not tobacco and boys were fools," attributed to him by Richard Baines in his list of charges against Marlowe sent to the queen three days after Marlowe's death. In "Sodomy and Society: The Case of Christopher Marlowe," Jonathan Goldberg treats some of the difficulties this last piece of evidence presents, which include the possibility that it was fabricated as part of a government action.[2] Since, as has seemed at least possible to many recent commentators, Marlowe's very death may have been a government-ordered assassination, we need put no great faith in the disinterested accuracy of Baines's report, which was clearly intended to discredit at least. Even as a fabrication, however, it bears some weight since its plausibility may be assumed. As with the anticlerical and sacrilegious remarks Baines also attributes to Marlowe, so with the remark about tobacco and boys: there is reason to suspect that Marlowe had behaved in ways that made it seem he could well have made the remark, whether or not he actually did make it. Baines's report, then, if not evidence of Marlowe's homoerotic stance, exemplifies the treatment of such "evidence": that is, Baines's or his superiors' confidence that pederasty (like any other homosexual practice) would discredit Marlowe manifests a stance apparent in the commentary on Marlowe (and writers such as Richard Barnfield) from the Renaissance to the present. With due acknowledgment that this stance toward "homosexuality" varies with time in weight and tenability, it appears in criticism past and present, antipathetic and ostensibly tolerant.[3]

A second way of processing Marlowe's sexuality is by ignoring it. This has been the most common response, both of detractors and proponents, from shortly after Marlowe's death to the present. Some detractors have ignored Marlowe's sexuality as part of a general downplaying of him, or because the subject in their opinions is per se inappropriate for discussion, or even because they prefer not to denigrate homosexuality. Most of the ignoring of Marlowe's sexuality, however, has been at the hands of his champions and proponents. In some cases they have doubtless shared the detractors' reluctance, for reasons of propriety, to discuss the matter at all; some must have been inclined to save Marlowe from the "taint" he had paraded in self-advertisement and self-destructiveness. Editors in particular have followed this line, usually providing in notes and commentary a kind of bowdlerized-into-wonderland Marlowe; nor does any edition to date yet take significant cognizance of Marlowe's sexuality. While the recent climate of criticism has made it less easy to paper over Marlowe's sexuality, we still have a widespread inability or refusal to grant its pervasive importance in his life and work, and in his reception. When that importance is granted, even now, it may be with the most surprising indirectness. Michael Goldman, one of Marlowe's most influential recent commentators, says almost nothing directly about Marlowe's minority sexuality, while indirectly acknowledging it—flaunting it, even—with the "ravished" acting style he recommends for Marlowe's drama.[4]

A third possible treatment of Marlowe's sexuality is to acknowledge it and its importance in an unprejudicial response to his work. To an extent we can see this treatment in the wave of homoerotic and largely Ovidian poetry that sweeps through the 1590s, which includes Shakespeare's *Venus and Adonis*, and which seems importantly initiated by the example of Marlowe's *Hero and Leander*. In Marlowe criticism and editorial procedures, however, some of which is otherwise of a very high order, this sort of response (which I take as a desideratum) appears as a scant glimmer. During the two-session seminar on "Marlowe and Shakespeare" at the 1985 meeting of the Shakespeare Association of America, virtually no attention was given to questions of sexuality and sexual preference.

As for Shakespeare's sexuality, while there seems to be more to go on, both in the life and in the works, the evidence is also more ambiguous and contradictory than with Marlowe. Apparent evidence from the life includes all the tantalizing facts we have about his marriage, fatherhood, and long absence from his family, as well as the complete absence of suggestions of any sort of sexual impropriety. Evidence from the work, too voluminous and complex for more than a glance here, includes: the celebration of heterosexuality in many of the plays, above all *Antony and Cleopatra*; the various sorts of protofeminism and celebration of the female in most of the same plays; the eruptions of what has been called sexual loathing or fear of the female, especially in *Hamlet*, *Lear*, and the dark lady sonnets; the loving sonnets to the young man; the narrative poems, one with rape as its titular subject and the other portraying something approaching a goddess's rape of a mortal male; and a multitude of *sexually* complex moments and situations in the plays and poems. Compared to Marlowe's, Shakespeare's sexual stance seems to me less misogynistic and sexist and far more protofeminist, less aggressively sensual, and generally if perhaps not exclusively heterosexual. Furthermore, still painting with broad strokes, I would say not only that Shakespeare is more retiring than Marlowe on the subject of sexuality (as on most subjects), but also that the subject itself is less prominent in Shakespeare.

My take on the evidence, of course, constitutes a part of the cultural processing of Shakespeare's sexuality. Given Shakespeare's early prominence and later canonization, stakes in the processing of his sexuality have been much higher than with Marlowe. Therefore, while in general Shakespeare's sexuality has not seemed so much at issue as Marlowe's, and in particular has not seemed so subversive, still where the subject has arisen there has been a hotter contest for its determination, more strident claims and charges, and heavier ammunition. Here I have in mind not merely the shadow-land of claims that Shakespeare actually was Marlowe, or that he was female, but also, for instance, the broad daylight Victorian manufacture of that sentimentalized Shakespeare of heroines fitted out with girlhoods. In our century the *Sonnets* have of course been prime battleground. Most recently Joseph Pequigney argues that Sonnets 1–126 detail physical intimacies in an amorous friendship that is "sexual in both orientation and practice," these sonnets comprising "the grand masterpiece of homoerotic poetry"; and Eve Kosofsky Sedgwick begins her *Between Men* with "Swan in Love: The Example of Shakespeare's Sonnets," a subtle and powerful treatment of relations among gender, power, and "homosocial" desire in the sonnets.[5]

When Shakespeare in *As You Like It* has the silly shepherdess Phebe quote Marlowe—"Dead shepherd, now I find thy saw of might, / 'Who ever loved that loved not at first sight?' "—the directness and the assured lightness of touch seem earned, since in itself the moment scarcely hints at how much of Shakespeare's energy during most of the preceding decade has been absorbed in a struggle with his mighty rival, before and after Marlowe's death in 1593. Whether or not Marlowe is, as some maintain, the "rival poet" of the sonnets, he was certainly a commercial rival even after his death, and he was also (insofar as the two can be separated) an artistic rival. While clarification of much about their tangled artistic relations must await more precise dating of their works in the years near Marlowe's death, enough is clear for us to be able to characterize the general dynamic as notably including Shakespeare's response to the challenge posed by Marlowe. Shakespeare's response to Marlowe is characteristically complex and delayed, in part considered and in part barely if at all conscious, and at once a containment of subversiveness and a creation of subtle new subversiveness.

Phebe's quotation serves as something of a valedictory from Shakespeare to Marlowe. Following it, Shakespeare's concern with Marlowe subsides markedly, and appears only in such sporadic traces as those in the Player's speech in *Hamlet*, which at "one or perhaps two points" seems to echo the *Dido* of Marlowe and Nashe.[6] Before Phebe's valedictory, however, Shakespeare's massive engagement with Marlowe shows, as is generally recognized, in the correspondence between three pairs of complete works by the two authors—the Ovidian poems *Hero and Leander* and *Venus and Adonis*, the history plays *Edward II* and *Richard II*, and the two plays *The Jew of Malta* and *The Merchant of Venice*, the one a kind of tragedy and the other a kind of comedy—as well as in numerous local features of Shakespeare, some of them of great interest. Marjorie Garber, for instance, has argued persuasively that in Hal's killing of Hotspur in *1 Henry IV* Shakespeare represents his dramatic victory over Marlowe.[7]

As I maintain in *Shakespeare's Mercutio*, using the character of Mercutio in *Romeo and Juliet* as a partial simulacrum of Marlowe, dead some two years, Shakespeare carries out a major and hitherto largely unremarked phase of his negotiations with the memory of the rival.[8] With Mercutio, those negotiations concern, among other things, sexual matters. Indeed, leaving aside questions of the sonnets, I would say that in the plays Mercutio plays the major and indeed virtually the sole part in Shakespeare's processing of the challenge presented by Marlowe's sexuality.

Before elaborating, it may be well to insert a few caveats. My claim is not that Shakespeare's Mercutio must be taken in any simple, obvious, or reductive way as really or merely "a homosexual" with the hots for Romeo, although I know he has been read and played that way. Nor am I claiming that *Romeo and Juliet* is a *drame à clef* wherein Mercutio is "really" Marlowe, nor even that Mercutio's Marlovianness is simple, uniform, or determinate. Nor finally do I claim

that Shakespeare was fully conscious in using Mercutio for a negotiation with Marlowe's homoeroticism. That negotiation seems to have
been partly conscious, given such a detail as the echo of *Tamburlaine*
in Benvolio's announcement of Mercutio's death, but here as with
much else in Shakespeare important operations seem to take place
beneath the level of full consciousness.[9]

Shakespeare, choosing what was already a fairly canonical story
of heterosexual love for his play, seems to have relied entirely on
the version in Arthur Brooke's *The Tragical History of Romeus and
Juliet* (1562).[10] Brooke's Mercutio is a rudimentary figure who appears
at the Capulet ball as a potential rival of Romeo's for Juliet. The
sketched figure, that is, exhibits some of the conventional heterosexual interest of a young gallant, and there is no suggestion that
he and Romeo even know each other. His main *raison d'être* in the
poem is to occasion the first words between Juliet and Romeo, for
after he and Romeo each have grasped one of Juliet's hands she turns
to Romeo to complain of Mercutio's "icy hand." Thereafter Brooke's
poem contains no mention of Mercutio.

Shakespeare's elaboration of Brooke's trace Mercutio begins, in a
sense, with the erasure of the potential Mercutio-Juliet bond. The
erasure is very thorough. At the Capulet ball, Shakespeare gives Mercutio neither lines nor stage directions, nor any acknowledgment of
his presence, not even where it might seem most natural, as when
the Nurse informs Juliet of the identities of guests as they depart at
the end of the scene. Shakespeare's Mercutio and Juliet never touch
hands or speak to each other, nor does either ever speak of the other.
Furthermore, while the play contains several occasions where one
might naturally be spoken of to the other, neither ever hears mention
of the other.

By a certain conservation of imaginative weight, the erased Mercutio-Juliet bond reappears in Shakespeare as the bond uniting Mercutio
and Romeo. Their friendship is, of course, a part of the camaraderie that also bonds each of these two with Benvolio, in a version of
the liminal fraternities studied by Victor Turner and others. Within
that fraternity, however, the Mercutio-Romeo bond is much the most
prominent and consequential. Soon after Mercutio's last exit, the
play twice comes close to naming the bond, when Romeo calls Mer-

cutio his "very friend" and when Montague says his son was "Mercutio's friend." "Friendship" will do as a name for the bond so long as we recognize that, on Mercutio's part at least, the affectional state might as easily be named love, and that, while what we would call homosexual desire plays no conspicuous role in Mercutio's friendship for Romeo, still the erotic and indeed the phallic figure more prominently here than in any other significant friendship in Shakespeare.[11]

Given all this, along with Shakespeare's great expansion of the role of a character whose Marlovian resonances extend even to his name, it would seem that Shakespeare's response to Marlowe's sexuality must be legible in Mercutio. The general nature of that response is summarized, *mutatis mutandis*, in Nicholas Brooke's remark about Marlowe's political heterodoxy:

> Marlowe seems to have been for Shakespeare . . . the inescapable creator of something initially alien which he could only assimilate with difficulty.[12]

While we might not wish to credit Marlowe as "creator" of homoeroticism (any more, perhaps, than as creator of his political heterodoxy), Shakespeare does seem to deserve credit for accepting the challenge of Marlowe's sexuality, at least in Mercutio.

The opening of *Romeo and Juliet*, with Sampson and Gregory talking of thrusting maids to the wall, drawing a tool, and having a naked weapon out, is the most relentlessly phallic opening in all of Shakespeare's plays, and in only a few passages from anywhere in his work is the phallus more prominent. The opening ranks the phallus alongside the feud as a major theme, and sets up equations between phallus and weapon, and between male heterosexuality and the violent subjugation of women. At the same time, since the two servants are comic, Shakespeare uses them to call into question the institution of patriarchal sexism, an institution some of whose costs Shakespeare recognizes in much of the play. The parodic heterosexual phallocentrism of the opening lines, that is, sounds a characteristic Shakespearean note, the note we call antisexist or protofeminist.

The point is worth making because commentators have sometimes blurred together with the play's opening its three additional notably phallic passages, all in Mercutio's speech, and all with the phallocentrism still more prominent and concentrated than in the opening: Mercutio's talk of sinking in love, pricks and pricking, and beating love down; his long bawdy interchange with Benvolio about raising a spirit; and his talk with Romeo and Benvolio, and then the Nurse, of love's bauble, of his own "tale," and of the prick of noon. Given that in each passage it is Mercutio who introduces the phallicism and primarily sustains it, and given the proportional prominence of such talk in Mercutio's total of lines, he is easily Shakespeare's most phallic character. And several points should be made immediately about his insistent references to the phallus.

While Mercutio's phallicism is as aggressive as the Capulet servants', his is in a thoroughly different key to start with, by virtue of his social class and friendships. Furthermore, while Sampson boasts to Gregory of the tool with which he thrusts maids to the wall, in Mercutio we find neither boasting nor envisioned male aggression toward women. Indeed he begins his first phallic passage with "And, to sink in it, should you burden love— / Too great oppression for a tender thing"—a mock counsel to Romeo against love on the grounds that heterosexual intercourse per se is overly aggressive against women. The roughness in the remainder of his counsel, "If love be rough with you, be rough with love; / Prick love for pricking and you beat love down," is directed not against women but against love, which has changed gender from female to male in Romeo's intervening speech. Nor do we find misogyny or particular aggressiveness toward women in Mercutio's other concentrations of phallic speech. Nor, it may be worth noting, is Mercutio's disapproval of Romeo's infatuation and heterosexuality at all sternly prescriptive. Rather it is genial and tolerant, and the increasingly sensual catalog of Rosaline's parts that introduces the second concentration of phallicism is appreciative throughout. In an important respect Mercutio's phallic talk reverses Sampson's. While Sampson talks boastfully and exclusively about his own phallus, and induces the compliant though not entirely credulous Gregory to talk about it too, only a portion of Mercutio's bawdy, and that not boastful, is about his own "tale." The other phalli that come up more or less explicitly in his speech are love's, noon's, a stranger's, and Romeo's. Mercutio, that is, very readily grants the phallus to others, notably including his friend Romeo.

Mercutio's references to his friend's phallus suggest the sexual dynamics of the friendship. The quibbling figurativeness of "If love be rough with you, be rough with love; / Prick love for pricking and you beat love down" makes the sentence exceptionally resistant to close paraphrase. Still, the exhortation is not only phallic but also opposed to heterosexual love, or antivenereal, so that (being rough with the sentence) we might paraphrase it as "Use your phallus against love." A lightened and, as it were, genially resigned antivenerealism appears as well in the context of "in his mistress' name / I conjure only but to raise up him" with its sensually appreciative but irreverent talk of Rosaline. But Mercutio's phallicism is the stronger and more apparent agenda. Mercutio here exhibits a generous and interested attitude toward Romeo's phallus, as if he has a personal investment, as we say, in his friend's erection. The nature of that investment might seem, on the basis of the line and a half quoted above, to involve the idea of Mercutio's taking Rosaline's place not only as conjurer but also as container of Romeo's phallus, and it is true that Rosaline has receded from active participation with the stranger, her circle around his spirit, to a mere deputizing name at Mercutio's raising of Romeo. But that fleeting, apparently subliminal trace of sexual desire on Mercutio's part for Romeo, which seems to reappear in Mercutio's image of biting Romeo by the ear,[13] is preceded by the genially explicit talk of Rosaline as sexually active and attractive, and is followed shortly by the third reference to Romeo's phallus, in Mercutio's mock wish that Romeo were a poperin pear, another image that (like "raise up him") reduces the friend to his genitals, while naming the phallus precisely for its use in heterosexual intercourse.

These references of Mercutio's to Romeo's phallus add up to a highly mercurial stance that combines an opposition to love, an amiable erotic permissiveness, and a phallocentrism that admits traces of homoeroticism. The stance amounts to an invitation, and it is one Romeo is unable to accept. His repartee with Mercutio never seems quite wholehearted; when Mercutio shifts into the bawdy Romeo hangs back and Romeo's love for Juliet is notably uncarnal and unphallic. Just as the play authorizes Romeo's greater allegiance to love than to family honor in the feud, so it also authorizes his greater allegiance to Juliet than to Mercutio. The generally neglected point, however, is that by radically expanding Brooke's minor Mercutio, Shakespeare gives Romeo's heterosexual love an opposition other than and different in quality from the opposition of the feud. That is, in *Romeo and Juliet*, while acknowledging the (here disastrous) power of heterosexual love, Shakespeare uses Mercutio and his appeal to entertain Marlovian homosexuality as fully as he can.

To elaborate this last point: through Mercutio, while Marlowe's sexual orientation is not paraded, neither is it cancelled, denied, or ignored. Rather, in this play at least, Shakespeare in the arena of the erotic demonstrates the sort of mastery that Stephen Greenblatt and others have taught us to see in him, as he admits and incorporates the subversive element, to some extent containing it, and to some extent rendering it still more subversive. Here, in other words, Shakespeare mounts his strongest case against the enshrinement of heterosexuality at the expense of homosexuality. The strength of the case is in part a function of the force of the general challenge of Marlowe's example as felt by Shakespeare, and in part a function of the strength of Shakespeare's general response.

With Mercutio, then, Shakespeare seems to carry out a profound and nonjudgmental acknowledgment of Marlowe's minority sexuality, and does so by way of what in 1595 is still for him an exceptional, even unprecedented, degree of imaginative identification. The identification shows in the warmth and generosity of Mercutio's fraternal bonding to Romeo, and in his phallic bawdiness, neither feature especially noteworthy in Shakespearean characters before Mercutio or, for that matter, after him either. The imaginative empathy may account for particulars of Mercutio's behavior as well, the most remarkable possibly being the wish he expresses to his absent friend, "O Romeo, that she were, O that she were / An open-arse and thou a poperin pear!" This seems to be the only direct and explicit reference to sodomy in the canon.[14] Of course the sodomy imagined in these lines is heterosexual, but its uniqueness in Shakespeare suggests that it derives from Mercutio's Marlovianness—as if Shakespeare has Mercutio wish for his friend heterosexual intercourse as it might easily have been imagined, in passing, by Marlowe. So understood, the moment marks an exceptional imaginative reach.

Mercutio, however, is about as far as Shakespeare goes with the con-

version of Marlovian homosexuality into phallocentric male friendship charged with erotic overtones and undertones. Shakespeare lets
the homosexual Marlowe into the realm of the canonical heterosexual, not only to give him some free rein but also to kill him
off. While the heterosexual lovers die too, their deaths are later and
their love is finally accorded the sanction of their society. In what
may be the next play, *The Merchant of Venice*, Antonio's melan-
choly manifests some lingering dissatisfaction with the accommoda-
tion achieved through Mercutio and his death, but while Antonio
lives to the end of his play much of the life has now gone out of the
Marlowe simulacrum. In *The Merchant of Venice* friendship is supplanted by undying heterosexual love; then Shakespeare is off and
running through a series of plays conspicuously deficient in celebra-
tions of male-male bonding, and generally without celebratory or
even acquiescent moments of the homoerotic.

Still, with Mercutio Shakespeare has entertained the Marlovian
stance. He has shown himself open to an alternate sexuality. The negotiation with Marlowe and his sexuality in the creation of Mercutio
may well have been instrumental in giving Shakespeare an exceptional freedom from the prescriptivism that must demonize homosexuality. As is well known, he seems not unsympathetic to the more
or less explicit homosexuality of Achilles and Patroclus in *Troilus and
Cressida*, and restricts derision of it to the "deformed and scurrilous"
Thersites.

The imaginative capaciousness and generosity with which Shakespeare comes to terms with Marlovian homoeroticism in Mercutio
has not usually been matched or even approached in our culture's
nearly four-hundred-year processing of Mercutio. In numerous and
changing ways that history has been one of suppression, reduction,
bowdlerizing, sentimentalizing, and denial of his fraternal phallocentric bawdy and of the nature and vigor of his bonding with Romeo,
as well as of much else about him. The manifold attack on Mercutio,
which may for convenience be termed a drive for his containment,
is visible in adaptations, in promptbooks, in editorial practice, in
records of performance (including film and video), and in critical

commentary on the texts and performances of the play. The drive for containment of Mercutio varies in scope and intricacy from Francis Gentleman's considered view that *Romeo and Juliet* would have been better if Shakespeare had left Mercutio out of it altogether, to the ingenious cutting in the 1906 production that reduces Mercutio's catalog of Rosaline's parts to her "bright eyes, / And the demesnes that there adjacent lie." [15]

At the same time, Mercutio through the four centuries has continued to exert the subversive appeal that, according to Dryden, made Shakespeare have to kill him off midway through the play, so that the drive for containment has always been opposed by forces working for the restoration and acceptance of an authentic Mercutio. The volatile and continuing contest that has been and continues to be waged over Mercutio may be seen as a small but not insignificant part of the dialectic of sexualities. Indeed, given Shakespeare's prominence, especially in the past two centuries, I maintain that the processing of Mercutio can serve as a useful series of bulletins from the front in the struggle over the privileging of heterosexuality. Before concluding, then, I wish briefly to consider three of those bulletins. While the academy's conservatorship of Shakespeare brings all of what I have said above into the general purview of the subject of Shakespeare and the academy, with these three matters I will try to lay open some more specifics.

In this century, and especially in the permissive climate of twenty years ago, Mercutio seems finally to begin to come into his own, after the centuries-long night of seldom remitting censorship. Franco Zeffirelli's 1968 *Romeo and Juliet*, with John McEnery playing Mercutio, was a landmark. Zeffirelli had directed a stage version of the play earlier, and some of what he had worked out there reappears in the film.[16] Still, the film manifests some fundamental rethinking of the play, rethinking especially evident in, and possibly originating with, the part of Mercutio. One of the important innovations was the choice of an actor appreciably older than those playing Romeo, Juliet, and Benvolio. The age discrepancy works with some subtlety to enlist audience interest in—and perhaps sympathy for, and perhaps anxiety about—"an aging manic-depressive, idling his time away in the company of men half his own age." [17] The Marlovian-

Shakespearean phallicism is abundantly present, as in the moment when Mercutio in the waist-deep watering trough raises the shank of his sword out of the water at a phallic angle. The strength and potential eroticism of his bond with Romeo also manifests itself, as in the two moments when they touch foreheads. Nor does the Zeffirelli-McEnery Mercutio exhibit any trace of the un-Marlovian hetero-sexual flirtatiousness the character shows in Shakespeare's source and often in adaptations and stagings of Shakespeare's play, though no-where in Shakespeare's dialogue.

While the great popularity of the film clearly derived from Zeffir-elli's playing to the sixties cult of innocent youth with his principals —and the film does celebrate and partly canonize youthful hetero-sexual desire—at the same time the influence of McEnery's Mercutio may prove to have been more consequential. Five years later, for in-stance, in the Terry Hands 1973 Stratford stage production of the play, Mercutio becomes, according to Evans, "an aggressive homosexual."[18]

Evans's reactions to both film and stage productions in his intro-duction to the 1984 New Cambridge *Romeo and Juliet* represent one sort of academic response to the late twentieth-century acknowl-edgment or exaggeration, in performance, of Shakespeare's engage-ment with Marlovian homoeroticism. Of the Hands production Evans writes,

> Such character perversion, all too common today in Shakespeare productions generally, is nothing more than a meretricious at-tempt, at whatever drastic cost to the integrity of the play, to make Shakespeare "our contemporary"; only if the friendship of Romeo, Benvolio and Mercutio can be given an exciting nuance of homosexuality does the play become relevant for a modern audience—so runs the directors' justification.

As for the Zeffirelli film, Evans disapproves of it as "narrowly con-ceived and reductionist" because of its "emphasis on youth" which seems to him to diminish "the larger aspects of their [Romeo's and Juliet's] love, its developing maturity and final dignity." Evans does not mention the Zeffirelli-McEnery Mercutio's strong traces of the protohomoerotic or indeed anything about the role.[19] His very neglect of it seems a function of his concern that the play be understood as enshrining a dignified heterosexual love.

Elsewhere in the academy reception has been more favorable to recent performances of Mercutio that counter the canonization of heterosexuality. Jack J. Jorgens appreciates the prominence Zeffirelli gives Mercutio, noting, for instance, that with Mercutio's death the entire film is "drained of its busy look and festive colors"; Jorgens acknowledges the depth of this Mercutio's attachment to Romeo:

> There is deep friendship, even love, between Romeo and Mer-
> cutio. Mercutio's mercurial showmanship seems aimed at Ro-
> meo, and his anger, when Romeo is off sighing for love or making
> a milksop of himself before Tybalt, is tinged with jealousy. How
> could a friend abandon his male comradery for "a smock"?

And E. A. M. Colman writes of the film that "*Romeo and Juliet* demands a good deal of critical reorientation if . . . Zeffirelli's . . .
presentation of Mercutio is justified by the text." Despite a certain
circularity here—not merely "the text" but also a particular given
critical orientation is necessarily implicated in determining whether
the presentation is "justified" or not—Colman clearly acknowledges
the disruptive importance of the Zeffirelli-McEnery Mercutio.[20]

Feminist and psychoanalytic critical treatments of Mercutio com-
prise a second index of the part Mercutio is currently playing in the
contest for and against the canonization of heterosexuality in the
academy. While the MLA Delegate Assembly's passage of a resolution
opposing discrimination on the basis of sexual orientation clearly
results from interrogation inside the academy of the received assumptions grounding such discrimination, all too often in academic discourse these assumptions continue to be promulgated as fact. Mercutio serves as an exceptionally good gauge of this discourse, by
virtue of his homosocial-homoerotic resonances and opposition to
heterosexual love in what has become far more canonical a story of
heterosexual love than it was when it came to Shakespeare's hand.

The strengths and weaknesses of both feminist and psychoanalytic
treatments of Shakespeare have been widely discussed. Most recently
Richard Levin has exposed widespread error and falsehood in femi-

nist thematic readings of the tragedies; he suggests that the deficiencies derive not only from the thematism but also from a fallacious feminist-psychoanalytic conception of masculinity.[21] Levin does not address the preconceptions about sexual orientation in the critics he surveys, but his admirable concluding call for the abandonment of psychoanalytic stances that must make one gender or the other inherently pathological may be immediately extrapolated to psychoanalytic stances that privilege heterosexuality by making adult homosexuality a pathology.

Levin's concerns resemble mine enough to lead him to notice some suppression of Mercutio in the criticism he surveys, as when he notes the misrepresentation by Coppélia Kahn of Romeo's motive in attacking Tybalt—not, as Kahn claims, to uphold the Montague honor, but rather "to avenge Mercutio."[22] If we shift focus from gender to sexual orientation, however, it is easy to see that, for feminist-psychoanalytic criticism espousing the doctrine that adult male homosexuality is either an irrelevance or a pathology, Mercutio has a good deal besides mere maleness working against him. And a conspicuous resurgence of the ongoing movement to contain Mercutio appears precisely in this body of criticism.

In "Coming of Age in Verona," for example, Kahn maintains that Mercutio "represents" the "attempted sublimation" of "virile energy . . . into fancy and wit," and that he "suggests" that feuding functions psychologically as a definition of manhood.[23] If these slippery and jargon-bound claims seem provisionally tenable, the same is not true of Kahn's "Love is only manly, he [Mercutio] hints, if it is aggressive and violent and consists of subjugating women, rather than being subjugated by them." In fact, Mercutio nowhere hints at approval of "subjugating women." Nor does he hint that a particular sort of heterosexual love is "manly." Indeed, as Kahn herself observes, Mercutio "mocks . . . all [heterosexual] love."[24] Kahn's otherwise helpful essay traduces Mercutio in such ways because he threatens the psychological dogma that prescribes the supplanting of homosexual by heterosexual bonding in the life of the "healthy" individual, and also because he stands outside the feminist reflex division of men into two sorts: those who wish to dominate women and those who love women in a way characterized by mutuality, a division that depends on the prescriptive assumption that only heterosexual men bear discussion. Mercutio serves, that is, as a particularly sensitive emblem of the extent to which current feminist and psychoanalytic modes of criticism constitute a new stronghold in the academic privileging of heterosexuality.

The bibliographical and critical history of a particular half-line of Mercutio's provides still another yardstick for measuring his changing phallic subversiveness and the varying acceptance and containment it elicits. At the beginning of act 2, Romeo enters alone and after two lines withdraws, hiding himself from the next two entrants, his friends Mercutio and Benvolio, whom he overhears summoning him wittily and in vain, until they give up the search and exit. The apostrophe "O Romeo, that she [Romeo's love] were, O that she were / An open-arse and thou a poperin pear!" in Mercutio's last speech in the scene contains, as I have said, what seems to be Shakespeare's only explicit reference to sodomy, but the "open-arse" does not appear in printed texts of the play before 1954.

The intricate and not yet fully understood story of the disappearance and recovery of what is now generally, though not quite universally, taken to be the phrase as Shakespeare wrote it may be summarized as follows. Shakespeare seems to have written something like "open-arse" or "openers," which the compositor of the Bad First Quarto (1597) understood in its reported form and replaced with the euphemism "open *Et cetera*," and which the compositor of the Good Second Quarto (1599), probably working from Shakespeare's foul papers, misread and set as "open, or." The Q2 reading reappears in Q3 (1609) and in the First Folio (1623), but since it makes no sense it is generally superseded thenceforth by the Q1 reading, until a flurry of independent restorations in the mid-1950s. In 1953, Kökeritz suggests the reading "open-arse"; the following year, Hosley prints the line as "An open-arse or thou a poperin pear"; and in 1955 Wilson and Duthie give the line the form, and thus the coherence, it has in virtually all subsequent editions.

There is no way to know how often in the three and a half centuries between Q1 and the mid-1950s the "open-arse" may have been divined, but we do know that it was suggested in print at least once, in Farmer and Henley's *Slang and Its Analogues* (1902), not an especially obscure work. So the reluctance of editors through half a century to adopt the reading may betoken not simply procedural conservatism but also a continuing drive to protect Mercutio, and through him Shakespeare, from what was perceived as scandalous, a drive that to the present day maintains the superseded line in one edition in general use, the Pelican.

Squeamishness about the "open-arse" continues even after its general adoption in editions of the play. In editors' notes on the passage a nearly uniform silence prevails about the envisioned sodomy, broken only by what seems a muffled pun in the note by Wilson and Duthie about " 'or' as the seat of the [textual] corruption."[25] Eric Partridge, writing during the last decade of the exclusive reign of "et cetera" in editions, glosses it confidently "Pudend," although in his notes on this phrase and on "medlar" he seems not only to foresee the imminent "arse" but also to attempt to bowdlerize it in advance.[26]

In 1974, well after "open-arse" has carried the day, Colman writes with a comparatively generous appreciation of Mercutio; nevertheless, he too goes to some lengths to detoxify the phrase:

> It is unlikely that Mercutios of Shakespeare's own day spoke the term "open-arse" here, as both the Bad and Good quartos . . . suppress it, and some such action as Benvolio's clapping his hand over Mercutio's mouth seems called for.

This ingenious bit of hypothetical stage business seems called for largely by Colman's disapproval of the implied image of sodomy, about which he remarks rather primly: "Clearly, all that Romeo needs to do about so broad a sally is to keep out of the way and flatly disregard it."[27] Furthermore, Colman is at best misleading about how the two Quartos "suppress" the offending phrase, since the Q2 "open, or" seems a compositor's misreading or misunderstanding rather than the sort of censorship that explains the Q1 et cetera.

Colman's expedients with Mercutio's image of sodomy may suggest what I believe to be the case: that the struggle over the canonization of heterosexuality is proceeding in his own thought, and perhaps beneath the level of full consciousness. In his summary discussion of homosexuality and sodomy, he restates conventional reassurances about the innocence of Elizabethan friendship, although here and in his chapter on the sonnets he does admit the possibility of homosexual eroticism. And a double standard is apparent in his discussion of the act implied by Mercutio's image: when heterosexual, the act is "anal intercourse," when homosexual, "sodomy."[28] Colman finds few references to either in Shakespeare; however, while he passes over the first scarcity without comment, of the second he remarks that when "the plays glance at sodomy it is with reticence and distaste. . . . Shakespeare seems to have shared in the conventional disapproval of sodomy."[29] True enough of Shakespeare, perhaps, and perhaps also truer of Colman than he acknowledges.

Hence the general screening out of homosexual bawdy for which Joseph Pequigney takes Colman, Partridge, and many other commentators on Shakespeare, to task. Pequigney is openly against the prescriptive privileging of heterosexuality, and at times he is not averse even to a certain privileging of homosexuality. Thus some of the screening Pequigney finds in Colman may seem as fabricated as a few of the more strained homosexual glosses Pequigney gives the sonnets. Still, partisanship of even the most outspoken sort is an intricate matter here, as witness Pequigney's passing treatment of Mercutio. This scholar, who finds many more homosexual meanings in the sonnets than do all previous commentators together, screens every trace of the sexual out of his understanding of the friendship between Mercutio and Romeo.

Because of his lineage and pedigree, and because of the manifold uses Shakespeare puts him to, Mercutio plays an idiosyncratic and comparatively prominent part in the ongoing struggle for and against the canonization of heterosexuality. Since the struggle goes on throughout our culture, Mercutio's part is only a small component of it, and would be vanishingly small but for Shakespeare's continuing prominence. Nevertheless, Mercutio's part in the struggle is complex, changing, and far from entirely predictable, and the same seems likely to be true to some extent of other Shakespearean characters— indeed of any other component of Shakespeare's or anyone else's art, and even possibly of any object of attention.

With Mercutio, while the struggle goes on outside the academy,

most notably in productions of *Romeo and Juliet* and in nonaca-
demic responses to them, the academy's custodianship of Shakespeare
means that the struggle proceeds within the walls at least as vigor-
ously as without, and of course the walls are permeable to the influence of defeats and victories. We in the academy, in any case, seem
best situated to read bulletins from all fronts. The task of reading
them demands patience, tenacity, imagination, and all other hermeneutic skills we can muster, but it can be done, and doing it will help
us avoid providing unintentional support for one contested doctrinal
position or another.

Notes

1 By "canonization" I mean what the term means generally in ecclesiastical and
   current literary-critical discourse; by "processing" I mean psychological and cultural reception, interpretation, response, and other sorts of treatments, whether
   they be conscious or not.
2 Jonathan Goldberg, "Sodomy and Society: The Case of Christopher Marlowe,"
   Southwest Review 69 (1984): 371–78.
3 See Alan Bray, *Homosexuality in Renaissance England* (London, 1982); Wilbur
   Sanders, *The Dramatist and the Received Idea* (Cambridge, 1968); and Judith Weil,
   Christopher Marlowe (Cambridge, 1977).
4 Michael Goldman, "Marlowe and the Histrionics of Ravishment," in *Two Renaissance Mythmakers: Christopher Marlowe and Ben Jonson*, ed. Alvin Kernan
   (Baltimore, 1977).
5 Joseph Pequigney, *Such Is My Love* (Chicago, 1985), 1; Eve Kosofsky Sedgwick,
   Between Men: English Literature and Male Homosocial Desire (New York, 1985).
6 William Shakespeare, *Hamlet*, ed. Harold Jenkins (London, 1982), 479.
7 Marjorie Garber, "Marlovian Vision/Shakespearean Revision," *Research Opportunities in Renaissance Drama* 22 (1979): 7. I would argue that the moment also
   figures the same irrationally assumed responsibility for Marlowe's death that first
   appears as a flicker of attribution of responsibility for Mercutio's death to Romeo,
   in Mercutio's dying words: "I was hurt under your arm."
8 Joseph Porter, *Shakespeare's Mercutio: His History and Drama* (Chapel Hill, 1988).
9 Benvolio's "brave Mercutio is dead, / That gallant spirit hath aspir'd the clouds"
   echoes the "And both our soules aspire celestiall thrones" in Tamburlaine's vow
   of undying friendship to Theridamas.
10 Arthur Brooke, *The Tragical History of Romeus and Juliet*, ed. J. J. Munro (New
   York, 1908).
11 Ronald A. Sharp, *Friendship and Literature* (Durham, 1986), treats with exceptional acuteness the subject of the erotic as a component of friendship.

12 Nicholas Brooke, "Marlowe as Provocative Agent in Shakespeare's Early Plays," *Shakespeare Survey* 14 (1961): 44.

13 Here and throughout I'm citing William Shakespeare, *Romeo and Juliet*, ed. Brian Gibbons (London, 1980); see Gibbons's note on 2.4.77.

14 See Eric Partridge, *Shakespeare's Bawdy* (London, 1948); E. A. M. Colman, *The Dramatic Use of Bawdy in Shakespeare* (London, 1974); Frankie Rubenstein, *A Dictionary of Shakespeare's Sexual Puns and Their Significance* (London, 1984); along with Pequigney, these and other critics find various indirect, inexplicit, and metaphorical references to sodomy in Shakespeare.

15 See my *Shakespeare's Mercutio*; Francis Gentleman, *The Dramatic Censor* (London, 1770); and Folger Shakespeare Library Promptbook, *Rom.* 29.

16 See Jill L. Levenson, *Shakespeare in Performance: "Romeo and Juliet"* (Manchester, 1987).

17 Colman, *Dramatic Use of Bawdy*, 70.

18 William Shakespeare, *Romeo and Juliet*, ed. G. Blakemore Evans (Cambridge, 1984), 45.

19 Probably these traces were lost on him, or on his conscious mind, as were the names of the leading actors, Leonard Whiting and Olivia Hussey, whom he has confused with John Stride and Judi Dench, performers in stage productions. See Evans's edition, 45–48.

20 Jack J. Jorgens, *Shakespeare on Film* (Bloomington, Ind., 1977), 89, 84; Colman, *Dramatic Use of Bawdy*, 171.

21 Richard Levin, "Feminist Thematics and Shakespearean Tragedy," *PMLA* 103 (1988): 125–38.

22 Ibid., 128; and see Coppélia Kahn, *Man's Estate: Masculine Identity in Shakespeare* (Berkeley, 1981). In more detail in *Shakespeare's Mercutio*, I discuss the effort to contain/suppress Mercutio and thereby to continue the canonization of heterosexuality.

23 Coppélia Kahn, "Coming of Age in Verona," in *The Woman's Part: Feminist Criticism of Shakespeare*, ed. Carolyn Ruth Swift Lenz, Gayle Greene, and Carol Thomas Neely (Urbana, 1980), 176.

24 Ibid., 176–77.

25 William Shakespeare, *Romeo and Juliet*, ed. John Dover Wilson and George Ian Duthie (Cambridge, 1955), 152–53.

26 In *Shakespeare's Bawdy*, Partridge's note on et cetera cross-references "medlar," where we find the oddly defensive claim that in "Shakespeare, 'medlar' means *either* pudend *or* podex *or* the pudend-podex area."

27 Colman, *Dramatic Use of Bawdy*, 69.

28 Ibid., 100, 7.

29 Ibid., 7.

John M. Clum

"Something Cloudy, Something Clear": Homophobic Discourse in Tennessee Williams

Throughout his career, Tennessee Williams was attacked from all sides for his treatment or nontreatment of homosexuality in his work. During the early years of gay liberation, gay critics complained that Williams was not "out" enough in his work and demanded that he stop writing around his homosexuality. One gay playwright went so far as to assert: "He has yet to contribute any work of understanding to gay theater."[1] Williams's response to such attacks was a series of candid personal disclosures culminating in the unfortunate volume of memoirs, and more explicit treatment of homosexuality in his later, often autobiographical works. This new candor led to attacks by heterosexual critics, one of whom even referred to one play of the seventies as "faggotty fantasizing."[2]

The first critic to deal intelligently with this aspect of Williams's work was Edward A. Sklepowitch, whose formulation was too simplistic, though typical of early work in gay studies:

> Williams' so-called "decadent" vision and his preoccupation
> with loneliness, evasion, role-playing, wastage, sexual reluc-
> tance and sexual excess are in many instances functions of a
> homosexual sensibility which has been evolving steadily in the
> more than quarter century since the publication of *One Arm
> and Other Stories.* In this period, Williams' treatment of homo-
> sexuality has undergone significant changes, moving from a mys-
> tical to a more social perspective, a personal, if fictional micro-
> cosm of the wider cultural demystification of homosexuality.[3]

I do not see such a steady evolution in Williams's "homosexual sensibility": rather, there seems to be a constant attitude toward homosexual acts, though Williams's presentation of homosexual persons
changed when public tolerance allowed a candidness in drama which
Williams had previously restricted to his stories and poems. That
change in presentation, alas, was also a function of his decreased
ability to convert memory or self-judgment into a controlled work
of art. But the constant in Williams's career is the dual vision that
shaped his presentation of the homosexuality he was always impelled
to write about.

Some relatively late statements issued by Williams demonstrate his
sense of a split personality which separated the homosexual artist
from his work, and they provide a crucial starting point for any discussion of the relation of Williams's sexual orientation to his work,
particularly his plays. This one is from an interview with Dotson
Rader:

> I never found it necessary to deal with it [homosexuality] in
> my work. It was never a preoccupation of mine, except in my
> intimate, private life.[4]

Quibbling with this statement becomes a matter of semantics. Williams may not have found it "necessary" to "deal with" homosexuality
in his work, but the fact is he did. His poetry is filled with homoerotic visions and encounters with "gentlemen callers." Indeed, no
poet has so vividly and poignantly captured the tension, excitement,
and loneliness of the anonymous sexual encounter as Williams, from
the wry humor of "Life Story" to the poignancy of "Young Men
Waking at Daybreak." The focus of these poems is not so much

homo*sexuality* as it is the peculiar alienation of the brief sexual encounter. Williams's best stories also feature homosexuals as central characters. The semi-canonization of the boxer/hustler/murderer in "One Arm," who dies with love letters from the men with whom he has tricked jammed between his legs, is typical in its combination of religion, mortality, and impersonal gay sex which pervades many of Williams's best stories. The plays, too, are filled with homosexual characters: from the offstage martyrs of the plays of the major period, to the happy, ideal "marriage" of Jack Straw and Peter Ochello in *Cat on a Hot Tin Roof*, to the writers, artists, and hustlers of the later plays for whom sex is a temporary cure for loneliness.

Williams's theoretical separation of his homosexuality from his work is in conflict with his many assertions of the highly personal nature of his work and of his close relationship with his characters. It does not conform with "I draw all my characters from myself. I can't draw a character unless I know it within myself," unless one factors in an essential variable: "I draw every character out of my very multiple split personality."[5] Split personality and split vision are recurring themes in Williams's work, particularly in references to himself. They suggest not only the multiple split personalities which allow such empathetic relationships with his characters, but also the split presentation of his own homosexuality.

Part of Williams's need to deny the homosexual element in his work is an extension of his need for validation as a writer (though he seldom got it in the last twenty-five years of his life). Admitting to the homosexual dimension of his work was a professional liability:

> You still want to know why I don't write a gay play? I don't find it necessary. I could express what I wanted to express through other means. I would be narrowing my audience a great deal [if I wrote for a gay audience alone]. I wish to have a broad audience because the major thrust of my work is not sexual orientation, it's social. I'm not about to limit myself to writing about gay people.[6]

While making clear his continued, though frustrated, interest in writing for a broad audience, this statement demonstrates Williams's political naiveté: for him, homosexuality was merely a sexual issue, thus incongruent with his "social" interest. This separation is impossible for the homosexual, for whom the sexual *is* social, as Williams implies when he passionately asserts that "I do not deal with the didactic, ever." For him, a gay play was bound to be didactic, a notion his later work all too often bears out.[7]

The split persona is seen again in a crucial quotation from his *Memoirs*: "Of course I also existed outside of conventional society while contriving somewhat precariously to remain in contact with it. For me this was not only precarious but a matter of dark unconscious disturbance."[8] While Williams is referring to himself as a social being rather than as an artist, this statement defines the problematics of Williams's stance as homosexual artist and of the gulf between private art (poetry and fiction) and public art (drama), and the corollary gap between private homosexual and public celebrity. For most of his career, Williams was extremely protective of this split. Homosexuality was not the only element of Williams's personality which placed him outside of conventional society, but it was the subject which in the 1940s and 1950s seldom spoke its name. Williams was privately open about his sexual orientation, but publicly cautious, as he was relatively willing to treat homosexuality directly in his nondramatic writings, which would reach a limited audience (he never until his later years strove for the money and publicity of a best-selling novel), but cautious in his dramas. His caution takes two forms. One is the clever use of what he calls "obscurity or indirection" to soften and blur the homosexual element of much of his work. The other is a complex acceptance of homophobic discourse, which he both critiques and embraces.

This reliance on and occasional manipulation of the language of homophobia is the basis of Williams's treatment of the subject of homosexuality in his plays, reflecting a split he saw in his own nature. Williams wrote of his vision problems in 1940:

> My left eye was cloudy then because it was developing a cataract. But my right eye was clear. It was like the two sides of my nature. The side that was obsessively homosexual, compulsively interested in sexuality. And the side that in those days was gentle and understanding and contemplative.[9]

This double vision, which always obsessed the playwright and led to the title of his last produced play in New York, *Something Cloudy, Something Clear*, defines the split Williams conceived between his homosexual activity and his "human" side. Even in his confused later novel, *Moise and the World of Reason*, in which he depicts himself as an eccentric aging playwright the narrator encounters, he fixes on a dual vision:

> He came back to the table and simultaneously two things hap-
> pened of the automatic nature. He kissed me on the mouth and
> I started to cry. . . .
> "Baby, I didn't mean to do that, it was just automatic."
> (He thought I was crying over his Listerine kiss which I'd
> barely noticed.)
> He slumped there drinking the dago red wine as if to extinguish
> a fire in his belly, the rate at which he poured it down him
> slowing only when the bottle was half-empty. Then his one good
> eye focussed on me again but the luster was gone from it and its
> look was inward.[10]

The outward gaze becomes linked to an automatic, impersonal homo-sexual advance while the inward gaze signifies the writer's now un-controllable withdrawals into memory, which form the basis of his later autobiographical work which, paradoxically, depicts his split vision and at the same time demonstrates the loss his work suffered when he blurred the public/private split which was essential to his control over memory and craft.

Williams's split vision, then, defines the internal conflict that compelled him to write of his homosexuality and, in doing so, to rely on the language of indirection and homophobic discourse. It signified a cloudy sense of his own sexual identity, but it enabled him to write clearly. On the other hand, as the sexual self became clearer, and the plays became more autobiographical, the writing became murkier.

=====

The story "Hard Candy" (1954), characteristic of Williams's fiction in dealing with homosexuality and its evasions, embodies Williams's split vision and attendant manipulation of language. "Hard Candy" centers on the last day in the life of an elderly man, Mr. Krupper, who habitually goes to an old movie palace with a bag of hard candy and a handful of quarters, his bribes to willing young men for their sexual favors. On the day of the story, Mr. Krupper dies while performing fellatio on a handsome young vagrant. Before describing Mr. Krupper's fatal visit to the movie theater, Williams offers this peculiar rejoinder:

> In the course of this story, and very soon now, it will be necessary to make some disclosures about Mr. Krupper of a nature *too coarse* to be dealt with very directly in a work of such brevity. The grossly naturalistic details of a life, contained in the enormously wide context of that life, are softened and qualified by it, but when you attempt to set those details down in a tale, *some measure of obscurity or indirection* is called for to provide the same, or even approximate, softening effect that existence in time gives to those gross elements in the life itself. When I say that there was a *certain mystery* in the life of Mr. Krupper, *I am beginning to approach those things in the only way possible without a head-on violence that would disgust and destroy and which would only falsify the story.*
>
> To have hatred and contempt for a person . . . calls for the assumption that you know practically everything of any significance about him. If you admit that he is a *mystery*, you admit that the hostility may be unjust.[11]

Mr. Krupper's "mystery" is contained in his afternoon visits to the Joy Rio movie theater; his sexual encounters there with poor, beautiful (of course) young men are acts which would brand him in the eyes of most people as a "dirty old man" or worse. Williams's rejoinder both shows his sympathy and understanding of his audience's sensibilities and prejudices, and plays with those prejudices. The language of mystery and evasion allows him to write about the forbidden in a sympathetic, even subversive way. That mystery, however, is also clothed in harsh authorial judgment, which places the narrator in a superior position to his central character and allies him with the "average reader's" moral judgment. As Mr. Krupper approaches the Joy Rio theater, the narrator describes it as "the place where the mysteries of his nature are to be made unpleasantly manifest to us." [12] Williams is both compassionate and judgmental: the story is both grotesque and touching. The "mysteries," however natural, are "unpleasant."

This dual vision functions in a number of ways in the story. There is the split between the physical grotesqueness and disease of the subject, which implies a connection between disease/ugliness and homosexual desire, and the shadowy beauty of the object of that desire. More important, the story embodies an intense consciousness of the split between the public persona and the private actor central to Williams's treatment of homosexuality:

> When around midnight the lights of the Joy Rio were brought up for the last time that evening, the body of Mr. Krupper was discovered in his remote box of the theater with his knees on the floor and his ponderous torso wedged between two wobbly gilt chairs as if he had expired in an attitude of prayer. The notice of the old man's death was given unusual prominence for the obituary of someone who had no public character and whose private character was so peculiarly low. But evidently the private character of Mr. Krupper was to remain anonymous in the memories of those anonymous persons who had enjoyed or profited from his company in the tiny box at the Joy Rio, for the notice contained no mention of anything of such a special nature. It was composed by a spinsterly reporter who had been impressed by the sentimental values of a seventy year old retired merchant dying of thrombosis at a cowboy thriller with a split bag of hard candies in his pocket and the floor about him littered with sticky wrappers, some of which even adhered to the shoulders and sleeves of his jacket. [13]

Mr. Krupper dies in a public place while engaged in a very private act that is never in any way literally described in a story which is a model of playful circumspection. Yet the gay reader immediately recognizes the significance of Mr. Krupper's position and the act of worship it denotes, as he understands the sticky papers from the candies which are stuck to Mr. Krupper's shoulders and sleeves. Characteristically for Williams, an act of pederasty satisfies two hungers simultaneously; the sexual hunger of the older man and the real hunger of the boy he feeds. (This pederasty/hunger nexus will reach its extreme in *Suddenly Last Summer* when the hungry, naked boys Sebastian Venable sexually exploits literally eat him.) In what amounts to a sexual pun underscored by the young cousin's final line in the story—". . . *the old man choked to death on our hard candy!*" —hard candy represents both hunger of the phallus and of the stomach.[14] But Mr. Krupper, unlike Williams, is also private, anonymous in the audience of a theater, not the public creator of theatrical and cinematic fantasies. Krupper is allowed an anonymity and mystery forbidden his creator whose late autobiographical work fixes on the unknown, still anonymous, private writer/homosexual.

The young cousin's final line speaks to the public misunderstanding of the private act. To the obituary writer, the old man's death was the sentimental extinction of a man with a sweet tooth and a love for westerns. To the child, a hated old man choked on the products of the family business. The real meaning of the death is a secret between the dead Mr. Krupper and the young men who shared his box at the Joy Rio. It is private and mysterious, reinforcing and embodying Williams's little treatise on mystery. Yet we also have the judgment of the narrator, the only reliable witness, who tells us that Krupper's "private character" was "peculiarly low." In making this harsh judgment on his own creation, the narrator both validates Krupper's story by telling it, and colludes with his "straight" reader by judging it harshly.

As the authorial judgment keeps Williams on the side of his reader, so the smokescreen of mystery, created with what Williams calls "obscurity or indirection," allows him to turn Mr. Krupper's death into something both tawdry and beautiful. While acknowledging his reader's possible scruples and prejudices, he manipulates them, luring his reader to see Mr. Krupper's life and death as at least pathetic. Still, Williams allows no space in this story for alternatives to Mr. Krupper's Joy Rio meetings. Homosexual encounters are furtive, impersonal appeasements of hunger. The operative word is "anonymous," matching Krupper's nonexistent public character. It is interesting to note as well that Krupper's partners enjoyed *or* profited from their encounters with him.

The devices Williams uses in "Hard Candy" are much more typical of his plays than of his fiction. One can see a miniversion of the public/private problem in Blanche's monologue about her husband in *A Streetcar Named Desire*. Blanche tells of "coming suddenly into a room that I thought was empty — which wasn't empty, but had two people in it . . . the boy I had married and an older man who had been his friend for years." This extremely discreet picture of Blanche's discovery of her husband's private homosexuality is followed by her public reaction to it on a crowded dance floor: "I saw! I know! You disgust me . . . ," and then by his public act of suicide.[15] Once made public, Alan's homosexuality becomes unbearable for him: he cannot deal with public disapproval.

Suddenly Last Summer weaves an interesting set of variations on the theme of exposure for the homosexual artist. Sebastian Venable has always been a private artist, wishing to be "unknown outside of a small coterie." The privacy of Sebastian's art is a corollary to his sense that his art is his expression of his religious vision; for the rest of his experience, living was enough: "his life was his occupation."[16] Yet that life was to be even more private than his work: "He *dreaded, abhorred!* — false values that come from being publicly known, from fame, from personal — exploitation."[17] But Sebastian's private life became a public matter when his cousin/wife witnessed his death and devouring at the hands of adolescent boys Sebastian had sexually exploited. To protect Sebastian's privacy, his mother will have Sebastian's widow lobotomized.

Homosexuality in *Suddenly Last Summer* is linked with Sebastian's brutal, carnivorous sense of life, but it is also linked with Williams's private sexual proclivities. Sebastian connects sex with appetite:

> Cousin Sebastian said he was famished for blonds, he was fed up with the dark ones and was famished for blonds. . . . [T]hat's how he talked about people, as if they were — items on a menu —.[18]

Donald Spoto argues convincingly for a strong autobiographical element in *Suddenly Last Summer*, nowhere clearer than in this speech. While in Italy in 1948, Williams wrote Donald Windham: "[Prokosch] says that Florence is full of blue-eyed blonds that are very tender hearted and 'not at all mercenary'. We were both getting an appetite for blonds as the Roman gentry are all sort of dusky types."[19] Sebastian's unfeeling sexual exploitation is as much a dramatization of the playwright as is Sebastian's pill-popping and confused sense of private and public personae.

Cat on a Hot Tin Roof, written around the same time as "Hard Candy," is the most vivid dramatic embodiment of Williams's mixed signals regarding homosexuality and his obsession with public exposure. *Cat* takes place in the bedroom once occupied by Jack Straw and Peter Ochello, a room dominated by the large double bed the lovers shared for thirty years. The plantation the ailing Big Daddy now controls, and which is now being fought over by his potential heirs, was inherited from Straw and Ochello. In ways both financial and sexual, the legacy of these two lovers lies at the heart of the play, and the love of Jack Straw and Peter Ochello stands as a counter to the compromised heterosexual relationships we see played out. Their relationship, the reader is told in the stage directions, "*must have involved a tenderness which was uncommon*,"[20] yet the audience never hears the relationship spoken of in positive terms. Straw and Ochello do not carry the freight of negative stereotypes other Williams homosexuals carry: they are not frail like Blanche duBois's suicidal husband; nor voracious pederasts like Sebastian Venable, the poet-martyr of *Suddenly Last Summer*; nor are they self-hating like Skipper, the other homosexual ghost in *Cat*. Yet, beyond the stage directions, there is no positive language for Straw and Ochello, who become in the action of the play the targets for Brick's homophobic diatribes.

Straw and Ochello's heir was Big Daddy Pollitt, the cigar-smoking, virile patriarch who admits to loving only two things, his "twenty-eight thousand acres of the richest land this side of the Valley Nile!"[21] and his handsome, ex-athlete son, Brick, who has turned into a drunken recluse since the death of his best friend, Skipper. The central scene in the play is a violent confrontation between patriarch and troubled son in which Big Daddy tries to get at the truth of Brick's relationship with Skipper.

Williams's stage direction tells the reader that Big Daddy "*leaves a lot unspoken*" as he tells Brick of his young years as a hobo and of being taken in and given a job by Jack Straw and Peter Ochello.[22] The implication of the stage direction, and other hints Big Daddy gives in the scene, is that homosexual behavior is not alien to Big Daddy, who "knocked around in [his] time." Yet Brick is so terrified of being called "queer" that he cannot listen to what his father is trying to tell him:

BIG DADDY: . . . I bummed, I bummed this country till I was —
BRICK: Whose suggestion, who else's suggestion is it?
BIG DADDY: Slept in hobo jungles and railroad Y's and flophouses in all cities before I —
BRICK: Oh, *you* think so, too, you call me your son and a queer. Oh! Maybe that's why you put Maggie and me in this room that was Jack Straw's and Peter Ochello's, in which that pair of old sisters slept in a double bed where both of 'em died!
BIG DADDY: *Now just don't go throwing rocks at —*[23]

The exchange is a brilliant reversal of expectation: the object of suspicion will not listen to expressions of understanding and tolerance, countering them with homophobic ranting. Brick is obsessed, terrified of being called a "queer," and conscious of the irony of being expected to perform sexually in Straw and Ochello's bed. Big Daddy will allow no attacks on Straw and Ochello, but his defense is interrupted by the appearance of Reverend Tooker, "*the living embodiment of the pious, conventional lie,*" an interruption that suggests that it is the pious conventional lie that forbids defense of Straw and Ochello.[24] The interruption is Williams's choice: it allows Brick's homophobic discourse to dominate the scene. In addition to "queer[s]" and "old sisters," Brick speaks of "sodomy," "dirty things," "dirty old men," "ducking [*sic*] sissies," "unnatural thing," and "*fairies*." Brick's acceptance of the pious conventional lie is heard in statements which sound like a caricature of the voice of pious respectability: "Big Daddy, you shock me, Big Daddy, you, you — *shock* me! Talkin' so — casually! — about a — thing like that." Yet his stated reason for his shock is not moral, religious, or psychological; it is public opinion: "Don't you know how people *feel* about things like that? How, how *disgusted* they are by things like that?"[25] Homosexuality to Brick is terrifying because it is inevitably public.

Brick's homophobia is part of his sexual/emotional malaise. He is painfully aware that his nonsexual, nominal marriage to Maggie is a far cry from the total relationship the bed signifies. Brick occupies a perilous middle state: he does not love his wife, with whom he claims never to have gotten any closer "than two people just get in bed which is not much closer than two cats on a — fence humping," [26] an echo of Big Daddy's loveless sex with Big Mama and an expression of Brick's inability to combine sex and friendship or love. Yet he is horrified at the thought of a sexual dimension of his friendship with Skipper: "Why can't exceptional friendship, *real, real, deep, deep friendship* between two men be respected as something clean and decent without being thought of as *fairies.*" [27]

Ironically, Maggie, Brick's frustrated wife, understands that Brick's friendship with Skipper "was one of those beautiful, ideal things they tell you about in Greek legends, it couldn't be anything else, you being you, and that's what made it so awful, because it was love that never could be carried through to anything satisfying or even talked about plainly." [28] Maggie knows that it is Brick's "ass-aching Puritanism" that puts him in such an unhappy position—that he would be better off if he had the courage to have a complete relationship with Skipper. But Skipper is dead as a result of his own internalized homophobia, and Brick has, as Big Daddy cogently puts it, "dug the grave of [his] friend and kicked him in it! — before you'd face truth with him!" [29]

The bed of Jack Straw and Peter Ochello represents an unstated ideal relationship which seems unattainable for the heterosexual marriages in Williams's play. In positing this ideal, the play is subversive for its time, yet the love of Jack Straw and Peter Ochello never seems a real possibility for homosexuals either. It is, to coin a phrase from Simon Gray's *Butley*, more a figure of speech than a matter of fact, and a rather paradoxical figure of speech at that, since the only positive words used to describe the relationship are silent hints in the stage directions. The only operative terminology for homosexuals the play allows is Brick's homophobic discourse.

Just at the moment that Big Daddy's dialogue with Brick reaches the crucial issue of Brick's relationship with Skipper, Williams offers a lengthy stage direction which echoes the rejoinder found in "Hard Candy":

> The thing they're discussing, timidly and painfully on the side of Big Daddy, fiercely, violently on Brick's side, is the inadmissible

thing that Skipper died to disavow between them. The fact that if it existed it had to be disavowed to "keep face" in the world they lived in, may be at the heart of the "mendacity" that Brick drinks to kill his disgust with. It may be the root of his collapse. Or maybe it is only a single manifestation of it, not even the most important. The bird that I hope to catch in the net of this play is not the solution of one man's psychological problem. I'm trying to catch the true quality of experience in a group of people, that cloudy, flickering, evanescent — fiercely charged! — interplay of five human beings in the thundercloud of a common crisis. Some mystery should be left in the revelation of character in a play, just as a great deal of mystery is always left in the revelation of character in life, even in one's own character to himself. This does not absolve the playwright of his duty to observe and probe as clearly and deeply as he *legitimately* can: but it should steer him away from "pat" conclusions, facile definitions which make a play just a play, not a snare for the truth of human experience.[30]

Williams begins this statement with a definite interpretation of Brick's panic that places responsibility on the false values of Brick's world, then hedges his bets by qualifying his interpretation, then moves the focus away from Brick to the problems of five people, and finally dismisses definite interpretations altogether in the name of "mystery." The last sentence of Williams's little treatise thickens the smokescreen: he wants to offer the truth of human experience without facile conclusions or pat definitions. Fair enough. But he seems to worry about such things only when homosexuality rears its problematic head. Of course, his printed warning is not shared by his audience, only his readers, but it allows him to proceed with a scene about homosexuality while denying that that is what he is doing. At the end of his statement, he directs that the scene between Big Daddy and Brick be *"palpable in what is left unspoken."* His concern for the unspoken dominates this scene, and what is unspoken here and in the rest of the play is the positive force of the love of Jack Straw and Peter Ochello and the unrealized possibility it represents of a nonhomophobic discourse.

Love is not an operative term for the men in *Cat on a Hot Tin Roof.* It is a word used only by Maggie and Big Mama—the men can only wonder, "Wouldn't it be funny if it were true?"[31] Not able to accept the love of women, neither can the men accept the unspoken option of sexual male/male love. Nor can Williams convincingly offer that option. The tenderness Williams sees as the clear side of his vision here exists only in a stage direction: the cloudiness of homosexuality remains an object of terror, not of the act, but of public exposure.

═══════

While elements of homosexuality suffuse many of Williams's major plays, his later post-Stonewall works deal more directly with his attitudes toward homosexuality. He moves from indirection and poetic image to didacticism and thinly veiled autobiography; the problematics of Williams's treatment of homosexuality become clearer, if less dramatically viable.

Small Craft Warnings (1972) establishes a formula Williams will use again in *Vieux Carré* (1977): the antagonism between a homosexual and a heterosexual "stud," and the placement of a troubled homosexual encounter in the context of a chaotic set of heterosexual relationships. In *Small Craft Warnings* the homosexual character, Quentin, is immediately seen as out of place in the Pacific Coast bar in which the play is set, not because of his sexuality, but because of his appearance, which announces him as a stereotypical homosexual out of a 1940s movie.: "dressed effetely in a yachting jacket, maroon linen slacks, and silk neck-scarf."[32] His face, "which seems to have been burned thin by a fever that is not of the flesh," makes him a brother to Williams's many aging male beauties, but here the wasting is an outward manifestation of the spiritual dessication which has resulted from Quentin's sexual promiscuity:

> There's a coarseness, a deadening coarseness, in the experience of most homosexuals. The experiences are quick, and hard, and brutal, and the pattern of them is practically unchanging. Their act of love is like the jabbing of a hypodermic needle to which they're addicted but which is more and more empty of real interest and surprise. This lack of variation and surprise in their . . . "love life" . . . [*He smiles harshly*] . . . spreads into other areas of . . . sensibility.[33]

The result of this emptying is finally the loss of the "capacity for being surprised," which is the loss of imagination and, potentially, of the possibility of creation. Quentin speaks of himself here in the language of textbook homophobic "objectivity."

Quentin is given the profession of screenwriter, and the experiences he recounts are those of Williams with MGM in the early 1940s. Moreover, he now writes pornographic movies, candid depictions of sex, even as Williams's plays have become more simplemindedly and candidly focused on sexual activity. These autobiographical clues enable the reader to see Quentin's emotional diminution not merely as the inevitable result of a pattern of homosexual activity, but as a corollary of Williams's fear of the draining away of his emotional and imaginative resources that would eventually cripple his writing. He wrote Donald Windham in 1955, the year of *Cat on a Hot Tin Roof*:

> I think my work is good in exact ratio to the degree of emotional tension which is released in it. In a sense, writing of this kind (lyric?) is a losing game, for steadily life takes away from you, bit by bit, step by step, the quality of fresh involvement, new, startling reactions to experience, the emotional reservoir is only rarely replenished . . . and most of the time you are just "paying out", draining off.[34]

The spiritual waning that cripples the artist becomes here the inevitable cynicism of the aging homosexual who is so self-hating that he can have sex only with boys who are not homosexual, thus emerging as the most articulate and least interesting older member of the typical Williams gay liaison: an older homosexual hungry for the flesh of beautiful, young, heterosexual men.

Williams felt that Quentin's monologue is "much the most effective piece of writing in the play," and one does see in it an effective duality.[35] Quentin is suffering the physical and spiritual ravages of time and mortality, the great nemeses in Williams's world. Yet he also suffers for his awareness of the brutality of his sex life. The attraction of youth is the attraction of what has been lost emotionally, and the attraction to heterosexuality is to the possibility of an alternative to the "coarseness" of homosexual activity. Part of that coarseness involves the need to keep sex on a financial basis, a matter of distancing and control which Williams well understood—even his beloved Frank Merlo was on the payroll. (Williams saw the male prostitute, homo- or heterosexual, as saintly.) Leona tells Bobby, the boy Quentin has picked up, to take Quentin's payment: "He wants to pay you, it's part of his sad routine. It's like doing penance . . . penitence." [36]

Quentin's expression of the homeless place of homosexuality as one cause for his sexual/spiritual malaise is reinforced by echoes from the other characters, who present an image of homosexuality Jerry Falwell would cheerfully endorse. The exuberant, sexually active Leona, tells Quentin:

> I know the gay scene and I know the language of it and I know how full it is of sickness and sadness; it's so full of sadness and sickness, I could almost be glad that my little brother died before he had time to be infected with all that sadness and sickness in the heart of a gay boy. [37]

And Bill, the stud who lives by his cocksmanship with women, who proves himself through fag-bashing—"Y' can't insult 'em, there's no way to bring 'em down except to beat 'em and roll 'em"—at least sees homosexuals as victims of determinism: "They can't help the way they are. Who can?" And Monk, the bartender, does not want gay men in his bar, because eventually they come in droves: "First thing you know you're operating what they call a gay bar and it sounds like a bird cage, they're standing three deep at the bar and lining up at the men's room." [38]

Williams, who did not want to "deal with the didactic, ever," has written here not the gay play he swore he didn't want to write, but a virulently homophobic play. The only positive possibility for homosexual experience resides with Bobby, the young man who accompanies Quentin into the bar. Bobby, Williams's typical fantasy youth, is omnisexual, able temporarily to equate sex with love and enjoy whatever experience comes his way. Bobby has the sense of wonder Quentin has lost, a function of youth; all he lacks is the sexual specialization he calls Quentin's "hangup."

Williams's relationship to *Small Craft Warnings* was complex. He saw it, in characteristically dualistic fashion, as "a sort of lyric appeal to my remnant of life to somehow redeem and save me — not from life's end, which can't be revealed through any court of appeals, but from a sinking into shadow and eclipse of everything that had made my life meaningful to me."[39] The play was originally titled "Confessional," which suggests a very personal relationship to the creation. And Williams, to keep the play running long enough to prove that he was still bankable, appeared as Doc through the last weeks of the show's run, though, as Donald Spoto points out, his drunken and drugged shenanigans and foolish ad libs "advertis[ed] the very condition for which he dreaded condemnation."[40] Ironically, Williams's performances in *Small Craft Warnings* were taking place at the same time as his creation of his most antic public performance, his *Memoirs*, in which the tables are turned and the public homosexual totally overshadows the private playwright.

Not ironically, but perhaps predictably, the equally confessional *Vieux Carré* is a desperate mining of memory and early fiction ("The Angel in the Alcove" [1943]) for material. As with Williams's first success, *The Glass Menagerie*, this late work is narrated by the playwright as a young man, here nameless and, alas, faceless. The time is the late thirties, when Williams finally had his first homosexual experiences, and the setting is a boarding house in the Vieux Carré. While the play seems to present Williams's "coming out," the liberation is, at best, conditional. *Vieux Carré* is the most vivid evidence for the consistency of Williams's attitude toward homosexuality: in the 1943 story and the 1977 play, homosexual activities are characterized as "perversions of longing" experienced by the young writer and an artist who is fatally diseased. Williams once again presents his past life and his past material in such a way as to expose himself to his audience while anticipating and affirming their homophobic reaction.

In his poem "Intimations" Williams states:

> I do not think that I ought to appear in public
> below the shoulders.
> > Below the collar bone

I am swathed in bandages already.
I have received no serious wound as yet
but I am expecting several.
A slant of light reminds me of iron lances;
my belly shudders and my loins contract.[41]

While the poem is about mortality, it also suggests Williams's sense of separation from his own physicality and sexuality as well as his confusion of private and public selves. In "Intimations" only the mind is public: the body, of which only the belly and loins are specifically mentioned—appetite and sexuality—are private and already "swathed in bandages" to cover their disease. This is a regrettably fitting self-image for Williams the homosexual and for the homosexuality he depicted throughout his career.

Notes

Thanks to my research assistant, Christopher Busiel.
1 Lee Barton "Why Do Playwrights Hide Their Homosexuality," *New York Times*, 23 January 1972.
2 Paul Bailey, "Dead Stork," *New Statesman*, 4 July 1975, 29.
3 Edward A. Sklepowitch, "In Pursuit of the Lyric Quarry: The Image of the Homosexual in Tennessee Williams' Prose Fiction," in *Tennessee Williams: A Tribute*, ed. Jac Tharpe (Jackson, Miss., 1977), 526.
4 Dotson Rader, "The Art of Theatre: Tennessee Williams," in *Conversations with Tennessee Williams*, ed. Albert J. Devlin (Jackson, Miss., 1986), 344.
5 Dotson Rader, *Tennessee: Cry of the Heart* (Garden City, N.Y., 1985), 153, 289.
6 Donald Spoto, *The Kindness of Strangers: The Life of Tennessee Williams* (New York, 1986), 319.
7 Ibid., 355.
8 Tennessee Williams, *Memoirs* (New York, 1975), 162.
9 Spoto, *Kindness of Strangers*, 81.
10 Tennessee Williams, *Moise and the World of Reason* (New York, 1975), 45.
11 Tennessee Williams, "Hard Candy," in *Collected Stories* (New York, 1985), 337; emphasis mine.
12 Ibid., 340.
13 Ibid., 345. "Hard Candy" is one of two stories ("The Mysteries of the Joy Rio" is the other) in which aging, diseased, fat homosexual men go to the former opera house, now a faded movie theater, to die while reliving their homosexual fantasies.

14 Ibid., 346.
15 Tennessee Williams, *A Streetcar Named Desire* (New York, 1947), 109.
16 Tennessee Williams, *Suddenly Last Summer* (New York, 1958), 15.
17 Ibid., 17.
18 Ibid., 40.
19 *Tennessee Williams' Letters to Donald Windham: 1940–1965*, ed. Donald Windham (New York, 1977), 215.
20 Tennessee Williams, *Cat on a Hot Tin Roof* (New York, 1955), 15.
21 Ibid., 88.
22 Ibid., 118.
23 Ibid., 117–18.
24 Ibid., 118.
25 Ibid., 121.
26 Ibid., 125.
27 Ibid., 122.
28 Ibid., 58.
29 Ibid., 127.
30 Ibid., 116–17.
31 Ibid., 80, 173.
32 Tennessee Williams, *Small Craft Warnings* (New York, 1972), 26.
33 Ibid., 46.
34 Windham, ed., *Letters*, 306–7.
35 Williams, *Memoirs*, 234.
36 Williams, *Small Craft Warnings*, 44.
37 Ibid., 40.
38 Ibid., 27–28, 50.
39 Ibid., 74.
40 Spoto, *Kindness of Strangers*, 334.
41 Tennessee Williams, *In the Winter of Cities* (New York, 1964), 62.

Ed Cohen

Legislating the Norm: From Sodomy to Gross Indecency

In the opinion of some, English homosexuality has become much more conspicuous during recent years, and this is sometimes attributed to the Oscar Wilde case. No doubt, the celebrity of Oscar Wilde and the universal publicity given to the facts of the case by the newspapers may have brought conviction of their perversion to many inverts who were before only vaguely conscious of their abnormality, and, paradoxical though it may seem, have imparted greater courage to others; but it can scarcely have sufficed to increase the number of inverts.

Following a paragraph which begins "as to the frequency of homosexuality in England and the United States there is much evidence," this quotation from the introduction to Havelock Ellis's *Sexual Inversion* (1897) addresses the implication that the number of "inverts" had grown as a result of "numerous criminal cases and scandals . . . in which homosexuality has come to the surface."[1] In formulating his response to this suggestion and to the underlying fears that motivated it, Ellis—nominally quoting a general, and hence unattributable, cultural voice—underscores the links between the "Oscar Wilde case" and the emergence of a "conspicuous" form of "English homosexuality." For, while ostensibly attempting to deny the validity of the contention that Wilde's conviction "increase[d] the number of inverts," Ellis's text paraleptically portrays Wilde as the example that defines the phenomenon and thereby represents him as a paradigmatic case of the very category that the book seeks to elucidate.

Without question, Wilde's trials and conviction were the most widely publicized events of their kind in the nineteenth century.[2] As such they were instrumental in disseminating representations of sexual behavior between men that were no longer predicated upon the evocation of a sexual crime that earlier in the same century was still named (often in Latin) as unnameable: "sodomy." However, in playing upon the word "conviction," Ellis's text also draws attention to the divergent and contradictory effects induced by the trials' newspaper coverage. Although the press reports may have given those men who had little knowledge about their feelings toward and sexual pleasures with other men a more concrete comprehension (a "conviction") of their sexual experience, it did so only by constituting this experience as a "perversion" or "abnormality" for which they could be "convicted." Yet, since the "conviction" which sent Wilde to prison for two years could not entirely efface his eloquent courtroom defense of his "conviction" that same-sex pleasures were "beautiful," Ellis concludes by conceding that "paradoxical though it may seem, [the newspaper reports on the trials may] have imparted greater courage to others."

As this brief analysis of the quotation from one of the first—and most controversial[3]—English texts on the subject suggests, the story of Wilde's trials crystallized the concept of "homosexuality" in the Victorian sexual imagination around his excessively unique, highly visible, male person(a). Indeed, Wilde was and remains so central to late nineteenth-century sexual iconography precisely because he became the figure around which new representations of male sexual behavior coalesced. For, although the opposition between "heterosexual" and "homosexual" has become so accepted that it now often seems to define a "natural" range of sexual expression, it was only during the last decades of the nineteenth century that this binary pairing actually emerged. Making their first significant appearance in the English language only three years before Wilde's conviction (in the 1892 translation of Krafft-Ebing's *Psychopathia Sexualis*), the words "heterosexual" and "homosexual" have always signified much more than just scientific descriptions of sexual practices. Even in its initial usage, "homosexual" was defined exclusively as the absence of a "natural reproductive instinct" that was supposed to direct desire toward the "opposite sex," while "heterosexual" was coined by symmetry to denote the "healthy" result that medical treatment should produce in the "pathological" male. In this schema, sexual desire for someone of the same sex could only be seen as a substitution for the real thing: "homosexual" came to imply a type of man—like Wilde —who negated normal "sexual instinct," while conversely "heterosexual" redeemed the pathological type by confirming the "naturalness" of the sexual norm.

Prior to this dichotomous conceptualization, sexual practices between men were almost universally understood as "sodomy"—a category deriving from canon law that referred exclusively to a particular kind of sexual act whether "committed with mankind or beast." Since sodomy was never conceived of as the antithesis of any normative sexual standard, it was perceived to be a ubiquitous, nonprocreative possibility resulting from the inherent sinfulness of human nature. While the transition from "sodomy" to the medico-legal category, "homosexuality," must be traced across more than three hundred years of medical, legal, religious, and moral writing, the results of these shifts were made most visible only during Wilde's lifetime. It was in 1861, fewer than ten years after Wilde's birth, that sodomy was finally removed from the British list of capital crimes, and a mere twenty-five years later that the Criminal Law Amendment Act created the first nonreligious category for such sexual offenses, labeling them "acts of gross indecency with another male person." It was under this statute that in 1895 Wilde was tried, convicted, and sentenced to two years' hard labor, becoming the most famous example —if not the literal embodiment—of the new definition.

In recent years the emergence of "the homosexual" as a pathological figure has received increasing attention from gay historians, especially in the wake of Michel Foucault's claim that:

> As defined by the ancient civil or canonical codes, sodomy was a category of forbidden acts; their perpetrator was nothing more than the juridical subject of them. The nineteenth-century homosexual became a personage, a past, a case history, and a childhood in addition to being a type of life, a life form, and a morphology, with an indiscreet anatomy and possibly a mysterious physiology. Nothing that went into his total composition was unaffected by his sexuality.[4]

Unfortunately, to date little research has been done on how the movement between the categories "sodomy" and "homosexuality" occurred, so that recent sexual histories have tended either to accept Foucault's claims by focusing exclusively on the emergence of "the homosexual" within the nineteenth century's discursive formation or to dispute this periodization by attempting to locate an ur-form of "the homosexual" at various points in Western history. However, if we begin to follow the transformations in the relation between legal, religious, ethical, and popular representations of sodomy from the time it entered English criminal law and to examine how these transformations articulated pronounced differences in who sodomy's "juridical subject" was at different historical moments, we find that the emergence of "the homosexual" in the late nineteenth century is intimately linked to fundamental changes in the legal/cultural interpretations ascribed to this sexual "crime." Indeed, a narrative that sketches how sexual relations between men were understood—both serially and simultaneously—as sin, crime, and moral transgression suggests that the shifting articulation of these categories created a juridical space within which popular representations of "the homosexual" could be legitimately written in late Victorian Britain. For it does not seem entirely coincidental that it was only after he was legally determined to have "posed as a somdomite [*sic*]" and was then tried and convicted for committing "acts of gross indecency with another male person" that Wilde could figure meaningfully as Havelock Ellis's iconic British homosexual.

During its brief session in 1533, the English parliament took time from its general preoccupation with Henry VIII's marriage disputes and its specific concern with such major issues as "the submission of the clergy to the king" and "the establishment of the succession of the king's most royal majesty in the imperial crown of the realm" to pass the first civil injunction against sodomy in British history.[5] Prior to this secularization, sodomy had been defined in strictly ecclesiastical terms as one of the gravest sins against divine law whose name alone proved such an affront to God that it was often named only as the unnameable.[6] As one in a constellation of liminal offenses (such as blasphemy, heresy, apostasy, witchcraft, prostitution, and usury, whose punishment merited religious execution), sodomy—or more precisely, the active exclusion of sodomy—provided an occasion for the Catholic church to violently mark "God's law" on the bodies of its "flock" and simultaneously to define the limits of its authority over Christian bodies and souls.[7] As Michael Goodich points out: "In English law, it would appear that sexual morality fell early under church authority, and crimes against nature were identified with heresy."[8]

Since sodomy, like heresy, constituted a transgression against the word/law of God, its punishment provided an occasion to reaffirm religious "truth" and thereby to reiterate the material human relations which that "truth" organized.[9] In this context, "sodomy" did not refer exclusively or even primarily to sexual relations between members of the same sex, but indicated a spectrum of nonprocreative sexual practices ranging from use of a dildo or birth control to anal intercourse (between men, or between men and women) and bestiality.[10] When Henry VIII's Parliament made "the detestable and abominable vice of buggery committed with mankind or beast" a felony in 1533, it transformed the broader implications of the religious offense into a specific legal injunction against a set of nonprocreative sexual practices.

Although the ostensive justification for this new legislation was that "there is not yet sufficient and Condyne punishment apoynted and limited by the due course of the Lawes of this Realme," the transformation of sodomy from an ecclesiastical to a secular crime must also be seen as part of a large-scale renegotiation in the boundaries between the Catholic church and the British state. Indeed, as the first in a series of statutes that recodified as felonies crimes which formerly fell under the jurisdiction of ecclesiastical courts, the creation of a legal injunction against sodomy provided a model strategy to curtail the power of the Catholic church by removing its right to try those offenses that directly reproduced its authority.[11] Yet, given that one of the primary conflicts in Henry VIII's struggle against papal authority concerned the church's right to insist that as a Christian subject the king was bound *body and soul* by the sacrament of marriage, the choice of sodomy as the first such state appropriation of canon law can hardly have been coincidental.[12] For the criminalization of sodomy would seem to have effectively transferred the power to define and punish "unnatural" sexual practices to the state and conversely to have made the state—in this case coextensive with a king who sought to abrogate his wedding vows—the sole source for establishing the range of acceptable, legitimate, or "true" relationships.[13] In particular, by claiming for the sovereign the right to punish and execute those convicted for the "vice of buggery," Parliament (here acting at the king's behest) not only claimed the right to define the legal culpability for "sinful" sexual practice but also negated the pope's authority over the bodies and the property—if not the souls—of the king's subjects. The criminalization of sodomy, then, can be seen both to have introduced a legal injunction that would remain a capital offense until 1861, and also to have consolidated the state's power to seize and control the bodies of its subjects.[14]

Less than a hundred years after the passage of this statute, Sir Edward Coke's *Third Part of the Institutes of the Laws of England* (the legendary jurist's highly influential systematization of English penal law) included "sodomy" in a volume "concerning High Treason and other pleas of the crown." Coke's treatise testified to the successful rearticulation of "the unnameable sin" as crime and simultaneously reapplied much of the offense's earlier religious interpretation to the civil code.[15] As the tenth entry in a list of over one hundred crimes against the state, the section "On Buggery, or Sodomy" situated sodomy's first extensive legal explication in the (con)text of

British legal doctrine's systematic reorganization, thus providing one of the most effective means for recouping this category derived from canon law. Since the opening sentence of Coke's account ("If any person shall commit buggery with mankind or beast; by the authority of parliament this offense is adjudged a felony") foregrounds the state's jurisdiction over the offending individual who undertakes the act rather than defining the offense per se, it constructs this person's adjudication as the point where civil procedures subsume ecclesiastical meanings. Hence, at the moment of legal intervention, the sodomite becomes both the person over whom the state's authority is made manifest and the text upon which the act's legal and cultural significance is inscribed.

Significantly, then, the body is conspicuously absent from Coke's ensuing definition of the crime: "Buggery is a detestable, and abominable sin, amongst Christians not to be named, commited by carnal knowledge against the ordinance of the creator, and order of nature, by mankind with mankind, or with brute beast, or by womankind with brute beast." Using the traditional canonical appellation to equate the "unnameable sin" (the "sodomy" already named in the chapter heading) with the named act ("buggery"), Coke's text elides the religiously execrable with the legally reprehensible.[16] Similarly, his formulation seems to introduce a distinction between "the ordinance of the Creator" and "the order of nature," only to reunite them as the ultimate ground for legal statute; it thereby enlists them both to legitimate the state's jurisdiction over the offense and to signify the state's authority over these realms. That Coke's reinterpretation reiterates the ecclesiastical form of the objections against sodomy in order to explain a law does not manifestly depend upon them illustrates the extent to which, by the early seventeenth century, legal thought had redeployed both the rhetoric and the authority of the increasingly superseded ecclesiastical courts in legitimating its condemnation of sexual offenses.

In turning from the transcendental/religious horror of the "abominable sin" to a historical digression on its philological and sociological origins, Coke deploys what he defines as the essential foreignness of the crime to inveigh against the very religious authority that first enjoined it:

> *Bugeria* is an Italian word, and signifies so much, as is before described, *paederastes* or *paiderestes* is a Greek word, *amator puerorum*, which is a species of buggery, and it was complained of in parliament, that the Lumbards brought into the realm the shamefull sin of sodomy, that is not to be named, as there it is said.[17]

The attribution of buggery to the Italians plays on the suggestion current by Coke's time that the Roman church was the hotbed of sodomy. As Louis Crompton suggests, this characterization permitted the mapping of sexual transgression onto national/religious differences and hence became an effective means of furthering the crown's struggles against the Pope's authority.[18] Indeed, the strategy was so successful that it engendered a metaphorical equivalence in which "the Papacy itself [was] a 'second Sodom,' 'new Sodom,' 'Sodom Fair,' nothing but 'a cistern full of sodomy.' "[19] Thus rerouted through civil law, sodomy loses its earlier clerical affiliations with heresy in order to be redeployed as a political charge against the very church which first produced it. By the early seventeenth century, it seems that sodomy had become an important element in the (ideological?) reproduction of the British government's temporal and religious sovereignty, reenforcing the state's right to adjudicate personal, social, and even spiritual limitations on the human body.

Having first provided this legal, cultural, political, and religious context for the crime, Coke's text finally moves on to consider what it had ostensibly sought to address all along: the criteria for determining legal culpability. In specifying the legal proof necessary for conviction ("So as there must be *penetratio* [penetration], that is *res in re* [the thing in the thing], either with mankind or with beast, but the least penetration maketh it carnall knowledge"), Coke's gloss on this criteria foregrounds the heretofore absent body as the site wherein the offense is written. Announcing a doctrine that would require judges and juries to decide whether the body (of man, woman, or beast) bore the marks of "*penetratio*," Coke proposes a somatic hermeneutic that provides specific guidelines for inducing the body to testify against itself. Since those convicted of sodomy on the basis of this testimony were liable to public execution, their deaths would transform their corpses into physical signs of the crime, producing a spectacle which reiterated the crown's absolute power to seize upon the bodies and the lives of its subjects.[20] By linking the offense and its punishment to the very life of the body, sodomy's status as a capital crime organized the meanings attributed to it as a property of the body itself and as such situated it as "part of a universal potential for disorder which lay alongside an equally universal order."[21] When the final lines of Coke's legal account return to "holy scripture" naming sodomy as a "detestable sin" that is at once a "crying sin," his classification comes full circle, making the sodomite's body the site for the reorganization of the relations between church (sin) and state (felony).

This legal imbrication of sodomy's secular and religious significance provides a frame for its representations in Renaissance culture. In *Homosexuality in Renaissance England*, Alan Bray extrapolates the implications of these overlapping meanings and indicates that sodomy played a complex role in the religious, political, and literary texts of the period. Noting that sodomy continued to evoke religious connotations even after its criminalization in the sixteenth century, Bray suggests that it retained a "mythic" association which often placed it in the company of werewolves, basilisks, sorcerers, and heretics. However, these meanings were now overlaid with references to social and political behavior, so that they came to signify moral as well as religious transgressions. Coke once again provides an index for this constellation when he remarks: "The sodomites came to this abomination by four means, viz. by pride, excess of diet, idleness, and contempt of the poor." While this list of inducements to sodomy continues to play on the religious and sexual implications of the earlier ecclesiastical charge, it also marks them out as deviations from the virtuous self-government propounded by Protestant theology so that, Bray argues, they begin to refer to an essentially moral concept: debauchery.[22]

As this moral association became a salient element of sodomy's cultural specificity, it linked notions of sexual and personal excess to the particularity of a criminal charge. Analyzing numerous references to sodomy in the period and especially during the reign of James I, Bray concludes that rather than providing evidence of actual

sexual or religious transgressions, attributions of sodomy functioned
as political accusations by underscoring implications of extravagance
and irresponsibility:

> It was the Court—the extravagant, overblown, parasitic Renais-
> sance court—not homosexuality which was the focus of their
> attention. What homosexuality provided was a powerfully dam-
> aging charge to lay against it; at what should have been the
> stronghold of the kingdom, there was only weakness, confusion,
> and disorder.[23]

That the theological meanings of the crime were subordinated to
the political context illustrates their continuing disarticulation from
a strictly ecclesiastical discourse and their rearticulation within an
emerging secular frame. Bearing the accreted significance of its cultural history—first as sin and then as crime—sodomy became an
index for a variety of "excessive" behaviors that were then referred
back to the body as their source and their proof.

The accounts of the trial, conviction, and execution of the earl
of Castlehaven in 1631 are among the few extant examples of how
this nexus of meanings was produced.[24] Mervyn Touchet, ninth Lord
Audley and second earl of Castlehaven in the peerage of Ireland,
was brought before an assize of his peers on 13 April 1631 to answer
charges that he "abetted a rape upon his Countess," "committed sodomy with his servants," and "commanded and countenanced the De-
bauching of his Daughter." Instigated by his second wife who claimed
that Lord Audley had impelled one of his servants to rape her in his
presence (in his own bed) and then later encouraged the same servant
to rape her daughter, the trial inspired several popular accounts over
the next seventy years, detailing acts of aristocratic extravagance,
sexual license, familial violence, and religious impiety that remain
shocking even today. Drawing on the sensational testimony presented
in the case, the narratives indicate in abundant detail that the earl's
menage had been marked by great excesses: sodomy was only one
of a number of transgressions that included rape upon his wife and
daughter and the keeping of a household prostitute, but it was the one
transgression which merited his death sentence. The representation

of the lord high-steward's address to the court concerning the severity of this charge makes its implications clear:

> As for the *Crimen Sodomiticum* . . . I shall not paraphrase upon it, since *it is of so abominable and Vile a Nature* (that as the Indictment truly expresses it, *Crimen inter Christanos non nominandum*) *it is a crime not to be named among Christians;* and by the Law of God, as well as the Ancient Laws of *England*, it was punished with Death. . . . As to this Indictment there is no other Question, but whether it be *Crimen Sodomiticum penetratione*, whether he penetrated the Body, or not; to which I answer, the Fifth of *Elizabeth*, sets it down in general Terms, and *ubi Lex non distinguit, ibi non distinguendum* [where the law does not distinguish, let there be no distinction made]; and I know you will be cautious how you give the least Mitigation to such abominable Sins; for when once a Man indulges his Lust, and Prevaricates with his Religion, as my Lord *Audley* had done, by being a Protestant in the Morning and a Papist in the Afternoon, no wonder he commits abominable Impieties; for when Men forsake their God, 'tis no wonder he leaves them to themselves.

Moving from a description of the indictment through a brief consideration of the legal proofs and then returning to religion, this passage provides an excellent illustration of the shifting meanings engendered by the charge of sodomy. Initially named only in Latin, sodomy enters the text in a legal form which recasts its traditional Christian nomination as "unnameable sin" in the language of "crime." Invoking the authority of both divine and temporal law, the lord high-steward's speech then legitimates the power of the court to pronounce the death sentence upon the offender. However, since he indicates that the crime is to be adjudged solely by the act of penetration and cites the appropriate parliamentary act, he underscores that it is secular (il)legality that places the body at stake and conversely mitigates any other religious criteria for such a decision. Thus, when he returns to the "prevarication" of Lord Audley's religious practice, it is not in order to reiterate Audley's violation of the law of God but to use the political/moral implications of Audley's "Papism in the afternoon" to substantiate the sexual charges against him. In narrating the announcement of the guilty verdict and death sentence, the text returns to the lord high-steward's religious admonishment (". . . as your Crimes have been Abominable, so let your Mortification for them be as remarkable. 'Tis not a flight and formal Contrition can obliterate your Offenses, for you have not only Sins against the Law of God and Nature, but against the Rage of man. . . .") and demonstrates the overdetermined significance that the rhetoric of "sin" plays upon.

The rhetorical positioning of sodomy between sin and crime continued to shift during the last decades of the seventeenth century, as the relationship between sin and crime itself was problematized by the emergence of popular "projects" to supplement and/or augment legal and religious injunctions against "immorality" and "vice."[25] Almost immediately after the abdication of the last Catholic monarch, James II, in 1688 and the ensuing coronation of the Protestants, William and Mary, attention was brought to bear on "licentious" behavior as an affront both to the precepts of religion and to the security of the state. Drunkenness, prostitution, violation of the sabbath, gambling, swearing, and other "corruptions of manners" were believed to abound; their unchecked proliferation seemed to testify to a loss of authority by the society's great institutions and to undermine the culture's very foundations. As one tract succinctly phrased it: "If there be no power in the Church sufficient to enforce a regularity of life, and the civil magistrate be remiss and negligent, great confusions and disorder will need ensue in the state."[26] Whereas for centuries the Catholic church had maintained a technology (the confessional) that linked the supplicant's necessity for self-knowledge to the priest's representation of God's omniscient knowledge, creating a dense epistemological nexus through which the minute details of individual experience (the "regularity of life") could be known, the procedures of the Protestant church (which situated the individual in a more immediate epistemological and ontological relation to God) provided few such opportunities for the faithful to inform upon themselves. Consequently, unlike the Catholic church, the Church of England was never able to orchestrate a continuous authority over its subjects, especially as the institutions and rituals of the "Roman faith" came to be increasingly associated with religious and political oppression.

As there appeared larger and larger gaps in what the Church of England could legitimately claim to know of each person's behavior, and as religious dissent challenged even this more restrained institutionalization, its ability to monitor and ultimately affect individual behavior was limited. By the end of the seventeenth century, the radical negation of Catholicism in England had removed the sole authority for moral supervision from the church and stimulated the development of a uniquely English approach to moral enforcement.

During the 1690s, groups of men made anxious by what they perceived as the moral and religious degeneration of their nation banded together to form the Societies for the Reformation of Manners.[27] Originally initiated by "private men"—primarily skilled craft workers or merchants—in the Tower Hamlets of London's East End to address the transgressions of their own community, the idea for such societies quickly spread throughout London and beyond. These groups looked to each other for support and advice, so that by 1701 Josiah Woodward noted that there were "near twenty societies of various qualities and functions formed in subordination and correspondency with one another and engaged in this Christian design in and about this city and its suburbs."[28] Coinciding with Queen Mary's admonishment to the Middlesex justices (in July 1691) that the courts be especially vigilant in prosecuting offenders against moral law, the Societies took advantage of the royal enthusiasm for their cause in order to press their complaints. Since they perceived that the legal process could do little without detailed information of specific infractions, they undertook to obtain and record such information; lists of their prosecutions included the name and address of the prosecuted, the offenses charged, the verdict and punishment, along with the names of court officials who participated in the case. In addition, and perhaps most strikingly, the Societies actively encouraged individuals to watch for and report violations among their neighbors and friends. As Dudley Bahlman observes:

> . . . the members [of the Societies for the Reformation of Manners] concluded that even if the justices were willing to issue warrants as readily as they issued their order against vice, they could do little without information. Therefore they resolved to

enlist as many informers as they could; and to make the work of informing as easy as possible, they had blank warrants printed at their own expense. A member of the society, upon the word of an informer, could fill out one of these warrants and take it to a justice, who, after examining the member under oath, would sign it and seal it.[29]

Mediating between the Church, the Law, and the public sphere, the Societies were instrumental both in propagating a new technology for moral enforcement and in attaching this technology to the exercise of the state. If, as Foucault has suggested, the rationality of modern state power was formulated along two axes which he labels "the doctrine of reason of state" and the "doctrine of police," the Societies can be seen to have significantly developed this rationality as a consequence of their efforts.[30] Since their organizational procedures necessarily led them to inspect individual behavior in its most mundane detail in order to produce, record, and manage information that could lead to public prosecutions, they undertook the function of policing the populace and thereby extending the range of experience that was visible to legal enforcement. Simultaneously, they legitimated their actions (often in the face of extremely hostile public condemnation and/or violence against informers) by claiming—in the words of John Disney—"it deserves to be somewhat more largely considered how far the public Interests of *Society* and *Civil Government* are embarqued in the Execution of those [moral] Laws; what fatal *Mischiefs* issue from the *Neglect* of this part of our Duty; and what *Advantages* both to the Prince and People from the *faithful Discharge* of it."[31] The prosecutions by the Societies for the Reformation of Manners provided occasions for recasting the legal instantiations of religious ordinance—from sabbath breaking to sodomy—in the language of "public interest" and thereby coordinating the extirpation of "sin" with the establishment policing techniques in behalf of a moral code for "*Society* and *Civil Government.*"

The effect of this coordination on the popular representations of sodomy is graphically demonstrated in documents describing a series of trials that resulted from raids on London's "molly houses"—raids quite likely initiated by the Societies for the Reformation of Manners whose agents also testified in the prosecutions—in the spring of 1726. Appearing in *Select Trials for Murders, Robberies, Rapes, Sodomy, Frauds, and Other Offenses at the Sessions House in the Old Bailey*, the representations of these cases both reveal the existence of a highly developed London subculture within which men engaged in physical and emotional intimacies with each other and illustrate the means by which the public attacks on this subculture consolidated a moralistic interpretation of sodomy.[32] While the information about these trials and their contexts is necessarily sketchy, the reports in the *Select Trials* indicate that several informers went regularly to the London pubs where these men congregated and passed themselves off as sympathetic to their activities. In so doing, the informers obtained not only the names of individual men who engaged in same-sex practices but also documented the elaborate rituals which accompanied these practices.[33] For example, the *Select Trials'* version of the proceedings against Gabriel Lawrence for sodomy indicates that Samuel Stevens (who appears to have been one of the informers for the Societies for the Reformation of Manners) testified:

> Mother Clap's house was in Field-Lane, Holbourn. . . . It was notorious for being a Molly-House. I have been there several Times in order to detect those who frequented it: I have seen 20 or 30 of them hugging and making love (as they call'd it) in a very indecent Manner. Then they used to go out by Couples into another Room, and when they had come back they would tell what they had been doing, which in their Dialect they call'd marrying.[34]

While this account depicts the activities of the Molly-house as a parodic reenactment of the sacramental *and* legal affirmation of reproductive monogamy—and other accounts go ever farther, referring to the inner room where sexual encounters took place as "the chapel," indicating that sexual partners were designated as "husbands," and suggesting that after intercourse some men enacted false childbirth, sometimes even going so far as to baptize their "offspring" —the attempt to characterize these practices as blasphemous or heretical is conspicuously absent.[35] Indeed, even the legitimizing invocation of the offense's ecclesiastical formulation found a hundred years earlier in the lord high-steward's indictment and summation at Lord Audley's trial is largely missing from the text. Instead, the *Select Trials'* focuses on representing in detail the activities of which the men named were accused and on recounting their responses to these charges. The one exception to this pattern occurs in the cases of men found guilty and sentenced to death; here, as a supplement to court proceeding, a narrative by the clergyman who attended the condemned man in his final days in prison is appended. Called "the Ordinary's Account" and entirely set off by quotation marks, the appendix provides a short biographical sketch and then indicates whether or not the man executed made a public confession of his crime; however, while this brief narrative often underscores the dead man's love for the Church of England, it rarely enters into a full-blown religious reinterpretation of the crimes for which he was killed.[36] Thus, by the time the *Select Trials* were published during the second third of the eighteenth century, the emergent focus on sodomy's legal prosecution as represented in the narrative accounts of the courtroom proceedings seems to have largely displaced a residual focus on the charge's religious significance, rendering its popular descriptions primarily as transgressions against the "laws of man" or, perhaps more accurately, against the "laws of manners."

In this context, it is interesting to contrast the representations provided by the *Select Trials* to a contemporaneous pamphlet entitled *Plain Reasons for the Growth of Sodomy in England.*[37] While the accounts of the trials indicate that those who participated in London's Molly-houses were drawn from a variety of occupations (woolcombers, ale-house keepers, tradesmen, cabinetmakers, fruitsellers, teachers, etc.), the anonymous author of *Plain Reasons* addresses his text to the social transgressions of "fine gentlemen" and abjures the discussion of legal proceedings. Instead his text frames "sodomy" as a description of the degraded manhood that he attributes to certain members of the wealthy classes and seeks to imbricate "unnatural vices" with "unmanly" behavior. To this end, the pamphlet begins by nostalgically lauding the ideal from which his contemporaries had fallen away ("Our Forefathers were trained up to Art and Arms; The Scholar embellish'd the Hero; and the fine Gentleman, of former days, was equally fit for the Council and the Camp") and blaming the education which young men of wealth receive for the demise of this former grandeur (". . . he was brought up in all respects like a *girl* . . ."). The consequences of this fall are unequivocal for the author:

> Unfit to serve his King, his Country, or his Family, this Man of Clouts dwindles into nothing and leaves a Race as effeminate as himself; who, unable to please the Women, chuse rather to run into unnatural Vices one with another, than to attempt what they are sensible they cannot perform.

Here the sequence of decay begins with the Man of Clouts's inability to perform his socially designated functions and then degenerates into the "effeminacy" of his progeny, resulting in "unnatural Vices one with another" when, at a tertiary level, the degraded offspring finds himself unable to satisfy a woman sexually. Thus, rather than being seen as the cause of social decay—as will be the case for "the homosexual" whose social pathology derives specifically from his choice of sexual object—"sodomy" here is merely the rhetorical designation for an extreme form of social dissolution predicated on the negation of the "manly" ideal: ". . . anything of *Manliness* being diametrically opposed to such unnatural Practices." Concomitantly, as the chapter titles indicate, the text addresses "sodomy" only as a symptom of behavioral deviations: "The Effeminacy of Men's Dress and Manners, particularly their Kissing Each other" and "the Evils of the Italian Opera," suggesting that the specific sexual/sinful significance formerly attributed to the charge has been rearticulated in the legitimation of an emerging masculine norm.[38]

When, during the second half of the eighteenth century, Blackstone's *Commentaries on the Laws of England* (1769) recategorized sodomy among "Offenses against the Persons of Individuals," sodomy's relation to these increasingly normative cultural meanings was recouped by legal discourse. Included in a chapter devoted to such crimes as mayhem, forcible abduction ("vulgarly called stealing an heiress"), and rape, sodomy—which Blackstone's delicacy forbade him from ever actually naming—at first appears somewhat anomalous. Unlike the other offenses listed which refer to acts of grave bodily harm, it is not readily apparent why "the infamous crime against nature" constitutes an assault "against the security of [the] person." In his analysis of the *Commentaries*, legal historian Alex Gigeroff suggests that Blackstone may have been drawing upon "the spiritual concept of a person" in determining sodomy's classification in order to say that "participation in this kind of act is an offense or an affront to the spiritual aspect of man."[39] Yet while Blackstone's brief section uses the quasi-religious euphemism *peccatum illude horrible, inter christanos non nominandum* and attributes the legitimacy of capital punishment against the crime to "the express law of God," his—albeit elliptical—analysis is not manifestly religious. Indeed, Blackstone's inclusion of sodomy among "offenses against the person" instead of among "offenses against God and Religion"—where he placed, for example, "open and notorious *lewdness*, either by frequenting houses of ill fame . . . or by some grossly scandalous and public indecency"—would seem to militate against interpreting his classification of the crime on a strictly spiritual basis. Rather, it seems more plausible to link Blackstone's categorization, at least in part, to a normative conception of legal culpability, so that the violation "against the person" can be seen as a violation against the specific cultural identification of what a *male person* should be. This interpretation would seem to be further corroborated by the fact that unlike Coke and the jurists following him, who defined sodomy as a crime applicable to both men and women, Blackstone specified that "the infamous crime against nature" was "committed either with mankind or beast." The narrowing of sodomy's purview to specifically male practices transforms the crime from a generalized injunction against a range of transgressive behaviors formerly labeled as "sin" into a particular "offense against the person" whose "offensiveness" derives from the cultural meanings ascribed to the male sex of the person(s) involved.

While it is well beyond the scope of this essay to address the larger transformations in legal standards framing such a redefinition of "the person," it is important to note that Sir Leon Radzinowicz, in his compendious study of English legal development, *A History of English Criminal Law*, describes the second half of the eighteenth century as the period during which the moral reform movements of the preceding hundred years were able to consolidate their impact on legal doctrine.[40] Stressing that the arguments for legislating and policing morals took on an overt middle-class bias during the period and that increasing numbers of middle-class officials (especially clerics, lawyers, and politicians) participated in "reform" activities, Radzinowicz suggests that by the end of the century it had been accepted that certain acts were "so unusually dangerous and grievous to individuals, and from their frequency so injurious to the whole public, that they were lifted up into scale, and became criminal offenses."[41] The normative notion of "unusual danger to the individual" provides a relevant gloss on Blackstone's interpretation of sodomy as an "offense against the person," especially when this interpretation was coincident with a marked increase in prosecutions against sodomy. As A. D. Harvey has shown, the number of arrests and the number of executions for sodomy rose dramatically in the first three decades of the nineteenth century.[42] Using the statistics from Middlesex as an indicator, Harvey states: "from less than one a decade in the second half of the eighteenth century, after 1804 executions for sodomy in Middlesex came to an average of one a year."[43] While the specific causes of this increase remain elusive, it appears that the coincidence of emerging definitions of normative sexual behavior (what Harvey calls "the massive reinforcement of sexual stereotyping") with aggressive private policing and prosecution by the reform societies (in an era before the state consolidated these activities under its jurisdiction) was instrumental in fomenting the legal and public execration of sodomy.[44]

The newspaper accounts of the arrest of thirty men at the White Swan in Vere Street, London, in 1810 prove excellent—and tragic— examples of this coincidence.[45] Apparently the result of a long period of surveillance and a carefully coordinated series of raids, the arrests of the "Vere Street Club" provided the occasion for massive public demonstrations against the offenders. If the press versions are to be believed, those men found guilty were subjected to violent abuse— both verbal and physical—as they were conveyed to and from the pillory, and even those men who were released because there was insufficient evidence to prosecute them were often lucky to escape without serious harm from the crowds which surrounded the police courts. Unlike the accounts provided in the *Select Trials* eighty years earlier, however, these newspaper texts focus almost exclusively on the public demonstrations against and harassment of the men convicted of committing sexual offenses in the case while censoring precisely those details which formerly would have generated interest in such crimes. In explaining this textual silence, the newspapers profess their advocacy of standards of public decency; for example, one paper notes: "The evidence adduced against these prisoners was of so black a hue, of so abominable a nature, that we cannot pretend to give any report of it." And another sputters: "The existence of a Club, or Society, for a purpose so detestable and repugnant to the common feeling of our nature that by no word can it be described without committing an outrage against decency." Constituting the crimes as beyond decent representation, the terms that the press used to castigate the offenders indicate that the basis for the crime's non-nomination was no longer predicated entirely on its "sinful" nature but also on its violation of certain standards of "decency." Invoking "the name of decency and of morality, for the sake of offended Heaven," one newspaper exhorted Parliament to quickly legislate further punishments in order to deter future violations. Another publicly named those found guilty, calling them "the execrable miscreants convicted of forming a club at the White Swan, in Vere Street, to commit a vile offense" and applauded "the disgust felt by all ranks in society at the detestable conduct of these wretches." As these phrases suggest, while the penumbra of religious condemnation continued to adhere to the popular representations of sodomy, the force of public condemnation was directed as much against "detestable conduct" as against "a most diabolical offense."

Throughout the nineteenth century, as religious dogma continued to lose its exclusive power to organize public knowledge and as the normative standards for male behavior were rapidly consolidated, sodomy's prosecution provided new opportunities to legislate normative behavior.[46] In 1828, an omnibus bill entitled "Offenses Against the Person," designed to repeal fifty-seven separate pieces of criminal legislation and reenact them under a single rubric in order to "simplify them and make them clear"—in the words of the Home Secretary, Robert Peel—was passed by Parliament.[47] This act reorganized the statutory basis for many serious crimes, including "the abominable crime of buggery" which was recriminalized as a capital offense along the line of Blackstone's earlier classification. Sandwiched between the definition of "a woman secreting the dead Body of her Child" as a misdemeanor and the specification of rape as a felony, paragraph 15 states succinctly: "every Person convicted of the abominable Crime of Buggery, committed either with Mankind or with any animal, shall suffer Death as a Felon." Yet beyond simply recodifying buggery, the bill also overrode earlier legal precedent which required (in cases of buggery, rape, and "carnally abusing Girls under the Age of Ten Years") two proofs—of penetration and emission—for conviction. Under the provisions of the omnibus bill, the requirement "to prove the actual Emission of Seed in order to constitute carnal Knowledge" was intermitted so that "carnal Knowledge shall be deemed complete upon the Proof of Penetration only." While arguing for this proposed change in the standard of proof, Peel focused primarily on alleviating "the suffering of the unfortunate female who was the victim of the offense," indicating that his inclusion of buggery with the other two offenses was part of a more general containment of male sexual violence against women. However, this rearticulation of the legal criteria necessary for conviction not only changed the specific evidentiary standards that defined the crimes but also shifted the doctrinal basis for criminalizing the acts themselves. As Peel's speech for the bill indicates: "It was his strong opinion that one of those descriptions of proof was unnecessary and that it was not necessary to a capital conviction to prove more than that which constituted *the moral offense* as far as the offending party was concerned."[48] No longer, then, was sodomy's criminalization as a capital offense designed to enforce a biblical injunction against nonprocreative sexual behavior (which was the motivation for the required dual proof), but instead to maintain a certain "moral" standard for individual behavior. By specifically linking the death penalty to the immorality of the charge—in the absence of any reference to earlier "sinful" connotations—Peel privileged socially determinant behavioral standards as legitimating state intervention on the bodies and lives of the citizenry and simultaneously characterized sodomy as such a normative transgression.

The development of normative standards for (male) behavior became a critical element in the self-definition of the British middle
class throughout the nineteenth century; at the forefront of this effort
were the energetic activities by numerous organic intellectuals of the
bourgeoisie (doctors, educators, clerics, alienists, parents, feminists,
evangelicals) not only to define but also to watch for and to enforce
new ideological articulations of sex, age, and class. Since sodomy's
legal definition necessarily mediated between an earlier organization
of sexual practices predicated on the ecclesiastical affirmation of reproductive monogamy and a newer configuration which sought to
enforce certain cultural limits on the deployment of the body, its
status as a capital offense provided the point at which these two
regimes overlapped. So long as sodomy continued to merit execution
—even if only theoretically—its punishment provided an occasion
for the state to inscribe the offender's body with/as a hieroglyph
signifying its power to use death in order to regulate the very basis
of life, even while it was in the process of creating and organizing
new technologies which reproduced a more diffuse, yet more minute,
exercise of power over all aspects of that life. However, after 1836,
the year that the last execution for sodomy took place, the volatility
of this juncture was attenuated, so that when sodomy was removed
from the list of capital crimes in 1861, it signaled an effective shift in
the legal interpretation of sodomy's criminality from a secularization
of canon law to an essentially normative transgression.[49]

This transformation was further consolidated with the passage of
section 11 of the Criminal Law Amendment Act of 1885 which created a new statutory category independent of any ecclesiastical connotations—"acts of gross indecency with another male person"—to
redefine the legal injunction against sexual practices between men.[50]
Following on the momentum developed by the campaign to repeal the
Contagious Diseases Acts which popularized the demand to legislate
proprietary standards for male sexual behavior (in order to redress
the sexual "double standard" that allowed middle-class men sexual
access to working-class women outside of marriage),[51] the Criminal
Law Amendment Act attempted to define limitations on a range of
male sexual behavior primarily with prostitutes and adolescent girls
on behalf of a middle-class familial norm. Named "An Act to make

further provision for the Protection of Women and Girls, the suppression of brothels, and other purposes," it was quickly passed in the fall of 1885 after a series of articles in the *Pall Mall Gazette* by William Stead catalyzed public opinion in its favor. Dramatically entitled "the Maiden Tribute of Modern Babylon" and purporting to describe the sale of a young working-class virgin into "white slavery," Stead's (mostly apocryphal) story so enraged public sentiment that over 250,000 people reportedly demonstrated in Hyde Park in support of the legislation.[52] While the main purpose of the bill was to raise the age of consent for girls from thirteen to sixteen and to provide police enforcement for the regulation of brothels, it also included in the now infamous section 11 the first legal classification of a sexual relation (as opposed to a sexual act) between men:

> Any male person who, in public or private, commits or is party to the commission of, or procures the commission by any male person of, any act of gross indecency with another male person, shall be guilty of a misdemeanor, and being convicted thereof shall be liable at the discretion of the court to be imprisoned for any term not exceeding two years with or without hard labour.

This legal injunction formally shifted the criteria for criminalizing sexual practices between men: whereas "sodomy" had enjoined a particular sexual act that was to some extent independent of the sex of the actors, "acts of gross indecency" were entirely unspecified in themselves and only derived their "indecency" from their appearance in the context of a relationship between two men. In so contextualizing the new misdemeanor, the law moved beyond its earlier historical concern with prosecuting a particular form of sexual transgression to policing a range of activities that could at different moments be interpreted as "indecent" if they involved two or more men. Hence, the Criminal Law Amendment Act constituted all such relationships as objects of legal scrutiny and thereby shifted the locus of culpability from a particular kind of act to a particular type of actor.

This metonymic slide from act to actor can be seen to have subsumed the moralistic (knowledge) effects emerging from earlier interpretations of sodomy in defense of a normative familial ideology. In arguing for the bill before the House of Commons, Sir R. Assheton-

Cross, the Secretary of State for the Home Department, succinctly stated the aim of the act: ". . . the purity of the households of this country shall be maintained and . . . those who wish to violate them shall be punished."[53] That the defense of "household purity" should provide the legislative context for reconceptualizing the illegality of a diverse set of sexual activities between men suggests that what was being legislated was a standard for male sexual behavior rather than a liminal form of sexual transgression. For, unlike sodomy, which specified the illegality of a limited range of sexual activities ("buggery with mankind or beast") whose transgressive character derived from a Judeo-Christian affirmation of monogamous procreative sexuality, "acts of gross indecency" had no particular specificity save for the sexual similarity of the sexual actors and were defined against a normative standard which deified the "purity" of the middle-class "household."

In the years that followed the passage of section 11, the public reporting of prosecutions under the new legal rubric provided an opportunity to produce new representations of sexual relations between men. To a large extent, such trials, by foregrounding sexual practices that challenged normative gender ideologies, constitute what Victor Turner has called "social dramas," insofar as they bring into play certain contested elements of social behavior and through this conflict allow individuals "to take sides in terms of deeply entrenched moral imperatives and constraints, often against their own personal preferences."[54] This definition seems particularly appropriate for those cases that so catalyzed public interest that they transformed news into "scandal." While it is impossible to rigorously specify what constitutes a scandal, perhaps the best way to define one is in terms of the reactions it evokes.[55] For clearly, a scandal differs from news per se inasmuch as it provokes readers "to take sides" usually in a highly emotional or affective manner. The volatility characterizing these processes of social division and judgment in turn suggests that a scandal's "content" must in some sense include behavior which confounds the very certainty of basic social distinctions and implies that there are no clear (moral, ethical, legal) boundaries for human action. By thematizing this sense of cultural indeterminacy, scandals open up a liminal period during which the normative values and practices of a culture are contested. Individuals and groups align themselves according to their responses to the behaviors at issue, thereby reconstituting hegemonic configurations and ideologies in relation to the previously undefined or transitional activities. Scandals would appear, then, to crystallize new configurations of social difference by articulating heretofore marginal elements of a social formation in relation to those normative standards against which positions may be taken, judgments may be formed, and alliances may be created.

In one of the rare attempts to theorize this ubiquitous yet universally overlooked form of social transformation, Max Gluckman suggests that scandals perform a unifying function within a culture by "creating a past history for the members in relation to one another" and by "competitively aligning [individuals and cliques] against each other." [56] While Gluckman's conclusion is based on analysis of precapitalist social formations, his suggestions seem adaptable to the context of nineteenth-century Britain with one major distinction: unlike the more contained cultures that both Turner and Gluckman consider, in which individual members have (more or less) immediate access to the actors in or at least the context of the "social drama," the national scandals occurring in Britain during the last half of the nineteenth century were necessarily mediated by the press. Indeed, the numerous sexual scandals played out in the press, at least from the 1870s on, constitute a common staple of the "new journalism"'s attention. The widespread newspaper coverage of the arrest and trial of Ernest Boulton and Fredrick Park for conspiracy to commit sodomite acts (1870), the Besant-Bradlaugh trial for republishing pamphlets offering birth-control instruction (1876), the ongoing coverage of the campaign to repeal the Contagious Diseases Acts, the scandal involving sex acts between high male officials at Dublin Castle (1884), the trial and acquittal of a notorious brothel keeper, Mrs. Jeffries (1884), and the "Maiden Tribute" affair (1885), among others, testify to the role that scandals play in consolidating popular understanding of a disparate set of sexual practices. An analysis of the newspaper reporting on each of these particular incidents would reveal much about the emergence of popular discourses on sexuality in Victorian Britain; suffice it to say here that, as an integral part of the emergence of mass journalism in the late nineteenth century, the coverage of sexual scandals was instrumental in articulating sexual behavior as an element of class and national identities and in unifying class and national identities in relation to normative appraisals of sexual behavior.

By way of concluding this narrative of (il)legalities, I'll consider one further trial, if only because it became (in 1889–1890) the first sensational prosecution under section 11 of the Criminal Law Amendment Act prior to Wilde's own.[57] Dubbed "the Cleveland Street Affair" after the small West End street where, at number 19, a male brothel proffering young postal employees to an upper-class and often titled male clientele became the center of a controversy that not only implicated several highly placed men (including Prince Albert Victor, second in line to the throne) in a web of—to use the public prosecutor's words—"unnatural lust," but also put both the state prosecution and the newspaper coverage themselves on trial. The circumstances of "the affair" are rather complex: on 4 July 1889, while pursuing an investigation of small theft from the Central Telegraph Office, the police interrogated a fifteen-year-old messenger boy named Charles Swinscow who appeared to have more money in his possession than his meager salary could account for. Under questioning Swinscow revealed that he had earned the money by going to bed with "gentlemen" at the house in Cleveland Street run by a man called Charles Hammond. He also volunteered that he knew of at least two other telegraph boys who had pursued similar outside employment and noted that they had all been introduced to the practice by another messenger, Henry Newlove [!?]. These revelations led to an investigation culminating in the prosecution of Newlove and an older man, George Veck, for procuring boys to "commit divers acts of gross indecency with another person." The third man, Charles Hammond, was also indicted but fled the country to avoid prosecution.

Although the indictments received cursory treatment by both the *Times* and the *Star*, by and large the press had paid almost no attention to the case up until this point. However, when testimony given in both the investigation and the trials suggested the involvement of persons of rank and, in particular, that of Lord Arthur Somerset (who upon learning of his implication in the case left for the continent), journalistic interest was aroused. Fittingly, on 11 September 1889, the *Pall Mall Gazette* was the first to make the connection explicit:

We are glad to see that Sir Augustus Stephenson, Solicitor to the treasury, was present at the Marlborough Street police court yesterday, when two prisoners were committed for trial in connection with a criminal charge of a very disgraceful nature. Mr. Hannay refused bail for both the accused, and no doubt if found guilty by a jury they will receive exemplary punishment. But the question which Sir Augustus Stephenson will have to answer is whether the two noble lords and other notable persons who were accused by the witnesses of having been the principles in the crime for which the man Veck was committed for trial are to be allowed to escape scot free. There has been too much of that kind of thing in the past. The wretched agents are run in and sent to penal servitude; the lords and gentlemen who employ them swagger at large and are even welcomed as valuable allies of the Administration of the day.

This account sketches out the terms within which the case was reported to the public. The specific criminal acts themselves were typically invoked euphemistically ("a criminal charge of a very disgraceful kind") if at all ("the crime for which the man . . ."), while the text elaborates with much gusto the inequities of the penal system. Thus, the sexual transgressions function here merely as a prelude to the political charges, metonymically infecting the latter with the immoralities generated by the former. When Veck and Newlove pled guilty on 18 September and received sentences of nine and four months' imprisonment, respectively, the stage was set for the next act in the scandal.

While the state attempted to determine the legal and political feasibility of pursuing charges against Somerset and other named individuals, sectors of the press became impatient with what was deemed the sluggishness of the proceedings. On 16 November 1889 a newly founded Radical journal, the *North London Press*, published an article under the banner "THE WEST END SCANDALS," publicly naming Lord Arthur Somerset and the earl of Euston as being "among the number of aristocrats who were mixed up in an indescribably loathsome scandal in Cleveland Street." The article then proceeded to claim that both men had been allowed to leave the country and "thus defeat the ends of justice, because their prosecution would disclose the fact that a far more distinguished personage [Prince Albert Victor] was inculpated in these disgusting crimes." Here again, as in the *Pall Mall Gazette* article quoted above, the nature of the sexual crimes seems only of interest insofar as it underscores the inequities of class privilege. The sexual practices are rendered as "indescribably loathsome"—itself a highly evocative description—and "disgusting crimes," but they take on significance not primarily in themselves but only as they become the opportunity for the "defeat of justice." Unfortunately for the editor of the paper, Ernest Parke, justice had not been quite so battered as he thought, and the earl of Euston whom he had publicly described as having absconded to Peru to avoid prosecution was in fact still in the country and was not heavily implicated in the case. Taking umbrage at the inclusion of his name along with Somerset's as an unfair defamation of his character, Euston quickly brought charges against Parke for criminal libel.

Parke's trial became the occasion for a flood of press coverage, since it was the press itself that was now in the dock. The case juxtaposed Euston's claim that he had visited the house in Cleveland Street just once in the spring of 1889—as his counsel said, "prompted it might be by a prurient curiosity which did him no credit"—after having been given a card advertising *poses plastiques* (the Victorian equivalent of a strip joint) while walking in Piccadilly. Upon learning that there were no *poses plastiques* but only young male prostitutes, the earl claimed that he quickly left the house and never returned. The defense for its part attempted to prove both that Euston had visited Cleveland Street on several occasions and that he had willingly entered into the specialties of the house. The proof of this latter charge came in the testimony of a rather notorious male prostitute, John Saul, who offered details of alleged sexual acts he had committed with Euston.[58] Since the defense focus was on proving the justification for the statements about Euston published in the *North London Press*, the accounts of the trial foregrounded the question of the credibility of the testimony while rendering the particular claims made about sexual activities in very obscure language. Thus, the *Times* could report Saul's account of the activities which took place between him and Lord Euston only by describing them as unfit for publication.

When Parke was found guilty on 17 January 1890 and sentenced to a year in prison, the press almost unanimously abjured from referring to the substance of the sexual charges and instead editorialized about the appropriateness of the libel conviction.

While the press coverage of the Cleveland Street affair provided the first major coverage of prosecutions under the Criminal Law Amendment Act for "committing acts of gross indecency," it represented these acts only to the extent that they constituted the necessary backdrop for a libel case itself predicated on a challenge to unequal execution of justice based on class. The sexual crimes, although very explicitly placed at the margins of the reporting (and indeed often represented only by their suggestive absences), provided indispensable atmospheric interest because they confirmed the "degeneracy" of the aristocracy who were perceived as getting away with them, while those less well off were punished.[59] Yet the peripheral nature of this coverage does not mean that the sexual acts were not themselves at issue, for clearly what was thematized in the subsequent references to the incident was not the question of legal justice but the sexual underpinnings of the case. When Wilde's *The Picture of Dorian Gray* appeared shortly after Parke's conviction in 1890, the *Scots Observer* concludes its damning review with an unmistakable reference to the Cleveland Street scandal:

> Mr. Wilde has again been writing stuff that were better un-written; and while "The Picture of Dorian Gray," . . . is ingenious, interesting, full of cleverness, and plainly the work of a man of letters, it is false art—for its interest is medico-legal; it is false to human nature—for its hero is a devil; it is false to morality—for it is not made sufficiently clear that the writer does not prefer a course of unnatural iniquity to a life of cleanliness, health, and sanity. The story—which deals with matters only fitted for the Criminal Investigation Department or a hearing *in camera*—is discredible alike to author and editor. Mr. Wilde has brains, and art, and style; but if he can write for none but outlawed noblemen and perverted telegraph boys, the sooner he takes to tailoring (or some other decent trade) the better for his own reputation and the public morals.[60]

This prescient alignment of Wilde's text (which during his trials would become a metonym for his own "decadent" sexual practices) with the events of the Cleveland Street scandal—five years before his own trials would entirely eclipse this earlier incident as a cultural marker of same-sex relations between men—indicates how the press coverage of such proceedings was important as a means of mediating the popular interpretation of the new legal category and thereby structuring public representations of nominally "unrepresentable" practices. To the extent that the press provided a context both for the dissemination of information about sexual relations between men and for the organizing of that information into legitimately "public" forms, it constituted an important nexus for the construction of popular concepts of male sexuality. Even though the press reports on the Cleveland Street scandal attempted to maintain the same-sex practices of the actors at the margins of its coverage, the marginalized practices still effectively structured the historical interpretation of the legal events, making it possible for the author of this review to impugn Wilde by association without any explicit reference to excluded acts. In the case of Oscar Wilde, no such pretense of marginalization was possible, and thus the newspaper accounts of his trials provided a critical site for articulating an emerging popular conceptualization of male same-sex relations in terms of a new moral and legal standard for sexual behavior.

Recent polemics within gay historiography (and I have already declared my interest by calling it "gay") have expended much intellectual, if not emotional, energy on determining or denying the birth date of "the homosexual." Some argue that "homosexual" denotes a set of sexual activities between men that have existed—transhistorically and cross-culturally—in a recognizably "modern" form for as long as several hundred to perhaps well over a thousand years. Others contend that "homosexual" acquired a unique specificity in the nineteenth century that marks it as a socially and historically determinant frame for comprehending and experiencing a set of sexual practices between men such that they are distinguishable from earlier ways of knowing/experiencing these "same" practices. While clearly my approach is more closely aligned with the latter than the former, it seems important to stress that the polemical divide is constructed upon a political question represented in the guise of concrete historical and semantic issues. For what appears to be at stake in the historiographic debates about "homosexuality" is how we ought to comprehend the limits of its effectiveness for organizing our own engagement with and experience of the current historical moment.

The fluidity of and interpenetration between categories derived from legal, moral, religious, and popular discourses foregrounds the extent to which the public representations of "sodomy" situate sexual activities between men as elements in shifting configurations of power and domination. The criminalization of these sexual activities crystallizes different historical meanings at different historical moments, and the prosecution of men for sodomy rearticulates these meanings within the processes whereby power is exercised. For me, such a descriptive paradigm seems far from "academic" in a nation that is experiencing the public redefinition of sexuality in the wake of AIDS and is simultaneously confronting the (knowledge) effects of the recent Supreme Court decision in *Bowers* v. *Hardwick*. In this conjuncture, as the legal interpretation of "sodomy" is being explicitly linked to public fears generated by the media representations of AIDS, we find once again that the interpretations ascribed to sexual activities between men are mediating new forms of medical, legal, religious, political, and moral authority designed to delimit the range of "legitimate" sexual practices. Yet the ability of gay men and lesbians to resist such authority is predicated upon our refusing the limitations of those categories that naturalize the power to name our experience as "unnatural" and upon comprehending the historical consequences that this power has in and for our everyday lives.

Notes

1 Havelock Ellis, *Studies in the Psychology of Sex* (New York, 1942), 63.
2 See H. Montgomery Hyde, *The Trials of Oscar Wilde* (New York, 1962). While purporting to provide verbatim transcripts of the legal proceedings, Hyde's text is in fact a pastiche (drawn from contemporary news accounts) that structures the events as an exemplary—if apologetic—tale of Wilde's meteoric rise and pre-

cipitous fall. In his long-awaited biography of Wilde (New York, 1988), Richard
Ellmann provides yet another rewriting of this chronology without altering the
now traditional narrative form. For a critique of Ellmann, see my "Nothing Wilde,"
The Nation, 13 February 1988, 203–6.

3 See Phylis Grosskurth, *Havelock Ellis* (London, 1980) and *The Woeful Victorian: A
Biography of John Addington Symonds* (London, 1965); Jeffrey Weeks, "Havelock
Ellis and the Politics of Sex Reform," in *Socialism and the New Life*, ed. Sheila Row-
botham and Jeffrey Weeks (London, 1977), 139–85; and Arthur Calder Marshall,
Lewd, Blasphemous and Obscene (London, 1972).

4 Michel Foucault, *The History of Sexuality*, trans. Robert Hurley (New York, 1980),
1: 43.

5 This legislative account is taken from H. Montgomery Hyde's *The Other Love*
(London, 1970) which provides the most detailed contextualization of sodomy's
criminalization. This historical process has been underanalyzed by gay historians;
note, for example, the absence of the bill's consideration in Alan Bray's *Homosexuality in Renaissance England* (London, 1982), a text which reviews literature
back to the very period of the law's passage.

6 While to date there is no work that comprehensively traces the history of this non-
nomination or its implications, John Boswell in his *Christianity, Social Tolerance,
and Homosexuality* (Chicago, 1980) indirectly illustrates that by the thirteenth
century it had entered ecclesiastical discourse when he quotes a letter from Pope
Honorious III to the archbishop of Lund (380).

7 On "the flock," see Michel Foucault, "Omnes et Singulatim: Towards a Critique of
Political Reason," in *Tanner Lectures on Human Values*, ed. Sterlin McMurrin (Salt
Lake City, 1981), 224–54; see also Boswell, *Christianity . . . and Homosexuality*,
who explores this nexus from the origins of Christianity through the Middle Ages.

8 Michael Goodich, "Sodomy in Medieval Secular Law," *Journal of Homosexuality* 1
(Spring 1976): 297.

9 On "truth" as a "system of exclusion" that arranges particular historical configurations of power/knowledge, see Michel Foucault's "The Discourse on Language,"
in *The Archaeology of Knowledge*, trans. A. M. Sheridan Smith (New York, 1972),
215–37.

10 Hyde, *Trials of Oscar Wilde*, 31. As Boswell notes: ". . . the word [sodomy] would
not necessarily imply homosexuality since by the early seventeenth century 'sodomy' referred to 'unnatural' sex acts of any type and included certain relations between heterosexuals—anal intercourse for instance" (*Christianity . . . and Homosexuality*, 98).

11 Sir James Stephen, *A History of the Criminal Law of England* (London, 1883), 2:
429. For an outline of the specific legal restrictions on papal authority generated
during Henry's reign, see John Reeves, *History of the English Law* (Philadelphia,
1880), 4: 542–54.

12 For Hyde, *Trials of Oscar Wilde*, the choice does appear arbitrary: "No doubt buggery appeared to Cromwell as suitable a subject as any other for the inauguration

of this process which was to continue and eventually lead to the practical aboli-
tion of all ecclesiastical courts a century later . . ." (39). However, given the range
of possible choices, it seems highly unlikely that "sodomy" should be randomly
singled out to initiate this strategy simply for lack of any better alternative.

13 See Ernst Kantorowicz, *The King's Two Bodies: A Study in Mediaeval Political
    Theology* (Princeton, 1957).

14 This movement provides an excellent example for Foucault's description of sover-
    eign power as essentially "the right to *take* life or *let* live": "Power in this instance
    was essentially a right of seizure: of things, time, bodies, and ultimately life itself;
    it culminated in the privilege to seize hold of life in order to suppress it" (*His-
    tory of Sexuality*, 136). See also Gilles Deleuze and Felix Guattari, *Anti-Oedipus:
    Capitalism and Schizophrenia*, trans. Robert Hurley, Mark Seem, and Helen Lane
    (New York, 1972), 192–222.

15 Sir Edward Coke, *The Third Part of the Institutes of the Laws of England* (London,
    1797).

16 See Foucault, *History of Sexuality*, 38.

17 Coke, *Laws of England*, 58.

18 Louis Crompton, *Byron and Greek Love* (Berkeley, 1985), 53–54.

19 Bray, *Homosexuality in Renaissance England*, 19.

20 This characterization of public execution derives from Michel Foucault, *Discipline
    and Punish*, trans. Alan Sheridan (New York, 1979), 48–49.

21 Bray, *Homosexuality in Renaissance England*, 26.

22 Ibid., 19, 16.

23 Ibid., 37. Bray's anachronistic use of "homosexuality" is based on his supposition
    that it is "directly physical—and hence culturally neutral." While this thesis is
    clearly at odds with the project of my essay, his analysis of historical materials
    still seems empirically if not theoretically sound.

24 My discussion of this case is based on an anonymous pamphlet published in Lon-
    don in 1699 entitled *The Tryal and Condemnation of Mervin Lord Audley, Earl
    of Castle-Haven, at Westminster, April the 5th 1631. For abetting a rape upon his
    Countess, committing sodomy with his servants, and commanding and countenanc-
    ing the Debauching of His Daughter* recently reprinted in *Sodomy Trials*, ed. Ran-
    dolph Trumbach (New York, 1986). See also Caroline Bingham, "Seventeenth-
    Century Attitudes Towards Deviant Sex," *Journal of Interdisciplinary History* 1
    (Spring 1971): 447–68.

25 Dudley Bahlman, *The Moral Revolution of 1688* (New Haven, 1957), 101; quoting
    Swift, Bahlman notes that during the period the word "project" connoted an ori-
    entation of the individual toward the public sphere for the improvement of civil
    society.

26 John Lacy, *A Moral Test* (London, 1704), 13.

27 Bahlman, *Moral Revolution*, is the most comprehensive source on the Reformation
    Societies.

28 Quoted in Bahlman, *Moral Revolution*, 38.

29 Ibid., 33.

30 Foucault, "Omnes et Singulatim," 245–50.

31 John Disney, *An Essay upon the Execution of the Laws against Immorality and Prophaneness* (London, 1708), iv. Bahlman, *Moral Revolution*, succinctly summarizes the position taken by many reformers: "at a higher level morality would be a social cement, an instrument of civil peace" (42).

32 Using material largely culled from the *Select Trials for Murders, Robberies, Rapes, Sodomy, Frauds, and Other Offenses, at the Sessions House in the Old Bailey* (London, 1734–35), Bray argues that the seventeenth century saw the emergence of a "new identity," i.e., "the molly," that crystallized a variety of cultural meanings not applicable to earlier definitions of "sodomite" and "bugger": "The identity existed rather as a possible lifestyle that integrated homosexuality, to the extent that it was adopted, into a broad range of other experiences and forms of behavior, into the kind of person that you were; it had as palpable an existence over and against the individual as the conventions and life of the molly houses themselves, which it repeated on a personal scale" (99). While it seems quite probably that the subculture which produced and was reproduced by/through the "molly houses" significantly transformed the meanings attributed to sexual acts between men— both by those who engaged in them and those who execrated them—Bray's conclusions are unfortunately based on highly problematic textual interpretations. Since he first ignores the cultural construction of the *Select Trials* as "popular fictions"—although he admits in a footnote that this is what they are—and then attempts to use them to produce a pseudo-phenomenology of what the "molly's" experience must have been like, his "fiction" interpolates a number of questionable assumptions about how these individuals made their lives meaningful in the context of a dominant culture that seemed to exclude them. Thus, for example, Bray argues that the effect of raids on molly houses made the members of the subculture more aware of their "identity": "Someone who was a molly might well, probably would, avoid arrest and the horrors that followed, but what he could not avoid knowing was the constant possibility of this fate. And the implication of that? He could not avoid knowing—he could not afford to avoid knowing—what he was and what he was part of" (93). This subjectifying approach necessarily leads Bray to conclude that the "molly" was an "identity" based in a "lifestyle" and leads him to suggest that "the molly" was the prototype for—though not the same as—"the homosexual." Here the anachronistic usage of terminology derived from contemporary gay culture illustrates the circularity of Bray's project: in order to demonstrate the creation of a cultural category not unlike one produced in the past one hundred years, he uses the rhetoric of this category to describe an earlier set of experiences and then concludes that they are structurally similar. Randolph Trumbach, "London's Sodomite: Homosexual Behavior and Western Culture in the 18th Century," *Journal of Social History* 11 (Fall 1977): 1–33, also uses the *Select Trials* to develop an account of what the "molly's" life was like, but he is much less speculative about the subjective aspects of this experience.

33 *Select Trials*, 195. Samuel Stevens reported at the trial of William Griffin that

his accounts were accurate since "Every night when I came from thence, I took memorandums of what I had observ'd, that I might not be mistaken in dates."

34 Ibid., 193.

35 See Trumbach, ed., *Sodomy Trials*, 17.

36 The most significant counterexample to this claim appears in the *Select Trials* synopsis of Gilbert Lawrence's trial for sodomy in August 1730. Here the text notes the indictment as: "Gilbert Lawrence of the Precinct of St. Brides, was indicted for that he not having the fear of God before his eyes, but being moved by a devilish Instigation. . . ." The "Ordinary's Account" indicated that while awaiting execution Lawrence refused to confess his crimes even though the narrator/confessor told him: "it was to no purpose to deny the fact, since there was no hope of a Repreive, and that he would glorifie God by a free Confession, which would also make him leave this World with greater peace of Mind, in taking Shame and Confusion of Face to himself, for so notorious, so heinous, so barbarous, so unnatural a crime" (375). However, this extended religious diatribe can to some extent be attributed to the indication that Lawrence was a French Catholic and therefore his execution merited this religious charge, while those of "good Protestants" did not.

37 *Plain Reasons for the Growth of Sodomy in England* (London, circa 1730). Although open to methodological criticism, George Rousseau's recent essay, "The Pursuit of Homosexuality in the Eighteenth Century," in *'Tis Nature's Fault. Unauthorized Sexuality during the Enlightenment*, ed. R. P. Maccubbin (Cambridge, 1987), 132 68, provides an incredibly rich bibliography of contemporary sources on eighteenth-century sodomy.

38 The final chapter of *Plain Reasons*, entitled "The Perfection of *Prudes*, and the Barbarities of Women to one another," provides an interesting coda to the arguments against male effeminacy. Here the author argues that children born out of wedlock should be legitimated since, in his estimation, so long as sex is procreative it is moral, while the immorality of sex lies in not providing for the children thus engendered. This advocacy of male sexual access to women beyond the constraint of (Christian?) marriage underscores the normative assumption upon which the attack on sodomy depends: i.e., that "manliness" is tantamount to virility with/ against women.

39 Alex K. Gigeroff, *Sexual Deviations in the Criminal Law* (Toronto, 1968), 13.

40 Sir Leon Radzinowicz, *A History of English Criminal Law* (New York, 1957), 3: 141–207.

41 Ibid., 202. This quotation occurs during Radzinowicz's discussion of the attempts to criminalize adultery. While he never explicitly refers to sodomy in this context, it seems plausible to extrapolate the doctrine for this offense as well.

42 A. D. Harvey, "Prosecutions for Sodomy in England at the Beginning of the Nineteenth Century," *Historical Journal* 21 (1978): 939–48. Radzinowicz, *English Criminal Law*, 72 and 330–31, also provides statistics concerning sodomy prosecutions during the first half of the nineteenth century.

43 Harvey, "Prosecutions for Sodomy," 939.

44 Ibid., 946: "As women became more and more confined to a narrow range of social roles, and an exhaustive code of manly behavior and manly attitudes became more established, so sexual ambivalence became more and more outlawed. . . ."

45 Clippings of these accounts along with Robert Holloway's sensationalistic pamphlet, *The Phoenix of Sodom or the Vere Street Coterie. Being an Exhibition of the Gambols Practiced by the Ancient Leechers of Sodom and Gomorrah, embellished and improved with Modern Refinements in Sodomitical Practices, by the Members of the Vere Street Coterie, of detestable memory* (London, 1813), are reprinted in Trumbach, ed., *Sodomy Trials*.

46 I have written on this consolidation at great length in my dissertation, *Talk on the Wilde Side: Towards a Genealogy of the Discourse on Male Sexuality* (Stanford, 1988).

47 *Hansard Parliamentary Debates*, n.s., vol. 19 (1828), 350–60.

48 Ibid., 354; emphasis mine.

49 The 1861 "Act to consolidate and amend the Statute Law of England and Ireland relating to Offenses against the Person," 24 & 25 Victoria, Cap. C, reiterates the definition of the offense and the required proof as specified in the 1828 act, amending the latter only by changing the penalty from death to "penal servitude for life or for any term not less than ten years." In addition, however, the 1861 statute defines a lesser crime: "the attempt to commit the said abominable crime" punishable by "penal servitude for any term not exceeding ten years and not less than three years, or any terms not exceeding two years, with or without hard labour." It is this last lesser offense that would seem to have provided the prototype for the 1885 criminalization of "acts of gross indecency," also punishable by two years' imprisonment with or without hard labor.

50 The most comprehensive discussion of the act appears in François Lafitte's "Homosexuality and the Law," *British Journal of Delinquency* 9 (July 1958): 8–19. For an account of the legislative history of sec. 11, see F. B. Smith, "Labouchere's Amendment to the Criminal Law Amendment Bill," *Historical Studies* (University of Melbourne) 17 (October 1976): 165–73.

51 Judith Walkowitz, *Prostitution and Victorian Society* (Cambridge, 1980), remains the best source on the Contagious Diseases Acts.

52 On the "Maiden Tribute of Modern Babylon," see Judith Walkowitz's *Jack the Ripper's London* (Chicago, forthcoming); also see Deborah Gorham, "The 'Maiden Tribute of Modern Babylon' Re-examined: Child Prostitution and the Idea of Childhood in Late-Victorian England," *Victorian Studies* 21 (Spring 1978): 353–79.

53 *Hansard Parliamentary Debates*, n.s., vol. 300 (1885), 578.

54 Victor Turner, *Dramas, Fields, and Metaphors: Symbolic Action in Human Society* (Ithaca, 1974), 35.

55 While almost no work has been done on this type of historical event, the one recent text which does take up the subject is woefully inept at characterizing its field of inquiry. Colin Wilson and Donald Seaman, in *Scandal* (New York, 1985), provide a series of platitudes by way of definition: "A scandal is any event that 'lets the cat out of the bag' and provides material for interesting gossip"; "it [scan-

dal] suggests that truth has finally triumphed and the hypocrite stands exposed";
"scandal is based on wishful thinking. The public wants to be shocked in order to
confirm its own sense of virtue"; "what interests us is the contrast between myth
and reality that becomes apparent when a scandal explodes." What these char-
acterizations do suggest, however, is that scandal is constituted primarily by the
public responses that it provokes and, indeed, to some degree is these responses
themselves. The authors of this text would probably vociferously deny this suggestion, however, since their project is designed specifically to provide a listing of
those "events" which provoke such response and does not address the responses
themselves at all.

56 Max Gluckman, "Gossip and Scandal," *Current Anthropology* 4 (June 1963): 313.

57 Of all the late Victorian "scandals," only the Cleveland Street affair has received
even the most cursory attention. My account is culled from two books, H. M.
Hyde, *The Cleveland Street Scandal* (New York, 1976), and Colin Simpson, Lewis
Chester, and David Leitch, *The Cleveland Street Affair* (Boston, 1976). The former,
which attempts to reconstruct the chronology of events, relies on newspaper accounts, but as in Hyde's *The Trials of Oscar Wilde*, fails to provide any analysis
of this coverage. The latter proceeds in much the same manner with a somewhat more detailed account of the behind-the-scenes machinations which led to
or didn't lead to prosecutions.

58 Saul is also reputed to be the anonymous author of a choice piece of Victorian
pornography entitled *The Sins of the City of the Plain* published privately in 1882.

59 A poem published in the *North London Press* (and quoted in Simpson, Chester,
and Leitch, *Cleveland Street Affair*, 117–18) makes these connections explicit:

> My Lord Gomorrah sat in his chair
> Sipping his costly wine;
> He was safe in France, that's called the fair;
> In a city some call 'Boo-line'
> He poked the blaze and he warmed his toes,
> And, as the sparks from the logs arose,
> He laid on finger beside his nose—
> And my Lord Gomorrah smiled.
>
> He thought of the wretched, vulgar tools
> Of his paederastian joys,
> How they lay in prison, poor scapegoat fools;
> Raw, cash-corrupted boys.
> While he and his 'pals' the 'office' got
> From a 'friend at Court,' and were off like a shot,
> Out of reach of Law, Justice, and 'that—rot,'
> And my Lord Gomorrah smiled.

60 Quoted in Stuart Mason, *Oscar Wilde: Art and Morality* (New York, 1971), 75–76.

William A. Cohen

Willie and Wilde: Reading
The Portrait of Mr. W. H.

When Oscar Wilde was brought to trial in 1895 for committing "acts of gross indecency," one of the most damaging pieces of evidence against him was a letter of his to Lord Alfred Douglas. In the letter, Wilde thanked Lord Alfred for sending him a poem and complimented his young friend in extravagant terms:

> My Own Boy,
> Your sonnet is quite lovely, and it is a marvel that those red rose-leaf lips of yours should have been made no less for music of song than for madness of kisses. Your slim gilt soul walks between passion and poetry. I know Hyacinthus, whom Apollo loved so madly, was you in Greek days.

The letter had been stolen, used in an attempt to blackmail Wilde, and finally became damning evidence. Poised at the center of the scandalous trials that brought Wilde's downfall was this purloined letter about a mediocre sonnet. From Reading prison, Wilde recounted the episode two years later in another letter to Lord Alfred:

> You send me a very nice poem, of the undergraduate school of verse, for my approval: I reply by a letter of fantastic literary conceits. . . . The letter is like a passage from one of Shakespeare's sonnets, transposed to a minor key.[1]

In contrast to its object, claims Wilde, the letter of commentary upon the sonnet is itself "like" a sonnet of Shakespeare's, diminished though it may be. Here is a prison letter (itself eventually published under the title *De Profundis*) about an evidential letter that is more poetic than the poem to which it replies—a pederast's letter about a poetaster's sonnet, and all to the tune of Shakespeare: this is how Wilde interprets his own tragedy.

Wilde clearly understood just how self-damaging his own lovely words had been, as he continues in *De Profundis*:

> It was, let me say frankly, the sort of letter I would, in a happy if wilful moment, have written to any graceful young man of either University who had sent me a poem of his own making, certain that he would have sufficient wit or culture to interpret rightly its fantastic phrases. Look at the history of that letter! It passes from you into the hands of a loathsome companion: from him to a gang of blackmailers: . . . every construction but the right one is put on it: Society is thrilled with the absurd rumours that I have had to pay a huge sum of money for having written an infamous letter to you: this forms the basis of your father's worst attack: I produce the original letter myself in Court to show what it really is: it is denounced by your father's Counsel as a revolting and insidious attempt to corrupt Innocence: ultimately it forms part of a criminal charge: the Crown takes it up: the Judge sums up on it with little learning and much morality: I go to prison for it at last. That is the result of writing you a charming letter.[2]

Wilde's condensed self-history is quoted here at length because it describes precisely the trajectory of an intercepted letter, of the real horrors that result when something akin to "a passage from one of Shakespeare's sonnets" is misinterpreted and mishandled.

Despite its pretention, the comparison to Shakespeare is neither

casual nor unjustified: not only was Wilde well acquainted with the
sonnets, but, in a certain interpretation, the sonnets themselves can
be read as letters sent to the poet's "own boy" in praise of his "red
rose-leaf lips . . . made no less for music of song than for madness
of kisses." Like the letter that is both commentary upon a poem and
itself poetic, Wilde's novella *The Portrait of Mr. W. H.*, written six
years before the trials, analyzes Shakespeare's sonnet sequence even
as it articulates its theory in a story that is, in its way, Shakespearean
(though again transposed to a minor key). Wilde's narrative folds
back upon its purported object, rendering its interpretation of the
sonnets upon the framing story. Like the "real" sonnet/letter sequence
that came to recapitulate it, Wilde's novella displays the inextricability of literature from interpretation.

At the center of *The Portrait of Mr. W. H.* is a theory that ostensibly
attempts what many others have sought as well: to suggest a positive
identity for the young man to whom at least the first 126 sonnets
(in the canonical arrangement) are addressed.[5] In Wilde's story, the
case is argued that the young man is the same as the "W. H." of the
printer's famous epigraph:

> TO. THE. ONLIE. BEGETTER. OF.
>
> THESE. INSVING. SONNETS.
>
> M^r. W. H. ALL. HAPPINESSE.
>
> AND. THAT. ETERNITIE.
>
> PROMISED.
>
> BY.
>
> OVR. EVER-LIVING. POET.
>
> WISHETH.
>
> THE. WELL-WISHING.
>
> ADVENTVRER. IN.
>
> SETTING.
>
> FORTH.
>
> T. T.

Based on an imputed narrative of the poems, Wilde claims that Mr.
W. H. was a lovely "boy-actor" in Shakespeare's company to whom

the poet was deeply devoted. Moreover, "working purely by internal evidence," Wilde's story discovers the actual name of this boy embedded in the sonnets. The name—Willie Hughes—is located in several famous puns in the sonnets where various senses of "Will" and "Hews" are brought into play.

The narrator begins the story by recounting his acquaintance with an older friend, Erskine. The latter, in turn, relates the story of his own youthful friendship with another beautiful boy-actor, Cyril Graham. This gifted boy originally developed the interpretation of the sonnets, claiming to solve the "riddle" of the famous young man's identity. Unable to persuade Erskine with his theory, Graham produces as incontrovertible evidence a painting of "Mr. W. H.," clearly identified as the young man of the sonnets. Although initially convinced, Erskine soon discovers the portrait to be a forgery, and upon this revelation, Graham shoots himself, charging Erskine in a note with proving the truth of the theory to the world. While Erskine still remains unconvinced, the narrator is enticed by the theory, and pursues the evidence to develop an even stronger case for Graham's interpretation. Presenting the evidence to Erskine several weeks later, the narrator manages at last to convince the older man of the theory, only to find that, in doing so, he himself has lost his faith in it. Two years later, he receives a note from Erskine in which the latter claims he is about to kill himself out of devotion to the theory. The narrator rushes to his friend, only to learn that he is already dead—not, however, by his own hand, but instead from consumption, which he knew would kill him when he sent the false suicide note.

Returning to the theory proper, the most urgent question facing us is: what might it mean for an analysis of Shakespeare's sonnets to focus on proper names encrypted within the poetic structure? It is, first of all, a project encouraged by the sonnets themselves: "Every word doth almost tell my name, / Showing their birth, and where they did proceed." Such an interpretation understands its object to be a puzzle, a surface on which coded information is inscribed; the information is clearly visible to the knowing reader, yet hidden from the untrained eye. The story's narrator enunciates just this method of reading as he gazes on the portrait of Willie Hughes for the first time: "I see there is some writing there, but I cannot make it out."[4] If the disguised referent of the sonnets is itself a proper name, then the poems are cast in a register different from their typical reading either as universalizable love poems or as biographical clues to the life of Shakespeare. For despite its initial claims, Wilde's project is exactly not to track down historical evidence about Shakespeare, but instead to produce a reading that is "literary" in the fullest sense.

In the realm of proper names, language induces the belief that the subjectivity of "I" and "you" (that is, where "I" designates the speaking subject) has been transcended; meaning appears anchored to identity when "Will" can speak his own name (as in Sonnets 135 and 136). Names implicitly propose the inextricability of signifier from signified because the one invokes the other even when they are temporally and spatially dislocated: a unique human identity and its concomitant proper name would seem to be mutually constitutive. But the difference between common words and proper names is a trick of language, a false representation. Naming is only the most basic instinct of language, for in the proper name the primal fantasy of language is replayed: a singular correspondence between word and thing is established. Such an arrangement suggests that a name is a false word, or, what amounts to the same thing, a word that is truer than the truth. Naming displays the fundamental desire of language; yet even as the primordial act of naming enables Wilde's story (in constituting the sonnet theory), the simultaneous hollowing out and overdetermination of names is what will ultimately structure it.[5]

In *The Portrait of Mr. W. H.*, the issue is further complicated by the fact that the name is encoded in specifically graphemic form: here the name is a written unit, abbreviated—as a name can be only when written—by its initial letters. Initials figure importantly in this text not only in what they stand for but also in the *way in which* they stand for something: initials are the truncated, synecdochical form of the material signification of a proper name. As it seeks to decode the initials, Wilde's theory of the sonnets becomes a determinedly visual one, in the sense that it proceeds by reading—or more precisely, looking at—the printed words on the page: "In the original edition of the Sonnets 'Hews' is printed with a capital letter and in italics," as is *Will*. The poems come to be more than just a hidden code: they are a *picture of a puzzle*, which must be interpreted as visual representation. Furthermore, if, as I've claimed, naming is the instance of language that wants to be truer than the truth, then the visual image of such a structure is located exactly where the story begins: with a discussion of artistic forgery. "I insisted," says the narrator in the story's second sentence, that "forgeries were merely the result of an artistic desire for perfect representation."[6]

The story is arranged around a forgery that operates in just such a structure: the portrait in the title is the "perfect representation" not of some referential reality but of the name figured in the sonnets; it is a palpably visual form of the name "Mr. W. H." Yet the portrait that is intended as final proof of the theory's verity ("I warmly congratulated him on the marvellous discovery") ultimately asserts only its fraudulence ("the theory is based on a delusion. The only evidence for the existence of Willie Hughes is that picture in front of you, and the picture is a forgery"). And like the name that is coded and hidden in the poems, the forgery—ocular proof of the theory—must be extracted from its unlikely location:

> [Cyril] told me that he had discovered [the picture] by the merest chance nailed to the side of an old chest that he had bought at a farmhouse in Warwickshire. . . . In the centre of the front panel the initials W. H. were undoubtedly carved. It was this monogram that had attracted his attention, and he told me that it was not till he had had the chest in his possession for several days that he had thought of making any careful examination of the inside. One morning, however, he saw that one of the sides of the chest was much thicker than the other, and looking more closely, he discovered that a framed panel picture was clamped against it. . . . It was very dirty, and covered with mould; but he managed to clean it, and, to his great joy, saw that he had fallen by mere chance on the one thing for which he had been looking. Here was an authentic portrait of Mr. W. H., with his hand resting on the dedicatory page of the Sonnets, and on the frame itself could be faintly seen the name of the young man written in black uncial letters on a faded gold ground, "Master Will. Hews."[7]

Just as Cyril is led from the initials of the printer's inscription to discover the name in the sonnets, so it is the initials that "attract his attention" to the chest in which he supposedly discovers the portrait. Cyril is a consistent reader: he moves from obscuring exteriors to revealing initials and finally to discovering written names ("on the frame itself could be faintly seen the name of the young man written").

The forgery is then a visual representation not only of the subject of the sonnets, but of the cryptographic hermeneutic that the theory proposes. Yet if the forgery represents the theory in visual form, it is only *as* a forgery—precisely not as a representation of the "real" —that it induces belief in the theory. For the forgery is, in Wilde's larger aesthetic project, a form of art higher than vulgar imitation of reality. In "The Decay of Lying," for instance, he writes of the liar:

> Nor will he be welcomed by society alone. Art, breaking from the prison-house of realism, will run to greet him, and will kiss his false, beautiful lips, knowing that he alone is in possession of the great secret of all her manifestations.

Similarly, in "The Truth of Masks," Wilde claims:

> Of course the aesthetic value of Shakespeare's plays does not, in the slightest degree, depend on their facts, but on their Truth, and Truth is independent of facts always, inventing or selecting them at pleasure.[8]

The forgery is as "true" as the name it represents, not only in lending it aesthetic form, but also in recapitulating the structure of the name: that form of language truer than the truth. The forgery is more self-consciously artificial—and therefore, in Wilde's scheme, truer to the ideals of art—than any "genuine" portrait. Cyril obviously knows as much, as Erskine notes:

> This was Cyril Graham's theory, evolved as you see purely from the Sonnets themselves, and depending for its acceptance not so much on demonstrable proof or formal evidence, but on a kind of spiritual and artistic sense, by which alone he claimed could the true meaning of the poems be discerned.[9]

The portrait represents the truth of the theory, regardless of its own status as forged. It is simply a tool for overcoming skepticism, as Cyril explains to Erskine: "I did it purely for your sake. You would not be convinced in any other way. It does not affect the truth of the theory."[10] Cyril regularly develops his theory by literalizing images from the sonnets: the character Willie Hughes bodies forth Shakespeare's puns, just as the portrait itself is already figured across the sonnets. For the young man in Shakespeare's poems is described throughout in terms of painting:

> Mine eye hath play'd the painter and hath stell'd
> Thy beauty's form in table of my heart.
>
> .   .   .   .
>
> My love's picture . . . the painted banquet.
>
> .   .   .   .
>
> I never saw that you did painting need,
> And therefore to your fair no painting set.

Cyril's coffered forgery simply dramatizes in fiction Shakespeare's repeated image of his friend as an "up-locked treasure" in a "chest": "Thee have I not lock'd up in any chest / Save where thou art not."

As we move from the theory out into the narrative frame, we can begin to see how the graphic value of names is inscribed all over the story, and, following Wilde's logic, apply to the object of interpretation its own hermeneutic model.

> His very name fascinated me. Willie Hughes! Willie Hughes! How musically it sounded! Yes; who else but he could have been the master-mistress of Shakespeare's passion . . . ?[11]

As the (significantly unnamed) narrator makes this gleeful exclamation, he entices us to attend to the names Wilde chooses for his own characters, if only to find "hidden" there the very strategies with which to decode them.

At the center of the story is Cyril Graham, instigator of the Willie Hughes theory and a near reproduction of Willie himself. Both young men are "of quite extraordinary personal beauty, though evidently somewhat effeminate"; like Shakespeare's presumed catamite, Cyril is "very languid in his manner, and not a little vain of his good looks. . . . He was always dressing up and reciting Shakespeare."[12] Also like Willie, Cyril's name is overdetermined: but not only does it signify multivalently, it also signifies multivalence itself—doing so precisely in the register of the written letter. Cyril conjures up Saint Cyril, originator of the eponymous alphabet, which, for the Victorian reader, is an unintelligible form of writing; appropriately, the coded alphabet's namesake is the character capable of deciphering the alphabetically reduced inscription. Bearing in mind the hagiographic allusion, we can rearrange the letters "c y r i l" to produce "lyric," which in its anagrammatic form comes to stand for the sonnet folded in on itself; encrypted in the decrypter's name is the object of interpretation.

To supplement the suggestion of foreign alphabetics and topsy-turvy poetry inherent in Cyril's first name is his surname, Graham—which we might rewrite as "gram," the supplement itself. The *Oxford English Dictionary* defines a *-gram* as "something written, letter (of the alphabet)," that is, the smallest, most atomized unit of scripted language. The *-gram*, of course, is not a meaningful word by itself, but only a suffix, a subatomic linguistic unit that signifies the atomic unit of material signification: it gains value only when attached to other words (*diagram, anagram*). If the name of the father—Cyril's father, that is—stands for the minimal written unit, then the name of the mother—or more accurately, the mother's father, Crediton (Cyril's guardian)—suggests the entrance of this minute but significant unit into the circuit of signification: only on the course of this circuit does the "gram" accrue meaning. For what is "credit" but the arbitrary, linguistic assignment of value to an absent referent? In Lacanian terms, the name "Cyril (Crediton) Graham" suggests that the law of the father (the literal name of the father) becomes meaningful upon (and is coincident with) the subject's entrance into the symbolic register, the circuit (the "credit") of signification.[13] In this all-too-literal reading of a name, we locate the order of written language (of grammatology), and it is from this figure *of* language *in* language that the story produces its literal, literary reading of the sonnets.

"Cyril Graham" bears forth the operations of written language, and is thus the necessary originator of the Willie Hughes theory: a "Cyril Graham" reading is one that attends to the sonnets' literal signification, one that can produce the name of the object of desire out of the printed matter of the poems. We might at this point recall the

earlier formulation of *The Portrait of Mr. W. H.* as both literary interpretation and literature. If in the first sense the story proceeds according to a determinable hermeneutic practice (to which I've given
the name "Cyril Graham"), then in the second it enacts and performs this practice in the narrated story that constitutes its frame.
The overdetermined name is the juncture of this putative difference
between interpretation and narration: just as within Cyril's theory,
where the hidden name "Willie Hughes" is manifested in a character,
so in Wilde's story is a "Cyril Graham" reading—bound up as it is in
the decoding of written text—amplified and announced in (written
all over, as it were) the thematization of writing itself.

Wilde's story is suffused with letters, signatures, and literature. It
begins and ends in a library, as if to figure the story itself between
the covers of a book, and from the opening—"when the question of
literary forgeries happened to turn up in conversation"—the written
word is at issue. In the portrait there is "crabbed sixteenth-century
handwriting" that can be detected only with a magnifying glass, and
writing on its frame that is visible only once it is cleaned; there are
two suicide notes as well as Cyril's initial invitation to Erskine to
learn of the theory—though the latter "was rather surprised at his
taking the trouble to write."[14] Writing *in* the novella comes to seem
like the displaced performance of the interpretive model I've identified, as if the story were compelled to keep secret its own method of
deciphering secrets exactly by broadcasting that method everywhere
in the image of writing.

The sonnet theory is committed to writing each time it is reinvented, until it takes on the tangible form of a letter—though a
letter that is by definition unrecoverable:

> I have not any copy of my letter, I regret to say, nor have I been
> able to lay my hand upon the original; but I remember that I
> went over the whole ground, and covered sheets of paper with
> passionate reiteration of the arguments and proofs that my study
> had suggested to me. . . . I put into the letter all my faith.[15]

To put the theory into a letter is not simply to transcribe it: more than
its literal epistolary location, the Willie Hughes theory has the material qualities of a letter, in that only one person at a time can pos-
sess (that is, believe) it. It can be passed from one person to another,

but it cannot be shared or divided. Yet as Wilde would painfully discover, letters are hardly inviolable: they are subject to stealing and misinterpretation, and can lead to criminal prosecution.

The theory's circuit through the story illustrates its indissoluble unity as epistolary object. In the first exchange, when Erskine begins to convince the narrator, he states, "As I don't believe in the theory, I am not likely to convert you to it." In the exchange that takes place twenty years earlier, when Erskine is the recent convert, he exclaims upon discovering Cyril's forgery, "You never even believed in [the theory] yourself. If you had, you would not have committed a forgery to prove it." In the third exchange—as the narrator returns the theory to Erskine toward the end of the story—the narrator confesses:

> No sooner, in fact, had I sent [the letter] off than a curious reaction came over me. It seemed to me that I had given away my capacity for belief in the Willie Hughes theory of the Sonnets, that something had gone out of me, as it were, and that I was perfectly indifferent to the whole subject.[16]

The theory's determining characteristic is this: to convince someone else is not to believe in it oneself. The repetition of this topos suggests that belief in the theory is material, exchangeable, and indivisible: its representational form is precisely a letter. Belief "goes out of one" only to lodge itself (for the moment) in the recipient. Like Lacan's formulation for the purloined letter of Poe's story, the theory passes through and locates the subject, but continues ever on its trajectory.

The story's most overt letters, however—the suicide notes—curiously subvert its pervasive insistence on writing. Cyril kills himself after the forgery is discovered, leaving behind a note for Erskine that claims "he was going to offer his life as a sacrifice to the secret of the Sonnets." The suicide note is a form of absolute writing: it is unidirectional, unanswerable. Yet the note is peculiarly ineffective, for in this story a man's suicide is precisely what testifies to the insincerity of his belief: Erskine responds to the death by saying that "a thing is not necessarily true because a man dies for it,"[17] and after Erskine's death the narrator comments, "no man dies for what he knows to be true. Men die for what they want to be true, for what some terror in their hearts tells them is not true."[18]

Yet Cyril's suicide fails in a more important way, too, as the performance of his death covers over the very name that he had hoped to sustain by killing himself: "he shot himself with a revolver. Some of the blood splashed upon the frame of the picture, just where the name [Willie Hughes] had been painted."[19] Cyril offers his life to the theory of the sonnets, but his blood literally obliterates the name he uncovered. The story's ubiquitous images of writing dramatize in "literature" the procedures of "interpretation," yet the interpreter's ultimate act of writing—his suicide note—would seem to traduce his interpretation by figuratively covering with blood the name it has worked to decipher.

If Cyril's interpretive methods finally undo themselves, how are we to account for Erskine's suicide note, at once a rehearsal and inversion of Cyril's? For Erskine's letter is a forgery: as the doctor reveals to the narrator, Erskine had known for months that he was to die of consumption. To answer this question, we need to know how an "Erskine" interpretation of the sonnets would read and how such an interpretation might be enunciated in its own register in the framing narrative; only then can we understand how his suicide stands in relation to the interpretive model that requires it. But to identify Erskine's hermeneutic strategy—distinct from Cyril's, and linked in certain ways to Wilde's own—we must return to the matter of naming.

When he comes to narrate the theory, Erskine occupies the position of sonneteer, adorer of his "very fascinating, and very foolish, and very heartless" friend;[20] he might thereby stand in for the poets, Will and Oscar, themselves admirers of lovely boy-actors. By name he is "kin" of the "Ers," defined as follows in the *Oxford English Dictionary*:

> In 18th c., *Erse* was used in literary England as the ordinary designation of the Gaelic of Scotland, and occasionally extended to the Irish Gaelic; at present [1893] some writers apply it to the Irish alone. Now nearly obsolete.

If "Erse" was nearly obsolete by 1893, its homophone, "arse," was obsolete only in "polite use," according to the *OED*. And who, more than Wilde, we might ask, is kin of the Erse and of the arse? Erse:

"The issue that the Wilde legend has obscured," one critic writes, "is that until the mid-nineties, literary culture had linked Wilde's sexuality to his Celtic ethnicity rather than to his homoeroticism."[21] Arse: "those red rose-leaf lips of yours"—once again Wilde's self-declared Shakespearean poetry, now comprehensible (as it probably was to the prosecution) as coded sodomitical language.[22]

The peculiar conjunction of Irish and homosexual discourses produces a certain poetics to which *The Portrait of Mr. W. H.* gives the name "Erskine." It is worth noting in this context that *Mr. W. H.* is the work that announces the arrival of Wilde's homosexuality for several critics.[23] And if Wilde progressed, in the popular imagination, from a tolerated Irish nationalist[24] to a scandalous homosexual, then "Erskine" is also the name for what he represented to the English public. By the same logic that produced the "Cyril Graham" hermeneutic as the decoding of scripted names, we might then expect to discover in "Erskine" a reading attuned to the operations of homoerotic desire through the written word. (The names for these interpretive strategies are kept between quotation marks as an indication that, although the story supplies the terms, it does not rigidly assign these hermeneutics to the characters per se: each strategy is rather suggested and represented by a character, but not necessarily articulated exclusively by him.) While the story endorses both interpretive projects, it would appear to privilege the latter, both in allowing it to frame the former (within the narrative) and in its evocative consonance with Wilde's own concerns.

The affinity between Wilde and "Erskine" becomes clearer if we turn for a moment to another of his letters, this one to Edmond de Goncourt, dated 17 December 1891. The context is Wilde's French having previously been misunderstood—though he is quick to admit "sans doute c'était de ma faute":

> On peut adorer une langue sans bien la parler, comme on peut aimer une femme sans la connaître. Français de sympathie, je suis Irlandais de race, et les Anglais m'ont condamné à parler le langage de Shakespeare.[25]

It is, appropriately, only in a foreign tongue that Wilde can name the language he is condemned to speak: not English, *bien sûr*, but "the language of Shakespeare." He adores French without speaking it too well, just as he could love a woman without knowing her: this French "heterosexual" discourse (which he would go on to use in *Salome*) is reserved for objects that are admired from afar, never really loved by "knowing."[26] The language of Shakespeare, which he claims the English forced upon the Irish, takes on the value of Wilde's homoerotic discourse: it is the language of men, for men, between men. When an Irishman is forced to speak in this Shakespearean tongue—a language different from the one that he adores like a woman—it surely has the sound of "Erskine's" voice.[27]

The homoerotic valence that Wilde attributed to Shakespeare's poetry becomes even more vivid if we recall for a moment his self-proclaimed Shakespearean letter to Lord Alfred, and the trials that exposed it. Wilde and his counsel repeatedly defended his obviously amatory letter by claiming that it was "literature"—not a mere love letter—and thereby exempt from the usual (i.e., bourgeois, "Philistine") norms of moral judgment. To this effect, Edward Clarke, Wilde's counsel, stated in his opening speech at the first trial:

> The words of that letter, gentlemen, may appear extravagant to those in the habit of writing commercial correspondence, or those ordinary letters which the necessities of life force upon one every day; but Mr. Wilde is a poet, and the letter is considered by him as a prose sonnet, and one of which he is in no way ashamed and is prepared to produce anywhere as an expression of true poetic feeling, and with no relation whatever to the hateful and repulsive suggestions put to it in the plea in this case.[28]

Despite the prosecution's insistence that the letter made "repulsive suggestions," Wilde maintained, "I think it is a beautiful letter. It is a poem. I was not writing an ordinary letter. You might as well cross-examine me as to whether *King Lear* or a sonnet of Shakespeare was proper." Yet Wilde's interpretation of Shakespeare's sonnets was hardly deemed proper by the English public, for when the prosecutor inquired, with reference to *Mr. W. H.*, "I believe you have written an article to show that Shakespeare's sonnets were suggestive of unnatural vice," Wilde responded, "On the contrary I have written an article to show that they are not. I objected to such a perversion being put upon Shakespeare." Where the court detected unnatural vice, Wilde instead argued for the "great affection of an elder for a younger man," an affection that he identified in a well-established literary tradition. It was through this tradition that he equated his own erotic language with that of Shakespeare's, as he made clear in the following impassioned speech from the second trial (which was met by "loud applause, mingled with some hisses"):

> "The love that dare not speak its name" in this century is such a great affection of an elder for a younger man as there was between David and Jonathan, such as Plato made the very basis of his philosophy, and such as you find in the sonnets of Michelangelo and Shakespeare. It is that deep, spiritual affection that is as pure as it is perfect. It dictates and pervades great works of art like those of Shakespeare and Michelangelo, and those two letters of mine, such as they are. It is in this century misunderstood . . . and on account of it I am placed where I am now. It is beautiful, it is fine, it is the noblest form of affection. There is nothing unnatural about it.[29]

The discussion of sonnets by Michelangelo and Shakespeare refers to the enlarged version of *The Portrait of Mr. W. H.*, in which Wilde included a dissertation on the history of poetry with themes of "platonic friendship." Wilde's consistent association of himself with Shakespeare centers precisely on their shared erotic themes;[30] yet *The Portrait of Mr. W. H.* extends the parallels between the two playwrights' poetry to include the very capacity of language to express or contain the erotic.

The trials hinged upon conflicting interpretations of Wilde's letters: while the prosecution argued that the letters were erotic (that is, criminally homoerotic), Wilde insisted on the purely aesthetic value of their language. *The Portrait of Mr. W. H.* similarly vacillates between two interpretive strategies, for while the "Cyril Graham" project is to decode names encrypted in the text, the "Erskine" method seems inversely to inscribe into the text secrets—which are nevertheless open—with particular homoerotic content.[31] As in many of Wilde's other works, the "secrets" are, paradoxically, entirely absent at the same moment they are everywhere present. The examples that immediately come to mind are Dorian Gray's mysterious vices, Algernon's unseen friend Bunbury, and, epigrammatically, "The Sphinx without a Secret." As usual with Wilde, however, the best paradigm is in his life: at the opening of *Lady Windermere's Fan* in 1895, he put out word that members of the audience were to don green carnations, knowing they would think it "must be some secret symbol," and asserting that it meant "nothing whatsoever, but that is just what nobody will guess."[32] An absent secret, certainly, but one with a particular referent: unknown to most of the audience, the green carnation was a symbol coded for homosexuality in Paris—and therein the logic of the open secret, inscribed everywhere upon the audience and yet apparent to no one. As Cecil Graham, a character in the same play, observes, "nothing looks so like innocence as an indiscretion."[33]

In *The Portrait of Mr. W. H.*, the open secret (to the extent that it is a secret) has similar characteristics, as, for instance, indignantly described by biographer Rupert Croft-Cooke:

> [The story] would have passed . . . if it had been put forward as a serious and rather boring literary theory, but to make a delightful spree of Shakespeare's homosexuality was unforgivable in the 1880s. It might fool the editor of *Blackwood's* who saw in it nothing but quaint antiquarian theorising, but it could not fool more knowing readers, who considered that Wilde was suggesting England's greatest poet was a bugger, and doing so by introducing as narrator "one of the pretty undergraduates who used to act girls' parts."[34]

But beyond the rather heavy-handed homoerotic imagery associated with cross-dressing in Shakespeare, there are in the story certain internal dynamics as well as interpretive practices that come to be homosexually charged—in much the same way that coded writing was both thematized and developed as hermeneutic practice around "Cyril Graham." Just as Cyril leads us to decode names, that is, Erskine will lead us to decode desire in the text. As Cyril extracts the hidden painting from a chest in order to verify his theory, Erskine seeks "to unlock the secret of Shakespeare's heart," to provide "the only perfect key to Shakespeare's Sonnets that has ever been made."[35]

At one level, erotic desire in this text is quite explicit: Shakespeare's sonnets are called "strangely passionate poems"; Willie is likewise evoked in "passionate" language: "so well had Shakespeare drawn him, with his golden hair, his tender flower-like grace, his dreamy deep-sunken eyes, his delicate mobile limbs, and his white lily hands." Erskine's initial gesture toward the narrator indicates a more-than-avuncular affection: "Erskine, who was a good deal older than I was, and had been listening to me with the amused deference of a man of forty, suddenly put his hand upon my shoulder." And Erskine depicts his earlier and deeper attachment to Cyril in striking terms:

> I was a year or two older than he was, but we were immense friends, and did all our work and all our play together. There was, of course, a good deal more play than work, but I cannot say that I am sorry for that. . . . I was absurdly devoted to him. . . . He certainly was wonderfully handsome. . . . I think he was the most splendid creature I ever saw.[36]

Cyril clearly knows as much about himself: "he always set an absurdly high value on personal appearance, and once read a paper before our debating society to prove that it was better to be good-looking than to be good."

The sonnet theory is always constituted between these erotically charged pairs of men. The originary couple, Willie and Shakespeare, comes to be replaced by Erskine and Cyril; the latters' relationship is reproduced by the narrator and Erskine, though now Erskine is the disbelieving purveyor of the theory rather than its credulous recipient; in the final configuration, Erskine and the narrator switch roles, and Erskine once more accepts the theory. If, as I've argued, belief in the theory has the qualities of material text, then it is not only *about* desire (since the content of the theory is the name of the object of desire), but it takes on the asymptotic language of desire itself: "It seemed to me that I was always on the brink of absolute verification, but that I could never really attain to it."[37] Again, like Lacan's version of the purloined letter, belief in the theory constitutes the subjectivity of the one who possesses it. Yet when we augment this analogy with the specific erotics of the story, we find that—precisely *un*like the oedipal triangle in which psychoanalysis situates production of the subject—Wilde's text (as well as Shakespeare's, read in this way) posits subjectivity only in a homoerotic duality. The oedipal myth appears to be supplanted by some version of projected narcissistic desire.

In this "Erskine" reading, it is homoerotic desire that is written all over the text: such desire is, predictably, the content of its "open secret." Yet homoerotic desire also provides the very hermeneutic model for exposing open secrets, as it has traditionally in our culture —from "in the closet" to "coming out," from coded manners and apparel to (Lord Alfred's best line) "the love that dare not speak its name."[38] Homosexuality provides the literary content and, at the same time, the hermeneutic practice for explicating that content, just as the topos "deciphered writing" was both the content and the strategy of the "Cyril Graham" reading.

I have suggested that the "Erskine" interpretation corresponds to an extent with Wilde's own, if only for the fact of a name. Proceeding by the same logic, we might expect evidence of this alliance to locate itself with a kind of seriousness in Wilde's "signature effect," as carefully attended to as the sounding of "Will" in the works of the bard.[39] Wilde invokes his own name three times in the story: first at a moment of uneasiness about gender, again at a point of imminent revelation, and finally at a moment suggesting both the one and the other. In the first instance, Cyril Graham is, "of course, *wild* to go on the stage"—that is, to transform himself into a woman, as he does so well: "Cyril Graham was the only perfect Rosalind I have ever seen." The second occurs at the moment Cyril presents his theory: "He told me that he had at last discovered the true secret of Shakespeare's Sonnets . . . had found out who Mr. W. H. really was. He was perfectly *wild* with delight." The last occasion returns us to the unanswered question of how to interpret Erskine's false suicide. In the story's penultimate scene, when the narrator learns of the "horribly grotesque tragedy" that Erskine has died, he admits:

> I said all kinds of *wild* things, and the people in the hall looked curiously at me.
>
> Suddenly Lady Erskine, in deep mourning, passed across the vestibule.[40]

The narrator still believes Erskine to have committed suicide when the latter's mother materializes. Here, around the representation of the only woman in the story, a kind of hysterical ("wild") self-reference arises. As if to perform the anxiety surrounding that most glaring absence from the Willie Hughes theory of the sonnets—the dark lady—Lady Erskine appears in funereal black, a figurative dark lady, seeming to necessitate the sounding of Oscar's own name.[41] If it is objected that Wilde's self-reference is altogether too marginal to be of much significance, it need only be pointed out that this is precisely the complaint often sounded by Shakespeareans faced with the Willie Hughes theory (at least when it is based on "internal evidence" and not, as it was for Lord Alfred, on historical data): "Why not 'Will Rose'?" some critics have replied, since *Rose* is capitalized and italicized in the sonnets as much as *Hews*. Obviously this misses the point, since what makes Wilde's theory compelling is that it can be obscenely literal (in deciphering the name) at the same time that it is thoroughly literary in describing and rehearsing the texture of the poems. That Wilde's theory operates at the level of the letter should encourage, not dissuade us from reading likewise.

The "Cyril Graham" reading of this scene would easily make reference to Shakespeare's play on words in Sonnet 132 about the dark lady in mo[u]rning. As with the depiction of Willie Hughes, it would understand the story to enact dramatically a pun that is purely graphic in the sonnets: the difference between "mourning" and "morning" is only a written letter, visually (not aurally) discernible. Its narrative representation takes the form of the figure across whose body the Shakespearean pun is executed. The "Erskine" reading, on the other hand, might discover an analogy between the undesirability of Shakespeare's dark lady—the paradoxically unattractive object of desire—and the unattainable dark mother as object of the dead son's desire. Here we seem to have returned to the (inevitable) oedipal mythology, hard as this story may have tried to swerve from it. In the first reading, the mourning mother acts out the language of Shakespeare's dark lady in an all-too-obvious way (implying that the visually determined "decoding" is another of this text's open secrets); in the second, she likewise manifests that all-too-obvious object—"mother"—who is the ultimate horizon for erotic desire in any version of psychoanalysis. Like Cyril's suicide, which upends his theory by spilling blood on the very name it disclosed, Erskine's death seems to disrupt (by exposing) the entire "Erskine" project of locating homoerotic desire in the text: his death can produce nothing but a dark lady as mother, that profoundly unattainable (and, to consciousness, undesirable) object of desire.

To reinforce this reading, I want to turn for a moment to the pornographic novel *Teleny* (1890), often attributed in part to Wilde, which has some close affinities with *The Portrait of Mr. W. H.* The narrative structure is strikingly similar: Des Grieux, the central character, tells his story (like Erskine) to an unnamed narrator, relating his youthful relationship with a brilliant, beautiful young artist, Teleny, who (like Cyril) kills himself after a "secret" is revealed. Given the essential explicitness of pornography, a reading of *Mr. W. H.* "through" *Teleny* produces a curiously explicit version of many elements of the present interpretation. The two men are much more nearly doubles ("I stared at myself within the looking-glass, and I saw Teleny in it instead of myself. . . . I could not feel him at all; in fact, it seemed to me as if I were touching my own body"), their relationship is overtly sexual (to say the least), and the parallel between the narrator and the artist (Teleny) is clearly articulated ("I think I can see him leaning . . . as you are leaning now, for you have many of his feline, graceful ways"), where the similarity between the narrator and Cyril Graham is only implied in *Mr. W. H.* The close association between the "key" to Shakespeare's art and homosexuality in *Mr. W. H.* is carried over to *Teleny* in the form of a clear correspondence between the sexual and the artistic: Teleny's brilliant piano playing is always contingent upon the erotic link with Des Grieux. Yet if the "secret" of *Mr. W. H.* is its homoerotic component, then *Teleny*, as a pornographic text, is implicated in a pervasively secretive readership, however explicit its content may be.[42]

What is particularly revealing about *Mr. W. H.* in terms of *Teleny* is the force of the mother. In *Teleny* Des Grieux's mother is finally what comes between the men, as she and Teleny carry on an affair behind Des Grieux's back. The mother is an expressly, irrepressibly erotic force, yet her sudden insinuation within the homosexual affair ultimately performs the same function as the startling appearance of the "dark lady" in *The Portrait of Mr. W. H.*: she suggests the closing in of an oedipally driven heterosexuality, even if "perverted" in this pornographic form. Des Grieux's mother performs and reveals (in the typically, excessively explicit manner of pornography) the function of Erskine's mother in *Mr. W. H.* That the "dark lady" in *Mr. W. H.* is so marginal as to be almost unnoticeable is thus in one sense testament to her very significance; given the weight of the opposing terms "trivial" and "important" in Wilde's aesthetic lexicon, moreover, a "woman of no importance," one suspects, will never be entirely trivial. However strenuously this text tries to establish a relation of desire outside of and against restrictive heterosexual-oedipal models from the "straight" world (and to whatever extent it is successful), it finally lets in, if only for a moment, that classic figure of oedipal desire.

Yet if the procedure of this reading has been throughout to display the mutual and simultaneous effects of "literature" on "interpretation" and vice versa, then Wilde's entire project—what can now be understood as "reading by inversion"—will in one sense have already exposed its homoerotic predilection. For it is well known that both the language and the trope of "inversion" were common figures for homosexuality in the second half of the nineteenth century;[43] and for a story that is centrally concerned with the interrelation of literature and interpretation, such a trope overarches the text even as it can never be articulated.

Returning to a place near where I started, I want to examine one more letter of Wilde's. In this one, from July 1889, to Robert Ross, Wilde discloses the origin of *The Portrait of Mr. W. H.*:

> Indeed the story is half yours, and but for you would not have been written. . . . Now that Willie Hughes has been revealed to the world, we must have another secret.[44]

It is apparently true that Ross gave Wilde the idea for the story, and rather fitting that it was both a "secret" and a collaborative project between the older poet and the pretty young man (Ross reportedly claimed to have been "the first boy that Oscar ever had").[45] After the story was published in *Blackwood's* magazine in July 1889, Wilde continued to work on it, completing (but not publishing) the much expanded version in 1893. The manuscript, stolen from Wilde's flat shortly after he was arrested, disappeared and remained unpublished until 1921, when a pirated edition appeared in the United States; it was not published in an authorized edition until 1958, by Wilde's son Vyvyan Holland.

In the longer version, Wilde made numerous additions to the middle chapters, where the narrator develops the sonnet theory, though most of the added material has little bearing on the theory itself. It elaborates and deepens the invented biography of Shakespeare, introduces a catalog of boy-actors through history, and adds an essay on platonic "friendship" and homoerotic poetry (of Michelangelo, Montaigne, and others). The effect of the later version is to alter the balance between framing narrative and sonnet theory greatly in favor of the latter. The only significant deletion in the 1893 edition is the highly compressed and suggestive image of Cyril's blood spilling onto the name etched in the portrait's frame. Between 1889 and 1893 Wilde's erotic preferences seem to have altered significantly as well, and I would therefore suggest that the first version—with its bloodied writing—is more nearly allied with what I've called the "Cyril Graham" reading, while the second—as a clearly identified treatise on homosexual poetry—is strongly weighted toward the "Erskine" interpretation. That the Willie Hughes theory came to be identified with homosexuality for both Wilde and his readers suggests his motivation for expanding just that component of the story, even at the expense of the thematics of graphic writing. The resulting imbalance produces a noticeably weaker, more diffuse narrative, though a correspondingly richer literary history.

Beyond the immediate circumstances of its production, moreover, we can now understand that the "real history" of Wilde's theory curiously reproduces the story's own internal "inverted" dynamic, suggesting the infinite regress (*mise en abîme*) of such a project. Probably the most hackneyed question of literary identity in English, the matter of the characters in the sonnets and of the dedication has received innumerable hypotheses. The Willie Hughes theory was first put forward in 1766 by Thomas Tyrwhitt, and Wilde's work is in one sense unabashed plagiarism. Samuel Butler published a similar theory in 1899, without acknowledging Wilde, and Lord Alfred joined the fray with the ostentatiously titled *True History of Shakespeare's Sonnets* in 1933 (though he "utterly rejects the notion that Shakespeare was a homosexualist").[46] Unlike Wilde, these and most other critics engage the theory as if it referred to a historical and biographical reality—though ultimately Lord Alfred had some success in this respect. If "the one flaw in the theory is that it presupposes the existence of the person whose existence is the subject of dispute," then Douglas may well have overcome it. Incredibly, after his book was published, Douglas learned from records in Canterbury of the existence of a William Hewes connected with Marlowe's company, exactly as the theory had predicted.[47]

The issue, of course, is not whether Lord Alfred had the final, incontrovertible proof of Willie Hughes's existence: at least that is never the interest of *The Portrait of Mr. W. H.* In Wilde's terms, Lord Alfred's discovery only demonstrates the ascendancy of art over life; in fact it illustrates quite nicely the claim Wilde makes in "The Decay of Lying":

> All that I desire to point out is the general principle that Life imitates Art far more than Art imitates Life, and I feel sure that if you think seriously about it you will find that it is true. Life holds the mirror up to Art, and either reproduces some strange type imagined by a painter or sculptor, or realizes in fact what has been dreamed in fiction.[48]

There is no indication that the volumes of discussion over identity in the sonnets will ever abate; yet Wilde alone seems to have engaged the question at just the literary register in which it is articulated. *The Portrait of Mr. W. H.* soundly repudiates the insistent referentiality of virtually every other Shakespearean scholar, for the story is inextricably self-involved in the same way that it is involved in the sonnets: its discovery of graphic writing and homoerotic desire as the sonnets' own issues are written, if always in "inverted" form, all over the story.

Notes

1 *Selected Letters of Oscar Wilde*, ed. Rupert Hart-Davis (London, 1979), 107, 169.

2 Ibid., 169–70.

3 Oscar Wilde, *The Portrait of Mr. W. H.*, in *Complete Shorter Fiction*, ed. Isobel Murray (London, 1979). This edition, which I rely on for the most part, reprints the story as it was published in 1889. When citing the expanded version of 1893, *The Portrait of Mr. W. H.*, ed. Vyvyan Holland (London, 1958), I include Holland's name.

4 Ibid., 140.

5 This discussion is indebted to Joel Fineman, "The Significance of Literature: *The Importance of Being Earnest*," October 15 (Winter 1980): 79–90, and *Shakespeare's Perjured Eye: The Invention of Poetic Subjectivity in the Sonnets* (Berkeley, 1986), 28–29.

6 Wilde, *Portrait of Mr. W. H.*, 148, 139.

7 Ibid., 150, 166, 149–50.

8 Oscar Wilde, *Intentions* (New York, 1930), 29, 246.

9 Wilde, *Portrait of Mr. W. H.*, 147.

10 Ibid., 151.

11 Ibid., 159.

12 Ibid., 140, 142.

13 Cyril's etymology is fruitful as well, for the name derives from the Greek *Kurillos*, "probably from *kurios*, master, lord," according to the *American Heritage Dictionary*. And its Indo-European root, *ku-ro-*, means "swollen, strong, powerful." What more vivid image of the phallic name of the father could we produce than that of a "master" who is "swollen"? Furthermore, both his effeminacy/hermaphroditism ("of course Cyril was always cast for the girls' parts") and the fact that his parents are dead ("they had been drowned in a horrible yachting accident off the Isle of Wight")—thus putting him in the care of Lord Crediton—suggest his immanent vacillation between "Graham" and "Crediton": he is the boy who plays the perfect girl, the man who bears his father's name in his mother's house, the figure of a written unit engaged in the circuit of signification.

14 Wilde, *Portrait of Mr. W. H.*, 139, 141, 150, 143.

15 Ibid., 164.

16 Ibid., 141, 151, 165.

17 Ibid., 152.

18 Holland, ed., *Portrait of Mr. W. H.*, 89. Wilde had expressed the same sentiment in a more personal vein in a letter to Harry Marillier from 1886: "I myself would sacrifice everything for a new experience, and I know there is no such thing as a new experience at all. I think I would more readily die for what I do not believe in than for what I hold to be true." Cited in Richard Ellmann, *Oscar Wilde* (New York, 1988), 270, 297.

19 Wilde, *Portrait of Mr. W. H.*, 151–52.

20 Ibid., 140.

21   Sandra Siegel, "Anecdotes, Scandal, and *Dorian Gray*'s Doubles" (unpublished, Cornell University/Payne Whitney Psychoanalytic Institute, 1986), 12. Siegel argues that Wilde's attachment to Celtic culture and his involvement in the radical wing of the women's movement (especially as editor of *Woman's World*) combined with a peculiar force in him that significantly threatened bourgeois English culture.

22   I am grateful to Christopher Craft for pointing out the allusion. If we pursued the homoerotic puns, we would eventually locate Willie Hughes—concatenating the famous Elizabethan play on "will" as both sexual desire and sexual organs, "use" as sexual intercourse—and finally the poet himself: for the image of "shake spear" is one of phallic thrusting.

23   Rupert Croft-Cooke, *The Unrecorded Life of Oscar Wilde* (New York, 1972), writes that Wilde's "comparatively discreet manner of existence during the years following his marriage [in 1884] was disturbed by a number of factors in 1889 and 1890, including [his] wilful and deliberate rashness in publishing a short story of homosexual interest called *The Portrait of Mr. W. H.* in *Blackwood's Magazine*" (111). Introducing the story, Isobel Murray writes: "At a time when homosexuality was considered one of the vilest human aberrations, severely punishable by law, to suggest that Shakespeare wrote his Sonnets to a boy actor whose personality dominated him was courting disaster. William Blackwood was either brave or a little out of touch when he wrote to Wilde accepting [the story]" (13). Likewise, in his introduction to *The Portable Oscar Wilde*, ed. Richard Aldington and Stanley Weintraub (New York, 1981), Richard Aldington cites allusions to a work of Virgil's in *Mr. W. H.*: "an exquisitely beautiful poem but flagrantly homosexual. To anyone who had read Virgil—and at that time most upper-class Englishmen had—*The Portrait of Mr. W. H.* was an unequivocal declaration and an insolent defiance. Prudent men began to drop Mr. Wilde's acquaintance" (23).

24   See, for instance, the *Scots Observer* review in Stuart Mason, *Oscar Wilde: Art and Morality* (London, 1912), 90–94, which compares *Dorian Gray* to a fine performance of an offensive song—namely, "God Save Ireland."

25   Hart-Davis, ed., *Selected Letters*, 100.

26   Roland Barthes strikes a similar note in *Roland Barthes* (Paris, 1975) when he describes French, his "mother tongue," as the "language of women": "Tout ce blocage [of other languages] est l'envers d'un amour: celui de la langue maternelle (la langue des femmes). Ce n'est pas un amour national . . . [je] ne croi[s] à la précellence d'aucune langue et [j']éprouve souvent les manques cruels de français" (119).

27   In addition to the confusion between Wilde's Celtic ethnicity and his deviant sexuality, the latter was conflated with class issues as well, as in the vitriolic review in the *Scots Observer* of *Dorian Gray* from 5 July 1890, which concludes: "Mr. Wilde has brains, and art, and style; but if he can write for none but outlawed noblemen and perverted telegraph-boys, the sooner he takes to tailoring (or some other decent trade) the better for his own reputation and the public morals" (Mason, *Art and Morality*, 76). Wilde is accused of "descending" to infernal re-

gions of both sex and class; the advice to seek "some decent trade" is an obvious class jab.

28 H. Montgomery Hyde, *The Three Trials of Oscar Wilde* (New York, 1956), 112–13.

29 Ibid., 133, 130, 236.

30 Ellmann, *Oscar Wilde*, relates the following anecdote, of a more personal association: "Wilde once explained, at Lady Archibald Campbell's, why he thought he looked like Shakespeare. He ended a brilliant monologue by saying he intended to have a bronze medallion struck of his own profile and Shakespeare's. 'And I suppose, Mr. Wilde,' said Lady Archibald, 'your profile will protrude beyond Shakespeare's' " (289).

31 My discussion of the "open secret" derives in part from D. A. Miller, "Secret Subjects, Open Secrets," *Dickens Studies Annual* 14 (1985): 17–38. Miller describes it as "the double bind of a secrecy which must always be rigorously maintained in the face of a secret that everybody already knows, since this is the very condition that entitles me to my subjectivity in the first place" (19).

32 Reginia Gagnier, *Idylls of the Marketplace: Oscar Wilde and the Victorian Public* (Stanford, 1986), 163–65.

33 *The Works of Oscar Wilde*, ed. G. F. Maine (London, 1948), 391.

34 Croft-Cooke, *Unrecorded Life of Oscar Wilde*, 111–12.

35 Wilde, *Portrait of Mr. W. H.*, 152. It is worth noting that the convergence of homoerotic themes, death, doubling, and narcissism on a "Will" is curiously anticipated in Edgar Allan Poe's short story "William Wilson" (1839). In Poe's gothic tale, the doppelgänger drives the narrator to a murder/suicide in which the homoerotic and the homicidal are completely identified.

36 Wilde, *Portrait of Mr. W. H.*, 144, 159, 139, 141–42.

37 Ibid., 163.

38 In "The Epistemology of the Closet (I)," *Raritan* 7 (Spring 1988): 39–69, Eve Kosofsky Sedgwick identifies this historically strong link between the secrecy/exposure topos in general and the homosexual secret in particular. "A whole cluster of the most crucial sites for the contestation of meaning in twentieth-century Western culture are . . . quite indelibly marked with the historical specificity of homosocial/homosexual definition, notably but not exclusively male, from around the turn of the century. Among those sites are . . . the pairings secrecy/disclosure and private/public . . . condensed in the figures of 'the closet' and 'coming out' " (43–44).

39 For a discussion of Oscar's self-conscious use of "wild," see Karl Beckson, "The Autobiographical Signature in *The Picture of Dorian Gray*," *Victorian Newsletter* 69 (Spring 1986): 30–32. Beckson's insights resonate, in a literal way, with the *Punch* review (12 July 1890) that describes *Dorian Gray* as "Oscar Wilde's Wildest and Oscarest work" (cited in Mason, *Art and Morality*, 159).

40 Wilde, *Portrait of Mr. W. H.*, 143–44, 168.

41 In the later version of the story, Wilde accounts for the dark lady sonnets by insisting that the sequence be reordered so that the young man sonnets contain,

and are not superseded by them. The narrator proposes that Shakespeare initially feigns love for the dark lady only in order to draw her away from Willie Hughes, but "suddenly he finds that what his tongue had spoken his soul had listened to," and he is helplessly in love with her, despite her ugliness. Eventually he recovers, she departs, and the poet and the actor are reunited (Holland, ed., *Portrait of Mr. W. H.*, 63–64, 60–73).

42 Oscar Wilde and Others, *Teleny*, ed. John McRae (London, 1986), 46, 110, 159. On the supposed "secret society" of men who wrote and read the manuscript by circulating it through a London bookshop, see McRae's introduction.

43 See, for instance, Havelock Ellis's *Sexual Inversion*, vol. 2 of *Studies in the Psychology of Sex* (Philadelphia, 1920). For a rather graphic account of Wilde's pathology, see "The Problem of Wilde's Inversion," Appendix E in Hyde, *Three Trials*. Sedgwick argues that "inversion" continues as strong as ever in the cultural imagination of gay life ("Epistemology of the Closet," 58).

44 Hart-Davis, ed., *Selected Letters*, 78.

45 Hyde, *Three Trials*, 371.

46 Lord Alfred Douglas, *The True History of Shakespeare's Sonnets* (London, 1933), 19.

47 Wilde, *Portrait of Mr. W. H.*, 166, 160. See Gagnier, *Idylls of the Marketplace*, 43–44. William Freeman, *The Life of Lord Alfred Douglas* (London, 1948), substantiates the claim with the report of one Mrs. M. A. Idiens: "Douglas said that he had discovered and proved to be a fact that Mr. W. H. was William Hughes, the handsome boy who for years acted the part of Shakespeare's heroines. Douglas had traced the family of the boy to Canterbury, where he lived with his parents and where Douglas obtained full particulars. He had not published his discoveries because his publisher had 'packed up' and he did not feel sufficiently energetic to obtain another" (282).

48 Wilde, *Intentions*, 39.

Michael Moon

Disseminating Whitman

Between the novel and America there are
peculiar and intimate connections." These
Sam Wellerish words are Leslie Fiedler's opening gambit in his 1960 study *Love and Death in
the American Novel.*[1] I propose to supplement
(dangerously, I would hope) Fiedler's thesis
by insisting on a third term—the homoerotic
—which is submerged in his neatly symmetrical linking of those two eighteenth-century
bourgeois creations, the novel and the United
States. In view of a large body of work
done in the past decade on gender historiography, one might revise the opening words
of Fiedler's book to read, "Between American literature and homoeroticism there have
historically been peculiar and intimate connections." In rewriting the sentence in this
fashion, one may be doing nothing more than
spelling out what was already at least implicit
in it as Fiedler originally wrote it, for his
use of the terms "peculiar and intimate" to
characterize relations between America and
its classic writing connotes "homosexuality"
in a readily recognizable, albeit euphemis-

tically encoded, fifties way. This would be in keeping with *Love and Death*'s once scandalous thesis: that in the body of writing which D. H. Lawrence had canonized in the twenties as classic American literature, "mature heterosexuality" (that shibboleth and ever-vanishing horizon of American postwar ego psychology and its ancillary schools of cultural and literary criticism) counts for little or nothing, and its allegedly central place has long been usurped in our literature by romances of interracial, male-homoerotic union—Natty Bumppo and Chingachgook, Ishmael and Queequeg, Huck Finn and Jim being among the chief prototypes of these. "Our great novelists . . . tend to avoid treating the passionate encounter of a man and a woman, which we expect at the center of a novel," Fiedler laments, asking, "Where is our *Madame Bovary*, our *Anna Karenina*, our *Pride and Prejudice* or *Vanity Fair?*"[2]

Thirty years later, amid an ongoing series of extraordinary changes in the ways many American women and gay men conceive of and perform our social and political roles, as well as a comparably radical reconception of literary studies in some influential quarters (in the same period, Afro-American studies, gender studies, deconstruction, Lacanian psychoanalytic theory, canon revision, the "new historicism," and other intellectual movements have transformed academic literary discourse), students of American cultural history are proposing new answers to the kinds of questions Fiedler raised at the beginning of the 1960s. The work of the past decade or so that has most directly empowered those of us concerned with overturning homophobic accounts (like Fiedler's) of the markedly homoerotic character of American literature has been Carroll Smith-Rosenberg's and Eve Kosofsky Sedgwick's critique of the dynamics of various forms of homosociality throughout the modern period.[3] Such influential framers of feminist critique of American literary history as Ann Douglas, Annette Kolodny, Jane Tompkins, and Cathy Davidson have also contributed significantly to a widespread reassessment of the cultural and, specifically, the gender politics determining and to some degree determined by American writing in its first century.[4]

Early attempts to work out the relation between American literature and homosexuality from a gay studies perspective—Robert K. Martin's *The Homosexual Tradition in American Poetry* is an important and characteristic example—were constrained by their thoroughly traditional and tradition-minded notions of literary history and by their tendency (one they shared with earlier, unsympathetic accounts of the matter like Fiedler's) to scant or ignore altogether the historicity of homosexuality.[5] This latter constraint was perhaps inevitable, since the historiography of sexualities, homosexualities certainly included, had not emerged from its subdisciplinary infancy ten years ago.

A generic divide yawns between Martin's and Fiedler's very different kinds of attempts to account for—one positively, the other negatively—the alleged focus of American writing on the homoerotic. Although he has since written a separate account of Melville's fiction, Martin's efforts to secure a male homophilic rather than homophobic American literary canon around Whitman ignore fiction and valorize poetry. Fiedler's procedure is precisely converse to this: he limits his study strictly to novels. There is much more at stake in such critical practices than simply a conservative desire to maintain the purity of genres. Fiedler makes one of his few forays outside the academic literary canon of the 1950s and 1960s to consider Whitman's early temperance novel, *Franklin Evans*, but never once mentions *Leaves of Grass* even in passing: not only an enormously more influential work of Whitman's, but also one that would figure in any extended consideration of "love and death" in American writing—and one that radically defies Fiedler's crude sexual typology (the Pale Maiden and the Dark Lady, the Good Good Boy and the Good Bad Boy) for American literature. Granted, Fiedler's book announces in its title that it is a study of prose fiction only, but his substitution of a narrowly defined body of "classic American fiction" (chiefly Brown, Cooper, Poe, Hawthorne, Melville, Twain, and Faulkner) for a canon conceived in any broader terms, generically or otherwise, has considerable extraliterary consequences. From its first appearance, Fiedler's book was taken by many to be not merely what it is—an archetype-slinging romp through the then fairly recently installed "strenuous" straight white male canon—but also a work of "general cultural" import. Lionel Trilling called it "a general cultural history of the nation" and George Steiner asserted that it bore as significantly on the study of "American morals" as it did on American literature.[6]

For the past several years I have been studying the work of a small number of American male writers—principally Walt Whitman, Horatio Alger, and Henry James—whose works taken together collectively violate many of the lines along which American history and literary history have long been organized. With regard to history, the work of these three authors represents widely divergent constructions of class, gender, and national identities. With regard to specifically literary-historical issues, they raise questions about the hybridization of genres as well as about canonicity; the relations of each of their respective bodies of work to popular and elite practices and audiences of the period are complex. As one might well expect, given the conspicuous differences in the social circumstances and aspirations of these three figures and the wide divergences among their literary practices, their writings engage questions of the history and theory of homosexuality in extremely various ways. Far from constituting a "tradition," homosexual or otherwise, their writings are divided from each other as well as within themselves. Without minimizing the violent contradictions with which their writings abound, I am interested in trying to resist the historiographical and literary-historiographical conventions which have tended to keep Whitman and James apart, and a writer like Alger away from either of them, and, in so doing, have tended to reify such conventional distinctions as those between fiction and poetry, between producers of popular and elite culture, and between bourgeois writers and those of lower-class origins.

≡≡≡

"Difficult as it will be, it has become . . . imperative to achieve a shifted attitude . . . towards the thought and fact of sexuality, as an element in character, personality, the emotions, and a theme in literature. I am not going to argue the question by itself; it does not stand by itself."[7] Whitman wrote these words a hundred years ago, in his 1887 preface, "A Backward Glance O'er Travel'd Roads," and the challenge they pose to students of sexuality, character, personality, the emotions, and literature has still not been fully met, although largely discrete discourses on each of these topics continue to proliferate today, as they had begun to in Whitman's youth. With the exception of a few figures like Carroll Smith-Rosenberg and Christine

Stansell, American historians have by and large been slow to perceive the extraordinary degree to which discourses on contraception, abortion, masturbation, prostitution, and homosexuality were engaged in furious dialogue with one another and with other predominantly nonerotic discourses like those of housing, public health, education, domesticity, and nationalism.[8] Whitman makes the point and suggests a method of analysis in his emphatic and axiomatic assertion that the question of sexuality "does not stand by itself," but is at all points interactive with other politics or economies which are for the most part not specifically or obviously erotic ones, such as the network of class- and gender-positions enforced in the culture, of people's various ways of inhabiting these positions, especially in their respective relations to their own and other people's bodies and bodily lives, to their work, and to language and writing. Whitman's writing is importantly representative of a range of counterdiscourses first launched in this period against his culture's elaboration of a phallogocentric, gender-polarizing code of political and social practices which tended to privatize, domesticize, and pathologize sexualities. These counterdiscourses kept insisting on the fundamentally political and representational character of sexualities within a historical situation in which predominant forces were tending more and more powerfully to repress the relation of sexualities to a wide array of other social relations, in significant part by means of a range of medico-forensic discourses which took as their founding assumption that the "truth" or "nature" of sexuality and of bodiliness in general was to be found in the figure of the body conceived of as an isolable and in fact isolated object of discursive analysis and control.

In the intervening century since Whitman articulated his unwavering political opposition to the cultural construction of "the body" as a monolithic entity subject at every point to regulation by the state, innumerable attempts have been made to "argue the question" of sexuality "by itself." But in asserting that "it does not stand by itself," Whitman repudiates the fantasy of the self-instantiated, self-instantiating phallus as center and ground of meaning which has been used to underwrite so many modern ideas of sexuality, and of power and politics in general—perhaps nowhere more so than in the United States, where, during the Reagan imperium, we have been witness to yet another revival of the Cold War rhetoric of "cocky" machismo, potent preparedness, readiness to strike, to show backbone, muscle, "starch," uprightness.

The vocabulary and conceptual framework which structure this notion of the state as a kind of monitory, perpetually turgid dirigible, and the image of its model (male) citizens as themselves a band of heat-seeking missiles poised at permanently rigid attention, entered American political discourse much earlier than my Top Gun metaphors may suggest—as early as the 1840s, during the wave of nationalist fervor which accompanied the outbreak of the so-called Mexican War, a thoroughly successful dress rehearsal for later American imperialist adventures.[9] The Mexican War culminated in the idea of the nation's manifest destiny and the imposition of its powerful new disciplinary culture of self-reliant male rectitude on the entire continent and eventually on the world. Whitman and other writers —Thoreau, Melville—whose work was to be canonized during World War II and after as having constituted "the American Renaissance" were young men when this historical process first got going; writers of James's and Alger's generation were born into a society in which it was already essentially in place.

Scholars have been aware of the young Whitman's strong public support of the Mexican War since the publication in 1920 of his conventionally patriotic Brooklyn *Eagle* editorials of the mid-1840s, when he was in his mid-twenties.[10] If these were all the writing Whitman had done, the title of Mauricio González de la Garza's study, *Walt Whitman: Racista, Imperialista, Antimexicano* (1971), might be justified. But Whitman soon moved from this conventional view to radically opposing positions—by following the logic of manifest destiny "otherwise," as it were. His critics have been slow to recognize this, for although the poetry continues to exhibit numerous signs of the conventional American political attitudes of its time, from the beginning of the *Leaves of Grass* project in the mid-1850s, and perhaps even before, the politics informing Whitman's poetry is not simply a party politics or a nationalist politics, but a radically materialist "body" politics based on novel ideas about the fundamental equality and interchangeability of human bodies and of the desirability of privileging claims to bodily well-being, health, pleasure, and "adventure" for the masses over more traditional kinds of political claims of power and interest.

Opposing his society's imposition of increasingly rigid constraints over sexualities was of course a central concern of Whitman's particular brand of corporeal utopianism. The terms of the mostly sterile debate over whether sexualities are fundamentally biological or cultural phenomena, whether they are inborn or learned, divinely ordained or casually picked up on street corners, were first set in this country in the disciplinary discourses of sexuality which began to pour from American presses in the 1830s and 1840s. The pseudo-physics concerning the dynamics of the "sex drives" and the pseudo-theology concerning which of these "drives" were healthy, natural, and creative, and which were perverted, sick, and destructive, were first worked out in the United States in a massive, only recently recovered, "advice" literature. Here, in the case of "advice," the scare quotes seem in order, since this "advice" was in fact ferociously, even terroristically, enforced with increasing relentlessness over the course of the century. As anyone who has read around in this literature knows, sexuality was vehemently made to "stand by itself" in the Jacksonian period, in a plethora of pamphlets, tracts, lectures, newspaper articles, conduct books and manuals which demonized all forms of nonconjugal, nonprocreative sexual desires and behaviors.[11]

Even as sexuality "[did] not stand by itself" for Whitman, neither had it stood by itself for his elders in the freethinking, artisanal social and political milieu into which he was born. Sean Wilentz, in his 1985 work on the labor history of early New York City, *Chants Democratic*—a book which is indebted to Whitman's writing not only for its title but for other crucial elements of its discourse— has provided an illuminating account of this milieu during the decades of Whitman's childhood and adolescence, showing the coherence of its nascent labor politics with, among other things, its radical new attitudes toward sexual behavior.[12] Robert Dale Owen, son of the reformer Robert Owen, was, along with the celebrated Scotswoman Frances Wright, the leading ideologue of this movement. Besides operating a "Hall of Science" with Wright which functioned as a social and political center for workers, and writing and publishing the newspaper *Free Enquirer* with her (Whitman's father was a subscriber), Owen contributed to the movement for workers' autonomy by publishing in 1830 the first book on birth control to appear in the United States, *Moral Physiology: or, a Brief and Plain Treatise on the Population Question*. The second work on birth control to appear here, Charles Knowlton's *Fruits of Philosophy*, followed in 1832. These books' treatment of conjugal union, and of sexual indulgence in general, as actions that could happily be detached from their hitherto supposedly inevitable biological consequences encountered furious opposition. The flood of books denouncing solitary sexual indulgence that followed in the immediate wake of the birth control manuals was no doubt a part of the general movement to resist fundamental changes in ideas of sexuality and in sexual practices that tended to be compatible with other practices promoting personal autonomy. The anonymous pamphlet *Solitary Vice Considered*, the first of countless nineteenth-century American efforts to identify masturbation as the cause of a wide range of disastrous effects, appeared in 1831, the year after Owens's birth control book. Three years later, Sylvester Graham published his *Lecture to Young Men on Chastity*, a founding document of the American male-purity movement. In his preface to the printed version of his lecture, Graham claimed to have set up shop as male-purity author in response to a widespread demand from young men that a strong counterdiscourse be produced to the wave of books that had recently begun to appear which tended (in Graham's words) "to encourage illicit and promiscuous commerce between the sexes." Rather than being the explicitly pornographic or "libertine" productions one might expect, the books in question undoubtedly included, according to Nissenbaum, Owens's and Knowlton's pioneering works on the practice of birth control. In 1835, the year after the publication of Graham's influential lecture, Samuel B. Woodward, sometime superintendent of the Worcester, Massachusetts, lunatic asylum, began making his much-discussed reports to the Massachusetts legislature and to the *Boston Medical and Surgical Journal* of his discovery that masturbation "caused" insanity; and in the same year, Reverend John Todd of Pittsfield, Massachusetts, published *The Student's Manual*, another milestone in the male-purity movement and a book that went through edition after edition in both the United States and in England for the rest of the century.

Carroll Smith-Rosenberg has argued that when male-purity writers threatened their readers with disease, disgrace, and premature death for masturbating, they were inveighing—with undecidably varying degrees of awareness of their actual targets—against a whole range of emergent social forms of male autonomy, including what was subsequently conceptualized (at the end of the century) as male homosexuality and the embryonic urban, male-homosexual subculture of streets, taverns, and brothels, for all of which "onanism" served as a highly elastic label.[13] The difficulty, indeed to a great extent the impossibility, of recovering much of the early social history of this proto-male-homosexual subculture and the behaviors and institutions it fostered and which in turn fostered it, has been widely recognized; what can still be recovered, however, are the discourses which structured people's perceptions and conceptualizations of the relations between erotic and nonerotic practices.

It is important for a historian of sexualities to see, for example, that homophobia was among the chief effects of the proliferating discourses of the 1830s and 1840s which condemned all forms of nonreproductive sexual behavior, as well as the chief effect of similarly and simultaneously proliferating discourses of "manliness" —masculine self-making and self-reliance—and nationalist-militarist practices. Although one of the most frequently employed euphemisms for masturbation was "the solitary vice," from the 1830s forward it was the social pursuit of this nominally solitary activity that is a constant target of anti-onanist writing. This discourse crystallizes around the figure of the depraved individual—servant, older relative, or older child—who, by teaching the young to masturbate, introduces sexual difference and sexual desire into what American moral-purity writers represent as the previously innocent—which is to say asexual—homosocial environments to which the young are committed. Even in supposedly super-repressive Puritan New England, attitudes toward extracurricular sex education seem not to have been as virulent as they became in the period I am discussing. In a letter of 1672, for example, the Reverend Thomas Shepard, Jr., of Charlestown, Massachusetts, son of the great Puritan preacher, coolly cautioned *his* son, who was about to enter Harvard, to avoid those of his fellows such as "there are and will be . . . in every scholastic society

. . . as will teach you how to be filthy."[14] Shepard's tone seems serious and casual at the same time; in comparison with the male-purity writers of a century and a half later, it is strikingly unhysterical about the fair certainty that his son will be sexually importuned by some of his associates at college. His tone suggests that he recognizes this as a structural feature, so to speak, of all-male environments—Puritan Harvard not excepted—and that while he strongly desires that his son avoid such sexual "instruction," he accepts without approving, as his society generally does, that boys will be "filthy"—not all boys, they imagine, but some. And as Roger Thompson has recently observed of Shepard's letter, "As a Harvard graduate himself, [Shepard] presumably wrote from experience."[15]

≡≡≡≡

To cast forward to a text from the very end of the nineteenth century, a full half-century after the first heyday of the anti-onanist writers, to Henry James's *The Turn of the Screw* (1898), one has only to recall how much in the tale turns on the mystery (or nonmystery) of little Miles's having been sent down from school for shocking misconduct toward some of his schoolmates—conduct into which he may have earlier been initiated by the literally haunting figure of Peter Quint —to perceive how resonant the figures of the boy and his corrupter, figures first disseminated on a mass scale in male-purity discourse, remained in the imaginations of James and many of his readers.

Before going on to consider further the dissemination of figures of anti-onanist terrorist writing through some of James's other work, I want to consider a text of Whitman's which was contemporaneous with the early male-purity discourse. This is a story entitled "The Child's Champion," which Whitman published in 1841 when he was twenty-two.[16] It initially appeared in a popular weekly called the *New World*, on which he was working as a compositor at the time. (The *New World* was one of the first two mass-circulation "story papers" established in the United States in the late 1830s.)[17] "The Child's Champion" tells a sentimental story about a twelve-year-old boy, the son of a poor widow, whose body and spirit are being crushed by the cruel master to whom he is apprenticed. On the way back to his master's from a brief visit to his mother, the boy Charles stops to gaze through an open tavern window at a rowdy drinking party taking place inside. He is hauled through the window by a drunken, one-eyed sailor who attempts to force him to drink alcohol. When the boy refuses because he has promised his mother never to drink, the sailor begins to beat him. Fortunately for Charles, telling the sailor about his mother's wish rouses a dissipated but prosperous-looking young man named John Lankton to come to his defense. Having taken an instantaneous and strong liking to Charles, Lankton promises to rescue him immediately from his cruel master and further resolves to mend his own dissipated habits, all on the strength of his newfound tie to the boy. Charles is said at this point to require "little persuading" to accept Lankton's invitation to stay with him at the inn and share his bed. The story ends with the apparition of an angel who blesses and kisses the boy and the young man in turn. In the closing lines, the narrator invites the "loved reader" to linger over the "moral of this simple story."

Perhaps the most striking quality of "The Child's Champion" as a literary text is its dense figuration in terms of liquidity—the story is full of figures of drinking, spilling, weeping, sweating, soaking, and flooding. In the context of the rest of Whitman's writing this text would be disseminated through a poetic practice designed to represent the "fluidity" of identities between males. The fantasy of male selves flowing in and out of each other and dissolving into each other is an impelling one in this and other early texts of Whitman's, including most of the poems that constituted the first, great 1855 edition of *Leaves of Grass*, poems that were later entitled "Song of Myself," "I Sing the Body Electric," "The Sleepers." The story's representations of "fluid" practices, including oral ones, and of "fluidity" between males take on as well the charged significance of drinking in antebellum culture (the first mass temperance movement in the United States was contemporaneous with the male-purity movement).

What particularly interests me about the story is the fidelity with which it projects the outlines of what would prove to be one of the most popular literary forms of the post–Civil War era, the rags-to-riches, or, more precisely, rags-to-respectability, stories of Horatio Alger: the boy's initial abjection—in "The Child's Champion," his weeping with his mother over his helplessness in the grip of his cruel master; his extremely labile relation to older males—the master who enslaves him, the sailor who beats him, the young gentleman who rescues him from them; the way in which his intensified abjection at the hands of an abusive older male (the drunken sailor) is represented as precipitating, as if with the force of a natural law, the boy's "rescue" from abjection, his being fatefully "drawn up," Ganymede-like, across previously intractable class lines, into the heaven of sentimental relationship between males and the predominantly masculine versions of domesticity and affluence which are the precincts of these privileged relations. Taken together, these formulae represent the dynamics of a male-sentimental master-narrative which is one of the principal forms of the counterdiscourse to the powerful new disciplinary culture of self-reliant male rectitude of the 1830s and 1840s—an oppositional dynamics which is as clearly delineated in Whitman's 1841 tale as it will be in Alger's "success" stories of a quarter-century and more later.

Each of Alger's books represents the intensely male-homosocial fraternity of proletarian streetboy life magically transformed for the "exceptional" boy—again, as in "The Child's Champion," by bourgeois-male intervention "from above"—into the scene of settled conjugal domesticity which the culture projected as its ideal civilian goal of male self-fashioning. James's disapproval of the child figures who emerged in the new postwar literature of children's series books produced by writers like Alger and Louisa May Alcott is registered, for instance, in his 1875 review in *The Nation* of Alcott's *Eight Cousins*, in which he complains that the little girls in such books "are apt to be pert and shrill, [and] the little boys to be aggressive and knowing." [18] Yet perhaps no other body of writing registers more extensively than James's frequently does the persistence in late nineteenth-century American culture of the scenes of boyhood abjection first elaborated in the male-purity writing of the 1830s and 1840s. In some ways, James tends to make his boy characters as definitively abject, as impervious to what Hugh Kenner has called (in relation to Alger's writing) "the paradigms of ascent," as similar boy figures are in the terrorist narratives of the antimasturbation tracts.

I have already mentioned Miles in *The Turn of the Screw*, who expires in the culminating moments of that story, as does the boy protagonist of James's 1891 tale "The Pupil," a story which is curiously and belatedly poised between a male-purity model of boyish abjection and the male sentimental model of rescue by an older male which was designed to sublate boyhood abjection: the "pupil" literally dies from the intensity of his emotional response to finally being released from his unhappy family to go make the home of his dreams with his beloved tutor, and from seeing the tutor hesitate momentarily when the boy's parents propose to him that he take the boy off. The homophobic implications of the figure of the abject boy in male-purity writing are palpable as well in the figure of the little boy who dies in James's "The Author of Beltraffio" (1884): the boy dies as a "punishment" for and/or a required "sacrifice" to his father's homosexuality—or, more precisely, the homosexuality of his author-father's writing. Yet in tales like "The Middle Years" (1893) and "The Great Good Place" (1900), in which the predominant subject position is neither that of the abject boy nor his adult male protector or corrupter but that of an older man who either lacks an articulated erotic focus or loves a younger adult male, there emerge scenes of male fosterage and male domesticity of the kind enshrined in texts like "The Child's Champion" and Alger's boys' books.

Alger admired James's fiction so much that he paid him a double *hommage* in his 1890 boys' book *The Erie Train Boy*, which briefly features a young female character from Albany named Isabel Archer and another young female character who, like Daisy Miller, mistakes a comely young Italian man of little or no social significance for an eligible gentleman.[19] Alger's apparent inability to perceive class differences in any terms other than the crude and inflexible ones of his mechanical "paradigm," which transforms sexually attractive street-boys into small-time corporate capitalists, results in the probably unwitting but nonetheless delicious irony of Isabel Archer's and Daisy Miller's unexpected and incongruous appearances in this late tale of his—delicious because the irony cuts two ways, not only against the banality and iron simplemindedness which characterizes Alger's fiction but also against the simultaneous suppression and promotion of class arrogance in much of James's fiction.

It is very unlikely that James was ever aware of Alger's tipping of his hat to him. James, who could admire so little of his contemporaries' writing, not even much of that of a supposedly kindred spirit like Edith Wharton, certainly could not admire Alger's work. Given this fact, it comes as a slight surprise to find James in 1902 proclaiming himself an extremely enthusiastic reader of a new pop genre that had emerged in that year: the first, and still the archetypal western, Owen Wister's *The Virginian*. In his only published letter to Wister (who was the grandson of a friend of James's youth, the celebrated actress Frances Kemble), James expresses his excitement in terms that may sound distinctly un-Jamesian: "What I best like in it," he writes Wister, "is exactly the fact of the *subject* itself, . . . the exhibition, to the last intimacy . . . of your hero." [20] Wister's tale relates the story of an ungainly, middle-aged eastern gentleman's life-transforming fascination and friendship "out west" with the first slow-walkin', slow-talkin' cowboy in fiction (the Virginian's most famous "line" is that quintessentially American-male response to homosocial provocation of many kinds: "*Smile* when you call me that"). When *The Virginian* shifts from its, for James (and no doubt for many other readers), idyllic male-male phase to its inevitable homophobic phase—the Virginian is finally represented as outgrowing his burdensome memories of his dead buddy Steve and marrying an attractive and spunky schoolmarm from Vermont—James does not hesitate to tell Wister that he has what he calls strong "reserves" about what is for him this problematic ending. "I am willing to throw out, even though you don't ask me, that nothing would have induced me to unite [the Virginian] to the little Vermont person, or to dedicate him in fact to achieved parentage, prosperity, maturity, at all—which is mere *prosaic* justice, and rather grim at that." James then really drops the veil, as it were, about the sources of his pleasure in reading Wister; he writes of the Virginian: "I thirst for his blood. I wouldn't have let him live and be happy; I should have made him perish in his flower and in some splendid noble way." James then directs Wister to Pierre Loti's *Pecheur d'islande* (1886)—perhaps the most pungently male homoerotic novel about a sailor before Jean Genet's *Querelle de Brest*—as a good example of possible ways of "improving" the ending of *The Virginian*.

In the context of the model of abjection and rescue between higher-class man and lower-class boy that I have been discussing, the interesting thing about James's vampiric rewriting of Wister's western ("I thirst for his blood") is the way it nakedly exposes the violent and sadistic fantasy of the pleasure James imagines taking in planning and carrying out the narratorial execution of the book's handsome hero ("I should have made him perish in his flower") alongside this fantasy's sublation into the traditional terms of the idealizing aesthetics of romance and/or tragedy ("in some splendid noble way"). James was writing *The Wings of the Dove* and *The Ambassadors* around the time he sent Wister his "suggestions" for *The Virginian*; although he foregrounds male homoerotic attraction and male homosocial competition more thoroughly in these two extraordinary novels than in any of his other writings, they contain no language to compare with the candidly sado-erotic relish of his revision of Wister's lower-class (in terms of genre) account of his lower-class hero.

In his youth, James wrote a famously dismissive review in *The Nation* of Whitman's Civil War poems; later, he expressed his deep appreciation of the poet in a review of a posthumously published volume of Whitman's letters to his boyfriend Peter Doyle.[21] In the long period between 1865 and 1898, the respective dates of these reviews, James seems to have remained silent about Whitman's work, even while some of his British friends and acquaintances were praising the poet in print, entering into correspondence with him, proclaiming him (if, for some time, only to one another) the heroic founder of the male homoerotic literary cult of "Calamus," and going so far as to visit him at his home in Camden, New Jersey.[22] Whitman, on his side, is on record as (quite unsurprisingly) having found James's writing all "feathers," as he put it. In his last years, Whitman several times in conversation contrasted what he called the "vogue" of the younger Henry James ("surely his vogue won't last," he says) with the far superior achievements of Henry James, Sr.: the elder James's free-floating reflections on metaphysics, mystical theology, and the desirability of society's rearranging sexual relations—a not uncharacteristic configuration of topics in elite discourse of the antebellum period —were understandably more to Whitman's liking.[23] The complex circuitry of the relations of Whitman's writings to the striations of class in late nineteenth-century American society are nowhere more evident than in his gesture of sending one of his working-class boyfriends

—once again, Peter Doyle—the uncharacteristic gift of a book rather than the usual dollar or a new shirt. When he did so, the book Whitman sent was notably not something like Alger's *Luke Larkin's Luck* or *Risen from the Ranks*; it was Regina Maria Roche's 1796 gothic romance, *The Children of the Abbey*.[24] Eve Kosofsky Sedgwick's reading of the shifting tensions between homophobia and homosexual panic in relation to changes in the writing of English gothic fiction of the late eighteenth and early nineteenth centuries provides one richly suggestive context in which to consider the possible significance of Whitman's gift. The persistence of a limited although fairly labile repertory of scenes of boyhood abjection sublated into sentimental male domesticity in some of the writings of Whitman, Alger, and James suggests another, not unrelated context in which to consider Whitman's gift.

Whitman's difficulties with the emergent realist fiction of his own time are well known: he disliked William Dean Howells's novels almost as much as he did James's. He remained a loyal partisan of the romances for which he had shared a passion with his mother in his boyhood—books like Scott's *Ivanhoe*, Cooper's *The Wept of Wish-ton-Wish*, and George Sand's *Consuelo*.[25] The most audaciously experimental poet of the English-speaking world in his time sustained to the end of his life what has generally been taken to have been a highly conservative, even reactionary attitude toward contemporaneous developments in fiction.

I would relate Whitman's refusal to admire realist fiction to his commitment to disseminating a different model of writing and of writing's determinate relations to sexuality and social class, a commitment which—as much as any other reason that might be advanced —because of the increasing predominance of homophobia in American society from the 1830s forward, could never be central to the realist enterprise. Certain forms of the romantic fiction Whitman and his mother read and regaled each other with in his youth seem to continue to represent for him, on the one hand, certain terrorized and foreclosed possibilities of collaboration between a range of feminine, feminist, and/or maternal counterdiscourses in his culture, and, on the other, a range of antimilitarist, antinationalist, antihomophobic counterdiscourses. In the master narrative I have described, the abject boy is inevitably "drawn upward" and recovered for a scene of male domesticity and affluence from which the equally abject mother —and, along with her, the femininity she metonymically represents —is excluded. To try to reread male sentimental and male domestic fictions through the lenses of female sentimental and female domestic fictions, and to try to understand if not to justify their often unedifying collusions and exclusions, is one way of participating in an effort that has been ongoing for a very long time: an effort to resist the political forces in the United States that have been deforming and destroying human lives inside and outside this country for the past century and a half.

Notes

1   Leslie Fiedler, *Love and Death in the American Novel* (New York, 1966), 23.

2   Ibid., 24–25.

3   Carroll Smith-Rosenberg's work on homosocial spheres has been collected in her book *Disorderly Conduct: Visions of Gender in Victorian America* (New York, 1985). Eve Kosofsky Sedgwick theorizes about the relations among male homosociality, male homosexuality, homophobia, and heterosexuality in *Between Men: English Literature and Male Homosocial Desire* (New York, 1985); see especially 1–5, 21–27.

4   See Ann Douglas, *The Feminization of American Culture* (New York, 1977); Annette Kolodny, *The Lay of the Land: Metaphor as Experience and History in American Life and Letters* (Chapel Hill, 1975) and *The Land Before Her: Fantasy and Experience of the American Frontiers, 1630–1860* (Chapel Hill, 1984); Jane Tompkins, *Sensational Designs: The Cultural Work of American Fiction 1790–1860* (New York, 1985); and Cathy Davidson, *Revolution and the Word: The Rise of the Novel in America* (New York, 1986).

5   Robert K. Martin, *The Homosexual Tradition in American Poetry* (Austin, 1979).

6   Trilling's and Steiner's encomia appear as blurbs on the back jacket of the 1966 Dell paperback edition of Fiedler's *Love and Death in the American Novel*.

7   Walt Whitman, "A Backward Glance O'er Travel'd Roads," in *Walt Whitman: Complete Poetry and Collected Prose*, compiled by Justin Kaplin (New York, 1982), 669.

8   Smith-Rosenberg, *Disorderly Conduct*; and Christine Stansell, *City of Women: Sex and Class in New York 1789–1860* (New York, 1986).

9   Henry Nash Smith, *Virgin Land: The American West as Symbol and Myth* (Cambridge, Mass., 1950), 44–48, provides a standard account of this topic. Robert W. Johannsen situates Whitman in the broader cultural context of American responses to the Mexican War in *To the Halls of Montezuma: The Mexican War in*

the American Imagination (New York, 1985), 38, 50–51, 97, 110, 115, 133, 308. I draw my "rehearsal" metaphor for the long-term political significance of America's Mexican adventure from Alfred H. Bill's centenary study of the war, *Rehearsal for Conflict: The War with Mexico 1846–1848* (New York, 1947). Some contemporary American historians have ceased to study "manifest destiny" as such, preferring to break down what they see as an enormously complex phenomenon into its component aspects. The entry for "manifest destiny" in the index of Richard Drinnon's *Facing West: The Metaphysics of Indian-Hating and Empire-Building* (New York, 1980) is significant; it reads simply, "*See* Racism; Nationalism; Imperialism; Colonialism."

10 Walt Whitman, *The Gathering of the Forces*, ed. Cleveland Rodgers and John Black (New York, 1920).

11 See Ronald G. Walters, *Primers for Prudery* (Englewood Cliffs, N.J., 1974); Carroll Smith-Rosenberg, "Sex as Symbol in Victorian Purity: An Ethnohistorical Analysis of Jacksonian America," *American Journal of Sociology*, supp., 84 (1978): 212–47; and G. J. Barker-Benfield, *The Horrors of the Half-Known Life: Male Attitudes Toward Women and Sexuality in Nineteenth-Century America* (New York, 1976); see especially 155–62 and 163–74. There is a rare original copy of the pamphlet *Solitary Vice Considered* in the collections of the American Antiquarian Society, Worcester, Massachusetts.

12 Sean Wilentz, *Chants Democratic* (New York, 1985). For Wilentz's account of the milieu of Wright and Owen's *Free Enquirer*, see especially 176–82.

13 See Smith-Rosenberg, "Sex as Symbol in Victorian Purity."

14 Shepard's letter is quoted in Roger Thompson, *Sex in Middlesex* (Amherst, 1986), 58.

15 Ibid., 58n.

16 "The Child's Champion" appears under its subsequent (1844) title, "The Child and the Profligate," in *Walt Whitman: The Early Poetry and the Fiction*, ed. Thomas L. Brasher (New York, 1963).

17 For more about the *New World* and the early years of the mass publishing market in the United States, see Michael Denning, *Mechanic Accents: Dime Novels and Working-Class Culture in America* (New York, 1987), 9–61.

18 James's review is reprinted in *Critical Essays on Louisa May Alcott*, ed. Madeleine B. Stern (Boston, 1984), 165–66.

19 Alger was acquainted with the James family. He interviewed Henry James, Sr., for the biography of the actor Edwin Forrest on which he collaborated with his cousin, the *litterateur* William Rounseville Alger. Alger had been expelled from the Unitarian ministry in 1866 for engaging in sexual activities with his boy parishioners. The members of the James family (at least the male ones) seem to have been aware of this, and William James, with whom he seems to have spoken about his troubles freely, may have been the last person with whom he ever discussed the matter. (See Gary Scharnhorst with Jack Bales, *The Lost Life of Horatio Alger, Jr.* [Bloomington: 1985], 70.) Henry James, Sr., wrote to his novelist son of Alger's visit: "Alger talks freely about his own late insanity—which he in fact appears

to enjoy as a subject of conversation and in which I believe he has somewhat interested William [James], who has talked with him a good deal of his experience at the Somerville Asylum." The younger Henry James quotes his father's letter in *Notes of a Son and Brother*, reprinted in Frederick W. Dupee, ed., *Henry James: Autobiography* (Princeton, 1956), 401.

20 Henry James, *Letters, 1895–1916*, ed. Leon Edel (Cambridge, Mass., 1984), 4: 232–34.

21 Both reviews are reprinted in *Walt Whitman: The Critical Heritage*, ed. Milton Hindus (London, 1971), 110–14, 159–60.

22 Perhaps we may take James's contribution to a collection for Whitman in 1885 as a sign of his private good will toward the poet. See Horace Traubel, *With Walt Whitman in Camden*, ed. Sculley Bradley (Philadelphia, 1953), 4: 210. Edith Wharton gives a well-known description of James reading Whitman aloud in fervent tones in her memoirs (title borrowed from Whitman's "A Backward Glance O'er Travel'd Roads"), *A Backward Glance*, which is "interesting, if true," as American newspapers used to head news stories they had not yet been able to verify at press time.

23 See Traubel, *With Walt Whitman in Camden*.

24 See *Walt Whitman: The Correspondence*, ed. Edwin Haviland Miller (New York, 1961), 2: 245.

25 Whitman compares Howells with James in Traubel, *With Walt Whitman in Camden* (New York, 1915), 1: 78. He invidiously compares the younger with the elder Henry James for a second time in the sixth volume of Traubel's *With Walt Whitman in Camden*, ed. Gertrude Traubel and William White (Carbondale and Edwardsville, 1982), 34–35. After this last devaluation of James's fiction, Whitman goes on to praise Cooper's and Scott's novels extensively, beginning by saying, "Cooper is way better than Hawthorne—50 percent better" (35–36). In Whitman's comparison of Hawthorne to Cooper he may be expressing a belief that as the cultural ascendency of the former over the latter developed and persisted in the second half of the nineteenth century, American fiction "got off the track" of the kind of sweeping social and political point of view which Cooper's writing represents for Whitman onto what seemed to him to be a different, inferior "track" of "Hawthornean" fiction, which valorized the introspective, the psychological, and the fragmentary—the kind of writing of which he saw James and Howells as notable young practitioners.

Robert L. Caserio

Supreme Court Discourse vs. Homosexual Fiction

D. A. Miller's essay on the role of the police in *Bleak House* is already a classic, five years after its appearance in *Representations*. The stature of the essay, collected now in Miller's *The Novel and the Police*, illustrates the thoroughness with which critics have turned from the formalist study of narrative to the study of narrative as a form of ideology. But there has been too little questioning of this latest trend's most significant element: suspicion of any novel's effort to provide an alternative to the ideologies and politics that prevail in the world in which the novel is produced and read.

In *The Novel and the Police*, Miller asserts that the narrative ideology of *Bleak House* participates in a general project of novelistic narrative—that is, to produce for readers a "sheltered space," outside the realms of public and institutional life. In fact, Miller says, "that sheltered space . . . is unconditionally taken for granted in the novel form, whose unfolding and consumption has not ceased to occur in such a space all along.

. . . [T]he novel counts among the conditions for this consumption the consumer's leisured withdrawal to the private, domestic sphere." Depending upon this situation of consumption, the novel thus constitutes "every novel-reading subject . . . within the categories of the individual, the inward, the domestic." "The domestic" is a term that brings together the privacy of individual life and the sphere of family influence. Thus "the only significant attempt to transcend the individualism projected by the novel took place precisely in Victorian England as the practice of *family reading*," but this attempt appears not to have succeeded, since it merely intensifies the privacy and inwardness underwritten by family and genre alike.[1] Unqualifiedly, then, the novel is the producer and the product of an ideology of privacy, understood as a liberating alternative to the public realm.

What is most at issue in Miller's analysis—as Miller sees it—is any novel's attempt, not just *Bleak House*'s, to make the individual, the inward, and the domestic into ideological alternatives to the ideological powers of the courts and the police. Thus Miller's Dickens means to set up an oppositional "outside" to established power, a sheltered space "occupied by an ideal of family," the variant of the individual and the inward. But Miller intends to shake up Dickens's ambition and to undo the novel's generic pride, its claim that it "views the world [from its self-appointed shelter] in better, more clear-sighted and disinterested ways than the world views itself." The model for this pride turns out to be a nefarious form of supervision, "a radical entanglement [of] the nature of the novel and the practice of the police." So Miller thinks that even the sheltered family space in Dickens harbors the antagonistic ideologies—the oppressive judging and policing—that the family is supposed to curtail. And the very narrative which carries *Bleak House*'s Esther and Allan to their ideal "outside" is only one of the voices in which Dickens "does" the police. Privacy and domesticity, supposed to be a refuge from power's oppressions, mime their opponent, and make the "outside" of power the twin of power. Miller concludes that Dickens's "rigorous reformism makes better sense as an undeclared defense of the status quo."[2]

When we read in *The Novel and the Police* that "whenever the novel censures policing power, it has already reinvented it, in the very practice of novelistic representation," we are to assume that narrative, one of the novel's principal representational modes, is also a nefarious policing agent.[3] This view is in step with the method and aim of the study of narrative as a form of ideology—ideological narrative poetics—which comes to us originally from Althusser, Foucault, and Pierre Macherey, Fredric Jameson and Terry Eagleton: narratives, they tell us, always make better sense if they are regarded as undeclared defenses of the status quo. And this, they say, is especially because novelistic narratives cultivate the categories of the individual, the inward, and the domestic. Miller glances nervously at Marxism—at Eagleton specifically—because Marxism appears to Miller to be self-deceptively optimistic about art's subversion of the world's all-supervising structures. But no less than Miller, Eagleton sees the individual and the inward as the other side of the coin of public and economic oppression. In *Criticism and Ideology* "the individual" appears to Eagleton as only a deadlocked categorical alternative to the sterile ideology of "organic" society. Although Eagleton sees "the fissuring of organic form" as a liberating step in the genre's progress, we can surmise how Miller's scrupulous skepticism would react to this alleged liberation.[4] Miller asserts that there is "a whole range of practices whereby our culture has become increasingly adept in taking benefit of doubt."[5] Would one of these profitable (hence conservative) practices be the doubting of narrative that issues in the fissuring of organic form and of one of organic form's possible models, the family?

Modern and postmodern novels would seem to be simultaneously antidomestic and antinarrative narratives. But the reader who oversees these doubt-created fissurings of narratives and organic forms must be a magisterial private detective. If he is not, he will be unable to read—to follow the tracks of, say, *Finnegans Wake* or, for another example, of Beckett's funny version of Bucket, the Moran of *Molloy*. The modern and postmodern reader, then, by virtue of his elite interpretative agency, arguably is still served by at least two categories constitutive of fiction: the categories of the individual and the inward. By opening up an ahistorical and apolitical "sheltered space" for their readers, antinarratives no less than narratives might be said to maintain an undeclared defense of the status quo. For such works would constitute their readers as private doubles of the agencies of detection and judgment that keep the established world weightily in place.

This critical method of seeing underlying productive likenesses below the appearance of exclusive antagonisms is a powerful one, to be sure. I make use of the same method in part of this essay. But insofar as the aim of ideological narrative poetics is to be in its own way a detective and a judiciary force dedicated to the arrest of equations of narrative with subversions of the status quo, I am skeptical. No less than Miller I too suspect the categories of the individual and the inward—especially when those categories give special privilege to "privacy." American judicial discourse, for instance, makes the inward and the private very suspicious allies of freedom. But I do not see compelling reason to identify *novelistic* form and *narrative* discourse with these categories or with the use of these categories in other discourses; nor do I see compelling reason to dissociate novelistic form and narrative from attempts to liberate us from public oppressions; nor do I see family structure as necessarily—and in every possible form—the ally of supervisory and disciplinary constraint.

My case relies on two contemporary novels of American homosexual and bisexual life: *The Talking Room* by Marianne Hauser and *The Story of Harold* by the pseudonymous Terry Andrews. If we think of homosexual and bisexual persons as men and women who have fared best under the shelter of inwardness and privacy, we will be surprised by Hauser and Andrews. Their narratives argue that, both in and out of storytelling, inwardness and privacy are inadequate housing. More surprisingly, these narratives cultivate an ideal of family at the same time as they subvert inwardness. Hauser's and Andrews's lesbians, gays, and bisexuals dream of parenthood as well as of Eros. Their stories feature philoprogenitiveness—nonsexual nurturing interest in offspring and children—and figure sodomite mothers and fathers as model parents. And why not? But we have also to ask why. If these narratives subvert some suspect categories only to return to domesticity and family, do they thereby collaborate homophobically with the status quo? In Miller's argument the family structure in *Bleak House* nowhere belongs to itself, or to any form of life alternative to the family's "outside," just as (apparently) Dickens's narrative does not belong to its own intention to counter the oppressive institutions it portrays. Do latter-day homosexual fictions, and homosexuals themselves, after the heyday of Wilde's, Gide's, and Proust's heroic combat against family and society on behalf of the individual and the inward, regress into the arms of the hegemonic Other by seeking out a new version of "the practice of the family"?

To work through these questions we need a procedure supplementary—if not alternative—to Miller's. Miller analyzes the relation of novelistic discourse and representational practice to non-novelistic, law-enforcing discourse and pragmatic practice. He does so by taking the novel's picture of the latter and the latter in fact *as identical*. One reason why Miller can then posit the similarity between the "discipline" of narrative novelistic order and the "discipline" of order outside the novelistic realm is that he does not compare side-by-side any specimens of the *two* discourses. What are non-novelistic discourse and practice really like; how exactly do they employ and enforce the individual, the inward, the domestic, or whatever categories might be under dispute, in comparison with the way fiction employs them? Miller's assumption is that separate realms of discourse and practice are only separate in appearance; that they are all the same in actuality, because they are cut from the same ideological cloth. This assumption is everywhere at work in ideological narrative poetics. Eagleton, for example, ultimately undoes the pains he takes to differentiate novelistic discourse from its ideological environment. On the one hand, he distinguishes—as Miller does not—different kinds of ideology (general, authorial, aesthetic) that layer a literary text. The co-presence of these layers suggests more than an ideological deadlock among them, or more than a deadlock between the literary text and the general ideology it might oppose: "The text is a theatre which doubles, prolongs, compacts and variegates its signs, shaking them free from single determinants, merging and eliding them with a freedom unknown to history"—and, I would add, with a freedom unknown to the ideological practices and discourses of the law and the police. But while Eagleton suggests that there is room to argue that the literary text is either not overcome or not compromisingly enabled by the text's ideological "outside," his argument tends nervously to bury the literary liberty it here and there invokes. In his analyses of specific novelists, Eagleton continually appeals to the general ideology that penetrates and makes tutelary this or that novel: "Eliot's fiction represents an attempt to integrate liberal ideology, in both its Romantic and empiricist forms"; "What is in question with all of those texts is the . . . over-determined character of their mode of insertion into the hegemonic ideological forms"; "The need for value, and the recognition of its utter vacuity: it is here that . . . Conrad's enterprise, . . . integral to the imperialist ideology he shared, stands revealed"; and so on.[6] Yet these instances of general ideology are always gestured to, and never concretely exemplified, so that one never comes to compare a practical and specific instance of general ideology with a fictional instance. The argument goes on in a realm of assumption and innuendo about the literary text's environment. It goes on thus about texts and "general ideologies" that are a century old and that are—for Americans—at a vast cultural remove. Whether or not novelists provide shelter or housing for censured experiences, discourses, and practices which are reinventions—in the very process of representation—of the censuring agency is a question that needs to be engaged with more empirical specificity than ideological narrative poetics has yet exemplified.

Unfortunately for our lives, but relevantly to my purpose, the 1986 Supreme Court decision in *Bowers v. Hardwick* furnishes an instance of general ideology in nonfictional, non-narrative or (at least) anti-narrative discourse, of both a judicial and policing kind. And the decision deploys the categories of inwardness, individuality, and familial domesticity in a way that affects all our stories. Since the categories at issue in *Hardwick* are the categories at issue for ideological narrative poetics, we can best measure what I would call the "liberty interests" of Hauser's and Andrews's narratives if we look first at the Court's majority and minority opinions.

By now the *Hardwick* decision is well known. Upholding the bizarre arrest of a Georgia citizen, Michael Hardwick, in his own bedroom, while he was performing private consensual sodomy with another man, the Court sanctioned a state's constitutional right to make and enforce antisodomy laws in relation to private, consensual, adult sexual relations. Currently twenty-five states and the District of Columbia have such laws. Because in 1961 all fifty states had them, we might surmise that the Court is worried about an erosion of moral standards implied by the declining number of these statutes. *Hardwick* shows that the Court is certainly concerned by the declining number of states willing to criminalize adult homosexuals for committing sodomy in consensual privacy. The Georgia antisodomy statute, dating from 1968, broadened the wording of earlier statutes, so that the definition of sodomy would not discriminate against either gender or against any combination of genders. For as of 1968 Georgia defines sodomy as "performance of or submission to any sex act involving the sex organs of one person and the mouth or anus of another." (Following Georgia's lead, this is my definition of sodomy throughout this essay.) But the Supreme Court ruling interprets the statute as primarily directed against private, consensual, adult homosexual relations, and the Court justifies discriminatory application of antisodomy statutes against these homosexual relations, rather than even-handed application to heterosexual and homosexual acts alike.

In the opinions justifying and opposing the *Hardwick* decision, the Court's sides pit the categories of the domestic and the private-individual against each other, and each side seeks to subordinate one category to the other. Thus Justice White's majority opinion claims that the Court's prior libertarian rulings about private consensual sexual conduct are rulings (including *Roe v. Wade*) that protect "family, marriage or procreation" from state interference. Hence adult homosexuals do not have a right to practice consensual sodomy in private, because "no connection between family, marriage or procreation on the one hand and homosexual activity on the other has been demonstrated."[7] To this emphasis on family, marriage, or procreation Justice Blackmun and the Court minority oppose the liberty interests of privacy and the individual. But while the decency of the dissenting arguments are a black-and-white contrast to the meanness of Justice White's, there is something unsettling in the strategies of argument on both sides.

What is unsettling is that both sides cannot permit to homosexuals a space of appearance in the public realm. While the Court majority justifies supervising—and even eliminating—homosexual privacy, and while the Court minority defends homosexual privacy, both sides agree that homosexuality is only a private matter. This exclusive identification of homosexuality with privacy guarantees that the judges, at their worst, will equate homosexuality exclusively with sodomite sexual intimacies (how *could* it be anything else, except perhaps acts of sodomy outrageously performed in public?); and, at their best, with emotional intimacies relevant only to the private sphere. Hence for both sides homosexuality has no public, no *political*, existence. Although Justice Blackmun makes an attempt to allow homosexuality a public place, his argument is weak, perhaps because half-hearted. So the arguments of both sides of the Court maintain a long ideological tradition: that homosexual life, whether supervised or not, is and should be a closeted life.

The White side of the Court's strategy is to make homosexuality more and more closeted, by insisting that—after all—the constitutional right to privacy is not a right in and of itself, but that it is a right determined by the measure of its public consequences. At least something like this reasoning seems to motivate White's bland sarcasm about there being "no connection" between homosexuality and family, marriage, or procreation. White brings forward *Griswold v. Connecticut* and *Eisenstadt v. Baird*, both cases about the right to practice contraception, along with *Roe v. Wade*, in order to suggest that they are not just defenses of doing as one likes in the name of the right to privacy. Rather, because these cases are connected with family matters, White sees them in the light of public issues. The family, his reasoning implies, is not just a private matter, but a halfway house between an individual's privacy and his public life as a citizen. Accordingly, private rights protect family rights, and family rights protect public rights. This connection between family and public categories, which lets go of privacy "in itself" is, as we shall see, shared with the sodomites represented by Hauser and Andrews. They too see the family as a Janus-like thing, at once private and public. Together, White and the sodomites suggest that parenthood makes the parent a less private, more public self, because the parent becomes the child's mediator vis-à-vis the public culture. But whereas the sodomites, given this line of thought, pursue homosexual philoprogenitiveness partly as an entry into the public realm, Justice White would block the pursuit by insuring an absence of connection between family and homosexuality. The individual, the inward, and the domestic belong to the public realm here, but homosexual inwardness does not. For White, the sodomite is thoroughly private —indeed so removed from and detrimental to public life that he has no right to be either public or private.

Justice Blackmun also believes that private rights belong to public issues; it is for this reason that he registers his and his colleagues' dissent from the majority. But with a curious inverted symmetry to White's arguments, Blackmun's defense of homosexual conduct attenuates the public and political place of homosexuality even as it tries not to. White suggests that *Roe v. Wade* supports public matters and values more than it does private rights; in reaction, Blackmun reasserts privacy, individuality, and inwardness. These were the categories operative, Blackmun says, in the abortion ruling. "We protect the decision whether to have a child because parenthood alters so dramatically an individual's self-definition." We can see the relevance of Blackmun's point to *Roe v. Wade*, but this is an odd way of defining what parenthood alters. Parenthood, it seems to me, abolishes the parent's *self*. Insofar as parenthood is antithetical to self, it is odd to see Blackmun suggest that parenthood is unqualifiedly subordinated to self-definition. It is by this elevation of the individual self as the darling of all rights that Blackmun comes to attenuate the public impact of private adult sexual consents, even at the moment when he praises that impact. He quotes the following sentence from a 1943 decision: "The test of the [freedom to differ] is the right to differ as to things that touch the heart of the existing order." He follows the quotation with this comment: "it is precisely because the issue [of private choice] raised [by *Bowers v. Hardwick*] makes individuals what they are that we should be especially sensitive to the rights of those whose choices upset the majority."[8] Thus, moving from the quotation to his commentary, the justice takes the phrase "touch the heart of the existing order" and rewrites it: "touches the heart of what makes individuals what they are." This revision makes the existing order an aggregate of private individuals; but we know that the existing order is a network of relations that, really, universally, stops nowhere. If the heart of this network can be touched, it is because private choices have public issue. But where homosexuality is concerned, the opposing sides of the Court in effect join hands in withdrawing homosexuality from the realm of the public.

To heterosexuals, whose command of public space is underwritten and assured by their sexual desire, privacy is a dear refuge from the omnipresence of inalienable community. To homosexuals, privacy is a dear refuge from oppression by the public—and is also a guarantee of "liberation" from public consequence. Due to their exclusion from appearance in public in any but a nominal sense, homosexuals and bisexuals have always had the private closet—and its scared, squalid freedom—for their status quo. Accordingly, we can see how in the Court's discourse the categories of the individual, the inward, and the domestic can be used—for libertarian ends!—to justify repressive and oppressive business as usual. What I fear to be the logic of Blackmun's position, no less than White's, is illustrated by a December 1987 AP story about Congressman Jack Kemp in the *Salt Lake Tribune*. The five-column headline about the then-presidential candidate reads: "Gays Have Rights, But Teaching Isn't One of Them." In the story Kemp explains his point, in a way that conveys the upshot of both Blackmun's and White's arguments: "We want all Americans to enjoy the right to privacy and we have to at the same time recognize that there have to be public standards." Presumably Kemp thinks —insofar as a member of the party of Jesse Helms can—that teaching, besides being a mere job, is a form of parenting, that it transmits culture via shaping personal influence, no matter how disinterested and professional the transmission. And I would agree with him. But apparently public standards, and the space of appearance we call the public, cannot tolerate or benefit from cultural philoprogenitiveness in nonheterosexuals. It does seem true, then, as Kemp's neat division of private and public shows, that the privilege—the legalized right —given by American ideology in the name of privacy to the categories of individuality and inwardness can co-opt the liberty they supposedly serve.

Of course, it might well be asked who would dispense with the right to privacy even if it is oppressively entangled. Have the women who benefited from *Roe v. Wade* (*pace* Byron White's understanding of it) been oppressed by the benefit? And AIDS victims would be more indifferent than astonished or even interested to learn that the privacy they depend on to protect them against punitive supervision is, after all, enabled by privacy's radical entanglement with the police or the judiciary. Yet it must be admitted that the all-suspecting method of ideological narrative poetics is well suited to reading Supreme Court discourse—even though this is to admit that the ideological study of fictional narrative is most fruitful when, oddly enough, it is applied elsewhere—to non-narratives or to antinarrative discourses that are not novelistic or fictional.

I should like to apply it once more to nonfiction before turning to Hauser's and Andrews's sodomite tales. *Hardwick* has already created double binds, indeed a discursive pathos, in judicial attempts to shift legal response to homosexuality away from a focus on privacy. But whether or not the shift can be achieved remains a doubtful question —in spite of a recently victorious attempt to do so. This attempt to wring out of the Constitution a place in public life for homosexuals is the majority decision written in February 1988 by Judge William Norris, of the Ninth Circuit Court of Appeals, in *Watkins v. United States Army*. In 1981 the Army issued new regulations disqualifying all homosexuals from all ranks, regardless of length or quality of service. So Perry Watkins, who had admitted to being homosexual when in 1967 the Army inducted him, and who had accumulated an exemplary service record, was told in 1981 that he would not be allowed to reenlist, and was remanded to the private sphere. Judge Norris declares in the decision of this case that the United States Army's ban on homosexual acts for all Army personnel is unconstitutional, not because it violates the homosexual's right to privacy or bans same-sex sodomy, but because it discriminates against homosexuals due to their orientation rather than their acts. By reason of such discrimination the Army violates the rights homosexuals have to equal protection under the law, since the alternative sexual orientation is not allowed to be discriminated against. Moreover, Norris asserts that homosexuals must be considered as a suspect class, as a disfavored group that is the victim of unjustified antipathy. As a suspect class, homosexuals must be protected by the judicial process— by a more than usually rigorous and judicial scrutiny of the motives of those who allege grievances against them. Norris finds the Army's grievances in this case to be unjustifiable.

In defending his majority decision, Judge Norris argues like a brilliant law student who brings a desperate youthful ingenuity to bear on the harm done to a just cause by legal precedent. I say *desperate* ingenuity because the precedential aspect of *Hardwick* surrounds *Watkins* like a brick wall, which Norris can only knock his head against—until by sheer cunning he knocks the wall down. He argues that the Supreme Court considered *Hardwick* in relation to substantive due process, and not primarily in relation to equal protection under the law; and that, insofar as the *Hardwick* majority did touch on equal protection, it did so by emphasizing "the fundamental rights branch" of the latter.[9] Hence *Hardwick* left untouched and still unargued the relation of gay rights to other branches of equal protection doctrine, including suspect class analysis. Moreover, Norris says that *Hardwick* backed up the states' right to legislate against sexual actions committed by every orientation, but that it did not condemn any specific orientation. Putting this claim together with a reductio ad absurdum of the Army's sexual prohibitions (the judge shows that the Army exonerates homosexual acts engaged in by men who are intoxicated, or curious, or coerced, and who *won't* perform such acts *again;* hence the prohibition discriminates against desire and orientation, not acts), Norris explains that *Hardwick* doesn't apply to Watkins, who never pleads that the right to privacy extends to homosexual sodomy. In this way Norris not only argues his way around *Hardwick*, but both condones and avoids some recent Ninth Circuit decisions—including one by new Supreme Court Justice Kennedy—upholding the Army's regulations against homosexual *conduct* (rather than against homosexual orientation).

But if the Supreme Court gets—or takes—the chance to review *Watkins*, I'll predict that Norris's courageous argument will not withstand the Court's precedent. In spite of the public life Norris tries to insure for Perry Watkins and for homosexuals in general, the way in which the *Hardwick* opinions, pro and con, make the right to privacy the be-all and end-all of discussion might yet destroy Norris's attempt. The dissenting judge in *Watkins*, Stephen Reinhardt, makes a breast-beating show about what he believes—as a private individual, in all inwardness—is wrong with *Hardwick*. The case has "egregiously misinterpreted the Constitution"; moreover, the Army regulations against homosexuals are "unfair and discriminatory." But, in spite of these private opinions, Reinhardt cannot join with Norris because of Reinhardt's duty to apply Supreme Court precedent. This duty leads Reinhardt not only to reassert precedent but also to characterize Norris's arguments as illogical and incredible. Reinhardt argues that Norris's distinction between suspect class and fundamental rights "branches" of equal protection analysis is factitious. And then he points out that homosexuality *is* sodomy, that homosexuality can mean nothing but sodomite action. Indeed, he instructs his colleagues on what homosexuals *must* do: "oral sex is the primary form of homosexual activity." Since homosexuality equals sodomy in his view, then *Hardwick* has made homosexuals—in twenty-five states and in the District of Columbia, at least—a criminal class, and criminal classification forecloses suspect class analysis. Most of all, it turns out, Reinhardt is worried that Norris's argument would abridge heterosexual rights to sexual privacy. The straight right to privacy, in other words, is the key to Reinhardt's pathos-burdened duty to enforce *Hardwick*. Norris's decision promotes "a serious retreat in the privacy area" for it suggests that, like homosexual sodomy, "heterosexual sodomy, including oral sex between married couples, is not protected by the right to privacy and may be criminalized." But for Reinhardt the fact that *Hardwick* singles out homosexual sodomy as its target, even though the Georgia statute does not, proves that heterosexual sodomy is protected—by the privacy right in the Constitution. Reinhardt here asserts his credo: "I believe the Constitution protects most, if not all, private heterosexual acts between consenting adults."[10] Norris would make such protection questionable—and so Reinhardt, in the name of *Hardwick*, finds it his duty to sacrifice homosexual privacy and homosexual public status to the Constitution, which, it now appears, speaks a definitively heterosexual discourse.

It does not take much distance from these debates to sense that the obsessive attention to privacy is not all that is wrong with them. The judicial discourse itself is impaired by its earnest ever-straitened logic, by a constant operation within it of limitations and discriminations. In fact, Norris's defense of Watkins's sexual actions seems another form of constraint: love the sinner but discriminate against the sin. The judicial discourse nefariously polices the liberties it means to serve. It does this by repressing its own potential to become narrative—by opposing antinarrative generalizations and discursive discriminations to the stories the judicial discourse seeks to rule. But if this discourse were a fully, openly narrative one, it would not suffer a deadlocking self-constraint. The liberty interest of narrative lies in its freedom to license any connection that crosses its path. Fictional narrative never runs a straight course. And a narrative bent for crookedness of relation makes the meaning of a narrative a law unto itself, antinomian in comparison to this or that general law—or general ideology. In regard to general law—including the general law of structure we believe rules the constitution of fictional narratives—even the saddest stories maintain a facetiousness, a kind of comic deviancy, in the face of regulation.

It is a sign of the self-constraint and of the antinarrative nature of the legal discourses I have surveyed that they appear to be incapable of anything but deadly earnest. In Norris an argumentatious glee plays through the footnotes, subordinated there as a sign of all the stories the law cannot tell or make sense of. Byron White condemns the pleas on behalf of Michael Hardwick as "facetious," but he sees nothing of the facetious relations in which a novelist's or storyteller's version of White against Blackmun would involve him. He tells us that private adult consensual homosexuality is a "victimless crime, such as the possession and use of illegal drugs"; that to protect it against prosecution would be tantamount to protecting "adultery, incest, and other sexual crimes even though they are committed in the home." And so "we are unwilling to start down that road," as the justice named Byron puts it, butchly avoiding the garden path his culture has gone down—not always to its harm—since the days of the justice's namesake. The very names in this discourse suggest a story that would stand the discourse on its head. When Justice Blackmun backs up his opposition to White he appeals to *Loving v. Virginia*, the case which—only twenty years ago—struck down state laws against mixed racial marriages. "The parallel," Blackmun writes, "between *Loving* and this case is almost uncanny," because Virginia used many of White's general arguments in *Hardwick* to defend antimiscegenation statutes.[11] (The parallel might be more uncanny if Richard Perry

Loving had been a black man, given the name of the judge who enlists him against White to suggest a tie between interdicted black-and-white love and interdicted sodomite loving.) But legal discourse cannot seem to make these analogies among cases have the impact narratives can make them have, because narratives can easily tie together what the judge must leave in a discriminated state. Judge Reinhardt objects to Judge Norris's drawing parallel relations between sodomites and blacks. True, he says "history will view *Hardwick* much as it views *Plessy v. Ferguson*"; but at the next moment he says that "no matter how appealing the analogy between [treatment of blacks and homosexuals] may be, we are not free to draw it. . . . Cases regarding blacks are simply irrelevant."[12] A narrative of *Watkins*, not so discriminating, would probably treat the fact that the plaintiff sergeant is a black man as no less relevant to his story than his homosexuality. Unable to permit or to make relations in the way live relations permit or make themselves, judicial discourse exhibits its self-imprisoning difference from narrative.

At first sight Hauser's novel gives us pause, and does not bode well for narrative's liberty interests. *The Talking Room* practices a high modern or high postmodern formalism that turns the text in on itself, as if to assert the text's artistic right to privacy, its right to shelter from the public altogether. Does the novel's farcical formal donnée not amount to reactionary ideological significance? As if instantly to satirize the love that will not speak its name, Hauser's story about lesbians and the child of one of them uses no names, only initials. B, a pregnant minor of thirteen and the novel's narrator, is the child of an unknown sire and of J, a lesbian. J's female lover, V, engineered J's pregnancy to shore up her relationship with J. As the domestic and familial relation unfolds, other initials move in and out of the drama. And since all of them are treated by the text with a consistent toughness, perhaps Hauser's pack of initials is only an alphabetic arrangement of loathing: a loathing that surfaces when V's mother, granny-anny, discovers that her daughter is a lesbian and performs naked a ritual dance of contempt, during which she invites V and her lesbian cohorts to kiss granny's ass. We find ourselves right where suspicious critics like Miller would lead us: to the possibility that granny-anny is the novelist, expressing contempt for sapphists who will not produce children via the acceptable channels.

But the novel's formalism is richer in relations than this suspicious accounting can tell. To begin with, in response to the suspicion that the formalism is a figure for privacy or inwardness, the treatment of the characters as initials immediately undoes the category of the individual. Not taken for granted, individuals here are only relational units. Their relations stop nowhere, and this narrative—I would say, like fictional narratives generally—cares for individuals only in order to exhibit their promiscuous interconnections. Hauser directs us as to how to use her formalism on the novel's first page. Installed above what she calls "the talking room," B, the minor-narrator who is pregnant, needs always to listen in, to overhear what is below, and so must the reader, to whom the novel's formal elements are offered as sounding boards or transmitters for what at first does not meet the ear. Granny-anny hears about V's lesbianism through her loathed hearing aid; the news prompts her to destroy the instrument, and her dance of contempt is a deaf one. *The Talking Room* does not condone deafness. The formal dance of its elements transmits a subtext, but we have to turn up our hearing aids to hear it—unless we want spitefully to play deaf.

What sounds or resounds below the normal level of audition is a transformation of the category of the domestic. It is a transformation that equates domesticity and family structure with the sodomite. To get her reader to hear this transformation Hauser puts the reader inside a peculiar situational pun. Eliciting a heightened aural response to talk, Hauser silently equates the aural and the oral. Demanding that we put ourselves aurally as close as possible to the vent of the text's significance, Hauser submits us subliminally to a writer's and reader's form of sodomite play. This play is appropriately at once sodomite and sublimated, because subaurally the text transmits the centrality of J's lesbian motherhood. Criticized though she is, J is the one figure in the text from whom Hauser does not withdraw the reader's approval. That approval is withdrawn from V, J's lover, because V enacts the female-oppressing role of a man in a woman's body; it is withdrawn from B, because B's ravening heterosexuality is a blundering attempt at identification with her mother; it is withdrawn from D, a gay man who dreams of liberating J from V and of being himself a mother, but who is too busy cruising to do more than dream. But perhaps it is D who makes the most significant comment in the novel, when he asks: "When [a little girl] plays mother [to her doll] where is the father? Absent most of the time or never invented."[13] Since B feels passionate toward D at the same time as she becomes pregnant by a boy named Ollie we can hear in her situation a girl playing mother to her dolly. Hauser's play with dolly makes the men absent or never invented, and makes the mother-figure nongenital. But Hauser's game has an earnest object: to transform the figure of the biological genital-centered mother of us all into an alternative figure of the cultural mother, a figure in whom sit side by side philoprogenitiveness and sodomite crime. And one further situational pun in Hauser's narrative must be noted. B's loving identification with J, the sodomite mother, invites the reader to read J and B, the minor mother-to-be, as interchangeable. We thereby see a minor-as-mother become a type for a minority motherhood, a type which is being presented perhaps as still premature for the bearing of culture. Yet this desire that the sodomite lesbian be the cultural mother is, according to the novel, as old as girls playing with dolls. This equivalence of the most new and the most ancient desire suggests, through the sounding board of B's pregnancy, that the heterosexual family is still in *its* minority. And since Hauser conjoins the girl-narrator B with heterosexuality and minority, B's love for her sodomite mother J transmits the idea that there is no difference between sexual majority and minority longings. They both share homosexual and sodomite inclinations, and these inclinations, sublimated, are the root of nurture.

What I see is that *The Talking Room* reduces the individual to an alphabetic sign, and that the novel transgresses a legally and culturally constructed opposition between domestic nurture and sodomy; what I cannot see is that Hauser's narrative mode of reformism makes better sense as an undeclared defense of the status quo. If Hauser uses the form of her work to maintain for it a certain privacy of meaning, this is to forestall an appropriation of the novel's scarcely audible ideology by an already publicly established one. We must hear the difference between the majority and the minority versions of motherhood. The majority version insists that authoritative maternity is heterosexually genital, inalienably biological. But the minority version puts us in mind of what persons of heterosexual genitality might want to forget: that every child depends for nurture, and for an entry into culture, upon the displacement of the sexuality by which the child has been biologically engendered. Within the sphere of that displacement, homosexuality is relatively closer to culture than to nature. If the sodomite parenting which is the cynosure of *The Talking Room* were to become a public possibility, the family heart of the state would be transformed. The more nurture might be removed from biological origins, the more philoprogenitiveness might be assured, since parenting would become increasingly a matter of choice. It is because the sodomite parent threatens the present allegedly natural and spontaneous constitution of domesticity that lesbians or homosexuals or bisexuals who seek to foster or adopt children and who present themselves openly to the appropriate agencies do not find themselves welcomed. Only three years ago, presidential candidate Governor Dukakis forcibly withdrew a child from a male couple in Boston publicly licensed to foster him; the Governor declared the licensing a mistake. Not surprisingly, Dukakis continues to insist that heterosexuals make better foster parents than homosexuals—and maintains that were he to become president he would not issue an executive order banning discrimination on grounds of sexual preference.[14]

But of course it will be said (and, at this point, no doubt it will be said impatiently) that it is on account of the threat to the welfare of children, and not on account of any other threat, that homosexual parenting ought to be questioned. Allow me to postpone this important consideration, albeit second to no other, for yet a while. Hauser's elevation of the sodomite mother is enabled by her absence of *piety* about parenting. This absence made me note at first the novel's apparent hostility toward its agents—an appearance which needs a final reconsideration. Hauser's B, momentarily on the run from the lesbian grown-ups who are weekending at granny-anny's, describes "the back of the house which juts out broad and bare like granny-anny's when she . . . told them in Croatian to kiss it." Then she reflects: "I run away from home, each time for ever. For ever is never, each time I stumble over the same looped root and the same fallen bird nest."[15] The house—domesticity—is a sign of contempt for outsiders; it is also the sign of entrapment. Is this designation of domesticity—even of domesticity presided over by sodomy—not a counterexpression of contempt for households? In the 18 April 1988 issue of *New York* magazine, devoted to "How We Live Now," a gay man interviewed by the journal is designated the representative of current mores. He is certainly averse to households. He objects to the present AIDS-related trend toward homosexual domesticity—"Sometimes they'll adopt a kid. They'll work on their relationship. . . . I'm not sure that's the ultimate answer for a fully evolved gay person— imitating the straight world." The interviewee, varying B's formula for entrapment, seems to have the hang of the narrative ideologists' method. But the same speaker is also an energetic political activist —and given the history of homosexuality's retreat into privacy, we can say that his activism imitates the straight world's traditions, its commitment to the public dimension of life. The house that appears to be inescapable now, for heterosexual or homosexual, for parent or child, is the public sphere. The return to this house, bleak though it be, is politically inevitable.

Hauser uses as a leitmotif in *The Talking Room* the story of a convict who is so hungry for liberty that, having the key to his cell door for his escape, he can't resist swallowing it, and dies with the key in his stomach. We could read this as a parable of many things—among them, of homosexuality's having swallowed the key to liberty by its craving for privacy as the medium "for a fully evolved gay person," as a liberation from politics altogether. But a better liberty might lie only in public politics, and only through the public sphere's halfway house, domesticity. To be sure, all the desires—for domesticity or for whatever—represented in this novel are modeled on the ravening hunger for the key to liberty that is a forever unfulfilled privation. Hauser's toughness comes from knowing that neither the sodomite mother nor her children nor their lovers can bring this ravening to a satisfied stop. But in this regard one aspect of J's lover V, B's self-styled "aunt," must be read also in a parabolical way. V is a real-estate agent who houses her "practice of the family" in a Greenwich Village building, close to a vantage point on the Statue of Liberty. Next door to the house is a dilapidated site V also owns, and means to restore. Is this neighboring site the traditional heterosexual domestic realm? Although V means to renovate this other house, she continually procrastinates. Perhaps this is because she secretly remains committed to the heterosexual domesticity of the site. Yet V does all her work for J and for the minor-mother. Hauser's novel opposes two radically different domesticities to each other, and one would be hardpressed to assert that the opposition ends in deadlock. Given V's objects of devotion, renovation work *is* under way, transforming the possession of conventional heterosexual housing into the dispossesssion of what is conventional. Under the ascendancy of the sodomite mother, the heterosexual site is and remains ruined, at least insofar as the heterosexual no longer has property rights on the engendering and the nurturing of the future.

In Andrews's book the renovation of the heterosexual household uses a narrative form that is more traditional than Hauser's. *The Story of Harold* is the title of a popular children's storybook written by the novel's protagonist, one Terry Andrews. Just as the novel's pseudonymous author (whom I shall refer to as Andrews) is made indistinguishable from the novel's protagonist (whom I shall refer to as Terry), so the storybook within the story is indistinguishable from the novel itself. Indeed the story of Terry's invented character Harold turns into an elaborate nest of tales, in which Terry's friends and lovers are dramatized by an array of fictions-within-fictions that fills the novel with self-reflexive play. Accordingly, the novel is perfectly traditional—even Dickensian—in its dedication to elaborate plottings; and it is at the same time perfectly modern or postmodern in the way it foregrounds narrative procedures, as if to meditate metacritically on storytelling. The conventional-traditional—in terms of story and family both—and the subversion of the traditional are side by side here. But the juxtaposition is not the sign of a deadlock between the two sides.

Story and narrative are portrayed by Andrews as crucially helping children to live, to get them through the perilous long time in which biology makes them wait for maturity. Narrative is thus given a parental nurturing role. "Not enough of the light from the idea of life has reached me," the narrator says in a despairing moment.[16] Narrative in the novel is this light from the idea of life. But *The Story of Harold* assigns the origin and operation of this nurturing idea to sources that are suspect (at least to the legal and civic police). Whereas Hauser figures her narrative as a play on oral sodomy, Andrews figures his as a play on anality, and of anality—although the figuration comprehends cunnilingus as well. Indeed the perversity of Andrews's narrator and storyteller knows few bounds. Emphatically of the pre-AIDS era, Terry carries on three simultaneous love affairs: one with a widow and mother, one with a married male surgeon who is the father of several children, and one with a single male social worker. The affairs with the men are confusedly sadomasochistic, which is partly the result of Terry's being more in love with the surgeon than with the others. Since this love is not equally returned, it is aggression-filled and desperate, and leads Terry into a suicide-murder pact with his other male lover, who has arranged a slave's masochistic love-death at the hands of his woeful master. But in the course of the novel the suicidal and murderous elements in the narrator are reversed, and he is freed from them.

The agency of the reversal is narrative. Although Terry is a professional writer of children's books, he appears to write so that he can keep children and his own childishness at a distance. This distance collapses when he is asked to help Barney, a friend's depressed seven-year-old. Terry undertakes to stimulate Barney by a chain of stories which allegorize his and Barney's reluctance to live. Along with Barney's terrors, all Terry's crimes against nature—appropriately disguised—enter into the fabulous narratives which come to overtake the novel. But it is this overtaking of reality by the narratives whose source is sexually illicit that in the end helps Terry and the child to come back to life. This happens, for one thing, because of the way the narratives disrupt the category of the individual. Terry becomes the sodomite cultural father, the male equivalent of Hauser's J, by the way his stories bridge the gap between the private and the public, and bring to Terry's closet for the first time a realm of public consequence. In fact the problem for Terry and Barney is that they experience the biological family as a purely private structure, hence as a deprivation of more extended and more vital cultural relations. The suicidal depression felt by both the man and the child results when they experience a loss of biological parents that has no compensation in the public cultural realm. In the American scene as Andrews portrays it there is no public; instead there is only an intense arena of private, mostly sexual interests. Here heterosexual biological parenthood creates privacy as a deprivation of public relation and consequence. In fostering and in effect adopting Barney, Terry links biological nurture to cultural nurture. He heartens the child—and heartens himself—because his stories invent and reveal a world that even in its familial dimension is no longer purely private or dedicated to privacy. In Andrews it is the family's jealous dedication to privacy that sickens children, for it gives them only biological family relations in which to live.

But it must be stressed that this entry into the public realm through the novel's interidentity of parenthood and narrative does not integrate or unify the individuality of Terry or of the child. The emphases on individuality and inward privacy in the Supreme Court's rights discourse would not be confirmed by Andrews's novel. *The Story of Harold* dramatizes not what Justice Blackmun would call the single decisional private self but the variety of selves which make up Terry and Barney, and life in general. Narrative can intervene in existing affairs because of the persistent open-ended and divided nature (both public and private) of personal identity and of the status quo.

But how is this creative intervention by fictional narrative equated in Andrews with anality and with a sodomite relation to the anus? This question needs answering before we can see how narratives arising from such a source can be related to philoprogenitiveness, and can escape representing the forces that repress these relations. Terry's stories to Barney are all oral narratives; they are therefore curiously related to Terry's romance with the widowed mother, Anne, since his sexual gratification of her is primarily cunnilingal. In this way Terry's storytelling mode is brought close to sodomy and maternity—his oral talent seems to have a clitoral and vaginal inspiration. But the content of Terry's stories—which, since it is for a child's hearing, displaces and desexualizes whatever sexual sources it has—derives largely from his male relations. And these relations are anus-centered. What Andrews leads us to make of this anality has a special force in turning aside the charge that novels produce and take for granted ("all along" their history) a sheltered, private space. Andrews is disrupting the most private of our bodily spaces and making narrative the agent of the disruption.

To explain Andrews's strategy I need to make use of Guy Hocquenghem's *Homosexual Desire*, published in France in 1972, and so a part of the era and ethos of *The Story of Harold*. Attempting to develop a theory of homosexual anal eroticism, Hocquenghem speculates that "ours is a phallic society," ruled by a "despotic signifier," the fetishized and sublimated penis. As a result, a structural social opposition between public and private realms founds itself on a kind of structural social mapping of male bodies. "Every man possesses a phallus which guarantees him a social role; every man has an anus which is truly his own, in the most secret depths of his own person." The autocracy of the phallus makes the phallus "essentially social," whereas in contrast "the anus has no social position except sublimation. The functions of this organ are truly private; they are the site of the formation of the person. The anus expresses privatisation itself"; it is "overinvested individually because its investment is withdrawn socially." Hocquenghem argues (so much for Judges Norris and Reinhardt) that "only homosexuals make such constant libidinal use of this zone," and, as a result, "homosexual desire challenges anality-sublimation because it restores the desiring use of the anus." This restoration in turn subverts the oppositional organization of social life into public and private categories. Homosexuality takes the erotic-organic anal space of privatization and of the constitution of one's proper self ("Control of the anus is the precondition of taking responsibility for property. The ability to 'hold back' or to evacuate the feces is the necessary moment of the constitution of the self"), and violates this sheltered space.[17] In practicing the desiring use of the anus, the homosexual liberates the foundation of privacy from public deprivation. He makes the anus a public competitor with the phallus; he unseats property and privacy by publicly exposing their source.

We can see at once in Hocquenghem a relevance to the Supreme Court's obsession with privacy, and to Andrews's use of narrative. Although the Court speaks up on behalf of intimate sexual privacy, insofar as that privacy concerns consensual heterosexuality, the source of its concern is deeper than nonsodomite genitality. Its source is the heart of the individual, but this heart's model turns out to be the anus. Justifying the outlawing of sodomy, the Court—and the public—can hide from themselves the equation of anality with cherished fundamental inwardness. Homosexual desire to liberate the anus from sexual prohibition threatens the purposive unconsciousness of this equation, and threatens individuation and privacy too. The judicial police cannot permit these threats. Allowing the states and the Constitution to supervise what men and women do with their anuses paradoxically insures privatization, and the withdrawal of the anus from any association with public value or significance. Thus the homosexual must not be allowed fundamental rights to consensual anal sodomy; that would be virtually to assign (in public!) an asshole to the Constitution. No such thing could be in the make-up or the makers-up of that document; and if it were there, it would be, naturally, insignificant—and utterly private. But the homosexual impulse is to advance this private insignificance, to connect more closely with the public this anal privacy upon which identity is founded. Of course the accomplishment of the connection would transform public and private alike.

As for fictional narrative, this transformational impulse is connected by Andrews with a contention between storytelling and other forms of discourse and ideology. Judicial discourse permits narrative only an inferior place in its adjudications: personal stories must submit themselves to the law's analytic structural discourse. The law expresses to Michael Hardwick's or to Perry Watkins's specific stories (in all their interrelations) an equivalent of the remark by one of Terry's lovers, who finds *The Story of Harold* in the bathroom and, beginning to read, exclaims: " 'Fuckin' Harold woke up one fuckin' morning'—what *is* this shit?"[18] For official discourse, that is to say, narratives are dross, useful only for spinning into strictly articulated nonfictional gold. Nevertheless, in Andrews's book the messiness of narrative (it can't control itself) and the lowness of its origin violate mature, reasonable order and discourse—and thereby prop up, extend, and transform life.

I am not using Andrews to say that narrative has always or essentially a relation to sodomy or anality. I am using him to suggest that narrative will attach itself to—and will shelter, in a kind of public housing—whatever narrative's environing general ideologies and specific discourses make homeless. If, thanks to the ideological and discursive environment, not enough light from the idea of life reaches the homeless, then narrative can attach itself to the anus and find us a solar consolation even there. But since I mention the home, and suggest a domestication of the homeless in the same breath as I allude to Bataille, I must again consider the homophobic hazards apparently courted (as ideological narrative poetics would point out) by *The Story of Harold*'s philoprogenitiveness. How can or does the novel draw upon sodomy for its very model of representation and not compromise its sources by linking the latter to family feeling? Hocquenghem the theorist of anal desublimation intends to undo two systematic economies of phallic rule: the economies of capitalism and of the modern family. For him Freudianism is a subset of these economies, and he defends sodomite anality against co-optation by a discourse about the family. He fears that the eroticized anus will be accounted for as a secondary consequence of an unresolved hetero-sexual Oedipus complex. Such consideration would reinscribe homo-phobia in any theory of the anus; it would desublimate anality by making it all too familiarly familial.

But the suspicion of discursive self-entrapment—the fear of that process of simultaneous self-enabling and self-undoing which is seen by ideological narrative poetics to be characteristic of all discourse—makes Hocquenghem's thinking falter. How does his theory fit—if at all—with lesbian desire? What matter if, as he says, "The anus is not a substitute for the vagina; women have one as well as men";[19] since in making this assertion so as to ward off "oedipalization," Hocqueng-hem overlooks the way male sodomites will gender the anus, careless that both genders "have one." If the theorist *worries* that the anus *is* a substitute for the vagina, is he not already oedipalized in thought? The fear of compromise with "oedipalization" and "family" leads the theorist not even to ask, let alone answer, questions that lie in his logic's path. In Andrews's light I suggest that the theorist's neglect of children underlies and intensifies this fear of the family. It is an odd neglect, since the fear seems to be itself based on a child's ter-ror of a grimly phallic parental figure. Precisely what this terrified child needs—i.e., another kind of parent—is forgotten in the theorist's terror-based hostility to the family in general. Clearly Andrews means to present Terry and his lovers Anne and the surgeon as such parental alternatives.

At first sight the surgeon Jim appears to be anything but an ideal. Seen in the light of Terry's angry and despairing fixation, Jim's refusal to declare his love for any of the men who sodomize him looks purely homophobic, an aggressive counterdefense against his pursuit of passive anal pleasure, usually in a dangerously masochistic form (because it includes penetration by the lover's fist). But the narrative suggests a curious motive (albeit not the only one) for this pursuit. The surgeon has a blind child (another version of Barney—and of Oedipus), whom he is desperate to help. This desperation appears to extend itself into an obsessive pursuit of sexual danger and transgression. It is as if the father is using sexual obsession and excess in his relations with men to push against all ordinary limits, and so is practicing a kind of sympathetic magic on his child's behalf. For if the adult can exceed the conventional constraints (even the constraints of physiology) upon adult sexuality, then he can take hope in his child's ability to overcome the constraints of blindness. The father's sexual activity with other adults is presented in this way as an extension of a desire to prop up a failing child's life. Jim does not love Terry for himself, but the reason for this is not homophobia. He loves him as part of a project that uses Eros to gain for his family more light from the idea of life.

Sexuality, domesticity, and narrative in *The Story of Harold* are alike derivatives, one is made to feel, of a pursuit of life more elemental than each. This pursuit is for the sake of children, and is also every child's own, in the face of the child's biological and emotional dependency that makes the pursuit especially vulnerable. In the face of Barney's and Terry's suicidal woes, what matters is any and every form of nurture that stimulates the child to keep on living. Domesticity is inevitably one of these modes; whatever griefs it causes children, if we condemn the ideology of parenting and of the family altogether, we are suggesting that supporting children's lives is not just politically but humanly reactionary, even anti-vital. Outside of academic discourse, this is a hard suggestion to swallow. Moreover, parental nurture is scarcely the monopoly of conventional domesticity or of heterosexuality—unless we agree with Jack Kemp's point of view. Terry's gradual commitment to being one of Barney's parents —a commitment that is terminated willingly upon the appearance of a stepfather for the boy—is and is not domestic.

One of the problems with Miller's picture of the family is that he does not see the family produce connections with anything but arms of the law. Presumably work and friendship are also disciplinary relations. But although Freud's darkest reflections on the murderousness of the supervisory superego influence Miller's kind of poetics, *The Story of Harold* reminds us of relations—the work of storytelling, the work of friendship—that escape punitive agency. Terry's and Barney's isolated privacies foster in them a killing sadism and masochism, but the work of nurturing friendship that brings them together, limiting their privacy, fosters in them a love of life that resists the destructive superego. The representation of Terry's growing parental stature shows no mere imitation of the straight world; it is rather an imitation of fantastic storytelling, which has here more nurturing power than any other form of vital organization. I might add, finally, that to suggest homosexual interest in nurturing children is a "pro-straight" sign of homophobia is the equivalent of suggesting that every homosexual's interest in children is the sign of pedophilia.

In *The Story of Harold* stories prop up, parent-fashion, the vital functions of children by displacing children's immediate concerns, and hence by making them feel liberated from those concerns' restraints and vulnerabilities. Bringing about "meetings of the unthinkable and the real," Terry's stories enact these liberations by dissolving and diffusing the identities and the inwardness of the narrator and his listeners.[20] In his narratives Terry's and Barney's "selves" appear in a metamorphic series—they are by turns the magical Harold (whose actions resemble the surgeon-lover's pushing against limits), a rancorously oedipalized Rumpelstiltskin, a sullenly and reluctantly antisocial Rat, an all-devouring rage called the Three-legged Nothing, a Family Jewel called Mama Pin. These fissurings of Terry's and Barney's "identity" escape Terry's narrative control, much to his own surprise. But it is the uncontrollable aspects of narrative that constitute its vitalizing effect—even when the effect is frightening. The Mama Pin character is intended to provide Barney with a sweet way

for him to come to terms with his real mother, but the intention mis-
carries into terror—as does another, later story, which provokes the
boy to swallow Seconal. But these dark turns of Andrews's narrative
exhibit a less dark assertion: that narrative courts the death of identity to make life more full of relations, hence more vital. In spite of
the dangerous confusions Barney and Terry muddle through, when
Barney begins to take over the storytelling he shows signs of having
gotten Terry's point: the sodomite above all wants the child to live,
in and through a realm that is not private.

The heterosexual world sees the homosexual's relation to children
as a version of *Rumpelstiltskin*. Presumably the canny homosexual
pariah wants the child not for the sake of extending the child's life,
but for the sake of a nefarious purpose, opposed to the natural family
and natural sexuality. In child custody cases where a homosexual
parent is concerned, the judicial tradition makes its overture to narrative by usually treating the gay parent as the nasty dwarf. But
what impact *do* homosexual parents have on children? A Brigham
Young University research team, reviewing the seventeen studies on
the subject since 1978, finds that there is no evidence substantiat-
ing heterosexual fears about the detrimental effects of homosexual
parents on children. "No evidence of aberrant gender identity, social
development, or sexual object choice" is reported.[21] Does this mean
that homosexual parenting and homosexual domesticity have no influence on the status quo? If the children of even the most modest
estimate of the number (1.5 million) of American homosexual parents can witness that their parents have wanted them above all to
live, with no nefarious intention, we might expect the heart of the
existing order—even its judicial heart—to be changed. We might expect homosexuals to be recognized as citizens of the public realm.
Even so, perhaps as long as the ideology of legal discourse resists
narrative, I cannot be sanguine about the transformation.

Andrews's Terry is fascinated by an ontological rather than by an
erotic triangle—"These three things: The Impossible, the Possible,
the Real."[22] In spite of attempts by judicial or critical police to straiten
narratives, narrative relations—as the great sodomite (or would-be

sodomite) storyteller says—stop nowhere in their traversal of the triangular dialectic. Because of the dialectic's open-endedness, the categories of the status quo can be transformed with the help of stories. Such transformation, however, can involve (as it does in *Andrews*) a further metamorphosis: one whereby the real, the possible, and the impossible change places. In relation to *Hardwick* and its legal progeny, homosexual fiction becomes a shelter for homosexual reality, a shelter from whose perspective the legal discourse appears to be a realm of shadow-puppets. The puppets argue about what homosexual identity is, determining to fix it, so that they can decide if it is "suspect" or criminal, can either liberate it or supervise it. To homosexuals, these debates appear to be exercises—whether sympathetic or not—in making up crude fictions, unacknowledged as such by their makers. Blacks and women know this experience, in which general ideology, and this or that institutional practice of it, becomes unreal to a whole segment of a population. It is not of much interest for those who know this experience to be told that, after all, every social order and conflict is entirely a network of arbitrary constructions in which the adversaries reinforce their dilemmas by a secret-yet-open likeness to each other. In the light (or darkness) of such knowledge, nothing changes; the powerful unreal constructions still do harm to those whom their powerful ideologies cannot engage as real lives. Against oppressive Victorian powers Dickens kept insisting that his fictions were true, for the stories unhoused by official Victorian discourse had to take up their abode in what was left them —the abode classified by the judges and the police as unreal. And now in contemporary American fictions, homosexual realities unhoused by official judicial discourse similarly take up abode in the realm designated officially as impossible, as narratives out of court.

I will put the idea that fictional narratives of homosexual desire for public life and of homosexual philoprogenitiveness might reproduce the homophobic impulses of their opponents next to one last judicial discourse, resulting from *Hardwick*, less than two months after the Court decision's announcement. *Appeal in Pima County Juvenile Action B-10489*, an Arizona case, tells us that an admittedly bisexual man, licensed by the appropriate Arizona state agency to be placed among prospective adoptive parents who wait to be matched with

adoptive children, had his license revoked by the Superior Court of
Pima County. Judge James D. Hathaway of the Court of Appeals
upheld the revocation. Hathaway says that he does not uphold the
Superior Court on the grounds that the appellant is bisexual. Instead
he claims that the appellant lives in a way not in the best interests of
a child who might be adopted by him. The evidence for this is that
the appellant "has held at least eight different employment positions
in eleven years; . . . has sought counseling for personal problems
repeatedly," and has a "limited" family support system. And then
there is *Hardwick*:

> Homosexual conduct [in Arizona] is proscribed. . . . Such statutes
> have been held constitutional. . . . Appellant testified that it was
> possible he . . . would have some type of homosexual relationship
> . . . even with placement of a child in his home. He also testified
> . . . he did not believe . . . continued homosexual activity would
> have an adverse effect on a child . . . he might adopt. It would be
> anomalous for the state on the one hand to declare homosexual
> conduct unlawful and on the other create a parent after that
> proscribed model, in effect approving that standard, inimical to
> the natural family, as head of a state-created family.[23]

The dissenting judge in this case, Lawrence Howard, is outraged.
Hathaway, Howard points out, distorts every point of evidence about
the appellant. With a specificity of detail that is absent in Hathaway's
decision, the dissent points out the grounds on which the appellant's
case worker had recommended certification. There *is* a support system, it appears; the appellant's changes of employment are explained
as the result of his listing various business consultant jobs on his
vita; the appellant is a teacher at Pima Community College, with a
salary of more than $32,000 a year (in 1985). As for the counseling
"problem," the appellant sought psychiatric help upon his honor-
able discharge from the Navy twelve years before; it turns out that
Hathaway is including in the appellant's "repeated" counseling needs
the appellant's statement that "I occasionally, probably two or three
times a year make an appointment with a pastoral counselor, to talk
about what's going on in my life." As for the welfare of the child
to be adopted in this case, Judge Howard points out that Hathaway

not only ignores everything the appellant's caseworker says about his parental ability, but makes a spectral, nonexistent child the measure of the court's decision. B-10489 seeks to adopt a school-age child, and the caseworker speaks to the court about the advantage for many adoptive children of a single-parent family. But Hathaway —the friend of the "natural" family—worries that B-10489 wants a child for the purpose of sexually abusing it. This idea, and the idea of a homosexual parent's "recruiting" a child for homosexuality, seems to be the focus of Hathaway's considerations of the child's best interest. What the caseworker has to say about the impact of parental homosexuality, which is along the lines of the *Bulletin of the American Academy of Psychiatry and the Law* article, does not matter. Nor does the fact that no specific child is yet at issue. But "until there is a particular child and a petition to adopt that child," Howard writes, the standards concerning the child's best interests do not apply.[24] And as for *Hardwick's* impact on the case, Howard believes it should not be used in a way that bears adversely on homosexual or bisexual adoptive parents if it does not bear on every parent. What shall the law do to investigate whether parents of any kind are sodomites?

But B-10489 has lost his case. And even the decent dissenting judge shows the biases of judicial discourse: he is pleased that B-10489 has nothing to do with gay rights activism, for *that* might well render an applicant unacceptable.[25] The homosexual must take no *politically* active, no *public* recourse against Whites and Hathaways; his virtue remains his privacy. In this note of Judge Howard's we see how the police maintain liberty by their intervening supervision of it. But what of B-10489, and his relation to the insights of ideological narrative poetics? How does his case exhibit his complicity with his adversaries? Having found B-10489's need for counseling to be suspect, Judge Hathaway's decision has probably intensified that need. So we might convey to B-10489 the following suspicious counsels derived from ideological narrative poetics: that he has perhaps desired a parental relation to a child in order to become one with his oppressors; that in losing the case he might be consoled to find that he is, after all, not one with the all-policing judiciary. Yet we must suggest to him, then, that in losing his case he has really not become the adversary of the court—in his privacy he inhabits the cherished right and the ideology of his oppressor, and becomes like him once more. And should he think of moving forward into public action again (but this time without "domestic" ideological baggage), we will remind B-10489 that this will cause him to become only another of the agencies of power to which he seeks to become an alternative. Of course, we cannot surmise what the hypothetical child who did not find a life support in B-10489 would think of these insights. As for the man, at least he has some alternatively consoling ways of thinking about his case, and even of carrying it on—ways that are not derivable from ideological narrative poetics. His impossible aim and appeal are housed already, have even succeeded, in novels like *The Talking Room* and *The Story of Harold*.

Notes

1 D. A. Miller, *The Novel and the Police* (Berkeley and Los Angeles, 1988), 81–82.
2 Ibid., 76, 85, 2, 104.
3 Ibid., 20.
4 Terry Eagleton, *Criticism and Ideology: A Study in Marxist Literary Theory* (Norfolk, 1976), 161.
5 Miller, *Novel and the Police*, 100.
6 Eagleton, *Criticism and Ideology*, 185, 124, 126, 140.
7 Bowers v. Hardwick, 106 S. Ct. 2841 (1986), 2844.
8 Ibid., 2851, 2854.
9 Watkins v. United States Army, 837 F.2d 1428 (9th Cir. 1988), 1442.
10 Ibid., 1457, 1461, 1455, 1454, 1454 n. 4.
11 Bowers v. Hardwick, 2846, 2854 n. 5.
12 Watkins v. United States Army, 1459.
13 Marianne Hauser, *The Talking Room* (New York, 1976), 42.
14 Douglas Jehl, "Dukakis Seeks Gays' Support, Draws Occasional Hisses," *Los Angeles Times*, 15 May 1988, sec. 1.
15 Hauser, *Talking Room*, 92–93.
16 Terry Andrews, *The Story of Harold* (New York, 1974), 318.
17 Guy Hocquenghem, *Homosexual Desire*, trans. Daniella Dangoor (London, 1978), 80, 82–85.
18 Andrews, *Story of Harold*, 42.
19 Hocquenghem, *Homosexual Desire*, 89.
20 Andrews, *Story of Harold*, 56.
21 David J. Kleber, Robert J. Howell, and Alta Lura Tibbits-Kleber, "The Impact of Parental Homosexuality in Child Custody Cases: A Review of the Literature," *Bulletin of the American Academy of Psychiatry and the Law* 14 (1986): 83.

22 Andrews, *Story of Harold*, 57.
23 *Appeal in Pima County Juvenile Action B-10489*, 727 P.2d 830 (Ariz. App. 1986), 832, 835.
24 Ibid., 836, 842.
25 Ibid., 840.

Lee Edelman

The Plague of Discourse: Politics, Literary Theory, and AIDS

In an article titled "The Metaphor of AIDS," published for a popular audience in the Sunday magazine of the *Boston Globe*, Lee Grove, an instructor of creative writing and American literature at the University of Massachusetts, reflects on the ways in which the AIDS epidemic has altered his understanding of literary texts and his relation to the teaching of literature. Referring specifically to the Renaissance pun that brought together, at least linguistically, the experiences of orgasm and death, Grove writes:

> "To die," "to have sex"—that coupling has always been figurative, metaphorical, sophisticated wordplay, a literary conceit, one of those outrageous paradoxes dear to the heart of a racy divine like John Donne.
> Outrageous no longer. The coupling isn't figurative anymore. It's literal.[1]

I want to consider the highly charged relation between the literal and the figural as it informs the discussion of AIDS in America and to explore the political uses to which the ideological framing of that relationship has been put. Toward that end my subtitle locates "literary theory" between the categories of "politics" and "AIDS" to indicate my belief that both of those categories produce, and are produced as, historical discourses susceptible to analysis by the critical methodologies associated with literary theory.

This is not to say that literary theory occupies some unproblematic or privileged position; to the contrary, literature, including that form of literature that is literary theory, is by no means distinct from political discourse, and thus from either the discourse on AIDS, or the politics that governs the discourse on AIDS. By the same token, politics and AIDS cannot be disentangled from their implication in the linguistic or the rhetorical. Indeed, one of the ideological oppositions I would call into question is that whereby the biological, associated with the literal or the "real," is counterposed against the literary, associated with the figural or the fictive. That opposition is already deeply and unavoidably political, which is to say, it bespeaks an ideologically determined hierarchy of values in which power—the power to speak seriously, to speak with authority, and thereby to influence policy—is very much at stake in the claim to be able to speak literally.

The AIDS epidemic, then, is not to be construed, as Grove asserts, in terms of its defiguralizing literality, but rather, and more dangerously, as the breeding ground for all sorts of figural associations whose virulence derives from their presentation under the aspect of literality. Indeed, one of the most disturbing features that characterizes the discourse on AIDS in America is the way in which the literal is recurrently and tendentiously produced as a figure whose figurality remains strategically occluded—a figure that thus has the potential to be used toward the most politically repressive ends. The often hysterical terms within which the Western discussion of AIDS has been conducted reflect an untenable, but politically manipulable, belief that we can separate biological science, and therefore the social policy based on that science, from the instability and duplicity that literary theory has increasingly identified as inherent in the operations of language.

Though my subject necessarily involves literature and AIDS, my focus falls not on those literary works wherein the urgency of AIDS achieves thematic inscription, but rather on the inevitable inscriptions of the literary that mark the discourse on AIDS. The text that provides the occasion for my analysis, the text on which my remarks will turn or trope, is a relatively brief one, "Silence = Death." This slogan has achieved wide currency, particularly—though by no means exclusively—within the gay community, both as a challenge to the murderously delayed and cynically inadequate official responses to AIDS and as a rallying cry for those who have borne the burden of death and suffering, calling upon them to defend themselves against the dangerous discourse of mastery produced by medical or legislative authorities in order to defend their *own* vested interests in the face of this epidemic. Significantly, issues of defense achieve an inevitable centrality in discussions of AIDS in ways that critically distinguish this epidemic from many others. Because the syndrome attacks the body's defensive mechanisms; because once it does so, science as yet can offer no defense against it; because in the West it has appeared primarily among groups already engaged in efforts to defend themselves against the intolerance of the dominant culture; because modern science and the national political institutions funding modern science feel called upon to defend their prestige against the assault on medical know-how represented by this disease; because individuals and groups, often irrationally, seek ways to defend themselves against contact with this disease; and because some politicians, in order to defend against political opposition, deploy the AIDS issue strategically to ensure their own political survival: for all of these reasons the question of defense is inextricably and distinctively inscribed in the discourse on AIDS. And as this preliminary formulation of the issues suggests, my focus is on the interrelations among the notions of discourse, defense, and disease—particularly as they intersect with the already activated ideologies of homosexuality and homophobia in the West to converge at the virulent site of discursive contention that is AIDS.

These last words seem to define AIDS in a way that few in the medical profession would recognize, so let me present a definition of AIDS at the outset that will seem more literal, or as students of rhetoric would say, more "proper." According to current scientific understanding, and I hasten to add that it is not my intention nec-essarily to endorse or validate that understanding, AIDS results from infection with some quantity of HIV or Human Immunodeficiency Virus, which attacks the cells of the immune system, particularly the T-helper or T-4 cells, and impairs the body's ability to defend itself against viral, fungal, and parasitic infections. Medical researchers would thus accept a characterization of AIDS as an infectious condi-tion in which the stake is "literally" the possibility of defense. As David Black puts it simply in *The Plague Years*, his "chronicle" of AIDS, "the immune system is the body's complex and still imper-fectly understood defense mechanism. Its job is to tell the difference between Self and Not-Self."[2] I will come back to the Emersonian im-plications of this description of the immune response, but for now I want to examine the notion of defense and its importance not only in the bio-logic articulated within the body by AIDS, but also in the re-active or defensive discourse embodied in the slogan Silence = Death. For if that slogan challenges those in the communities most affected by AIDS to defend themselves, it does so by appealing to defensive properties that it implicitly identifies as inherent in discourse. The slogan, after all, which most frequently appears in a graphic con-figuration that positions the letters of its text, in white, beneath a pink triangle on a field of black, alludes to the Nazi campaign against homosexuals (identified in the concentration camps by the pink tri-angle they were required to wear) in order to propose a gay equiva-lent to the post-Holocaust rallying cry of Jewish activists: "Never again." At the same time, Silence = Death can be read as a post-AIDS revision of a motto popular among gay militants not long ago —"Out of the closets and into the streets"—and as such it similarly implies that language, discourse, public manifestations are necessary weapons of defense in a contemporary strategy of gay survival. For if we assert that Silence = Death, then one corollary to this theorem in the geometry that governs the relationship among discourse, de-fense, and disease must be that Discourse = Defense, that language, articulation, the intervention of voice, is salutary, vivifying, since discourse can defend us against the death that must result from the continuation of our silence.

But to speak of mechanisms of defense, particularly in terms of linguistic operations, is necessarily to invoke the specter of Freud, who offered us a taxonomy of psychic defenses in his studies of the unconscious and its operations. And here, as always, Freud calls into question the basis for any naive optimism about the success of our defensive maneuvers. Here is a passage from H. D.'s memoir of her psychoanalysis by Freud that speaks to the relation between discourse and defense in a particularly telling way: only once, according to H. D., did Freud ever "lay down the law" and that was when he said "never—I mean, never at any time, in any circumstance, endeavor to defend me, if and when you hear abusive remarks made about me and my work." H. D. then goes on to recall: "He explained it carefully. He might have been giving a lesson in geometry or demonstrating the inevitable course of a disease once the virus has entered the system. At this point, he seemed to indicate (as if there were a chart of the fever patient, pinned on the wall before us), at the least suggestion that you may be about to begin a counterargument in my defense, the anger or frustration of the assailant will be driven deeper. You will do no good to the detractor by mistakenly beginning a logical defense. You will drive the hatred or the fear or the prejudice in deeper."[3] Defense of this sort is necessarily failed defense; far from being salubrious, it serves only to compromise further one's immunity and to stimulate greater virulence. Interestingly enough, this corresponds to the process whereby, according to some medical researchers, HIV moves from a state of latency in an infected cell to active reproduction. The defensive "stimulation of an immune response" seems to be one of "the conditions that activates the production of new" HIV that can then go on to infect other cells.[4] Since defensive maneuvers may have the unintended effect of disseminating or intensifying infection, the relationship between the two can be rearticulated in the formula: Defense = Disease.

Freud's argument in warning H. D. against engaging in defensive interventions significantly echoes the logic sounded centuries earlier by Plato in the *Timaeus*. Writing specifically about the wisdom of medical interventions to defend the body against the ravages of disease, Plato offers a cautionary note: "diseases unless they are very dangerous should not be irritated by medicines, since every form of disease is in a manner akin to the living being, whose complex frame has an appointed term of life. . . . And this holds also of the constitution of diseases; if any one regardless of the appointed time tries to subdue them by medicine, he only aggravates and multiplies them."[5] The word here translated as "medicine" derives, as Jacques Derrida argues in "Plato's Pharmacy," from the Greek word *pharmakon* signifying a drug or philter that occupies an ambiguous position as remedy and poison at once. Commenting on this passage from Plato, Derrida observes: "Just as health is auto-nomous and auto-matic, 'normal' disease demonstrates its autarky by confronting the pharmaceutical aggression with *metastatic* reactions which displace the site of the disease, with the eventual result that the points of resistance are reinforced and multiplied."[6] Thus for Plato, as for Freud, gestures of defense can aggravate rather than ameliorate one's condition. Freud, of course, is referring explicitly to language or discourse as a mechanism of defense against one's enemies or detractors; H. D.'s reference to the "course of a disease once the virus has entered the system" is clearly presented only as a figural embellishment. Plato, on the other hand, is referring explicitly to medical defenses against disease, but considerations of discourse are decisively at issue in his discussion as well.

In the long and complicated argument unfolded in "Plato's Pharmacy," Derrida shows how Plato identifies writing with the *pharmakon*, thus rendering it simultaneously a poison, a remedy, a fantastic or magical philter, and a rational medical technology. If writing as *pharmakon* is already, at the beginning of Western culture, producing an entanglement of literary and medical discourse, its antithesis, the true voice of speech, is identified by Plato in the *Phaedrus* with the vital force of *logos*. Thus Derrida characterizes Plato's notion of *logos* in the following words:

> *Logos* is a *zoon*. An animal that is born, grows, belongs to the *phusis*. Linguistics, logic, dialectics, and zoology are all in the same camp.

In describing *logos* as a *zoon*, Plato is following certain rhetors and sophists before him who, as a contrast to the cadaverous rigidity of writing, had held up the living spoken word.[7]

Derrida's strategy in deconstructing the opposition between speech and writing is to show how the living word of speech is already informed by or predicated upon a form of writing or an *archi-écriture*. But of particular importance for my purposes is the way in which Derrida's reading of Plato insists upon the inextricability of the textual and the biological even as it uses rhetorical or literary techniques to subvert or dismantle the rational edifice of the Western philosophical tradition.

Consider again Derrida's gloss on Plato's wariness about the *pharmakon* in *Timaeus*: "Just as health is auto-nomous and auto-matic, 'normal' disease demonstrates its autarky by confronting the pharmaceutical aggression with *metastatic* reactions which displace the site of the disease, with the eventual result that the points of resistance are reinforced or multiplied." Bearing in mind that Derrida's reading of the *pharmakon* explicitly invokes the critical conjunction of discourse and biology informing the platonic opposition between writing as supplement and speech as living word, his gloss suggests that defensive strategies deployed—in the realm of discourse or disease—to combat agencies of virulence may themselves be informed by the virulence they are seeking to efface, informed by it in ways that do not produce the immunizing effect of a vaccine, but that serve, instead, to reinforce and even multiply the dangerous sites of infection. Derrida makes explicit this pathology of rhetoric when, elsewhere in "Plato's Pharmacy," he remarks that "metaphoricity is the contamination of logic and the logic of contamination."[8] In other words, Disease = Discourse. Derrida's diagnosis of metaphor as contamination makes clear that the rationalism of philosophical logic— a rationalism that provides the foundation for Western medical and scientific practice—is not untainted by the figurality that philosophy repudiates as literary, and, in consequence, as deceptive, inessential, and expendable. Both logic and contamination are very much at stake in the unfolding of these infectiously multiplying equations. Perhaps by returning to the germ of these remarks it will be possible to see how the logic of equations distinctively contaminates the discourse on AIDS.

Against my initial text, Silence = Death, let me juxtapose a passage from an open letter written by Larry Kramer, AIDS activist and author of, among other things, *The Normal Heart*, a play about the difficulties of getting Americans—gay and straight alike—to pay serious attention to the AIDS epidemic. Outraged by dilatory and inadequate responses at the early stages of the medical crisis, Kramer is quoted as having addressed the following words to both the press and the leaders of the gay rights movement: "That all of you . . . continue to refuse to transmit to the public the facts and figures of what is happening *daily* makes you, in my mind, equal to murderers."[9] Beside Kramer's remark I would place a graffito that David Black describes as having been scrawled on a wall at New York University: "Gay Rights = AIDS."[10] A somewhat less overtly homophobic but no less insidious version of this notion is offered by Frances Fitzgerald in her analysis of the effects of AIDS on San Francisco's Castro Street community: "The gay carnival, with its leather masks and ball gowns, had thus been the twentieth-century equivalent of the Masque of the Red Death."[11] And finally, here is a quotation from a "26-year-old-never-married woman" cited by Masters and Johnson in *Newsweek* magazine's excerpt from their controversial book on AIDS: "No sex, no worries. No sex, no AIDS. It's really a very simple equation, isn't it?"[12] Even this brief list indicates that it is by no means a "simple equation," but rather a complex pattern of equations that must lead us to consider just what is at issue in this effort to translate differences (such as silence/death, leaders/murderers, gay rights/AIDS) into identities through a language that invokes the rhetorical form of mathematical or scientific inevitability (A = B), a language of equations that can be marshaled in the service of homophobic (Gay Rights = AIDS) or antihomophobic (Silence = Death) discourse.

In thinking about this we would do well to recall that it is precisely the question of equality, the post-Stonewall demand for equal rights for gays, that has mobilized in unprecedented ways both of these discursive fields. Indeed, the already complex matter of AIDS is exponentially complicated by the fact that the homophobic response to the demands for gay equality, long *before* the phenomenon of AIDS, was largely predicated on the equation of homosexuality with the unnatural, the irrational, and the diseased. The logic of homophobia thus rests upon the very same binary that enables Plato in the *Phaedrus* to value speech at the expense of writing—and lest this assertion seem too frivolous or far-fetched an association, let me cite another passage from Derrida's reading of Plato: "the conclusion of the *Phaedrus* is less a condemnation of writing in the name of present speech than a preference for one sort of writing over another, for the fertile trace over the sterile trace, for a seed that engenders because it is planted inside over a seed scattered wastefully outside: at the risk of *dissemination*."[13] If Derrida displaces the opposition between speech and writing by identifying speech itself as just another "sort of writing," he thereby calls into question the logic of the Western philosophical tradition that claims to be able to identify and distinguish the true from the false, the natural from the unnatural. In so doing he enacts the law of transgression that he sees as operative in "both the writing *and* the pederasty of a young man named Plato," a "transgression . . . not thinkable within the terms of classical logic but only within the graphics of the supplement or of the *pharmakon*."[14] Deconstruction, as a disseminative project, then, can be subsumed beneath the rubric of the homosexual and one can read, by contrast, in the emphatic equations cited earlier as politically antithetical responses to the AIDS epidemic, an insistence on the possibility of recuperating truth, of knowing absolutely, even mathematically, some literal identity unmarked by the logic of the supplement or the indeterminacy of the *pharmakon*. So homophobic and antihomophobic forces alike find themselves producing, as defensive reactions to the social and medical crisis of AIDS, discourses that reify and absolutize identities, discourses that make clear the extent to which both groups see the AIDS epidemic as threatening the social structures through which they have constituted their identities for themselves.

Of course heterosexual culture in the West has long interpreted homosexuality as a threat to the security or integrity of heterosexual identity. In our dauntingly inconsistent mythology of homosexuality, "the love that dared not speak its name" was long known as the crime "inter Christianos non nominandum," and it was so designated not only because it was seen as lurid, shameful, and repellent, but also,

and contradictorally, because it was, and is, conceived of as being
potentially so attractive that even to speak about it is to risk the
possibility of tempting some innocent into a fate too horrible—and
too seductive—to imagine. One corollary of this fear of seduction
through nomination is the still pervasive homophobic misperception
of gay sexuality as contagious—as something one can catch through
contact with, for instance, a teacher who is lesbian or gay. Thus even
before the historical accident of the outbreak of AIDS in the gay communities of the West, homosexuality was conceived as a contagion,
and the homosexual as parasitic upon the heterosexual community.
One chilling instance that may synecdochically evoke the insidious
logic behind this homophobic ideology was produced in 1977 in a dissent written by William Rehnquist, now chief justice of the United
States, in response to the Court's refusal to grant certiorari in the case
of *Gay Lib v. University of Missouri*. As an essay in the *Harvard Law
Review* described the case, "the university had refused to recognize a
gay students' organization on the ground that such recognition would
encourage violation of Missouri's anti-sodomy statute. In support of
the university's position, Justice Rehnquist argued that permitting
the exercise of first amendment rights of speech and association in
this instance would undercut a legitimate state interest, just as permitting people with the measles to associate freely with others would
undercut the states's interest in imposing a quarantine."[15] Here, in
1977, the ideological configuration of both homosexuality and discourse in relation to disease, and the invocation, albeit in metaphor,
of quarantine as an acceptable model for containment, is offered as
an argument against the right to produce a nonhomophobic public
discourse on homosexuality.

If such a context suggests the bitter urgency of the activists' assertion that Silence = Death, it does not suffice as a reading of the
slogan or of the slogan's relation to the historically specific logic
that governs the interimplication of discourse, defense, and disease.
For what is striking about Silence = Death as the most widely publicized, gay-articulated language of response to the AIDS epidemic
is its insistence upon the therapeutic property of discourse without
specifying in any way what should or must be said. Indeed, as a text
produced in response to a medical and political emergency, Silence

= Death is stunningly self-reflexive. It takes the form of a rallying cry, but its call for resistance is no call to arms; rather, it calls for the production of discourse, the production of more text, as a mode of defense against the opportunism of medical and legislative responses to the epidemic. But what can be said beyond the need to speak? What discourse can this call to discourse desire? Just what *is* the discourse of defense that will immunize the gay body politic against the opportunistic infections of demagogic rhetoric?

An answer to this question can be discerned in Kramer's accusation: "That all of you . . . continue to refuse to transmit to the public the facts and figures of what is happening *daily* makes you, in my mind, equal to murderers." Kramer's charge explicitly demands the production of texts in order to defend against the transmission of disease. In so doing it makes clear that the defensive discourse is a discourse of "facts and figures," a discourse that resists the rhetoric of homophobic ideologues by articulating a truth that it casts in the form of mathematical or scientific data beyond the disputations of rhetoric. In a similar fashion, the textual prescription offered in Silence = Death takes the form of a formula that implies for it the status of a mathematical axiom, a given, a literal truth that is not susceptible to figural evasions and distortions. In this light, the pink triangle that appears above the slogan in the graphic representations of the text functions not only as an emblem of homosexual oppression, but also, and crucially, as a geometrical shape—a triangle *tout court*—that produces a sort of cognitive rhyme with the equation mark inscribed in the text, thus reinforcing semiotically the scientific or geometric inevitability of the textual equation.

At the same time, however, the very formula of mathematical discourse (A = B) that appeals to the prestige of scientific fact evokes the paradigmatic formulation or figure of metaphoric substitution. A = B, after all, is a wholly conventional way of representing the process whereby metaphor improperly designates one thing by employing the name of another. Though Silence = Death is cast in the rhetorical form of geometric equation, and though it invokes, by means of that form, the necessity of articulating a truth of "facts and figures," the fact remains that the equation takes shape as a figure, that it enacts a metaphorical redefinition of "silence" as "death." What this means, then, is that the equations that appear to pronounce literal, scientifically verifiable truth cannot be distinguished from the disavowed literariness of the very figural language those equations undertake to repudiate or exclude. The truth of such equations can only pass for truth so long as we ignore that the literal must itself be produced by a figural sleight of hand.

The rhetorical form of Silence = Death thereby translates the mathematical into the poetic, the literal into the figural, by framing the call to discourse in terms that evoke the distinctive signature of metaphoric exchange. It would be useful in this context to recall for a moment Harold Bloom's identification of trope and defense and to cite yet one more equation, this one actually a series of equations proposed by Bloom in his essay "Freud and the Sublime": "Literal meaning equals anteriority equals an earlier state of meaning equals an earlier state of things equals death equals literal meaning."[16] Silence = Death, read in light of this, would gesture metaphorically toward the process of tropological substitution that resists or defends against the literality that Bloom, following Freud, identifies with death and sees as producing the reductive absolutism that informs the reality principle. Indeed, Silence = Death would seem to cast itself as that most heroic of all texts: a text whose metaphoric invocation of textuality, a text whose defensive appeal to discourse would have the power "literally" to counteract the agencies of death by exposing the duplicity inherent in the false equations that pass for "literal" truth and that make possible, as a result, such virulent formulations as Gay Rights = AIDS. In this case, for trope to operate as defense would involve, in part, the repudiation of what passes for the "literal truth" of AIDS by attending to the ideological investments that inform the scientific and political discourse about it and by articulating the inevitable construction of the disease within a massively overdetermined array of figural associations.

But such a defensive discourse can claim no immunity against contamination by the figural—a contamination that is nowhere more evident than in its defensive production of the figure of literality, the figure of mathematically precise calculation implicit in the equation

Silence = Death. For the politics of language governing the claim of absolute identity in such a formula as Silence = Death aligns that formula, despite its explicitly antihomophobic import, with the logic of natural self-identity implicit in Plato's binary oppositions, a logic that provides the ideological support for the homophobic terrorism Plato himself endorsed in order to defend the "law of restricting procreative intercourse to its natural function by abstention from congress with our own sex, with its deliberate murder of the race and its wasting of the seed of life on a stony and rocky soil, where it will never take root and bear its natural fruit."[17]

The proliferating equations that mark the discourse on AIDS, then, suggest that in the face of the terrifying epistemological ambiguity provoked by this epidemic, in the face of so powerful a representation of the force of what we do not know, the figure of certainty, the figure of literality, is itself ideologically constructed and deployed as a defense, if not as a remedy. (Note one manifestation of this deployment of the figure of knowledge or certainty in the way that political debate about AIDS in America has been counterproductively fixated on proposals to divert millions of dollars from necessary research toward compulsory testing of various populations for the presence of HIV antibodies. Given the persistence of the identification in America of AIDS with the gay male community, it is hard not to see this fixation as part and parcel of the desire to combat uncertainty not only about who has been infected by the so-called "AIDS virus," but also, and perhaps more deeply and irrationally, about how it is possible to determine who is straight and who is gay.) Precisely because the defensive appeal to literality in a slogan like Silence = Death must produce the literal *as a figure* of the need and desire for the shelter of certain knowledge, such a discourse is always necessarily a dangerously contaminated defense—contaminated by the Derridean logic of metaphor so that its attempt to achieve a natural or literal discourse beyond rhetoricity must reproduce the suspect ideology of reified (and threatened) identity marking the reactionary medical and political discourse it would counteract. The discursive logic of Silence = Death thus contributes to the ideologically motivated confusion of the literal and the figural, the proper and the improper, the inside and the outside, and in the process it recalls the biology of the human immunodeficiency virus as it attacks the mechanism whereby the body is able, in David Black's words, to distinguish between "Self and Not-Self."

HIV, scientists tell us, is a retrovirus that reproduces by a method involving an enzyme called reverse transcriptase. This "allows the virus to copy its genetic information into a form that can be integrated into the host cell's own genetic code. Each time a host cell divides, viral copies are produced along with more host cells, each containing the viral code."[18] At issue in the progress of the disease, then, is the question of inscription and transcription, the question of reproduction and substitution. The virus endangers precisely because it produces a code, or speaks a language, that can usurp or substitute for the genetic discourse of certain cells in the human immune system. AIDS thus inscribes within the biology of the human organism the notion of parasitic transcription. And this metastatic or substitutive transcription of the cell is particularly difficult to counteract because HIV, like metaphor, operates to naturalize, or present as proper, that which is improper or alien or imported from without. Subsequent to the metonymy, the contiguous transmission, of infection, the virus establishes itself as part of the essence or essential material of the invaded cell through a version of metaphoric substitution. It changes the meaning of the cellular code so that each reproduction or articulation of the cell disseminates further the altered genetic message. Moreover, one of the properties of HIV is that it can change the "genetic structure of [the] external proteins" that constitute the outer coat by which the immune system is able to recognize it; thus it can evade the agents of the immune system that attempt to defend against what is alien or improper. Even worse, since HIV attacks the immune system itself, depleting the T-4 or T-helper cells, it prevents the immune system from being able to "recognize foreign substances (antigens) and . . . eliminate them from the body."[19] Even as it works its tropological wiles within the infected cells, HIV is subverting the capacity of the immune system to read the difference between what is proper to the body, what is "literally" its own, and what is figural or extrinsic.

But these metaphoric flights of fancy that are at work in the scientific discourse on AIDS, just as they are at work in my own metaphorizing discourse, the flights of fancy in which the failures of discourse as defense are already inscribed within disease, have no literal warrant in "nature." Reverse transcriptase and immune defense systems are metaphoric designations that determine the way we understand the operations of the body; they are readings that metastasize the metabolic by infecting it with a strain of metaphor that can appear to be so natural, so intrinsic to our way of thinking, that we mistake it for the literal truth of the body, as if our rhetorical immune system were no longer operating properly, or as if the virus that is metaphor had mutated so successfully as to evade the antibodies that would differentiate between the inside and the outside, between the proper and the improper. This once again brings to mind Derrida's analysis of the parasitic relation of writing to Plato's living word of speech: "In order to cure the latter of the *pharmakon* and rid it of the parasite, it is thus necessary to put the outside back in its place. To keep the outside out. This is the inaugural gesture of 'logic' itself, of good 'sense' insofar as it accords with the self-identity of *that which is:* being is what it is, the outside is outside and the inside inside."[20] But since, as Derrida says, "metaphoricity is the logic of contamination and the contamination of logic," no discourse can ever achieve the logic of self-identity, the logic of scientific equations, without the infection of metaphor that finds the enemy or alien always already within. As Emily Dickinson declared in anticipation of Derrida's reading of the *pharmakon*, "infection in the sentence breeds."[21] And in the case of AIDS, infection endlessly breeds sentences—sentences whose implication in a poisonous history of homophobic constructions assures that no matter what explicit ideology they serve, they will carry within them the virulent germ of the dominant cultural discourse.

If my conclusion presents the somber circularity of Discourse = Defense = Disease = Discourse, I cannot conclude without trying to locate the zone of infection within these remarks. What I have been suggesting is that any discourse on AIDS must inscribe itself in a volatile and uncontrollable field of metaphoric contention in which its language will necessarily find itself at once appropriating AIDS for its own tendentious purposes and becoming subject to appropriation by the contradictory logic of homophobic ideology. This essay is not exempt from those necessities. As much as I would insist on the value and urgency of examining the figural inscriptions of AIDS, I am sufficiently susceptible to the gravity of the literal to feel uneasy, as a gay man, about producing a discourse in which the horrors experienced by my own community, along with other communities in America and abroad, become the material for intellectual arabesques that inscribe those horrors within the neutralizing conventions of literary criticism. Yet as painfully as my own investment in the figure of literality evokes for me the profound inhumanity implicit in this figural discourse on AIDS, I am also aware that any discourse on AIDS must inevitably reproduce that tendentious figurality. At the same time, I would argue that the appeal of the literal can be an equally dangerous seduction; it is, after all, the citation of the pressing literality of the epidemic with its allegedly "literal" identification of homosexuality and disease, that fuels the homophobic responses to AIDS and demands that we renounce what are blithely dismissed as figural embellishments upon the "real," material necessities of human survival—embellishments such as civil rights and equal protection under the law. We must be as wary, then, of the temptations of the literal as we are of the ideologies at work in the figural; for discourse, alas, is the only defense with which we can counteract discourse, and there is no available discourse on AIDS that is not itself diseased.

Notes

The earliest version of this essay was presented at a session on "The Literature of AIDS" at the 1987 MLA Convention. I would like to thank Michael Cadden and Elaine Showalter, the other panelists, for offering helpful suggestions. In revised form the essay was delivered at Bowdoin College and I am happy to thank those who sponsored me there, the Lesbian/Gay/Straight Alliance and the Bowdoin Literary Society. Finally I want to express my gratitude to Joseph Litvak for his invaluable assistance.

1   Lee Grove, "The Metaphor of AIDS," *Boston Globe Magazine*, 28 February 1988.
2   David Black, *The Plague Years: A Chronicle of AIDS, the Epidemic of Our Times* (New York, 1986), 80.
3   H. D., *Tribute to Freud* (Boston, 1974), 86.
4   Johns Hopkins University, Population Information Program, "Issues in World Health," *Population Reports*, series 50, no. 14 (1986): 198.
5   Plato, "Timaeus," in *The Dialogues of Plato*, trans. Benjamin Jowett (Oxford, 1953), 3: 89.

6 Jacques Derrida, "Plato's Pharmacy," in *Dissemination*, trans. Barbara Johnson (Chicago, 1981), 101.

7 Ibid., 79.

8 Ibid., 149.

9 Cited in Black, *Plague Years*, 17–18.

10 Ibid., 30.

11 Frances Fitzgerald, "The Castro—II," *New Yorker*, 28 July 1986, 50.

12 William H. Masters, Virginia E. Johnson, and Robert C. Kolodny, "Sex in the Age of AIDS," *Newsweek*, 14 March 1988, 48.

13 Derrida, "Plato's Pharmacy," 149.

14 Ibid., 153.

15 "The Constitutional Status of Sexual Orientation: Homosexuality as a Suspect Classification," *Harvard Law Review* 98 (1985): 1294.

16 Harold Bloom, "Freud and the Sublime," in *Agon: Towards a Theory of Revisionism* (New York, 1982), 107.

17 Cited in Derrida, "Plato's Pharmacy," 152–53.

18 Johns Hopkins University, "Issues in World Health," 198.

19 Ibid.

20 Derrida, "Plato's Pharmacy," 128.

21 Emily Dickinson, "A Word Dropped Careless on a Page," in *The Complete Poems of Emily Dickinson*, ed. Thomas H. Johnson (Boston, 1960), 553.

Notes on Contributors

JOSEPH A. BOONE, Associate Professor of English at Harvard University, is the author of *Tradition Counter Tradition: Love and the Form of Fiction* (1987) and is working on a companion volume, *Sexuality and Narrative: Issues in the Psychology of Sex and Self in Modern Fiction* (forthcoming, Chicago).

RONALD R. BUTTERS is Associate Professor of English at Duke University. He is editor of *American Speech*, the journal of the American Dialect Society, and has published extensively on social and regional variation in contemporary English.

ROBERT L. CASERIO is Associate Professor of English at the University of Utah and co-director of the university's Humanities Center. He is the author of *Plot, Story, and the Novel* (1979). His recent essays have appeared in *Antaeus, Grand Street,* and *Novel*; and he is at work on *The British Novel since Conrad: Theory and History*.

JOHN M. CLUM is Associate Professor of English and Professor of the Practice of Theater at Duke University. His recent essays are on gender politics in contemporary drama and film.

ED COHEN is Assistant Professor of English at Rutgers University. He is currently completing a manuscript entitled "Talk on the Wilde Side: Towards a Genealogy of the Discourse on Male Sexuality" from which the current essay is taken. His articles have recently appeared in several places, including *The Nation and Clio*; his *PMLA* article received the MLA's 1987 Crompton-Noll prize.

WILLIAM A. COHEN is a graduate student in English at the University of California, Berkeley.

LEE EDELMAN is Associate Professor of English at Tufts University and the author of *Transmemberment of Song: Hart Crane's Anatomies of Rhetoric and Desire* (1987). He is currently working on *Homographesis*, a study of lesbian and gay literature and literary theory.

JONATHAN GOLDBERG is Sir William Osler Professor of English Literature at the Johns Hopkins University; his most recent book is *Voice Terminal Echo: Postmodernism and English Renaissance Texts* (1986).

JOHN R. LEO teaches literature, theory, and communications at the University of Rhode Island, where he is Associate Professor of English. He was founder and is area chair of the Gay and Lesbian Studies Section of the American Culture Association and has published widely on media, theory, and American studies.

MICHAEL MOON is completing a book on the first four editions of *Leaves of Grass* as cultural critique. He teaches American literature at Duke University.

STEPHEN ORGEL is the Jackson Eli Reynolds Professor of Humanities at Stanford University. His books include *The Jonsonian Masque, The Illusion of Power,* and, in collaboration with Sir Roy Strong, *Inigo Jones: The Theatre of the Stuart Court.* His edition of *The Tempest* for the Oxford Shakespeare series has recently appeared, and he is currently editing *The Winter's Tale* in the same series.

JOSEPH A. PORTER is the author of *The Drama of Speech Acts: Shakespeare's Lancastrian Tetralogy* (1979), *Shakespeare's Mercutio: His History and Drama* (Chapel Hill, 1988), and articles on Shakespeare and speech-act theory. He teaches at Duke University.

EVE KOSOFSKY SEDGWICK, a Professor of English at Duke, is the author of *Between Men: English Literature and Male Homosocial Desire* and the forthcoming *Epistemology of the Closet.*

Author Index

Library of Congress Cataloging-in-Publication Data
Displacing homophobia : gay male perspectives in
literature and culture / edited by Ronald R. Butters,
John M. Clum, and Michael Moon.
p.   cm.
Essays originally published in the winter 1989 issue of
the South Atlantic Quarterly, v. 88, no. 1.
Includes bibliographical references.
ISBN 0-8223-0962-9 (alk. paper). — ISBN 0-8223-0970-X
(pbk. : alk. paper)
1. Men in literature.   2. American literature—History
and criticism.   3. English literature—History and
criticism.   4. Sex roles in literature.
5. Homosexuality and literature.   6. Homosexuality,
Male.   I. Butters, Ronald R.   II. Clum, John M.
III. Moon, Michael.   IV. Title: Gay male
perspectives in literature and culture.
PS173.M36D5   1989
810.9'353—dc20   89-27584